THE EVENING
OF THE WORLD

THE EVENING
OF THE WORLD

A Romance of the Dark Ages
being the first volume of the trilogy
The Matter of Eternal Rome which is also
The Matter of Europe.

Allan Massie

Weidenfeld & Nicolson
LONDON

First published in Great Britain in 2001 by Weidenfeld and Nicolson

A CIP catalogue record for this book is available
from the British Library.

ISBN 0297 816 97 7

Typeset by Deltatype Ltd, Birkenhead, Merseyside
Printed by Clays Ltd, St Ives plc.

Weidenfeld and Nicolson
The Orion Publishing Group Ltd
Orion House
5 Upper Saint Martin's Lane
London, WC2H 9EA

For Robert Nye,
melior faber

Introduction

One day in September 1999 I got a telephone call from Sando Clanroyden.

'Been digging about in my grandfather's papers,' he said. 'Have come on something that might be just your sort of whatsit.'

Sando, I should say, though still in his early thirties, affects a vagueness that some find charming and others, among them frequently his wife Tatiana, intensely irritating. It is not all affectation; he was just as vague when at the request of his father, a Trinity contemporary of mine, I crammed him for Eton more than twenty years ago. But he does put it on a bit too, in order perhaps to mask a powerful will.

'What sort of thing?' I said.

'You'll love it. Come to lunch.'

And he rang off.

Lunch at Laverlaw is hit or miss. It will be delicious if Tatiana is in cooking vein, or you may get only bread and cheese and a pickled herring if she isn't. But it was a beautiful autumn day, with the Border countryside at its marvellous best. So we went over and were greeted as usual by a troop of Dandie Dinmonts, so that the first half-hour was spent reintroducing them to our spaniels – a Clumber and a black-and-white Springer – and walking in the woods which Sando's great-grandfather planted.

It was a good lunch day: a dish of macaroni with anchovies, black olives, capers, onions and hard-boiled eggs (Tatiana's family are Genoese), followed by a blaeberry tart with cream; and it wasn't till we had finished eating that Sando was ready to talk about his find.

'You remember that old scandal of the Three Hostages and the Tory MP Medina, in which my grandad played a part?' he began, knowing I did and had indeed once written a piece on Medina's sub-Housman verses for Alan Ross's *London Magazine*.

'*Sit vini abstemius qui hermeneuma tentat aut hominum petit dominatum*.' I quoted the line Medina had spoken at a dinner of the Thursday Club, the line indeed which had put Sando's grandfather on the alert; he identified it as coming from Michael Scott's *Physionomia*, his manual of the arts of spiritual control.

'Snap,' said Sando. 'Michael Scott's rather one of your subjects, isn't it?'

'In a small way,' I said. 'An interesting fellow. I agree with old Sandy that it's absurd to call him "the Wizard", even if legend has it that he divided the Eildon Hills where Arthur waits his second coming in a cavern surrounded by his knights, and that he was really a very subtle and original thinker. But I've never done any real work on him.'

I drew on my Toscano – that cigar made from what looks like twisted tarry rope, which these days I find so much more satisfying than Havanas. Low taste, I suppose, but my own.

'No,' I said, 'the chap I'm really interested in is the Emperor Frederick the Second, *Stupor Mundi*. I've long thought he might make the subject of a novel. And of course you know, don't you, that he was Michael Scott's pupil.'

'Well, yes. Dante put Michael in the *Inferno*, didn't he? Why was that, d'you suppose?'

'Oh, reputation as a magician. *Michele Scotto fu, che veramente/ delle magiche frodo seppe il gioco*.'

Sando nodded and sipped his coffee. (Laverlaw is one of the few houses in the Borders where the coffee is good. Tatiana gets the beans sent down from Valvona & Crolla in Edinburgh.)

'You never heard of him writing a novel, did you?'

'Who? Michael Scott? Sounds unlikely. Novelists were thin on the ground in the Middle Ages.'

'Well, a sort of novel . . . look . . .'

He indicated a pile of typescript on his desk.

'It's a copy, of course. A copy of a copy if we are to believe it. My grandfather's hand was vile, but . . .'

He passed me a note in that vile hand, which I had encountered previously when Sando had showed me a portion of a memoir, too slight, we concluded, for publication.

The note was brief.

> This manuscript was copied by me from the original in the archives of the Bibliothèque Nationale in Paris, October–December 1938, and subsequently typed up for me by Mlle Jeanne-Marie de Lorenzac. She kept it throughout the years of the German Occupation, and handed it over to me in September 1945.

'The old man died a couple of months later, you'll recall,' Sando said. 'Heart failure. And my dear old dad wasn't a man for the library, as you know. Kept the books dusted and that was about the size of it. So this just lay in a drawer for more than fifty years. It was pure chance I came on it.'

'And you say it's a novel – written by Michael Scott. Ridiculous.'

'Just my impression. What it looks like. Course, I haven't read it. It's in Latin, you see, medieval Latin, I suppose. Sandy never had a translation made. So it's beyond me. I dropped Latin after O level. But up your street. Why don't you take it away, translate it, and see if it's publishable?'

I sighed. I'm sure I must have sighed.

'You don't know what you're asking, dear boy. I'm swamped with work, swamped. I've three columns to write every week, not to mention reviewing and trying to get a couple of my own books done. Impossible.'

Sando smiled. He has a sceptical sort of smile. Then he went and found a box for the typescript.

'Michael Scott,' he said, 'written for the edification of the young emperor. I've made that much out.'

Well, yes, indeed, ridiculous or not, that is what it seems to be: a novel, a medieval novel – or, better, Romance – set in the Dark Ages, and written by the scholar, mage and philosopher for his pupil, the young Frederick. Sando was right: my curiosity overcame my disinclination. I let other work slide. When I had translated half the first volume – purely, I told myself, for my own amusement and as an intellectual exercise – I even paid a visit to Paris to hunt up the original. And it exists, it really does, though it took the wonderfully helpful archivist, M. Albert Saniette (a distant connection of Proust's palaeographer), two days to unearth it. No one, he said, appeared to have consulted it since the English milord before the war. Well, of course, it would have been grotesque otherwise – to have imagined that Sandy Arbuthnott, 16th Lord Clanroyden, should have gone to the trouble of concocting a fraudulent manuscript.

On the other hand, somebody, sometime, may have done so. It's quite beyond my powers to establish whether Michael Scott was truly the author of this strange farrago, a mixture of history, romance, myth, legend, magic and, occasionally, nonsense. But there is no reason why he shouldn't have written it. He was certainly a remarkable man.

A brief biographical note may be of interest.

He was born, probably in Upper Tweeddale (John Buchan country), around 1175. He is sometimes styled Michael Scott of Blawearie. He studied mathematics, law and theology at the universities of Oxford, Paris and Bologna. By his middle twenties he was master of all the knowledge of Christian Europe. Around the year 1204 he was in Palermo as tutor to the young Emperor Frederick, grandson of the great Frederick Barbarossa and hope of the House of Hohenstaufen. Palermo was then the most brilliant court in Europe, open to Greek, Roman, Arab and Norman influences. At some point Scott added a knowledge of Greek and Arabic to the Latin in which he wrote and thought; he would reintroduce Aristotelian philosophy to the West by way of translations from the Arabic of Avicenna and Averroes. His translations were censured by the Church. A strong anti-papalist vein runs through this Romance. No doubt it contributed to Frederick's lifelong challenge to the pretensions of the Pope. Scott, in addition to this book (if it is his work), wrote for Frederick a handbook on astronomy and another on physiognomy; he believed that "the inward disposition of the soul may be read in visible characters on the bodily frame". (There are shadowings of this doctrine in the novel.) Scott also instilled in the the young emperor a love of natural history, dedicating to him his translation of Aristotle's work on animals. Frederick later made a fine collection of elephants, giraffes, dromedaries, etc., and rare birds; he introduced the pheasant into Calabria, and probably into Europe. Generations of English landowners and sportsmen have therefore reason to be grateful to him – and, by extension, to Michael Scott.

Scott later taught for some years at Toledo, where he pursued his Arabic studies, before returning to Palermo as the Emperor's physician and astrologer. He was offered the Archbishopric of Cashel, but declined on the grounds that he knew no Irish. This shows, a scrupulousness rare among medieval clerics.

In later life he is said to have suffered from depression. He returned to Scotland – seeking a cure? – and died there around 1235, perhaps at Melrose.

Dante, as Sando remarked, put him in the *Inferno*, placing him in the fourth chasm of the eighth circle among the sorcerers and enchanters. Nevertheless, Dante was not above borrowing from him – or so this manuscript suggests. There is a passage in its last chapter so uncannily like that narrative which Dante puts in the mouth of Ulysses that one can scarcely doubt that Dante had read what Scott wrote. Nobody in the Middle Ages thought twice about borrowing from other writers. It was indeed regarded as a sort of compliment. Compare Chaucer and his borrowings from Petrarch and Boccaccio.

The manuscript seems to have had two previous editors, or rather commentators. The first declares himself to be a knight of the Order of the Temple. He wrote after the dissolution of the Order on trumped-up charges of heresy, homosexuality, and idol worship. One may conjecture that he was one of those knights who escaped to Scotland, where they found a protector in the St Clair family and were established at Rosslyn (or Roslin) Chapel near Edinburgh. It is not difficult to understand how a Scottish-based Templar might have access to Scott's manuscript, or to a copy of it.

The second commentator, by his own account, would seem to have been a Rosicrucian scholar, perhaps living at the 'magic court' of the Emperor Rudolf in Prague. How he came to have possession of the manuscript must remain a mystery. There are suggestions, however, of a hermetic tradition linking the Templars and the Rosicrucians, however loosely.

Because the observations of these two commentators have their own peculiar interest, I have left them in the text. The Templar's interjections are signalled thus: *(...)*; the Rosicrucian's: **(...)**.

As to how the manuscript, thus annotated, found its way to the Bibliothèque Nationale, again one can do no more than guess. There was, however, a seventeenth – and eighteenth-century French Brotherhood of the Rosy Cross (Les Frères de la Croix Rose), which influenced, or is associated with, eighteenth-century Illuminist writers such as Fabre D'Olivet and Louis-Claude de Saint-Martin, and it is not perhaps a rash supposition to suggest that it was deposited in the library among some of their papers. Unfortunately not even the most assiduous researches of M. Saniette have succeeded in establishing when or how it was deposited in the library. Nevertheless, he does not dispute my hypothesis, and I am eternally grateful to him for his enthusiastic co-operation.

What then of the novel itself – for novel is, I think, what we must call it, the term fortunately being one of almost infinite elasticity?

It is tempting to offer a critique, tempting but unnecessary. Novels should be read before criticism of them is read, for criticism prejudices the reader. All I shall say, therefore, is that it is a narrative of the Dark Ages, more imaginative than historical; and that what now appears is but a third of the whole, the other parts being reworkings of the Arthurian Cycle (the Matter of Britain) and the Charlemagne cycle (the Matter of France). The whole, it may be said, is the Matter of Eternal Rome, for its theme is the nature and necessity of Empire: *imperium sine fine* – limitless empire – as Vergil wrote.

Finally I must thank Sando Clanroyden for giving me the opportunity to undertake this arduous but fascinating task, and I am happy to say that, in his opinion, 'the old boy may have been a bit off the wall, but it's good stuff, highly enjoyable'.

I hope that you, Michael Scott's readers across the silent centuries, agree.

Allan Massie
Thirladean House, Selkirk
The day of the Winter Solstice in the Year of Our Lord 2000

I

Know, most noble Prince, that the Holy Apostle John, he who was loved by Christ, and who is the Guide and Inspiration of all who seek after the knowledge that is born of the Spirit, knowledge which yields itself only to those who, by courage and insight, have broken the veils of Time and Flesh, wrote of the Last Days thus:

'And God shall wipe away all tears from their eyes; and there shall be no more death; neither sorrow nor crying; neither shall there be any more pain; for former things shall have passed away. And he that sat upon the throne said: behold, I make all things new. And he said unto me: write, for these words that I speak are true and faithful.'

And so I write, for this is the story that I have to impart to you, my Prince, now in the apple-blossom of your beauty, youth and strength. For it is necessary and meet that you learn of these things which are the nature of your inheritance and so the burden you bear for all mankind.

You must learn that this world is a battlefield where the Forces of Light and those of Darkness contend for mastery. You must learn that it is needful and proper on occasion for the wise man to conceal his wisdom and purpose, as a wary traveller will hold his lantern concealed under his cloak when he ventures into a forest, even of night. No enemy can be defeated till he is thoroughly known, and it is for this reason that even the Godly may be required to traffic with the Prince of Darkness, author of all Sin and Death, and of that suffering and misfortune which goes beyond the understanding of the unlettered.

For myself, who have been entrusted by Almighty God (and also by your most pious mother, Constance, Princess of Sicily, to whom I now make expression of my most reverent gratitude and duty) with your education in worldly knowledge and understanding of the Great Mysteries, let me say merely that, reared in the wintry extremity of the North, at that point where the armies of imperial Rome wavered and fell back, and having subsequently sojourned many years here in the land where the lemons bloom, I have, in the avidity of zeal for understanding of the spirits that move and order the world of men, delved deep and perilously. Nothing human or natural, nothing that goes beyond the human and natural, has been alien to me.

I am therefore, as I may testify in the face of malignant foes (sadly numerous, on account of envy), the choicest guide you might have, one qualified not only by the dangers I have confronted in my search for knowledge, but also by the ardent love I bear to your lustrous person, of which, as you will grant, I have given abundant proof.

The story I am about to relate to you is both that of your illustrious and puissant forebears, like you God's Regents here on earth, companions of the archangels and especially of the most glorious Archangel Michael who, on the mountain in whose shadow I now write, appeared before Laurentius, Bishop of Sipontum, by way of whom he delivered the charge which it is your destiny to keep. But it is also the History of Thought as revealed by God's Grace, in that most noble institution, the image of Paradise here on Earth, the Holy Roman Empire.

II

Our tale begins in a rude farmstead set on an island in the marshes that surround imperial Ravenna, now fallen from its former glory. It was four centuries to the day since the birth of Our Lord Jesus Christ. As dusk fell, a thin winter rain slanted landwards from the Adriatic, succeeded by a mist creeping over the reed-beds. In the farm's stable, for the dwelling-house had long fallen into desuetude, a woman turned, twisted, and howled in labour. Towards midnight she gave birth to a son. Before the dawn broke the Lord took her soul into his keeping.

The woman was Julia, daughter of the senator L. Julius Corvinus, a staunch conservative who held by the old ways, prized the honour of his family and his noble order, and was the author of an epic poem in the manner of Vergil, celebrating the expulsion of the kings from Rome and the establishment of the Republic. For this exercise in poetry and patriotism he was, by imperial order, blinded and exiled to the island of Pandeteria, where however he long survived, before dying none knows how or when. As a member of the Julian *gens* he claimed descent from the kings of Alba Longa, who flourished before Rome was, and so from Aeneas, father of the Roman people, who had carried his aged sire Anchises from burning Troy. According to pagan legend his heredity was still more distinguished, for an original ancestress was the goddess Venus. But you are not to believe this, my prince; the line was already sufficiently noble and impressive.

The paternity of the new-born babe is, in contrast, uncertain and disputed.

Julia had a husband, also of noble Roman birth, for he was descended on his father's side from Marcus Antonius, the avenger of the murdered Caesar and rival of the Emperor Augustus, and on his mother's from Marcus Aurelius, wisest of emperors and of pagan philosophers, possessed, in the opinion of the learned Ambrosius, Bishop of Milan, of a soul 'naturally Christian'. But this marriage, it is said, was never consummated, either for reasons too disreputable to be related in writing, or, conversely, because the young husband was visited on the wedding night by a vision of the saints and in consequence took a vow of lifelong chastity. Both versions were current in Ravenna for several hundred years and are recounted impartially by the chroniclers.

Some, however, maintain that the child was fathered by Stilicho, the great Vandal general who defended the Empire against the barbarian Visigoths. Certainly, when Stilicho, abandoned by the ignoble Emperor Honorius whom he had served with the utmost loyalty, was put to death, he was accused among other crimes too numerous to relate of the rape of one Julia, described in the indictment as 'a Bride of Christ'. And so it is averred that this is that same Julia who gave birth that Christmas in the Ravenna marshes, and that she was a nun of candid beauty whom the rude Stilicho ravished. But many deny this.

Others relate a still more scurrilous story, of which the origin might once have been overheard in the low taverns of Trastevere.

A day's journey from Rome the little town of Aricia looks over the golden Campagna. I have myself spent choice hours in its gardens, and know it well.

A dark and gloomy wood climbs the steep hill behind the little town, and if you follow the winding path to the summit, your gaze is held by a deep lake, black as pitch and of sinister import. Descend the hill, wary of emanations, and you come upon a grove wherein you will discover, to this very day, ruins of a pagan temple.

In former days this was dedicated to the goddess Diana, whom some call also the Great Mother. On a certain tree within the grove hung a Golden Bough which must be plucked by any man brave enough to seek entry to the underworld; for this lake, now called Nemi, was the Ancients' Avernus, the gateway to the nether regions. The shrine of Diana was guarded by a single priest who was both runaway slave and murderer, for he won his position of honour and peril by slaying the previous incumbent. And it was said, by some, that the father of Julia's child was none other than a household slave of her father's who had escaped to become the priest of Diana at Nemi, and who caressed his mistress with bloodstained hands.

But others, believing with a tender faith that no Christian hero could have such terrible pagan origins, maintain that he was fathered by the Archangel Michael in that cavern on Mount Gargano where he alighted to reveal himself to the Greek bishop of Sipontum, Laurentius by name.

Certainly this is the most pleasing of the legends that have encrusted our hero's birth.

Be that as it may, the boy Marcus survived his mother and was reared by an aunt, in a mighty castle set on a crag on the north-facing flank of Mount Gargano, and grew up strong in body and mind, and as beautiful as if St Michael was indeed his father. Of this there is no dispute. All chroniclers and commentators praise his golden aureole of hair, his countenance in which was combined the strength of men and the delicacy of women; they speak of his eyes blue as cornflowers, his rosy lips, his smooth skin and strong straight legs. His courage was as wonderful as his beauty. At the age of twelve he slew a marauding wolf, and yet he was so gentle that the nightingales came at his call. He studied deeply, being well versed in languages, though – it is reluctantly admitted – his attention to the Holy Scriptures was less than it might have been; and there are suggestions that he even preferred the pagan authors of Greece and Rome. Nevertheless his tutors were unanimous in declaring that they had never known a youth who so exemplified all the Christian virtues.

In short, he was a prodigy. But it may be the accounts we possess are partial.

Even as a youth, in those years when the sap runs strongest, he is reputed to have had no inclination towards vice. The maidens of his aunt's household flashed their black eyes at him in vain, and when the aged Bishop of Benevento laid a too exploratory hand on his smooth thigh, Marcus removed it with a calm remon-strance.

5

Reports of his virtue and heredity being carried to the Emperor Honorius, he was summoned to the imperial court at Milan.

III

Marcus set forth on his journey on a lambent May morning as the sun's first rays touched the escarpment of the Apennines with pink. We may suppose that his soul danced with the morning, but that he was also not free of that mood of tingling apprehension proper to a youth embarking on his first adventure. He had with him three companions: his chaplain Father Bernardo; Chiron, a Calabrian Greek, who had charge of the horses; and young Gito, his page, who was also the child of his old wet-nurse. The priest was pious and timid, the groom taciturn and cunning, deep-dyed in the deceits of horse-trading, and young Gito bold, impudent, and merry and skittish as a kitten.

As they journeyed, the priest told his beads, the groom scanned the horizon and drew rein at every turn of the way, and Gito chattered till Chiron gave him a buffet with his leathery fist, and bade him be silent. But Marcus rode as if in a dream, pondering the adventures that must lie before them.

Towards noon they found themselves in a thick wood which eclipsed the light of the sun, and where the way was beset with briars and long strands of twining reeds. It was such a wood, Gito said, as was known to be the habitation of dragons; and indeed, as they penetrated further, he saw their eyes flashing like demons amongst the trees. Though Father Bernardo, having made the sign of the Cross, stoutly declared that dragons were but pagan fancies of which no true Christian should be afeared, still Gito trembled with terror, which, however, in the manner of boys he appeared also to enjoy. Marcus himself felt the sinister allure of the dark wood, and, less than convinced by the assurances of the priest, who for his part kept his eyes closed, his lips moving as if in prayer while his fingers rattled his beads, had to summon all his fortitude to maintain his calm.

'For,' he told himself, 'this is but a test of manhood, and there will doubtless be more severe trials to come.'

On the subject of dragons, if I may interrupt my tale scarce yet begun, there is much to be said. That there be dragons is denied by no learned man, for their existence is well attested to by the Ancients. Hesiod, the Greek poet whose works are lost to us, is reported to have insisted on the dragon's terrible eyes. Other writers say that the dragon feeds on poisonous herbs, sure sign of its enmity to man. The habitat of dragons is varied. Some lurk in thick forest, through which their fiery breath cuts a path. Some dwell in deep waters, or in vast roomy caverns under lakes. Others lie, ever watchful, concealed amidst reeds and rushes.

The dragon never sleeps, which renders him fit companion for the Great Enemy of mankind. Indeed it was in the form of a dragon, mistranslated as serpent, that Satan first seduced Eve, the ancestress of all, and so condemned us to Sin and to expulsion from Eden.

Other dragons are known to guard the gold that is lodged in the bowels of the earth, and these dread creatures scorch with fiery breath any mortal bold enough to seek the treasure over which they stand sentry. And it is for this reason that gold itself, being tainted by the dragon's breath, is noxious. No man can satisfy a lust for gold without suffering corruption.

(Here, it may be said, our learned author errs. The *Fortalitium Scientiae*, of Hugo de Alverda, erudite *praepositus* of the Sacred Brotherhood of the Rosy Cross, has demonstrated that a man, schooled in the mysteries, may himself make gold, and that indeed this is but the least of the many feats of which the truly learned who have delved deep in search of knowledge are capable. Therefore it is evident that the metal itself is innocent of all malignity and has no need of dragons to guard it. Which nevertheless is not to deny the existence of such monsters, but merely to show that another explanation of their purpose is necessary. That they have a purpose, like all other created things, is certain. A learned Persian – it may be Zoroaster – maintains that dragons are rather guardians of the Divine Wisdom which wise men seek and yet wisely fear.)

Plunging more deeply into the wood, they came at last to a clearing where the overarching trees, oaks and chestnuts, hid them from the sky. There they saw an altar which, declaring it to be pagan, as was indeed the case, for it had been raised in honour of the goat-foot Pan, the good Father Bernardo would have had Chiron strike down. But he drew back and refused saying that, while he was a baptised Christian, he yet feared the ancient gods who had not abandoned their power over men. He was wise in this, though it be heresy to say so, for there are powers beyond our understanding, and Chiron felt the *numen* of that place. The priest was angered by his refusal and would have struck him before himself advancing to smite the altar, but Marcus laid his hand on him, and bade him desist. 'It does us no harm,' he said, 'and besides it is solidly constructed. Let us wage war only on evil men, and not on images.'

Scarcely had he spoken when they were surrounded by a troop of wild-looking fellows who emerged from the shadows of the trees. They were dressed in the skins of wild beasts, and on their heads they wore the masks of wolves. They babbled in a tongue long abandoned by citizens, and incomprehensible. Paying no heed to Marcus's questions, they seized the bridles of the horses, and led them out of the clearing.

Gito whimpered with terror, but Marcus said:

'There is nothing to be afraid of. This is merely the beginning of the first of our adventures.'

Their captors led them for many hours through the forest along tracks twisting like serpents, until at last they emerged on to an open plain and saw in the distance the ramparts and battlements of a mighty castle. Touched by the rays of the declining sun, it sparkled like fine glass. It was protected by a moat, filled with black water, but on their approach a drawbridge was lowered, and they proceeded into the courtyard. There, the sign was given that they were to dismount. An old man with a long white beard, like one of the Patriarchs, recognised Father Bernardo as an ecclesiastic, and, taking him by the hand, led him away. Meanwhile his three companions stood amazed, for they had none of them seen so splendid a castle before.

Then the wild fellows who had brought them there departed, as if satisfied to have performed their duty, and seeking no reward or payment. So they were left alone, with the gate shut behind them, and night falling.

The castle now appeared deserted. Tying the reins of their weary horses to the rail of a water-trough, they advanced, with a trepidation that was only natural, into the first hall of the castle. It was richly adorned with tapestries depicting acts of heroism and representing mysteries; but there was no living person to be seen. They proceeded to the next hall, and that too was empty. They advanced into the Great Hall of the castle and found evidence of an abandoned or interrupted feast. Here half a dozen men, in loose blue tunics, lay on the floor amidst gazehounds and large dogs like those mastiffs of Naples, the colour, men say, of English fog. But they could not tell whether they slept or had departed this life. Chiron stirred one with the toe of his boot, but met no response. Gito seized Marcus's hand and again whimpered with fear. There was no other sound.

Chiron turned to the table that ran round the room, for there was one at the far end that stood upon a dais, and two others on either side of the hall which was itself of some two chains in length. He picked up a goblet of wine, sniffed, and drank.

'It is but recently poured,' he said, 'for it is good wine, and not sour.'

'Perhaps it is poisoned,' Gito said, pointing to the bodies on the floor.

'No,' said Chiron, 'it is not poisoned unless poison has no taste of its own. It is good wine, I tell you.'

He drank again, and took from one of the gold plates before him a raised pie, and bit into it.

'And this pie, though the pastry is not as fresh as the wine, is made of good savoury venison. Eat and drink, Master, for it appears to me that this feast is prepared for ourselves alone.'

'Ourselves alone?' Marcus said. 'I mislike the import of these words. Surely some calamity has fallen on the people of this house and land.'

'And we look like to share it,' Gito said.

'All the better then to meet it with a full belly,' Chiron said, 'and wine, I tell you, gives a man courage.'

So saying, he settled himself on a bench and ate and drank heartily. In a little Gito released Marcus's hand and made bold to drink of the wine, and even nibble a piece of pie. But Marcus felt himself restrained by some force he did not understand.

Leaving them to their meal, which Gito was now addressing with signs of appetite, he ventured beyond the hall, and mounted a twisting stair. At the second landing a cold wind blew on his face, and caused him to pause, for it puzzled him that it should blow where there was no window or aperture to admit it.

He climbed higher and came to a door embossed with iron studs. He pushed it open, and entered into a chamber. It was lit by the risen moon, and he saw that it too was hung with draperies; they were made of the finest silk and floated in the wind, which blew more strongly here.

'So,' a voice said, 'you have come, and you have resisted the feast.'

The speaker rose from a high-backed chair and stood before him. She was dressed in a white gown, once magnificent, now dirty and ragged. Her face was chalked white and her head shaven, shining pale in the moonlight. To Marcus it seemed like a deformity, and he stepped backwards. But she took him by the wrist and drew him towards her, and kissed his lips; hers were cold as snow and the chamber chill as the Devil's sperm.

'I saw you in my glass,' she said, 'and I sent word that you were to be fetched. My father whom you have come to heal lies in the next room.'

'There is some mistake,' Marcus said, trying to disengage himself. 'I am no physician. I am but a young knight journeying to Milan at the command of the Emperor.'

'It is not medicine such as physicians know that we have need of. Throughout the land of which my father is king there is weeping and sorrow: tears for the plants that grow not; tears for the flocks that bring forth no young, and for the fruit trees that are barren of fruit. There is wailing for the great river that does not run; there is weeping for the fields of men and for the fish-ponds; wailing for the forests and the mountains; for the honey that does not flow and for the vines that wither on the hillsides. The wine which your servant drinks below is last year's vintage; there will be none this coming season. It is the month of spring but grim winter holds the land in thrall. There is wailing for the meadows and the gardens, for all the children of men. . .'

She chanted her lament and all the time her eyes did not leave his face and he found he could not look away.

'Surely,' he thought, 'this is uncanny.'

She led him to the next chamber, where a bier stood, illuminated by candles of the finest wax, and on the bier lay an old man with a crown of golden thorns on his brow, and a face that was wrinkled, yellow and soft as old parchment.

'This is my father,' she said, 'the King, and his wound is deep. If he is not healed he will die, and the land with him. Until he is healed I am held here, prisoner in this chamber, with the shaven head of mourning, and forbidden to eat or drink.'

Again Marcus protested that he was no physician, and again she paid no heed to what he said. Instead she held him there, gazing on the body of the King (for it seemed to Marcus that it was indeed a corpse, since there was no breath and all was still as the grave). She carried Marcus's hand forward so that it touched the King's cheek, and the flesh was cold as frosted grass.

'What is his illness?' Marcus said. 'For I see now that he is not dead as I had thought.'

'It is the sickness of a world condemned,' she said.

Then the Princess, for such Marcus knew she must be, lay on a couch covered with purple velvet, and drew up the skirts of her gown, and beckoned to Marcus indicating that he should lie with her. But Marcus had sworn a vow never to know woman till he had proved himself in battle, and so held back, and would not consent. When she understood his refusal she cried out three times, as women do when they watch over a deathbed, and he pitied her but yet held his ground.

*

*(It would appear that a leaf of our author's manuscript is lost, for this episode comes to an abrupt halt. Its chief interest is to be found, however, not in what subsequently might or might not have occurred, but rather in the interpretation of events so far. Concerning which, our author disappoints the reader by recording in a tone of incurious acceptance that which demands interpretation.

It is evident to the initiated in the Mysteries that our hero is being charged with a task the nature of which he does not at this point of the narrative comprehend. Whether the events related here happened as told, or whether, as seems more probable, they belong to a dream or vision of our hero, their significance is great and the same.

Consider that the hero is on a journey to the court of the Emperor, and then consider the parlous state of that once-mighty Empire, now fallen into decay.

Consider then the vision of a king sick even unto the point of death, so that he wears the appearance of Mortality even while the refuge of the grave is denied him.

Are we not approaching the True Mysteries, for it is written in the Gospel according to St Philip – which, however, orthodoxy repudiates:

'Those who proclaim that they will die first and then arise, err profoundly. If they do not first receive resurrection while they are yet alive, they will receive nothing after death. Even so is it said of Baptism, "Great is Baptism. For if one receives it, one will live."'

Verily, resurrection is brought us on the wind that bloweth from Heaven to sweep the world. The angel who rides with heavy-feathered wings on that wind from heaven does not cry out, 'Arise, ye Dead'. His thrilling message is, 'Let the living rise and live anew'.)*

13

IV

When Marcus awoke and rubbed sleep from his eyes he saw to his amazement that they were in that same forest clearing where stood the altar to the goat-foot Pan. He looked around, and their horses were there too, feeding on the grass and standing quietly though they were not tethered. He roused his companions.

'I have a head as though I had drunk deep,' Chiron said, 'and yet my throat is as dry as a Jew's Sabbath.'

'My skin smarts as though I had been whipped with thorny branches,' Gito said, rubbing his thighs.

'I have wrestled with evil spirits and been assailed by demons,' the priest said, and made the sign of the Cross.

But Marcus smiled, and said only,

'We have lost a day in this dark wood and must make haste for Milan.'

All day they rode, and it seemed as if the forest would never end. Yet Marcus no longer depended on Chiron to act as guide, but followed a light that glimmered before him, and led them by twisting paths through the obscurity. He trusted this light, which no other saw, till, towards evening, they emerged from the trees on to a misty plain where they heard the sound of running water. And all day, in the forest, they had seen neither man nor beast.

When they came to the river, Marcus, for the first time, consulted Chiron as to whether they should journey upstream or down.

'Let us go with the water,' he said, 'for in the plains they are like to be civilised folk, but in the mountains barbarous and hostile to travellers.'

So, judging this good, Marcus directed that they follow the water, and, as darkness fell, they came to a village.

Chiron offered to ride ahead to determine whether the people

14

were friendly, while Father Bernardo said his office, Gito sighed and moaned from weariness of body and hunger, and Marcus withdrew apart, and, wrapping himself in his cloak, gazed upon the tranquil flow of the stream.

When Chiron returned to announce that all was well and the inn hospitable, they gathered up their possessions, and followed him with light hearts.

The innkeeper was indeed happy to make them welcome, for, he said, travellers were few in that wild season and the wars had disturbed the pattern of trade. He set wine and bread and a cheese made from the milk of buffaloes, like that which we eat in Naples, before them, and roasted a pike, caught that very morning as he assured them, on the spit over a great fire.

When he learned that they had come through the forest, he was amazed and crossed himself, which action pleased Father Bernardo mightily, for he had been afraid on account of the mean appearance of the village in which bronze-haired pigs ran loose, even entering the inn parlour, that they had fallen among pagans.

Gito made to speak, but Marcus, loth to have the boy recount their experiences in the forest, stilled him, and assured the innkeeper that they had encountered nothing remarkable therein.

'Well, that is mighty strange and surprises me no end,' the man said. 'For there is not a fellow in this village who will venture beyond the trees, though all, save for Naso the ferryman, are accounted brave men.'

'And why is that, friend?' asked Chiron.

The innkeeper turned his single eye upon him, and laid his forefinger along his nose.

'In the forest there are wolves and there are men, and they are known to mate with each other, and so give birth to monsters, half-wolf and half-man.'

'I have heard of such tales from old women,' Marcus said, 'but whether they be true or not, we encountered no such beings.'

In saying this, as he later assured Gito, he did not believe he lied, for he was not persuaded that the strange creatures which had led them to the castle were indeed such montrous hybrids. And whether he was right or wrong we cannot guess, for, certes, on the one hand travellers since ancient times have met with Nature's unnatural offspring, such as the Centaurs against whom Hercules struggled, while on the other hand, it is well attested that the Author of all Darkness and Mischief may often assume shapes out of nature, as also may those deluded men and women who have surrendered themselves to his service. Wherefore, the wise man stays incredulity and dismisses nothing as impossible merely because it appears improbable, or has not hitherto entered into his experience.

When they had eaten and drunk, Chiron grumbling that the wine was thin and sour, they made ready to sleep. Marcus retired with Gito into an inner chamber where a palliasse had been stretched on the damp earthen floor, taking the boy with him because he had observed the lewd and lascivious glances which the innkeeper had directed at him, and the coarse-handed manner in which he had ruffled the lad's cherubic curls; and also because Gito feared to sleep alone. So, in a little, when they had toyed with each other, they fell asleep and the house was still. Not even the cry of wolves from the forest and the answering barks of the village dogs could hinder them from slumber, for they were exhausted by their journey.

Sleep is but another world which we inhabit, and which offers the ignorant only puzzlement and glimpses of its nature which they are unable to comprehend; but the wise man or adept reads its message differently.

Now it happened that, as Marcus slept, he was carried into that other world, which, for our convenience, we term the world of dreams. Concerning which, men have long – mistakenly as I aver – interpreted them as prophecies. Such was the opinion of the learned Tully among many others. Moreover the evidence of the Testaments leads many to this same conclusion, for, they say, do we not read there how Joseph dreamed of his future greatness in Egypt and of the obeisance which his jealous brethren would be compelled to offer unto him; and do we not also read of how he interpreted the dreams of Pharaoh in a manner that came to pass? So, acknowledging this, although I pronounce such interpretation or understanding of dreams to be erroneous, I cannot altogether dismiss it. Life is not mathematics, and few things have only one correct answer. Yet I affirm that a true understanding of dreams forbids one to regard them as mere vulgar prophecy.

So, for instance, when the ghost of the murdered Caesar appeared, the night before Philippi, to the sleeping Brutus, and displayed his many wounds, that vision did not foretell Brutus's own death in the next day's battle; it bore witness to his troubled soul. For this is the gist of the matter: a dream reveals more of the dreamer than it does of the world around him or of what is to come.

Now, as he slept, Marcus was vexed and troubled by lustfulness. First, a slender Indian youth danced before him to music that was sinuous in rhythm and played upon distant pipes. The boy lowered himself over the couch where Marcus lay, and turned his body gracefully, and his skin, soft as roses to the touch, gleamed. He extended his lips, pushing his face between Marcus's thighs, all the while murmuring endearments in an tongue that was yet unknown. Then, as Marcus reached towards him with an inexpressible yearning, the boy slipped from his encircling arms, and all was dark.

Next the music quickened and a woman rose before him. She moved like one in a trance, and she disrobed before his eyes as the Princess had done. But, on this occasion, Marcus, bewitched by her beauty – the pearly skin, the ruby lips, the long streaming black hair and the rounded perfection of her limbs – rose from his couch and approached her. She leaned forward to kiss him on the lips, and taking his hand pressed it against her breasts, which were three in number. She arched her back and drew him forward, and with eager words besought him to enter her and pleasure her, which in his intoxication of desire he hastened to do. Yet, even as his ardour swelled, he was seized from behind and restrained. Opening his eyes, he found the woman vanished and in her stead were three angelic figures, with stern faces and golden wings. One took him by the arms, another by the feet, and they laid him on a table or altar. The third angel, now smiling, drew near, a sickle in his hand. He murmured words which Marcus could not under-stand, and drew back the sickle, and then, with swift certainty, mutilated Marcus, who cried out in terror though he felt no pain.

His screams woke Gito, who enquired tenderly what was amiss. For a little Marcus could make no reply. When at last he was able to speak he told Gito what had happened. The boy was dismayed till he was able to assure Marcus that the mutilation had been performed only in phantom fashion.

'It was only a bad dream,' he said to console him.

'One that commenced so beautifully and ended so horribly,' Marcus said. 'It is either a judgement or a warning.'

(Such dreams are more common than our author may have supposed. A certain Pachomius and his disciple Theodore were once strolling through the cloisters of their monastery on a night when the moon was full. They saw before them, illuminated by its pale rays, a woman of indescribable beauty, for whom both simultaneously experienced intense and urgent desire. Yet, being pious and obedient monks, both prayed that their lustful desire be removed from them. Whereupon, the woman or phantom laughed and addressed them in tones of mockery: 'You must know,' she said, 'that I am the daughter of the Great Master of the infernal regions, and yet you think to resist my charms. Do you not know, ignorant men, that it was I who brought down the power of the stars and enticed Judas Iscariot from the Order of the Holy Apostles. I have been commanded to assail you, most holy Pachomius, that you may learn the feebleness and frailty of faith when at war with the flesh.' But Pachomius answered that he trusted indeed in the strong hand of the Lord which would uphold him against all temptations. Then, in anger, she spat liquid fire, but did not desist from her efforts to seduce him till he held the crucifix against her breast. When she felt the Holy Rood press upon her, she screamed thrice, and shrivelled before his gaze, and writhed on the earth like a serpent. Seeing this, he thanked God and was free of the lust he had felt for her even till that moment when he saw scales appear on the flesh of her legs.)

(It is not clear what my precursor among commentators intends us to understand by this anecdote, the relevance of which is questionable. Moreover, inasmuch as its import is apparent, it is founded in misapprehension. For it is evident that the angels who assailed Marcus were false, being in reality devils set to inspire in man a fear and hatred of the flesh that they may feast on cruel intercourse with men and women, boys and girls. No human soul is at any moment solitary; it is ever watched over by the invisible lords of darkness who seek and desire communion and congress, to use it, pervert it, and so triumph by taking possession. It is a victory for such evil spirits if men come to contemn their natural lusts and appetites, and, thus perverted, find satisfaction only in unnatural congress with demons. Fear of the flesh is the beginning of sin.)

Marcus rose with the dawn, troubled in mind and spirit, despite the consolations which Gito had offered him. But being one of great fortitude and intelligence, he turned these matters over in his mind, not shrinking from them, but seeking to extract significance. He formed an understanding of a connection between his dream and his refusal of the invitation held out to him in the castle by the maiden who watched over the living corpse.

'Surely,' he said, 'I am destined to some great work, that I am become the object of such attention from spirits. But as to the meaning of such attention, time alone can tell. Nevertheless, though it be a trial, it is also an honour, since an insignificant man would not receive such notice.'

So saying, he armed himself and prepared for the road.

V

Naso the ferryman shook his head when asked to carry them across the river. He did so knowing that it was necessary for them that they should cross, and so hoped to extract a higher price. Therefore he pretended that there was a curse on his boat. Father Bernardo said his office over the craft and assured the boatman that this had removed the curse. But Naso mumbled and shook his head again. He was afraid, he said, for he saw that in Marcus that foretold fatality; and so he would not take them. Marcus offered silver. Naso's eyes glinted with avarice, but still he shook his head. So Chiron, beckoning to Marcus, withdrew him a little from the company, and said, 'Leave me to deal with this rogue.'

He thrust his hand into the bag which he wore on a ribbon round his neck and took out a handful of ash. He hurled this in the ferryman's face, and when he cried out in terror and pain, protesting that he could no longer see, Chiron propelled him to the boat and put the pole in his hand. So, standing in the bows (which is the manner in which they punt in these parts, though elsewhere, in Cambridge where I have studied for example, the puntsman stands in the stern), he carried them over the water. When they arrived there and had disembarked, Naso asked plaintively for money, but Chiron assured him that he had already been paid in full with good silver.

'Why, so I have,' Naso said, though he had in truth received nothing; and he wished them godspeed.

'What was it that you threw in the knave's face?' Marcus asked.

'The ash from the burnt body of a blind cat,' Chiron said. 'It is a remedy which never fails.'

All day they journeyed through a waste land, starved of life-giving rain; an empty land, a barren, rock-strewn plain, where no crops were sown nor ever reaped, where no flocks or herds fed, and there was no sign of human habitation.

'Surely some great evil has been done here,' Marcus said.

'How far are we from Milan?' Gito sighed.

At noon, when the sun beat heavy upon them, they rested in the shade of a great rock, and drank the sour wine of the inn from their goatskins and ate dry bread and hard cheese. Before them, on their road, they saw only rock and the sandy track winding beyond towards red mountains in a land where there was no sound of water. Marcus touched his cheek and felt the flesh burn and the sweat streaming. He licked his finger and it tasted of salt. Thunder crackled, but, though the sky was now heavy and purple as a day-old bruise, there was no smell of rain in the air, and no rain fell. The horses suffered from their great thirst, and Father Bernardo knelt and prayed that they would come upon a pool. But there was no water, and they heard only the dry sound of the grasshopper, clicking in the yellow scrub amidst the thorns.

Then in the far distance figures appeared. For a long time, into the afternoon, they watched them. But, though they seemed to advance, they came no closer. At last, weary and fearful, they remounted, and urging their beasts into an unwilling trot moved towards the long, dark column.

Black-hooded figures stumbled on the cracked earth across the scree dotted with thorn-bushes. When they saw the horsemen approach, they halted and formed themselves into a ring, and sent up a psalm to heaven.

'We have nothing to fear,' Marcus said, 'for they are pilgrims. Let us ask them if they can set us on our way.'

So they drew near and the pilgrims straightway ceased singing and looked on them in silent apprehension.

Marcus in gentle and courtly fashion said: 'Well met, my friends, for we are travellers who have lost our way.'

One stepped forward and replied, 'Why, sir, so are all suffering humanity unless they find the Christ.'

'You mistake me, friend,' Marcus said. 'It is no spiritual path that we are in search of.'

'But it is that which we seek: the path of the living Christ. We were assured that we should encounter him in this wilderness, but we see him not. When we observed you in the distance, we hoped that you were He, but, alas, you are not. We are in haste to find Him, for the last days are upon us and on all mankind.'

Chiron plucked at Marcus's sleeve, and said:

'There is nothing for us here, my lord. These men are mad.'

'Nevertheless even a madman may set us on our way. And why not, since our sober wits have led us, as I fear, astray? Tell me, friend,' he said to the pilgrim, 'whence have you come?'

'Far have we journeyed, further must we go.'

Then Marcus, understanding that Chiron was wise, turned his horse's head, and the four rode towards the red mountains.

'Truly,' Chiron said, 'we might well believe ourselves that the last days are upon us, for I see the world has become the common ground of madmen. Be that as it may, however, it will not serve us for a dinner.'

To recount all the stages of their journey from that time on were wearisome. Suffice therefore to say that they endured hunger, thirst, much weariness and some hardship before they saw the golden towers of Milan rise before them. And when they did so, Father Bernardo and Gito both wept, the priest because he was ashamed of the fear he had felt, and the boy because he was now free of fear. So true is it that the same action is open to different interpretation; for which reason wise men judge their fellows not by their outward bearing but by their essence.

'Who, Father, were those pilgrims?' Marcus asked.

'It is my belief,' said the priest, making the sign of the Cross, 'that they were fallen angels in search of the route back to Paradise.'

At which Gito sniffed.

*(It is probable that Father Bernardo's words were prompted by his memory of the Book of Enoch, which only the initiated read well. Here we learn how two hundred angels fell to earth, where they descended from Mount Herman, their place of landing, lusting after the lovely daughters of men. Their leader was

22

Semyaz, whom the Greeks know as Orion, the mighty hunter, and spurred on by him, they took women with such rapacity that the children thus engendered were born monsters of terrible and unholy appetite. Enoch was therefore sent by the Archangel Raphael to warn his former comrades of God's mighty anger, and of his intention to send a Deluge upon the earth and to bury them under the stones of the wilderness. We may surmise that in the Father's opinion, the so-called pilgrims whom he encountered with our hero were all that remained of that fallen troop of angels, forever doomed to wander the waste places of the earth, and striving to deny the sons of men knowledge of the way of Truth and Enlightenment. But of this, more, as it may be, at some future date.)*

VI

You must know, beloved Prince, that at the time of which I write the mighty Empire of Rome had fallen on evil days.

Its unity was but nominally maintained, though one emperor resided in Constantinople and another in Milan. The fierce barbarian tribes had broken through the now fragile barriers erected against them.

You, my Prince, being both German and Roman, are heir to both Germany and Rome. It is in you that unity of Christendom is at last to be achieved, or rather restored, for in your person are united Roman virtue and German vigour.

In the years of Marcus's childhood, the great Empire was briefly held by a single person, the mighty and ever-glorious Emperor Theodosius, who repelled the tribes, suppressed the heresy taught by Arius, who maintained against all reason that the Son was not co-equal or co-eternal with the Father; and also exerted himself to extirpate the last vestiges of pagan superstition. His deeds were recorded on tablets of stone, still to be seen in the cathedral of Milan, but the words of praise outlasted the achievemnt that inspired them. Indeed, it is probable that the sculptor who carved them outlived it also.

The emperor to whom Marcus now made his approach was Honorius, unworthy son of Theodosius; a man of sloth, comfortable in body, dull of understanding, ardent only for ignoble pleasures, weak and irresolute as a feather blown in the wind. Yet this creature received in his palace acts of degrading homage such as would have disgusted the sturdy republican and manly soul of Augustus. So low had Rome fallen.

Marcus was therefore advised by a eunuch dressed from head to toe in yellow taffeta that he must prostrate himself before the

Emperor and kiss his foot in its green velvet slipper. But Marcus declared that he was a Roman nobleman and Christian knight and would fall at no man's feet; therefore, he said, he would do no more than bow to his lord, as civility demanded. This virtuous reply caused consternation, and guards seized him rudely and would have beaten him or thrust him into prison, had he not, with mental reservations, given way.

'For,' he said to himself, 'if I do but prostrate myself in form, while remaining upright in mind, then I do not in reality prostrate myself at all.'

(So casuistry is not, as ignorant men assert, an invention of the Jesuits, enemies of honesty and free thought.)

Therefore Marcus did as he was bid, and even, after kissing the slipper, struck his head three times on the marble floor.

The Emperor, who had heard of his great virtue, greeted him with the appearance of warmth. Yet the glances he shot at Marcus were full of suspicion. For it was as it ever is: the ignoble man felt reproached in the presence of virtue. For a little, Honorius toyed with the idea of corrupting that virtue, for the sight of Marcus's fair person – the curling hair, the soft red lips, the strong straight thighs – filled him with lust. But even while he played with lascivious thoughts, he feared to keep Marcus at court, where all could observe how in every way he outshone the Emperor and diminished him. So he determined to dispatch him on some mission of great danger, not reckoning that if Marcus won success in such an enterprise, his sun would shine still more brightly and quite eclipse the faint rays which Honorius himself emitted. But the truth was that Honorius, on account of his cowardice and addiction to wine and all vices, was incapable of sound judgement or of estimating the consequences of his actions.

Know then that forethought is a necessary attribute of princes.

Now it happened that the western Empire was then threatened by a barbarian people known as the Visigoths. They had indeed been admitted within its boundaries by Theodosius, and their war band incorporated in the Roman army. But either because they had been denied the rewards they had been promised, or because their chief, the great king Alaric, despised the indolence and effeminacy of Honorius, or merely because their warlike nature craved new satisfactions, they were discontented, and now threatened to make war against those they had formerly sworn to protect.

Honorius now resolved to send Marcus as an ambassador to Alaric, to test him and determine how he might be prevented from the war he contemplated. For Honorius was greatly terrified. Indeed he could scarce utter the name of Alaric without stammering in his fear, and only the layers of golden paint on his face disguised his pallor.

If it appears remarkable that he should have chosen one so young and come so lately to his court for so urgent an embassy, you must remember that all the world spoke well of Marcus, though few knew him. And in any case Honorius told himself that if the boy failed, he would be free of one whose virtue being apparent to all served as a rebuke to his own vice and incapacity. Moreover he feared that others might seize on Marcus and set him up as a rival who should supplant him on the throne. For Honorius was not altogether blind to his own deficiencies, and for this reason existed in a state of fear and apprehension.

Marcus understood the danger of the charge he had been given. Yet he welcomed the opportunity it offered to display his virtue. Only a craven knight could refuse such a challenge.

On the night before his departure was due, Marcus received a summons from the Emperor's sister Honoria. She commanded him to attend her in her private apartments, for she wished, as is reported, to see what manner of youth had undertaken so perilous a duty. You must understand, my Prince, that in those days women played a more active part in public life and the affairs of State than Holy Church now considers it proper for them to do. Whether this is a wise judgement, or whether the way of the Ancients was superior, is matter for debate it would too long delay my narrative to embark on.

Marcus was received at the door of the Princess's apartments by a comely African page. Having checked what the Greeks call his 'credentials', the boy led him into a long low chamber, lit by candles gathered in groups of six, and a fire burning in the hearth. This fire had been carried thither in secret from Rome when the Princess's pious father had laid waste the pagan temples, among them that of Vesta; and it was indeed the flame that had burned and never been extinguished in the Temple of Vesta, guarded by an order of priestesses sworn to virginity, throughout all the centuries since the foundation of the city. And it was this flame which was held by the Ancients to have secured Rome's impunity from all attacks. Whether there was some degree of impiety in removing it to the chamber of a princess, admittedly still virgin but not sworn to virginity, is a question that need concern no Christian. Honoria, however, who was, as legend tells us, 'tender to the memory of the old rites', cherished the flame while finding that same question disturbing.

When Marcus beheld her he stood still in amazement, for, except that she had a head of abundant golden hair, she was the very image of that princess who had led him to the bier on which the not-dead king had lain. Indeed it was some moments before Reason – that most divine of faculties – reasserted itself, and persuaded him of the deception which his senses played on him. Yet, in so persuading himself, he did not, being as yet unskilled in philosophy, comprehend the true relationship between what he had seen then and what was now before his eyes.

Observing him hesitate, the Princess smiled, and commanded him to draw near to where she reclined on what we have learned from the Saracens to call a divan.

He knelt and kissed her hand.

'No further ceremony,' she said, and gestured to a stool on which he was to sit.

'So,' she said, 'you are the young man my brother is sending to brave the terrible Alaric.'

'I have that honour, ma'am,' Marcus said.

'My brother is a fool.'

He made no response.

'Why,' she said, 'will he not permit the Visigoths to settle as they wish in Noricum, since he cannot prevent them from seizing all Italy if they so choose?'

'I am but his ambassador,' Marcus said.

'And one with honey in his mouth, that's clear.'

Then, seeing that she had embarrassed him, she laughed and ruffled his hair, and said she would explain why she had sent for him.

She wished him to carry a letter from her to Alaric. No one was to know of this letter. It would be death, or at the least blinding, for her if Marcus betrayed her.

So she withdrew a packet from her bosom and passed a letter sealed with her own seal. Then she gave Marcus two rings. The first, she said, he was to offer to Alaric, and report to her how it was received. The second, which was a garnet and a ring with great and curious properties, he was to wear himself. If his life was in danger while in the Gothic camp he was to show this ring to a certain Greek eunuch, by name John the Adept, who had fled from the Byzantine court to the camp of Alaric to escape charges of sodomy, 'Concerning which,' she said, 'I have no doubt but that he is guilty.

'Nevertheless,' she added, 'this John is an old ally of mine, on account of his being formerly a favourite of my mother, herself, as you must know, a princess of Byzantium.'

This information puzzled Marcus. He could not, in his innocence, comprehend how a eunuch could commit an act of sodomy. More perplexing still was the thought that, since the Princess already had an ally in the Gothic camp, she could have no true need of his services. With some hesitation, and in that tone of mild and polite apology which commended him to all men and women in whom virtue was not yet extinct, he voiced this doubt.

'Your uncertainty does not surprise me,' she said. 'Indeed, the possession of an understanding sufficiently acute to permit you to fathom my plans would consort ill with the frank and youthful beauty of your appearance. It is not, and never was, my intention to burden you with what you need not know in order to play the part I have assigned to you. So I shall say just this. First, though this John is an old ally, which is why I have told you to turn to him for help in any extremity, yet he is a man of cunning and devious nature and not such as I am prepared to trust in any great enterprise, and especially not in one which must remain secret. Second, the content of the letter I have entrusted to you is not for his eyes, but I could not trust him not to break the seal and then, having read the letter, refashion it, all the time awaiting the moment when he could put the knowledge thus gained to his own use, perhaps to my danger, I do not know. There is in this letter matter which may save the world from much torment and restore the glory and the power of the Empire itself. I tell you this only because you are pure in heart.'

With this explanation Marcus saw that he must be content, for no other was forthcoming.

Then she clapped her hands, and a maidservant entered bearing a jug of wine and golden goblets on a richly embossed silver tray. The girl was naked but for a thin chain of gold round her gleaming ebony hips, and as she leaned over Marcus to pour him wine, her skin glistened, little drops of eager perspiration shone on her pointed breasts, and she exuded a scent of musk-rose and cinnamon. But Marcus, mindful of his oath, averted his gaze, and when she saw this, the Princess was glad, for he had passed the test which she had set; and she believed he would serve her purpose better if his innocence remained intact. It is well known that a young man who has not lain with women inspires confidence in others more readily than one who falls victim to beauty and is ever eager to satisfy his lust. So the Princess knew that she had judged wisely. They drank the wine, which was spiced with cloves and nutmeg; and, in a little, while the moon was still up, Marcus left her chamber and set out on the next stage of his travels.

VII

For three days they journeyed through the mountains, knowing cold, weariness and fear. They were ever in danger from the fierce tribes that inhabit these inhospitable regions, and from the evil spirits that hover in the misty heights and assume strange enticing shapes to lure the unwary to their doom. Father Bernardo travelled in apprehension, but Chiron said, 'We are safer here than we shall be among the barbarians.' Which thought afforded no comfort to the priest.

But the spiced wine he had drunk with the Princess Honoria sang all these days in Marcus's veins, and it seemed to him that it was a potion which bound him to his lady, and her to him likewise, so that they had formed between them a bond of love which neither time nor any future affections could sever.

On the fourth day, they breasted a ridge, and below them extended a great plain that stretched eastwards till it merged with the sky. And all the plain over its immensity was dotted with black tents, and wagons, and the movement of men. There rose to them the lowing of oxen, the neighing of horses, the rattle of armour and the cries of women and children. So they knew that the whole army of the Visigoths was encamped below them; and the sight was terrible.

You must remember, my Prince, that Marcus had not yet known war, and he had never seen an army drawn up for battle.

As they descended the steep and winding path, they became aware that it was not only an army that lay exposed in the plain. It was a whole people that was on the move. This cheered both Chiron and Gito, for they reasoned that in so great a multitude there would doubtless be rich pickings and many occasions for amusement.

They were challenged by sentries who, however, waved them by in such negligent manner that it seemed to Marcus they had come upon a settled habitation rather than an army on the march. This impression was fortified when he found no difficulty in being directed to the pavilion of the King. There was an air of informality which he found pleasing, and which made an agreeable contrast to the elaborate ceremonies with which he had been constrained to approach his emperor. Indeed, my Prince, great men are more distinguished by an easy and welcoming confidence than by stiff ritual and solemn pomp.

The Gothic king was seated on a bench and apparently engaged in dispensing justice. Marcus saw a figure that had once been tall but was now bowed by labours and exertions. Alaric's hair was grizzled at the temples. He was bare-headed and wore no mark of office. His face was scarred with sword-cuts, but relieved from a fierce appearance by kindly eyes and an understanding smile.

(This description of the barbarian king is purely fanciful, unless our author is drawing from some manuscript long since lost. We have little evidence as to either Alaric's appearance or his manner. It may be assumed that our author is inventing, first to point a contrast with the decadent and fearful Honorius, and second to provide a pattern for his pupil, the young Hohenstaufen emperor.)

When Alaric saw Marcus approach, he immediately indicated that he should sit awhile on a stool which an attendant had brought forward, until he himself had finished the business with which he was occupied. Marcus did as he was bid, and another attendant provided him with a mug of dark sweet ale, such as he had never drunk before. Meanwhile he watched the King and was further impressed by the care he was evidently taking to enquire into the details of the case before him, and by the quiet manner in which he questioned the litigants. Being ignorant of the Gothic language he was of course unable to understand what was being said; but the King's manner was sufficient to persuade him that he was in the presence of a ruler whose sense of responsibility for the welfare of his subjects was profound.

At last the matter was determined, or suspended for the time being, and Alaric turned to Marcus and made enquiry concerning his journey and the purpose of this visit which, he said, did him such honour. He spoke in Latin, and though inclined to disregard or lop off case-endings and to frame his speech inelegantly (by the standards of Tully, whose work Marcus had studied in his Rhetoric classes), his fluency was considerable, and his meaning perfectly clear.

Marcus then explained that he had been dispatched by the Emperor to urge the King to remember that he had always been a friend of the Roman People, had indeed been invested with the title *magister militum illyricum*; that reports of an intended incursion into Italy had disturbed the Emperor; and that – here Marcus hesitated, attempting to frame the Emperor's words in more diplomatic language than had been employed – Alaric was to understand that Honorius would regard such an incursion as an affront to his dignity and to that of the Senate and the Roman People.

'And this is your message, the purpose of your embassy?' the King said.

'It is.'

'Have you no offer to bring me, no proposals to satisfy my grievances?'

'I merely repeat the words I was bid to speak.'

Alaric took a piece of what the Goths call, in their language, *biltungha* – thin slices of beef dried in the wind that scours the endless plains – and chewed it. His brow wrinkled as he pondered what Marcus had said.

'When the Sarmatians pressed hard upon the frontiers of the western Empire, it was I and my Visigoths who drove them back and diverted their course. Your emperor lay weeping in purple, terrified in his gilded palace. And when I had achieved so great a victory on his behalf, he showered me with praise and with honours and titles. And now he sends me this bare message to tell me, Alaric, King of the Visigoths and master of the Host, to obey him. Your emperor is a coward and a liar and an ingrate and, young man, between you and me, a shit and a degenerate. That is my reply. Now let us go and dine.'

It was after they had feasted on the flesh of oxen and goats, and drunk deeply of the sweet dark ale, that Marcus, stretched on a couch covered with goatskins, was approached by a tall stout figure, dressed in a robe of yellow silk, who introduced himself his as the eunuch John the Adept. His head was shaven and his skin was soft as a young girl's and pale as a winter dawn. Marcus, who had as yet found no suitable moment to offer the Princess's letter to the Gothic king (which he was reluctant to do since he had realised that Alaric would be unable to read it himself), welcomed him cautiously, for he remembered the ambiguity of the Princess's words concerning him.

The eunuch settled himself beside him on the couch, and his gaze was such that Marcus, with an appearance of casualness, drew one of the goatskins across his legs, remarking that he was unaccustomed to the chill of these northern nights. John the Adept rewarded him with a smile of infinite sweetness, in which the young man nevertheless read deep, and disagreeable, design, and complimented him on the manner in which he had conveyed the Emperor's message to the King, and the air of indifference with which he had responded to Alaric's angry outburst.

'I see,' he said, 'that you have the makings of a courtier. But if you are to make headway in your embassy, then I am the man in whom alone you can safely confide.'

Marcus replied that he was honoured, and enquired of the eunuch concerning the manners of the Goths of which, as he said, he was ignorant.

'I am puzzled,' he said, 'for they appear to be noble-minded and generous, and yet I am told that they sacked the temples of Eleusis, home of mysteries which all should surely revere.'

'It is good to hear a Christian, for such I suppose you to be, talk with reverence of the Old Religion,' the eunuch said.

'And are you not yourself a follower of the true Christ?' Marcus asked.

Again the eunuch smiled.

33

'That there is truth in Christ's message I would not deny,' he replied. 'And yet, I am one who has travelled to India, and throughout the great empire of Persia, and have heard wise men in different lands dilate on the nature of reality. This being, as it were, so, how can I yield to the vain belief that there is one central unchallengeable truth, which has been denied to all mankind, till it was revealed a few short centuries ago to a handful of Jews in a tiny corner of Judaea, which is itself but a dot in the vastness of Creation?'

Marcus shifted under the goatskins, excited by the implications of the eunuch's words.

'I was reared,' John said, 'in Oblia on the Euxine, where, long before Christ was conceived, my ancestors paid special reverence to the shade of the great Achilles. Near the mouth of the great river Danube lies the island of Leuke, which belongs to the hero's shade. There a white cliff rises sheer from the sea, and on the island is no dwelling of mankind, no sound of human voice; only flocks of white birds soar to the heavens, calling out or emitting cries which may be hymns of praise; or were long understood as such. Sailors who pass the island are stilled with reverent awe. It is forbidden to those who venture on to that sacred shore to pass the night there, but when they have visited the tomb and temple of the hero, and made votive offerings, they must embark again before the dark closes in and the sea-birds fall silent. This island was gifted by the god Poseidon, whom you Romans style Neptune, to the nymph Thetis not only for the last earthly resting-place of her son, but for his continued blessedness. And there were gathered there also other heroes whose blameless life persuaded Zeus that they should not be abandoned in the gloom of the underworld. It was believed that the white birds, called halcyons, were the visible manifestations of the souls of departed heroes, which was why they were left unmolested and regarded with devotion.'

As he spoke, Marcus experienced a feeling that had visited him before, for he caught the beauty of that world which he had been schooled to dismiss as locked in pagan superstition, and set in opposition to the true religion of Christ. It seemed to him that the

34

world of the spirit was stranger than he had yet known, and that truth was not single but might wear many faces.

Then the eunuch, sensing that he had awakened the interest of the young man, told him that the destruction of the temples of Eleusis was the sign of a terrible lust for simplification, a protest against the manifold variety of experience.

'I myself,' he said, 'have delved deep in the realms of spirit, and so I know how myth – or what may be dismissed as myth – may encapsulate profound truths that reason cannot attain. The exercise of reason, which we may call rationalism, is the furious denial of the diversity of experience and true knowledge. It may be that this world of sense is but a dream, but that thought is intolerable to those who live wholly in it. As a young man I studied the Orphic mysteries and was initiated into the rites of Orphism.'

'Even the name has been hidden from me,' Marcus said, 'for I have never heard it.'

'Very well,' said the eunuch, moving more closely towards the young man, and lowering his voice. 'Very well, you must know that the God, for such he was thought to be, Dionysos, was born of the union between Zeus, and his daughter Persephone, herself the child of Zeus's coupling with Demeter. Zeus was held to be both creator and sovereign of the world, and of his plenitude set up the child Dionysos as the ruler of this physical world which we feel we inhabit. But then Zeus's old enemies and rivals, the Titans, paid court to the child, and distracted him with a mirror by means of which he might delight in his beauty, as you, my dear boy, might take pleasure in yours. While he was so engaged, the treacherous Titans killed him, dismembered his fair body, and devoured his flesh. It is this terrible slaughter and dismemberment which is re-enacted, and was so re-enacted over the ages, by his devotees. But Zeus – omnipotent lord of the universe – struck the Titans with lightning, and restored his son Dionysos to life, health, beauty and wholeness. You would be wise to ponder on that. At the same time, out of the ashes of the wretched Titans, man was formed or emerged. He inherited, as we all do, the elements of both Dionysos and his destroyers, the Titans. Man has therefore a dual nature, a soul formed of the divine Dionysian element and a body formed of the base material of the Titans. And so we bear within us a dual desire also: for the divine harmony of the spheres and also for whatever will satisfy the greedy and destructive demands of the body, which holds our soul in its living prison . . .'

So saying, the eunuch slipped his hand beneath the goatskin that covered Marcus's legs, and felt him – doubtless so that he might prove the involuntary impulses of the flesh, which man inherits from the unruly and rebellious Titans.

VIII

Though the Gothic king had so indignantly rejected the message or rather instruction which Marcus had carried to him from the Emperor, yet he showed no eagerness for the young Roman to depart from his camp. Chiron scratched his head and told Marcus he didn't like it.

'The King's a barbarian,' he said, 'and you can't trust them barbarians. They even shit in spirals, they're that devious. If you ask me, sir, the only good barbarian's a dead one, and I don't mind who hears me say that, so long as he's not a barbarian hisself.'

But Marcus met with only kindness and consideration from Alaric. The King spoke of his enjoyment of the young nobleman's company, and regularly placed Marcus on his right hand at meals, and also when he dispensed justice before his tent. Marcus was impressed by the frequency with which the King undertoook this duty, and, as on the first day, by the calm and assured manner in which he executed it. There could be no doubt, he thought, that Alaric exhibited the true nature of monarchy as Honorius didn't. Which was in itself puzzling and even distressing, since the one was a barbarian and the other a Roman.

Many days they rode out to hawk, and again Marcus delighted in the King's mastery of the most noble art of falconry. In this he was wise, for in no other bodily activity does a king show himself more god-like than in the exercise of his authority over these birds which a wise man has called 'the most free and magnificent of God's creation'. And the King was pleased to see the young Roman's intuitive sympathy with his falcons.

Nothing was said for many days of the Emperor's message, and Marcus saw no sign that the King was restless or preparing for war. On the contrary he found in the Gothic camp an atmosphere which in some remarkable way appeared to recover the simpler and more noble days of the youth of the world such as Homer sang.

He did not choose to disturb this by presenting the King with the Princess's letter; and indeed there were many days when, caught up in the pleasures of the moment, he forgot it entirely.

Truly, he thought, there is something fine in the primitive simplicity of these people. Could it be that we, in this evening of Empire, have followed the wrong path, one that leads us further from that knowledge of the Divine Purpose, which it should be our constant goal to attain? And may it not be that these noble savages are better attuned to the Divine Harmony of the spheres?

It was natural that being young and innocent, Marcus should have felt the attraction of barbarian simplicity. He did not yet understand that the pursuit of knowledge, though arduous, is enjoined on us by our very nature.

He would come to know this when his task was revealed to him; and yet the secret object of his search, which is that of all who seek wisdom, would be obstinate in its refusal to disclose itself.

(Here our author trembles on the verge of illumination. The pursuit of wisdom, which leads to a true understanding of the forces that shape our being and our fate, may be likened to the journey of a traveller, bearing only a lantern, through a dark forest. The light shed falls short of revelation; yet when light is added to light, as one age succeeds another, we at last enter into the true light that scatters darkness.)

One day, guiltily mindful of the manner in which the Princess Honoria had looked upon him, and of the importance of her charge, Marcus told Alaric that he was the bearer of a secret letter. The King enquired if he knew its matter.

'How should I?' he said. 'For the seal is unbroken.'

Whereupon the King commanded him to break the seal and read the letter to him.

'It is,' he said, 'for the messenger to deliver the message in full, and, even if I could read script, I should still wish to hear it from you.'

Marcus made ready to read, but first gave Alaric the ring which the Princess had entrusted to him, saying that his instructions were to do so at the same time as he delivered the letter. The King examined it closely, tried to force it on his finger, and, failing to do so, tucked it into the pouch which dangled from his belt.

He then commanded Marcus to commence his reading; and the text was as follows:

'My lord king, I send you this by the hand of one who, should he prove unworthy of my confidence, will doubtless be the cause of my death, so jealous and fearful is my brother, the Emperor. It is of him that I wish to speak. Cowardly and yet boastful, he has denied you and your Goths your most modest request, and commanded you to withdraw beyond the frontier of Empire. It is folly to command what one cannot enforce, and, in consequence, knowing this, all Romans fear your righteous wrath. But consider, my king; it is not Rome that has offended you; it is only Honorius. Why then should Rome suffer? Now, my lord king, I have friends who can turn the key that will unlock the gates of Empire for you, without the shedding of much blood or the waste and torment of war. I seek only your word, returned to me by this same messenger, that you will make me your wife, consort, and empress; and I shall straightway set in motion that which will make you master of the Empire and successor to the great Caesars themselves. As for my brother . . . but you need not, my lord king, be burdened with my plans for him. Say but the word.'

Marcus stopped reading and looked up. Alaric's face darkened, he frowned, and bit his lips. Marcus himself was troubled, for, on the one hand, he had seen sufficient of Honorius to despise him, but on the other, as the Emperor's envoy, he could not think it right to be party to a plan that would destroy him. Moreover, though this was the least of his anxieties, he had heard tell that the penalty for treason was death in most horrid and painful and shameful form.

Alaric looked at him, and his eye was as keen as a soaring falcon's.

39

'So, my child, you speak with double tongue. In your master's voice you order me to quit the bounds of Empire; and in your mistress's to join in conspiracy against your master. Is this honourable?'

Marcus flushed, for he valued nothing more highly than his honour.

'My lord king,' he said, 'believe me that I was wholly ignorant of the matter of this epistle.'

'That may be so,' the King replied. 'And yet how can I tell whether you speak truth or not? You have a fair face and a pleasing manner, but these are attributes such as anyone hoping to deceive would choose to have in their messenger. How can I tell whether this letter and the offer made to me are not a vile trick? The iniquity of Rome knows no limit. Moreover, now that you are no longer ignorant – if indeed you ever were – of the proposal made to me, you have become a danger to yourself and to my people.'

He gave orders to those standing by that they should seize Marcus and bind him and carry him to a hut which served as a prison and which stood at the northernmost extremity of the camp, hard against the great river. There Marcus, for the moment dumbfounded by this reversal of fortune, was shackled and chained to the post which supported the hut's roof.

Who can blame the young man for having been cast into dismay, almost indeed despair? Child of good fortune, favoured by nature, accustomed to the ready winning of the love and admiration of all he encountered, he had never experienced adversity. The King's abrupt change of mood, from sun to stormy thunder, had taken him by surprise. In a little, however, his resolution returned, he ceased to bewail his fate, and found a truer and more manly cause of concern in wondering how his misfortune would rebound on his friends. Unfortunately his guards, ignorant of Latin, were unable to enlighten him. Their surly looks suggested they were in any case unwilling.

So, for many days and nights while the moon that governs the shifting fortunes of men shrank and then swelled again, Marcus languished in the mean hut, shivering in the hours of darkness on account of the emanation of damp vapours from the river. His spirits were often low, sore oppressed. He felt keenly the injustice of his imprisonment and the uncertainty of his fate. But it was not long before the natural ardour of youth resumed its sway; for it is not in the nature of the young and virile to be long cast down, since they cannot believe what old men know: that evil fortune is man's lot, and that all earthly glory crumbles into dust, a grim reality which only those who have learned, and had the courage, to delve deep in the mysteries may survive and transcend. But I digress.

Be that as it may, Marcus soon recovered his buoyancy of spirit, and said to himself: 'The worst is not yet come, so long as I may conceive of something more terrible than my present condition.' Nevertheless he could not still the anxiety he felt for his companions; it is the nature of true royalty to care for those dependent on it; and they are not to be cast aside like chaff.

One night, his guards, after they had brought him the bowl of porridge and the mug of ale which was his supper, unfastened the chains that bound him, and indicated that he could now take his rest on a rude couch covered with skins, at which he had indeed often directed a longing gaze. He was so weak that he fell to the ground and was there seized with cramp. They rudely helped him to his feet, and one brought oil and water that he might cleanse himself of the filth that encrusted his lower limbs. Another then fetched a clean tunic, and all the while Marcus wondered for what he was now being prepared; this sudden accession of care for his comfort and appearance puzzled him, all the more so when the guards departed and left him alone.

In a little he heard the sound of the door of the hut being unbarred. The eunuch John the Adept entered, a lantern in his hand. He was followed by two slaves carrying a table, a jug of wine and two tankards. John spoke to them in Greek and they left with much bowing and scraping. The door was not barred behind them.

Marcus, mindful of the advances the eunuch had made at their first meeting and conscious of his unprotected condition, received him doubtfully. But he was made easy when John, having poured the wine (which was spiced with cloves), seated himself on the stool some distance from the couch where Marcus lay. So it was with a calm voice that he enquired of the eunuch the purpose of this visit.

'When we talked previously,' John said, 'I advised you to trust me if you wished to make headway with your embassy. You chose to disregard my words, and so you find yourself a captive, your life in danger.'

Marcus explained that he had obeyed the instructions given him by the Princess. Had the matter been left to his own judgement, he would naturally have consulted John.

'You speak like a courtier,' the eunuch said, and sniffed deeply. 'But you must learn, dear boy, that the judgement of women is ever faulty, and has been so since Eve first ate the apple. Had you spoken to me, and broken the seal of the letter, which I should have found no difficulty in repairing, we would have approached Alaric in different fashion, and he would have assented to the Princess's proposal. But now, because he thinks his honour besmirched, and because like all barbarians he attaches an absurd importance to that concept, he is determined to carry war into Italy.'

'And is this my fault?' Marcus cried out in distress. 'Is it on account of my folly that the horror of war is to be loosed on Italy?'

The eunuch smiled and said nothing.

'Then I am the most miserable of men and deserve to die,' Marcus exclaimed; and the very thought brought tears to his eyes.

'Such was indeed the King's intention,' John said, 'for he felt what he termed your treachery deeply. He declared himself sorely deceived in you, and was all the more angry because he had formed an affection for you. But, using all the arts at my disposal – and I must tell you they are considerable – I have persuaded him that you were but an innocent instrument, and so he has agreed to spare your life. More than that, he has determined that you will accompany him on the march, and even serve as his aide-de-camp.'

Marcus was astonished by this new reversal of fortune, and at first scarce convinced that this was the King's way. Yet, when he reflected how Alaric's early friendship had been transformed in an instant into hostility and repugnance, it seemed less strange that he should be so abruptly restored to favour. Conscious of the debt he owed the eunuch, he asked how he could repay it. He was all the more eager to do this quickly because he could not hide from himself the distaste he felt for him.

Again John smiled, and gave a quick lick to his lips.

'I seek no reward, no immediate reward,' he said. 'My highest ambitions are not of this world. As for my lower ambitions, your boy Gito came to me in great fear and distress, and so in comforting him I satisfied those.'

He kissed the tips of his fingers to express this satisfaction, and continued:

'Nevertheless, I do have matter of great import which I must now reveal to you. Alaric intends to march on Rome, for it is only by seizing the city that he can fulfil his now burning ambition to humiliate Honorius. Now listen carefully, dear boy. The Palace of the Holy Father, styled the Lateran, for it was formerly the property of the Laterani, a noble family since the earliest days of Republican Rome, contains the most sacred relics of the Christian Faith. The chapel of the Bishop of Rome is approached by way of the Scala Sancta. Do you know what that staircase is, young man? No? Then listen and be amazed: the Scala Sancta are those holy stairs which Christ mounted in order to be examined before Pilate, and which the Empress-Dowager Helena of York, mother of the great and fearful Constantine, carried from Jerusalem to Rome. In that chapel too may be found a portion of the Holy Cross, which she also rescued from the Place of Skulls called Golgotha. These facts are widely known. But there is one other relic there of which the world is ignorant. This is none other than the Cup from which Christ drank at the Last Supper, and which is known also as the Holy Grail. Whoever drinks of this will receive everlasting life and escape the chains of Death.

'Think of that, dear boy.

'Some admittedly maintain that the Cup is not in the Lateran but in the nearby Basilica of San Lorenzo beyond the walls that

43

the Emperor Aurelius caused to be thrown up around the city. They say so for this reason: that when the saint was seized by agents of the still-pagan emperor and commanded to surrender the treasures of the Church, he was burned on a gridiron because he tried to fob off his inquisitors by presenting them with the sick and destitute of the city, whom he declared to be the true treasures of the Christian Faith and Holy Church.

'Wise men, however, are not deceived by such rhetoric, and therefore many have concluded that the Holy Grail, choicest of all treasures, was then in the keeping of this Lorenzo, and must now lie concealed in that basilica which houses his martyred bones. But this I do not believe, for I have been vouchsafed secret information which persuades me that the Cup is to be found in a vault of the Lateran Palace, and I have learned in a dream that it is our destiny – yours and mine, dear boy – to recover it, and so reap the rich rewards promised by its mysteries. And the intention of Alaric offers us the opportunity.'

IX

For weeks the Gothic horde trailed down Italy on the roads the legions had built. The Emperor Honorius, whimpering in Milan, dared not move to impede their progress or resist their arms. Every day, foraging parties scoured the countryside for supplies, food for the tens of thousands of knights and men-at-arms and their still more numerous camp-followers, fodder for the shaggy ponies. Not a granary was neglected, and in the wake of the host the farmers and peasants were reduced to eating acorns, beech-nuts and even grass. The herds and flocks which the Goths drove with them spread over all the fields. Towns were required to surrender their stores of food, for which they received no payment. Any that refused or even deliberated were stormed and sacked, and the wretched citizens put to the sword or driven into the mountains, where many starved. The march was slow, little more than ten Roman miles a day, for it was not only an army, but a whole people on the move: women went into labour, infants came mewling into the world every day; and still the advance continued.

Marcus was filled with both horror and exultation. On the one hand he could not but respond to the magnitude of this great adventure; he was caught up in the surge of purpose. As he lay on the bare ground under the stars of night, and listened to the murmur of the camp, the clank and shuffling and whinnies that came from the horse-lines, he felt himself to be a part of something that had gone on since the beginning of time. This, he told himself, was how the great Achilles had felt as he made his way to the ships that would carry the Greeks to Troy; this was how Alexander's soldiers sniffed the air as they ventured to the rising of the sun. He was at one with Caesar and Antony and Trajan, makers of empire.

But on the other hand, it was towards the destruction of that empire that the Gothic army was advancing: against eternal unconquered Rome, that city which had never yielded to a foreign foe (as he had learned from his reading of Livy) since that awful day, centuries past, when the Gauls pulled the beards of senators sitting impassive but defiant on their thrones on the Capitol.

Often in the evenings Alaric would ask Marcus, as they sat over their wine, to tell him stories about the great days of Rome; and indeed he could not hear enough about that empire which he revered even as he prepared its destruction. When Marcus told him how Aeneas had been promised for his descendants 'empire without limit of time or place', as Vergil relates, Alaric, deeply moved by these lines of immortal poetry (which, however, had to be repeated several times before he fully understood them, for his Latin was so much simpler than the poet's), sat for a long while in silence; then remarked that if the promise was true, then he himself was its heir. Marcus wondered whether, in saying this, Alaric turned over in his mind the offer made him by the Princess Honoria, whom, however, he on no occasion mentioned.

No story more impressed and puzzled the noble barbarian than that of Sulla the Dictator. When he learned that Sulla abdicated power and retired into private life, he could not understand how Sulla should then have lived unmolested.

'He had made so many enemies,' he said. 'There were the families of those he had condemned to death. And yet they did not take their revenge when there was no obstacle to doing so. Truly, you are a strange people, you Romans.'

At last, soon after dawn on a lovely morning in June, they came within sight of the city. Marcus had never seen anything as beautiful as the fabled walls touched with the first pink of morning light. He reined in his horse, amazed to see the great aqueducts that marched from the hills across the Campagna to slake the city's thirst and supply water to the imperial baths. As they approached, the seemingly impassable barrier of the Aurelian Wall reared up before them. He recalled, tenderly, the noble lines of the poet Rufus Namatianus:

46

> To number the glories of Rome is like counting
> The stars in the sky . . .

'Surely,' he said to himself, 'it were sacrilege to assault this stupendous work of man. And vain too, I should think.'

John the Adept plucked at his sleeve.

'You wonder at the task before us,' he said, 'and indeed I am not surprised that you look amazed.'

'The eternal unconquered city,' Marcus murmured. 'Now I see indeed why it is so called.'

'Yet the city will fall,' John said. 'All is arranged. Last night emissaries whom I had sent in advance, weeks ago, returned to assure me that we have friends within who will open the gates to us. There will be no need to scale these mighty defences, no need to endure the rigours of a siege. More than twenty years ago, despite the protests of the famous Senator Quintus Aurelius Symmachus, last defender of the antique virtues of Rome and its old Religion, the Emperor caused the great winged statue of Victory to be removed from the Senate House on the grounds that its presence was an insult to the one true God. A little later all forms of pagan sacrifice and the worship even of household gods were prohibited by imperial decree. Rome that was, no longer is, as Symmachus lamented, though Rome itself will be forever. Truly, reality wears many faces, but those that were once gods of this city rightly named Caput Mundi dwell now with owls and bats under their dark roofs.'

'How is it,' Marcus said, 'that under the protection of these false gods, Rome was inviolable, but now, when only the true God, Father of all Mankind, is worshipped there, the city should be exposed to invasion and sack?'

John smiled but offered no reply. Indeed there was none that he could give, for no man can explain why the Lord permits evil fortune to be the lot of those who seek after truth and righteousness, while infidels may flourish like the green bay tree, and, as the Psalmist says, may grin like dogs.

But even if John had been about to suggest an answer, he was prevented by the arrival of Alaric.

47

The King was pale, as if, Marcus thought, he was abashed by the enormity of the enterprise. Marcus, appalled by the prospect of the sack and rapine which he imagined was about to follow, entreated the King to spare the city. But Alaric replied:

'Young man, you may suppose that my men are rude barbarians. Let me remind you that we are baptised Christians, though adhering to that form of the Faith which the Bishop of Rome obstinately condemns as a heresy, in that we follow the teaching of the saintly Arius, priest of Alexandria, who taught that the Son is not of the same substance as the Father, nor is he co-eternal with him. Nevertheless, as Christians we revere Rome, where Peter and Paul suffered. Do not suppose therefore that I have come here to destroy. My purpose is but to take possession.'

With this, Alaric frowned, and ordered his troops to advance against the Flaminian Gate.

They moved forward in close order at a smart trot. A shower of arrows was released from the wall to the left of the gate, and a roar of fury rose from the body of the Gothic army in reply. But this was quickly stilled when three bodies were seen to be hurled from the wall to crash on the stones below. Then the gate swung open and the Gothic army entered Rome.

Marcus, who had studied Vegetius and other masters of the arts of war, was impressed by their perfect discipline. They marched in silence, shoulder to shoulder, down the street which he later learned was the Via Flaminia. The main body of the Gothic host remained, however, beyond the walls, and it was only the elite troops whom Alaric permitted to pass through the gate; for he could rely on their absolute obedience.

As they passed along the street, a few cheers were raised from the rooftops and upper windows, but for the most part the citizens remained within, and silent, lurking behind closed shutters, and doubtless many on their knees praying for a deliverance that they scarce dared hope might be granted them.

Towards noon the Gothic vanguard was drawn up in the Field of Mars, once, in more virtuous times, the parade-ground of the armies of the Republic. Then Alaric, displaying the sublime confidence which is the mark of greatness of soul, himself advanced at the head of only a small body of picked men, his household knights, beyond the bloodstained magnificence of the Colosseum, where so many martyrs had proved their Christian Faith, till they came to the Lateran Palace, where, as the King had commanded, the Holy Father waited to receive him and surrender the keys of the city. Marcus knew both shame and excitement as he saw the successor to St Peter bow the knee to the Gothic king. But then Alaric extended his hands, raised the Holy Father to his feet, and himself knelt and kissed the ring which the Pope held out to him.

For a little they spoke together, and then music sounded, brave and holy music, and together King and Pope led the company into the great basilica for the celebration of the Mass. Marcus, deeply moved, would have followed them, but John the Adept took him by the arm in restraint. When the whole company had moved away, he led Marcus to a little door in the corner of the basilica, which opened on to a narrow staircase. They descended this, carefully, for it was ill-lit, only by tapers placed at intervals along the slimy walls, and so came to a dim cavernous chamber deserted and empty but for a great tomb raised in the centre of the stone-flagged floor. Passing by this, they approached an iron-studded door concealed behind a curtain at the far end of the room. Marcus waited while John struck the door three times with the brass head of his staff. The sound echoed round the vacant chamber and there followed a long silence. Marcus looked at the eunuch. There were flecks of white froth on his lips, and the sweat stood out on his temples.

A shuffling of feet broke the silence. The door swung open, creaking at the hinges. There stood before them a lean bald man in a yellow robe. He embraced John and without speaking indicated that they were to follow him.

Once more they descended a flight of steps worn with age and slippery. The fetid air made Marcus gasp for breath. He felt sick to the stomach. He would fain have turned back, for he knew in his heart that their enterprise was impious. Yet he was impotent against the eunuch's will.

Their guide conducted them into a little room. Four men sat at a table playing cards which were divided into four suits: Cup, Lance, Sword and Dish. But the men who played at the cards wore the mask of Death, and so Marcus crossed himself as they passed by them.

And still no word was spoken, nor had been since they were admitted to the vaults.

(Our author recounts this scene without explanation, or indeed, as it appears, purpose. I hold this to be proof of its authenticity. In any study of the Mysteries that underlie the search for eternal truth, there is ever that which appears contrary to reason, or which does not seem to fit the story being told. Some maintain that this is because all stories have but one origin, and that narrative itself is therefore but the attempt to devise a metaphor that illuminates what cannot be named. Be that as it may, it would appear, and may be perceived by the initiated, that these figures representing Death were playing with the very cards of Life. For it is clear from the naming of the suits that they employed the pack called the Tarot, now vulgarly put to use by the Egyptian race for the purpose of divination, as is justified by the assertion that the twenty-two keys of the Tarot pack correspond to the twenty-two columns that support the Great Hall of the Palace of Medinet Abou, on the ceiling of which the learned may read astrological designs, and thus ponder the Lost Wisdom of Ancient Egypt. But others affirm that these cards have no such significance, but represent symbols of Fertility. What is well attested, and beyond dispute, is that they correspond in detail to the Mystery of the Holy Grail. Nevertheless, in the opinion of the Wisest Scholars, the Grail itself is but a Metaphor, and was never a Real Object. This our author does not comprehend.)

If, most dearly beloved, I was now to expatiate on the fears which seized Marcus, your ardent spirit might find matter for condemnation. But you are to understand that he was engaged on no mere knightly adventure, but had ventured into an enterprise which imperilled his immortal soul. It was terror of what they might discover which he felt, not the mere temporal fear that they might be apprehended in their undertaking, which was certainly unsanctioned and which bore the appearance of a vulgar crime.

They came to an inner chamber, and, to his amazement, Marcus saw there a bier on which lay, still in the image of death, that old king whom he had first happened on in the Castle of the Lovely Maiden on the first day of his adventure. He could not stay himself from crying out. Whereupon there emerged from behind a tapestry curtain the Maiden or Princess herself.

'You are tardy,' she sighed, 'and I fear too late indeed.'

When he heard these words, John the Adept swore and, thrusting the Princess aside, laid his right hand on the King's face. And when he did so, the flesh crumbled, like paper which has been burned in a low fire and which still retains shape and semblance till a hand is laid on it. Again the eunuch gave vent to an exclamation, in which Marcus heard rage and bafflement, and, all at once, like a dream escaping as one wakes, the figure of the King, and of the Princess, dissolved before them. Nothing of what had been remained. Marcus heard the door of the chamber clang shut behind them. The light was extinguished. He found himself alone with John in the most profound darkness.

His first instinct was to upbraid his companion whose greed and ambition had carried them into such great danger. And he would have done so if the chill silence had not been broken by the eunuch's whimpering. This aroused the young man's pity; he felt superior to his companion in crime.

So, when John moaned that they were betrayed and destroyed, he did not reproach him, but instead remarked that, however dire their predicament, they would be best employed in seeking a way out of it.

'There is no way,' the eunuch said. 'When we passed through that chamber where four dead men sat at cards, I should have known what was to be our fate, and have drawn back.'

'If it is indeed our fate, we could not have drawn back,' Marcus said. 'But I do not believe it is my destiny to die here.'

So he set himself to explore the chamber in search of some means by which they might escape. The task was difficult on account of the deep darkness, but, very slowly and with great care, he ran his hands up and down the walls, moving, ever to his left, around the chamber. When he came to the door, he felt its iron hinge, and came close to despair. But his natural fortitude forbade that, and he resumed his search.

At last, having made his way round and returned to the door, his one point of certainty, and found nothing, he got on his hands and knees and examined the floor, inch by careful inch. It was made of flagstones, and that gave him hope. He crawled over it, seeking any crack between the stones. Then it seemed that one moved under his knee. He drew back, leaned on it with his hands, and was certain that it stirred. He drew the dagger which he wore at his belt, and tried to dig it into the join between that stone and the next. For a little he met with no success. Then, using the point of the dagger, he scraped a few crumbs of cement away. For a long time, hours it seemed, he worked at the task till the knuckles of his hand streamed with blood. And all the while John whimpered and would not help.

Marcus knelt again on that part of the stone which had first moved, and the movement was greater. He called out to John to come and feel that the stone moved.

'What if it does?' the eunuch said. 'Why should one suppose that the movement of a stone should be of aid and comfort?'

'It would be none,' Marcus said, 'if we were held here, as you fear, by some supernatural agency. But in my opinion it was the man who admitted us and who embraced you in the manner of friendship who has played us false; and therefore we are captives of no occult force, but only of man's malignity. For which reason, if we apply ourselves, we may escape.'

His bold words could not stir the eunuch. His feebleness enraged Marcus, and, unbuckling his belt, he began to belabour his companion, crying out that he would prove to him the power of man's will. He beat him with mighty strokes till at last the eunuch's howls of pain and terror persuaded him to desist.

'Will you then help me raise this stone?' Marcus said. 'For, if you do not, let me assure you that death will come speedily at my hands.'

The eunuch still moaning and whimpering and making no move

to help, Marcus struck him again, with the back of his hand across the face. He returned to his stone and now he could hear water move below. Then at last the eunuch crawled across the room and muttered that he was willing to do as Marcus wished, for indeed he now feared him more than all that had affrighted him before.

So Marcus learned two lessons which I commend to your attention, my Prince: that bodily pain (and also pleasure) may be so intense as to subdue the mind and spirit; and that, where one man has a will to action, he may achieve mastery over those who lack it.

For a long time they wrestled with the stone, and at moments even Marcus came close to despair, for it seemed that it could not be dislodged. But he would not surrender, and at last they shifted it so far that he could thrust his hand under it. Then with a mighty rending, as if the earth itself was being torn apart, the stone was raised, thrown back, and a faint glimmer of light came from the depths. And the sound of water was now a roar.

John drew back.

'No, no,' he said, 'no, it is the gateway to the underworld.'

'It is a way out,' Marcus said, 'wherever it may lead. And I am resolved to venture on it. If you have courage, you will follow me, but if you are still afraid you may remain here and die.'

He lowered himself into the cavity, till he hung at full stretch, his fingers still clinging to the floor, and his feet kicking in the empty air. He uttered a short prayer to such angels as might watch over him, St Michael first among them, and, lifting his hands, plunged into the unseen.

He fell, deeper than any plummet might sound, but, as he continued to descend, he was filled with exhilaration. He knew a freedom of body never experienced before, and this delighted him, as dreams of flying do. His fall was so prolonged that when he hit the waters and sank under them, and then rose, cork-like, to the surface, it occurred to him that perhaps the eunuch was right and he had indeed struck one of the rivers of the underworld; for he could not suppose that so great a fall could leave him still in the world he knew. But, there being no choice, he let himself be carried on the teeming foam, which stank somewhat of all things corrupt, though the sensation of rapid motion was not unpleasant. Then he was dashed against a rock, covered with slimy weed to which he clung till a wave lifted him and he was able to heave himself out of the water, and so discovered that he was in a fair country.

In truth any country would have seemed beautiful to Marcus having escaped so terrible an ordeal. But when he had got his breath and rested a moment, and found his limbs were torn and bleeding on account of the force with which they had been struck against the rocks, and when at last he had recovered so that he could gaze around him, he saw that the landscape was desolate and bare. Though it was summer, yet there were no leaves on the trees, the crops were twisted or laid flat, and the sky was empty of bird-life.

'Is this,' he asked himself, 'that waste-land of which the Princess spoke in the house of death?'

There was no sign of house or any habitation, and the sun was already sinking behind the hills.

He looked back at the river, in the hope of seeing his companion being carried to join him. But it roared by, dark and untenanted.

Marcus cursed John for a coward who had preferred to wait for punishment, even death, in that noisome chamber, rather than trust himself to the fall and the great water.

And so, leaving the refuge where he had been cast, he set his face to the hills.

He had not travelled half a league when he found the path blocked by a barrier of thorn-branches placed across a narrow defile in the rocks. While he was considering how to get by it, a voice hailed him from higher up the cliff.

'I am a traveller, lost in these desert parts,' Marcus answered. 'I pray you, have pity on me, for I am weak with hunger and exhaustion.'

For a moment there was silence but for the wind. Then a figure leapt from the rock and landed nimbly at his feet. Marcus saw a boy a couple of years younger than himself, with matted hair and

54

an impudent eye. The boy looked him up and down, then, putting two fingers in his mouth, emitted a piercing whistle. This was answered by other whistles, and Marcus was surrounded by half a dozen youths, who, pulling at his wet clothes and leading him by the hand, brought him by a circuitous route to a cave higher up the mountain.

When they spoke, Marcus had difficulty at first in understanding what they were saying, for their Latin was poor and vulgar, and ungrammatical, and they used words and phrases which were either rustic and archaic or the slang of the poor quarters of cities.

He explained to them that he was lost.

'Why so were we all when we came here,' said the boy who had first accosted him, Lycas by name. 'We are the tribe of the Lost.'

Some were slaves who had escaped from cruel masters. Others had been cast out by their own families. Some were orphans. A number were on the run from the Law.

'I myself was accused of theft by the keeper of the inn where I worked as a serving-boy,' Lycas said. 'He was for giving me a good whipping. I didn't fancy that, and so here I am.'

Marcus questioned them about the whereabouts of the Gothic army, though he could not decide whether to try to rejoin it, or whether that would be dangerous on account of the folly into which the eunuch had led him. But the boys knew nothing of events in Rome, and had never heard of the Goths.

'How do you live?'

'As birds and beasts do, on birds and beasts and the wild produce of the earth. We are a free company who take what is free.'

'And have you lived like this for long?'

'What is long?' was the reply. 'We live from sunrise to sunset, and then sleep, unless we choose to hunt by night. But tell us what danger or wickedness you have escaped from, for none comes to us who has not some horror behind him.'

'I was imprisoned and escaped by throwing myself into the river, and so find myself here.'

'Then you are one of us.'

Marcus was impressed by the innocence of these boys, some little more than children, who lived in perfect amity and communion with each other, despite what they had experienced of the cruelty of the world. He said to himself, 'If mankind has indeed fallen from high estate, and if we are all, as the priests aver, subject to the curse of original sin, how can it be that these Lost Boys have escaped this contagion?'

Even when they lay, as some did, with each other by night, there was no guilt in it, and they exchanged partners without displays of jealousy or anger. Nor did any one of them exercise command over the others. All were equals, and when there was a decision to be made, as to where they should hunt, for instance, they sat in a circle round the fire, and debated the matter like so many senators. A vote was seldom taken, for the argument was rarely pushed to the point where that was necessary. But if no consensus was arrived at, then the outvoted minority gave way graciously to the decision of the majority, bore no grievance, and never raised the matter again. Marcus thought how different this was from all that he had heard of disputes within Holy Church.

They were utterly free from any superstition, and – which amazed Marcus above all else – felt no need to sacrifice to any gods to secure the success of an enterprise. When Marcus asked Lycas, who had quickly become his special companion, if they did not fear that such neglect would incur the wrath of Almighty God, or indeed of the old pagan gods, should they exist and have power, the boy smiled and said,

'Since we don't trouble the gods, they've no need to trouble us.'

And Marcus wondered at the good sense of this observation.

X

For three days the sack of Rome continued, but, obedient to the King, the Goths spared churches and servants of God. Even women – of the respectable classes, that is – escaped the horror of rape, though many feared this, while a few, it is said, ventured into the streets in the hope of encountering lusty and ardent barbarians whose native vigour might supply to the children that might result the virility and virtue no longer to be found in their decadent and feeble consorts. But others say this is gross calumny and slander. Be that as it may, in the spring following, an unusual number of infants were born to noble and equestrian families, and many had the blue eyes and yellow hair of the Gothic invaders.

Some historians assert that there was no indiscriminate burning, looting and rapine, but that all was directed according to the will of the King, and supervised by his most trusted officers. Such authorities argue that Alaric had no wish to render his name infamous by subjecting the city to the extremity of horror, but that only those Romans who were known to be the most obdurate defenders of the Ancient Ways and loyal subjects of the Emperor were condemned to suffer. It was also, they say, the intention of the King to demonstrate both by his power and his clemency, in which virtue he took the great Julius as model, that he was a more fitting protector of the Empire than the degenerate and cowardly Honorius, who had not even dared to try to resist his passage through Italy, but remained craven and quivering in Milan. And indeed, inscriptions dating from that time and bearing this message have been discovered.

Finally, even though Alaric subscribed, as I have recorded, to the Arian heresy, which had been condemned by Holy Church, yet the Holy Father himself, displaying an intelligent suppleness of mind (absent, alas, too often subsequently and especially in the present occupant of St Peter's seat), received him honourably and with decorum, so that Alaric would have been truly cruel and vicious had he not responded to this approach, and honoured the request of the Holy Father that only pagan temples be despoiled. And indeed the riches of these temples were such that they would have satisfied a far more greedy conqueror than Alaric. When he eventually departed from the city on his march to the south, a mule-train of three hundred animals was required to carry off the treasures once offered to Jupiter and Apollo, Juno, Mars, Venus, Diana, and lesser deities, from the city which they had themselves abandoned, or from which they had been driven by the great wind of pure doctrine.

And so the grandeur of imperial Rome was borne away. Thus passed the glory of the world.

But before leaving the city, Alaric ordered a search to be made for Marcus.

'For,' he said, 'I have formed an affection for that young man in whom I see the last vestiges of antique Roman virtue, and I should be sorely grieved if he had come to harm. Moreover, since he gave me his word that he would not attempt to depart without asking my permission, I fear he may have been overtaken by some misfortune.'

Enquiries being instituted – to use a phrase beloved of the Holy Office – it was established that he had been last seen in the company of the eunuch John the Adept near the Basilica of St John Lateran. So a band of Gothic legionaries penetrated the sanctuary and discovered in, it is reported, the seventh crypt, the unfortunate eunuch, who was promptly carried before the King.

Being examined, he babbled in witless terror, unable or unwilling to say anything of what had happened to Marcus. Indeed it seemed, to those onlookers who have left report of his interrogation, that the boy's name induced in him extreme terror. 'When it was spoken,' one writes, 'the eunuch gibbered and shook in every limb.' The King, angered by his silence, ordered him to be more thoroughly and painfully examined, which was done by the pressing of his body between great weights. But still there was no useful answer. Alaric supposed that John could have answered had he been willing, and concluded that he had committed some crime too terrible to be confessed. So he commanded that the eunuch's eyes be put out with a poker heated in the fire and that his tongue be torn from its lodgement in his mouth, for, he said, 'If he will not speak, then let him be deprived forever of the power of speech, and if he has gazed on abomination, let him go blind through life.'

All those who knew the villainy of the eunuch approved this action, and those who did not were awed by the authority of the King.

But Alaric mourned the loss of Marcus, and some say that from this day on the King sank into a decline, refusing to eat and consoling himself with liquor.

Whatever the cause, it is certain that when the Gothic host marched from the city, and took the road to the south, whence he intended to cross over into Sicily and thence to Africa, to prove that there was no corner of the Empire in the west that could withstand his power, he no longer rode merrily, as had been his wont, at the head of his troops, but was carried in a litter and surrounded by wailing women.

So they journeyed till they came to Cosenza on its hilltop above the river Crathis, and there Alaric died, towards noon of a summer's day, but whether through melancholy, on account of the loss of Marcus, or by poison, as some assert, I cannot tell.

Though it was the custom for the bodies of barbarian chiefs to be burned on a pyre, with their most prized possessions, and, according to several authorities, with their wives also, this was deemed unfitting for Alaric, since he was a Christian monarch, albeit an Arian heretic.

So it was decided that Alaric should be given Christian burial, and this has been taken as evidence of the sincerity of the Gothic conversion to True Religion. Yet other authorities declare that it was the shortage of timber in the immediate vicinity of Cosenza (for the country around had been deforested on account of the number of goats kept by the farmers) that determined the mode of disposing of the body of the great King. For myself, I regard this as

59

nonsense, since there was nothing to prevent the Goths as masters of the town from tearing the doors from the houses, and seizing tables and chairs with which to make a pyre for the dead king. And I mention this interpretation merely to demonstrate to you, my Prince, that there is no explanation so far-fetched that some historian or apologist will not seize on it, without pausing to consider whether it accords with good sense or the dictates of reason. You will understand that my readiness to treat such explanations with a lively scepticism – that most beautiful and necessary of intellectual qualities – means that when I myself advance any theory, it has been exposed to the most stringent of tests; that is, it has been held up to the light of pure reason. I may add also that coming from the Borders of Scotland, inhabited by a people famed for their sturdy good sense, whenever I approach strange matters, I do so critically. This does not mean that I reject any manifestation of the supernatural, but that I accept such only when it is well attested, and does not fly clean contrary to my experience or to what Reason convinces me may be regarded as feasible, if not probable. I say this all the more emphatically since much in my narrative, treating of remarkable experiences and probing the utmost limits of our knowledge, is likely to be dismissed by my enemies and critics – not few in number, but men of dull wit and mean spirit – as inconceivable or improbable. Therefore I take this opportunity to affirm that there is nothing of invention in my narrative; that what I set down as truth may be accepted as such; and where I entertain scepticism as to the intelligence or veracity of the authorities on whom I have drawn, I make this abundantly clear.

I digress. But a digression is not to be condemned. A certain old poet, whose name I forget, said that truth is the daughter of time; and a digression gives the daughter time to mature.

Where then was I?

Ah yes, the Gothic chiefs, having resolved to give their king Christian burial, yet retained sufficient of the barbarian temper to think it unbecoming that he would journey into the world beyond bereft of great possessions, which would show the angels how great a man he had been here on earth. So they chose some of the treasures they had carried from Rome, not meanly reserving the best for their own use, but bestowing on the King the richest gold plate, silver ornaments and rare jewels – amethyst, onyx, rubies, porphyry, amber and topaz, with also many weapons encrusted with costly gems. And they buried these with him in the grave.

Then, because they feared that the King's grave would be robbed when they had departed from the land – for his death had caused them to despair and they were resolved to return to their homelands beyond the frontiers of the Empire – they set a gang of slaves and captives to work to divert the course of the river Crathis, that it might flow over the grave of Alaric, which would lie inviolate for ever.

Then they slew those who had been employed in diverting the river, that none might reveal where he lay. The bodies of more than five thousand of these reluctant artisans lay on the plain, and the river ran red with their blood.

Some authorities claim that that portion of the True Cross which the Empress Helena, daughter of King Coel and born in York, mother of the great Constantine, found in Jerusalem, being guided in her digging by the Holy Spirit, and carried to Rome, was among the treasures buried with Alaric. But this I do not believe, and not only because the Goths were Arians denying the divinity of Christ. For it is against Reason that they should have sent Alaric to meet the Almighty in the company of such a testament of the shame to which man's iniquity subjected Jesus, his only son. Moreover, it is well known that a portion of the True Cross is kept in the Chapel of St Helena in the church of Santa Croce in Gerusalemme in Rome, this chapel being part of the Sessorian Palace, where Helena lived. And it is displayed once a year on the day of the feast of the Invention of the True Cross.

Another vile assertion is a still grosser calumny. For some declare that the Holy Grail itself, object of John the Adept's greed, was also buried with Alaric. This is manifestly false, as my narrative has proved and will further substantiate. Marcus escaped the crypt empty-handed. Had John happened on the Grail, which he didn't, he would have confessed, in his terror, to

Alaric. But there is no record that he did so, though I have read the report of his examination.

It serves the cause of History ill to hand down frivolous and empty rumours as if they were fact. And fact, my dear Prince, is the currency of my narrative.

**(Our author protests too much. We do not know whether he convinced his pupil, who may well have received much that his master imparted with that scepticism which the said Michael himself recommends.

But this much is certain. In the year of Our Lord 1242, after his master's death, Frederick, now emperor and already known as 'the Wonder of the World', even in the midst of bitter war with the Papacy, employed a brigade of his Saracen bodyguard in again diverting the course of the river Crathis so that he might search for Alaric's grave. His biographers represent this as an example of their hero's intellectual curiosity, which it may well have been.

Yet, considering his financial difficulties at that time, it is probable that he sought Alaric's treasure the better to prosecute his war against the Pope. The claim of one biographer, the renegade monk Bernard of Sipontum, that the Emperor also hoped to find the Holy Grail may be discounted.)**

When word came to the Emperor Honorius, cowering in his silken sheets, that Alaric was dead, his mean heart was filled with joy, for it seemed to him that his throne was now secure. He gave orders that as many of the demoralised and retreating Goths should be apprehended as his legions were capable of seizing, for he had resolved to award himself a Triumph and required captives to walk in chains. A very ridiculous and shameful affair it was too. Honorius, as ever afraid of meeting the gaze of his subjects, whom he knew to despise him, fortified himself with wine, became intoxicated, and passed the triumphal journey in amorous dalliance with an Egyptian dancer, to the disgust of the sober citizens of Milan.

The Emperor now felt himself strong enough to move against his sister Honoria, whom he suspected of conspiring against him.

Yet, cruel as he was, either cowardice or prudence prevented him from putting her to death, though it was his dearest wish that she should die. He knew that she was popular with the people and feared their anger should he lay violent hands on her. So he merely ordered that she be immured in the Convent of St Agatha, which stood in one of the wildest Alpine passes, and forbidden male company. And this was done.

Honorius was also eager to know what had become of Marcus, of whom he was now inordinately jealous and fearful, since many who had admired the young man's bearing on his visit to the Court said that the Goths' retreat was his work; and some even plotted to make him emperor.

So Honorius dispatched bands of freedmen, culled from the most violent and depraved of his entourage. They were to seize Marcus and bring him to Milan. They were to bring him there alive, he insisted. The truth was that, reproached by Marcus's virtue, he wished to destroy that through the infliction of pain and torture. This is ever the way of the mean in spirit. They cannot endure virtue and so take pleasure in corrupting or breaking the spirit that informs it.

XI

Life with the tribe of Lost Boys was so enjoyable, gave Marcus so warm a sense of fellowship, such as he had never known before, that had he not been conscious of his duty and destiny, he would have chosen to remain with them for ever. For their part, they recognised his talents, and soon Lycas approached him with the suggestion that he should become the captain of their band.

But Marcus replied: 'My dear Lycas, while I'm more honoured than I can say, I must decline. I know I cannot commit myself to remain with you, perhaps not for long, but must return to my own world and resume the task set before me. Then, nothing, except for your friendship, has pleased me more than to see the perfect equality in which you all live together. But if you made me your captain or leader, then when I depart, as I must in time, someone will come forward claiming the right to take my place, and so this perfect fellowship, which is now such as should be a pattern to all chivalrous men, will dissolve, destroyed; and you will fall, like others, into bitter strife and partisanship.'

Lycas understood Marcus's reasoning, and was all the more impressed by his wisdom and judgement.

The boys lived, as they had told Marcus, off the country, and with them Marcus learned to bring down a running stag with a single arrow. He learned how to confront and outwit the savage boar, how to snare the wildfowl at the water's edge, how to track the deer and judge their movements. He learned which herbs were good and which noxious, where to find the most tasty mush-rooms, and how to dress wounds (for the boys were daring and sometimes rash) with the medicines which nature provides. He learned to catch fish by tickling them and how to sniff the wind so that he might judge the changing weather. He learned that life was good.

It seemed to him that he had been granted a sublime blessing; that these blithe children – for some were no more than children – and these joyous youths inhabited a world of prelapsarian innocence. Though all had known hardship and cruelty, yet all had escaped its grip, and a merciful heaven – or some such agency – had expunged the memory from their minds, so that they dwelled in the innocence of perpetual morning, in a recovered Age of Gold before the quarrels of gods or the disobedience of men brought death into the world and all our woe. It was true that some of what they did would have been accounted sinful by the priests, and that daily and nightly many, had their deeds been known, would have made themselves liable to penance and severe punishment. But, as he said to himself, since they feel no sense of sin, and are blithe and comradely to each other, can their actions be accounted wrong? Is not sin to be defined by consciousness? Such questions occupied Marcus's mind in moments of meditation.

It was his sole regret that, while sharing their happy life, he could not wipe out from his memory the knowledge which he had acquired of the world. And yet, he thought, surely some day, a company of noble knights might be formed which would live in like comradeship, devoted to generous deeds?

Another matter perplexed him. When he compared Lycas with his old companion John the Adept, he found the boy superior to the eunuch in manner and conduct; yet John excelled him in knowledge and learning. Thinking of the eunuch's cowardice and dishonesty, he asked himself whether that which the philosophers taught was of no value, and whether it was not better that men should live, like Lycas and the other boys, indifferent to intellect and things of the spirit. What profits it, he thought, to explore mysteries, when I see how happily we can live without such knowledge? My friends here may be savages, and would doubtless be accounted as such by John and others still more learned than he, but are they not noble savages, unspoiled, untainted, untarnished by the world of affairs?

Yet these meditations were soon to be interrupted, and he

discovered that the most fair beginnings may have a foul and horrid outcome.

One evening, returning from a hunting expedition in the forest, a party of the Lost Boys fell in with some village maidens, themselves journeying home – some say, though wrongly – from a pilgrimage to the shrine of the Archangel Michael, whither they had resorted (I believe) to pray that by his intercession they might obtain mates. For it happened that, on account of wars and pestilence, there were no young men in their village.

So when they chanced on the Lost Boys, in the lovely vigour of their youth, they cried out that their prayers were answered, for the ignorant sluts regarded the appearance of the boys as a miracle. They approached them with eager cries, and competed to display their charms. You may well image what ensued. Within minutes coupling was effected, and the glade rang with shrieks of pleasure. Nor were the boys loth, for even those who were accustomed to lie with each other were happy with this new diversion, while those who slept solitary by night went to it like lusty colts. The moon rose in the sky, as if the pagan goddess, Diana, gazed with approval, envy or longing on the scene of happy carnality.

Meanwhile Marcus and Lycas, who had ventured further in search of a wounded stag, remarkable for its milk-white colour, heard the sounds of pleasure as they descended the steep and winding path down the mountainside. Then, as they drew near, they heard also loud cries of anger. These smothered the shouts of joy and moans of pleasure which were indeed succeeded by screams of terror and cries of pain. Marcus and Lycas with one accord broke into a run, and so came upon the glade.

They found their comrades being struck and pinioned by wild-looking women, the mothers or grandmothers who had set out in search of their delinquent daughters. Naturally Marcus and Lycas hastened to the rescue. But Marcus was floored by a knobbled club and Lycas was tripped and pinned to the ground by a sinewy dame of remarkable strength, who, having got him there, had her way with him, to his great distress and anguish, since she employed nails and such teeth as she still possessed. In a little all the boys were overpowered, and this was done the more easily because their paramours, hoping doubtless to still the wrath of the old women, joined as eagerly in subduing them as they had formerly in acts of pleasure. And so, the band of unhappy boys were carried, prisoners, to the caves dug into the mountainside where these wild folk had their homes. And they were pinioned with ropes made from the hairs of wild beasts interwoven with stout reeds.

Marcus, ignorant of the dialect spoken by these mountain folk, could only speculate on their intentions towards them. But when they were alone, shut up in a cave over the mouth of which a great boulder had been rolled, Lycas told him, between sobs, of what he had understood as their captors' intent.

'We are to be kept as slaves,' he said, 'first to satisfy the lusts of these wild girls and beget children on them.'

'Why, that, though shameful, is no terrible fate,' replied Marcus, who had observed that some of the girls were comely.

'Aye,' Lycas said, 'that's as may be, though for my part I have long determined to have no truck with women, since, before I became one of our company, I saw how my father suffered at the hands of his second wife, my stepmother. Worse indeed, for I fled from home because of the lustful advances that woman made to me, which displeased me greatly, and frightened me too. And I fear, Marcus, that two of these witches – for women who attack and overpower young men like us can be none other than witches, in my opinion, leastways – well then, two of them I heard remarking on your charms and mine, and they were resolved that we should be reserved for their pleasure and be denied the young girls. And I could not help but note that both stank of worse even than female flesh.'

Marcus said, 'I have read somewhere of how the lusts of older women for young men are terrible, and how they exhaust their prey and yet are not satisfied, and how then . . . but no, it is too horrible.'

'Nevertheless,' Lycas said, 'such is our fate, I fear.'

Then he wept, for love of his own beauty and for what he feared to lose.

'In that case,' Marcus said, 'we must devise a means of escape.'

He clasped his friend to him, and, to aid thought, buried his face in Lycas's lustrous curls.

'Men have escaped from worse predicaments than ours,' he said, and told how Odysseus (whom the Romans call Ulysses), imprisoned with his companions in just such a cave as they now found themselves in, had eluded his captor, the Cyclops Polyphemus, by thrusting a burning brand into his single eye, and how then Odysseus and his friends had escaped by clinging to the under-fleece of the sheep which were driven every morning from the cave to their pastures.

'That,' Lycas said, 'is a fine story, and your Odysseus was a clever fellow, but I cannot see how it will help us. For one thing, our captors all seem to have the normal complement of eyes, and for another, there are no sheep in this cave.'

'These are indeed good points,' Marcus said. 'Nevertheless we have no reason to despair. This may be the worst situation you have ever found yourself in, but, though I have not lived much longer than you, dear Lycas, I have endured much hardship and danger, and this has taught me to know one thing for certain.'

'And what is that?'

'The worst is not yet on us, so long as we can say "this is the worst".'

'That would be some consolation,' Lycas said, 'if I understood it.'

So, finding comfort in one another's arms, they prepared for sleep.

Lycas indeed slept, though he shivered all the hours of night and gave vent to piteous moans and many sighs. But Marcus lay wakeful, pondering their plight and endeavouring to resolve his perplexities. In the first place, he thought, it is evident that these women will not kill us immediately, since they hope that we shall pleasure them; and that is good. But, in the second place, I have taken a vow that I shall lie with no woman on account of the love and duty I bear and owe to the Princess Honoria, who is my sworn mistress that I shall serve, and none other. So that is bad.

But, thirdly, all philosophers that I have ever read recognise the force of Necessity, which loosens other bonds and which it is no sin to submit to. Furthermore, the definition of sin, as I have learned from many tutors, is not inflexible. It is possible, when subject to Necessity, to commit what would be at other times a sin, and even to break vows, so long as one makes a mental reservation. Then it is unquestionably my duty to escape, and it may be that in order to find an opportunity, I must (again) yield to Necessity, and undergo this ordeal. Fifthly – or is it sixthly, for I have lost count – I observed even in the hurly-burly that one of the young girls was of delectable appearance, with shapely limbs, soft yielding thighs and active hips, and such a smile as would seduce an angel. That smile she directed at me, even in my humiliation, and I read pity and even admiration in her eye. I don't deceive myself there, I'm sure. If I cannot make her our accomplice in the matter of our escape, well, I'm not the man I think I am. None of this answers poor Lycas's repugnance for female flesh, which he says is insuperable. But, as my old friend Father Bernardo used to say, no horse can be put to cross a river in the middle of a desert. Which is a comforting thought.

In the morning they were led, still shackled, from the cave and lined up as if on parade to await inspection.

'This reminds me of the slave market in my home town of Brindisi,' said one boy whose name was Ascyltos. 'Well, I observed then that those slaves who made the bravest show fared best.' So he stood straight and pushed his black hair away from his eyes, and attempted to smile with lips that were bruised and broken.

Marcus thought the advice good. So he also drew himself up and assumed a brave countenance, and whispered to poor Lycas to do the same

Meanwhile the women came forward, some grim, others giggling, and muttering what Marcus guessed to be obscenities as they prodded the boys and squeezed their arms or nipped their young legs. None of the young girls were in sight, which disappointed Marcus, who had looked for the one that had smiled at him.

Yet, though the women seemed eager to make a selection and carry off their chosen one, none did so, but all waited.

Then there came a roll of drums, and from one of the caves emerged eight old men carrying a litter. The women raised a chant, which, as Lycas later told Marcus, went like this:

> When thou thunderest, Diana's double,
> Before thee all men tremble,
> Let not blight and rain fall upon us,
> Stay thy scourge,
> Queen of the deluge.

The shoulders of the greybeards who carried the litter bore the mark of many lashes, and they shuffled sadly on account of the iron shackles that showed they were slaves.

They halted before the line of boys, and a harridan with lank hair like rat's tails or wet flax stepped forward and withdrew a curtain to reveal the interior of the palanquin. Marcus now saw that it was occupied by a woman of such remarkable obesity that it seemed impossible she should ever rise by her own unaided motion from her bed of cushions. The other women now redoubled their song of praise, which echoed from the rocks that surrounded the clearing where they were assembled. But the woman on the bed of cushions did not deign to acknowledge their homage.

The lank-haired harridan advanced to the litter and conversed in a low voice with its occupant, goddess or queen or whatever she might be in the eyes of this alarming tribe.

The other women showed some signs of impatience during this colloquy but still made no move. The harridan turned away from the litter and took first Marcus and then Lycas by the hand and led them to her mistress, who indicated that they were to join her on the bed of cushions. Ascyltos was then led forward and ordered to mount the litter. The curtains were drawn back, and the swaying motion told Marcus they were being carried up the mountain. Behind him he heard shrieks of glee and cries of protest as the women fell on the remaining boys.

No word was spoken in the litter. Marcus wondered at the endurance and strength of the slaves, who now carried four persons, one of whom was larger and heavier than the other three together.

When at last the litter was deposited on level ground, Marcus heard the slaves withdraw, and only then did the woman address them. To his surprise she spoke in correct Latin and in a manner which suggested that she was well-born or had at least known finer company than that which she now appeared to command. What she said was too horrible to relate in detail, and she employed many obscenities which it is not proper that I write for you, my Prince, and which consorted ill with her well-bred voice. Furthermore, she spoke rank blasphemy, for when she informed them that she had from her great goodness at – which word she chuckled, shaking like a blancmange – selected them for her especial delight, and that it was their great good fortune to have been chosen to pleasure her, she added, with a seismic laugh, that she had several orifices and so great a body that she could accommodate all three boys simultaneously: 'It is,' she said – and I report her words with reluctance, merely to show, briefly, the depth of depravity in which she was sunk, like a great fish preserved in thick oil – 'it is truly godlike, three in one, and one,' she chuckled, probing Marcus with fingers thick as the salami of Milan, 'in three.'

You will understand why my chaste pen revolts from further description. It is enough to report, with pity and disgust, that none was able to defy her monstrous will, though poor Lycas was seized with a fit of vomiting, to the creature's vast amusement, and was then compelled to swallow anew what he had disgorged.

In short, if Marcus had already been subjected to horrible experiences, what he now endured surpassed them all. It seemed impossible to satisfy the woman, for each time any of the boys sank back exhausted, she set herself to revive them, either by angry words, lewd caresses, or the infliction of pain; for she kept by her a knotted whip which she freely employed to spur them on.

And so the day passed, most vilely.

In the evening the boys were brought by the greybeards back to

71

their cave. Once more the boulder was rolled across its mouth. But this time they found a wineskin and a stew of savoury kid awaiting them, for, as one greybeard told them, 'You must sustain yourselves to resume work tomorrow.'

'I would rather die,' Lycas said, and at first refused to eat, till Marcus persuaded him that he must try to maintain his strength if they were ever to escape.

On the evening of the third day, as the boys rested, without appetite but fortifying themselves with wine, they were surprised to find the stone eased aside, which had never previously been moved till the morning.

Ascyltos, whose natural courage had been worn away by their ordeal, cried out in alarm, for he feared that either the greybeards had been sent to kill them, their diminished performance that day having indicated that their time of use had passed, or, still more horribly, that they were being summoned back to the litter after so little time to recover. But Lycas said, if this was death, he for one would welcome it.

Three tapers now advanced into the cave, and the boys, who huddled in its furthest recess, clung together. But the voice which addressed them was sweet and gentle, and they saw that the tapers were carried by three girls, one of whom was the maiden who had attracted Marcus's attention on the night of their capture. They now came to the boys and, embracing them tenderly, began to bathe them with unguents and run light fingers over their worn and exhausted bodies. They murmured in sweet and musical tones.

For a little Marcus feared that this was merely the prelude to some new torment, but the gentleness of the girl was such that this fear soon left him, and he enjoyed her ministrations. Soon delight drove out all other feeling, and he was locked in love with the girl. He recalled his vow of chastity, but was able to excuse this new breach, on grounds of Necessity. Then the girls, with kisses light as the breeze of a sweet morning in May, slipped away. And this was repeated the next night.

When the girls left them that second evening, they debated what such visits might mean. Ascyltos, who was ever hopeful, declared that the girls had fallen in love with them, and so could afford a means of escape. 'Now that I have discovered this new pleasure and have learned that women may offer unparalleled delight, sufficient even to expunge the horror that monster has subjected us to, why, I shall be happy to take these girls with us.'

Lycas sighed and said: 'If only I could believe that you are right. I have to confess that I have come close to overcoming my repugnance for female flesh, which I had thought invincible. Nevertheless, in my opinion, this is but a trick, a device to restore our natural ardour so that we may more satisfactorily pleasure that filthy and obese creature.'

Marcus listened to what his friends said, and then remarked, 'What we need are the ashes of a blind cat.'

For he remembered what Chiron had said, and how he had employed this device against Naso the ferryman.

Then he said: 'I have considered your opinions, and find justice in both. Lycas is surely correct in his judgement of the purpose of these visits, which have, after all, we must assume, been sanctioned by our captors. But Ascyltos is wise also. I say this because I cannot believe that girls as sweet and delectable as these are capable of so dissembling their feelings, as would have to be the case if they were insincere in the loving acts they perform with us. Admittedly history and scripture give us many examples of the treachery of women. There was Delilah, who deceived Samson and robbed him of his strength, and there was Cleopatra, who, by her wiles, brought my noble ancestor Mark Antony to his doom. Yet my opinion of womanhood is, despite our sufferings, too exalted to allow me to entertain so vile a suspicion of these girls. Therefore, I submit that whatever their original purpose may have been, it is one they no longer subscribe to. And the tears which flowed from the lovely eyes of my utterly delicious Pulcherrima as she departed this evening persuade me that these girls may afford us the means of escape.'

And so it turned out. The following night, when the girls came to resume their play, Marcus, after expending all his tenderness, talked long with Pulcherrima. She, fearful at first, laughed happily at last, and promised she would do as he bid. So, on the night which lies black between the Old Moon and the New, she brought to him a little satchel, which, in the morning, he concealed beneath his tunic.

They were led as usual to the litter, and as soon as the greybeards had withdrawn, Marcus pulled out the satchel and hurled its contents in the many-folded face of their tormentor.

For a moment nothing happened. Then her eyes opened wide as the Gates of Hell, and her flesh shrivelled, the great mountainous body dissolved before their eyes and crumbled into dust, giving off a vapour rank with the stink of corruption.

Even as this happened there rose from the surrounding caves and hovels wails of dismay and cries of terror.

'Well,' Marcus said, 'Chiron assured me it never failed, but even he cannot have supposed it would meet with quite such success.'

Descending from the litter, they found the greybeards stretched out on the ground in a stupor or dead faint. They prodded them and they did not move. Then Pulcherrima and the other girls came to them and embraced them, and those of the tribe of Lost Boys who had survived their ordeal crowded round, cheering and rejoicing.

And so Marcus escaped from this peril.

**(Of all the stories our ingenious author relates, none is stranger or more absurd. It reads indeed like the silliest tale of Romance; on first reading, I jaloused that it was an interpolation made by a previous commentator on the manuscript, perhaps by that one who belonged to the heretical and sodomitical Order of the Knights Templar, amusing himself by confusing the matter of the narrative, and inserting his own disgusting and salacious fantasies.

But there is internal evidence that suggests this may not be a just reading. Perhaps our author had merely seized on one of these stories which attach themselves, though no more than idle and ridiculous fancies, to the skirts of greatness. But, if so, how could he bring himself to present it to the noble prince who was his pupil?

Yet, if we assume that our author, whose sagacity and learning are beyond dispute, includes nothing without a purpose and nothing for mere wonder alone, then it must be interpreted as allegory or metaphor.

So this reading is therefore suggested:

Though it is, on account of the requirements of the narrative, set ostensibly in Italy, I hazard that the true landscape is Thessally – a plain surrounded by mountains as high as the sky, as the Greek proverb has it. Now Thessally is known to have been the abode of Pheraia, also known as Hecate, Queen of Darkness, who, never seeing the light of day, is forever illuminated and only visible by torchlight. Pheraia's lusts were insatiable – she was *damnosissima luxuriosissimaque*, and moreover the daughter of Admetus, King of the Dead, that innkeeper whose gates are never closed to any traveller.

So, we may assume that Marcus and his friends are employed in these noisome activities by Pheraia-Hecate not, as might first seem, for the promotion of fertility, but rather in a parody of fertility in a land where divinity brings forth no fruit, but presents itself merely as a malign but sterile force. Lust and coupling divorced from purposes of procreation are vile, shameful, damnable.

Yet, while this interpretation is eminently satisfactory, there is yet an omission in our narrative. For while it is proper that Marcus should choose life (Pulcherrima) over death (Pheraia), there should be a passage in which he too feels the temptation of death, a temptation so powerful in the early Christian era that martyrs abound. But in this version only Lycas feels death's magnetism, and that on account of cowardice. Therefore there are lacunae, unexplained, and the passage must be deemed corrupt and defective.)**

XII

After their escape, Marcus and his friends sojourned some time in the forests and knew much happiness. But eventually Marcus was oppressed with the sense that he was neglecting the public duty for which he had been raised. He gazed on his companions stretched out on the turf, taking their ease in the afternoon sun, and knew temptation. Why struggle, he asked himself, when life lived so naturally was so sweet? Why shoulder the burden of obligation when contentment was so easily at hand? He envied Ascyltos, who, after their ordeal, had resumed his former way of life and felt no call to any other. But it was no good; he could not be easy. So, with a heavy heart, he resolved to part from his friends – all but Pulcherrima and Lycas, who both swore that they would rather die than be separated from him – and repair to the court of Honorius. For he did not know that the vicious emperor regarded him with fear and loathing and had resolved on his destruction.

So, taking leave of the rest, they came to the great city of Perusia, and there Marcus intended to consult with a councillor, a cousin of his mother's, who had formerly taken an interest in his education. He left his friends at an inn and sought directions to the councillor's house.

The councillor, whose name was Aemilianus Spocca, was amazed to see him, and indeed at first appeared also distressed.

'Have you forgotten me?' Marcus asked. 'Have you forgotten how we read Vergil together, and how you urged me to be worthy of my ancestor Aeneas?'

'Forgotten?' Spocca said. 'Forgotten?' He sniffed, briefly, from a little jar of sweet-scented salts. 'Dear boy, how could I? I am of course delighted to see you. It is merely that I am also surprised. But have you come here alone? Who knows – does anyone know – that you are in Perusia?'

'I have two companions with me,' Marcus said, 'and I left them at the Inn of Mercury, the sign of the Winged Heel.'

Spocca nodded. He pressed the tips of his fingers together, and then tapped them against each other.

'Dear boy,' he said. 'Oh, this is difficult. It is best perhaps if I ask you to read this instruction which I have received together with my appointment as imperial prefect of Perusia, a post which, I need hardly tell you, I would never have sought but dared not refuse. To such depths have we sunk, that office is a burden and the preference for a private life regarded as treasonous.'

Marcus took the document, authenticated with the imperial stamp. His own name leaped from the page. He was disturbed to see that the prefect was commanded to seek out, apprehend and dispatch him to Milan under armed guard. Am I so terrible, he thought, and what is my crime?

'I would rather you had not come here,' Spocca said.

'But here I am, and here' – Marcus held the imperial prescript aloft – 'is your duty. Here are your orders.'

'You have changed a great deal since I knew you as a boy and eager scholar,' Spocca said. 'Had you not given me your name, I would not have recognised you. It may be that I misheard it, for I confess that I am not a little hard of hearing. Not deaf, you understand, merely hard of hearing.'

He clapped his hands, and ordered the slave-boy who answered his summons to fetch them wine. Then he got to his feet and crossed over to the window. He stood with his back to Marcus, looking out over the olive groves that tumbled down the hillside to the river, and to the mountains beyond, hazy in the hot sun of noon.

'Italy,' he said, 'beautiful Italy, my beautiful Italy,' and he murmured lines of poetry which Marcus scarce overheard, about the springs of Clitumnus and the white oxen which bathed in its cool stream. 'Ravaged by barbarians, because the Emperor, the creature who calls himself emperor, who gave me this loathed commission, and who would condemn a boy I used to love to death, sat cravenly in Milan not daring, as my ancestors would have dared, to confront their army.'

The slave slipped from the room, which was cool but yet surrounded by the baking heat of noon. Spocca poured two cups of wine, pushed one to Marcus, and settled himself at the table, looking Marcus in the face.

'I am told,' he said, 'that the noble youth I am commanded to arrest journeyed to Rome with Alaric the Goth.'

'He did,' Marcus replied. 'But as a prisoner, if one honoured and treated with respect.'

'Just so,' Spocca said. 'Just so I had supposed.'

He drank wine, and holding his cup still aloft said,

'I am fifty-five, childless. Had things been other than they are, I would be ashamed of that condition. My line is long. The Aemilian *gens* can boast consuls from the great days of the Republic. My twelve-times great-grandfather, Marcus Aemilius Lepidus, was Master of the Horse in the great Caesar's time, and, after his murder would, with Mark Antony, the ancestor of the noble youth I am commanded to arrest and whom you somewhat resemble, have restored the Republic had the degeneracy of the times and the ambition of Octavius Caesar, later styled Augustus, not prevented him. I tell you this because now I am careless who knows that I am a Republican, a Republican, a Roman, and no Christian. Rome has been destroyed and Italy betrayed by the emperors, low-born men for centuries now. The final blow to the great edifice was delivered by that brute Constantine, when he adopted a slave's religion, an offshoot of Judaism, as the official religion of the state. So I live on my estates and take as little part in the debased public life of our times as I may.'

He spoke absently, disconnectedly, as if in a dream, and seemed to Marcus to speak as much to himself as to him.

'It is finished,' Spocca said, and sighed deeply. 'Rome is finished, Italy lies waste-land. The Gothic army has withdrawn to the north, and the man, the creature who calls himself emperor, Honorius, has established such a tyranny that men cry out for the return of the barbarian. His spies are everywhere, which is why I could not receive my kinsman Marcus, whom I knew and loved when he was a child, even if he should present himself to me. Honorius commands that he be delivered to his agents. You,

78

stranger as you must be, may have heard, or you may not have heard, that Honorius has arrested his sister, Honoria, whom some call the Princess – though that is a title never known in the days of the Republic – and confined her in a prison-convent in the northern mountains. There would be neither justice nor hope of mercy for Marcus here in Italy – if he should be still here.'

Marcus looked at the worn face and hooded eyes of the prefect and could read nothing in his expression. He drank some wine. For a moment there was silence, broken only by the lapping of water in the fountains of the courtyard below the window.

'If you were to chance on this Marcus . . .'

'As I pray not to do . . .'

'As you pray not to do . . . what would you advise?'

'That he withdraw to wherever he had come from and remain there in such safety as concealment may offer.'

'But if this Marcus had made a certain vow to the Princess, as some call her, Honoria, and would feel shame if he deserted her in her time of trouble, what then would you advise?'

'In evil times,' Spocca said, 'it is better to listen to the wind than to brave the storm, but if the nobly born Marcus cannot follow this advice with an easy mind, then I should advise him to depart from Italy, and journey to Constantinople, and set his case before the Emperor Arcadius there. Arcadius is brother to Honorius and Honoria, and hates and despises the former. Perhaps he has an affection for his sister. I do not know. But that he hates Honorius I know for certain.'

He sipped his wine.

'And I should advise that he travel incognito, in disguise, for the secret agents of the Emperor are everywhere.'

Marcus smiled. 'The keeper of the inn took me and my companions to be strolling players,' he said.

XIII

Marcus left Perusia with his companions and travelled, by night stages, to Ravenna, and thence took ship for the east. His meeting with Spocca had saddened him; he felt the pain and humiliation that the older man had tried to conceal beneath his languid and careful manner. Spocca's last words remained with him: 'We must play the comedy to the bitter end, dear boy.' He was horrified by the pessimism which made the old nobleman welcome his childlessness and the extinction of his line, and he brooded on these matters as he lay sleepless on the deck of the boat.

It is no part of my purpose to describe the city of Constantinople, and its wonders have been recited by more able pens than mine. The first stone had been laid by the great Constantine himself at the extremity of what was to be the western wall where it joins the sea, for the New Rome stands, as you may know, at the junction of Europe and Asia, which is the Middle Point of the Earth. It was inaugurated by ceremonies both pagan and Christian, for Constantine himself, despite Spocca's strictures, hung like a wavering star between the old faiths and the new. He had conquered empire at the Battle of the Milvian Bridge, where the Cross appeared to him in the morning sky, and he had liberated the Christian Church from the persecutions it had suffered since the time of the Emperor Nero, whom some denominate the Antichrist; though he was not that, since the prophecies of the Book of the Revelation of St John the Divine are not yet fulfilled.

Constantine, you must know, summoned on his imperial authority Councils of the Church, and made its bishops his chief ministers and advisers; in every way he established Christianity as the chief and dominant religion of the Empire. Yet he himself, being also Pontifex Maximus, High Priest of the old Roman cults and head of the state religion, and being worshipped as a god by all those among his subjects who did not humble themselves before the one True God and follow Christ, declined to receive Christian baptism, until, as some say, he was received into the Faith on his deathbed. But whether this is so, or whether it was a pious invention of the priests around him at that awful moment, none but the Almighty now truly knows.

Be that as it may, founding his new Rome at the Middle Point of the Earth, Constantine chose not to disdain the old pagan deities; and perhaps he feared to do so.

(Was it not that he was caught in that duality, that perfect scepticism, which is the character of all who have dwelled long in their imaginings among the ultimate mysteries; and this even though he was not, by report, a man of a speculative turn of mind but rather given to abrupt and violent action?)

Wishing that he himself and his New Rome should encompass all religions, and be all things to all men, he had that most sacred of Roman talismans, the Palladium, that statue of the goddess Pallas brought originally (as was believed) from burning Troy, torn from the Old City and carried to the New, to be placed by the base of the mighty statue of himself raised in the Forum. I may remind you that the learned and judicious pagan Symmachus believed that the later misfortunes which befell Rome and which I have recounted were the consequence of this act of perfidious impiety, indeed theft. No doubt he was mistaken, for greater forces than impiety directed at gods who existed, as may be supposed, only in men's minds were at work. Nevertheless Constantine, though he gave precedence to Holy Church and, as it has been claimed, made the Pope his legate in the western Empire, was eager, being superstitious, to draw all varieties of religion to his bosom in his new city. So, on the day of its inauguration, prayers to the goddess Tyche, the Greek version of the Roman Fortuna, mingled with the Christian chant of *Kyrie eleison*.

All this Marcus knew. Yet he was not prepared for the magnificence of the city, shining with the brightness of noon in comparison with the twilight that had fallen on Rome. He was amazed by the magnificence of the Circus, where contests between the Blues and the Greens divided the populace into fiercely partisan camps. He was dazzled by its seven theatres and one hundred and fifteen public baths, its fourteen Christian churches and fourteen imperial palaces, its eight granaries and six aqueducts, and the four thousand private residences listed as buildings of supreme artistic merit. He was enraptured also by the treasures of Greece which the rapacious Constantine had caused to be brought thither: statues of Apollo, Zeus, Hera, Pallas Athene, and a great wide-legged figure of Herakles slaying the Nemean lion, all filled him with wonder. He knew sadness too, for, gazing on the riches here assembled, he felt more deeply the degradation of his beloved Italy; and swore again to devote his life to its renaissance.

The sight of pagan and Christian symbols brought together caused him to remember how John the Adept had spoken, movingly, of his journeying in the world of spirit, and how myth might yield truths which unsupported Reason could not attain. And he felt the complexity of the world, and asked himself whether indeed any knowledge could be certain.

While he stood pondering these matters, Lycas tugged at his sleeve and remarked that magnificence was all very well, but would not fill their bellies; and that they should therefore seek out an agreeable tavern.

So they came to an inn which was full of boisterous fellows making merry. But Lycas, who had been appointed their purse-bearer, held back, saying it was better they found a quieter place where food, wine and lodging might cost less. Pulcherrima agreed. Some of the merry fellows had cast lewd glances at her, and she was afraid. So they turned into a side-street, and happened on a mean tavern with strings of beads serving as a door, and Lycas, thrusting his head through these, announced that all was quiet, and that this would serve them better.

When they had settled there, Marcus, who spoke Greek, though with an accent that was somewhat antique – for it was the Greek of Plato and Aristotle that he had learned, and not the demotic – enquired of the dame who kept the house what formalities would be necessary in order that he might present himself at the imperial palace. She laughed and said that none who were accustomed to frequent her house had ever entertained such an ambition. Therefore she could not tell, but surmised that he might be prudent to get himself a decent suit of clothes.

'For,' she said, 'while I can't tell where you've come from, it's easy to see you are a foreigner, and look, if you don't mind me saying so, a perfect fright and freak in those clothes. All the same,' she added, 'you've a bonnie face and a sweet smile, and that goes some way, even in Constantinople.'

'Thank you,' Marcus said. 'I'm sure your advice is good. But, since it's now evening, I'll leave that till tomorrow, and meanwhile we shall eat and drink.'

She laughed and clapped her hands and told the serving-boy to bring them fish and beans and bread and wine. They were all hungry and set to eagerly, though Lycas said that the wine, flavoured with resin, was disgusting.

The serving-lad also laughed, and said:

'That's 'cos you drink it the wrong way, like all foreigners. You're all ignorant bastards, aren't you? It's not to be sipped at as if it was a fine vintage, but swigged. Our wine, which we call retsina, is for hearty drinkers.'

'Thanks,' said Lycas, and followed this advice, then declaring that, as a drink, it wasn't half bad.

So they learned that the customs of one country may differ from those of another, but are not to be despised for that reason alone. Only provincials suppose that the only right way to do anything is the way it's done in their own town.

The next morning Marcus went to a tailor, and, having enquired what sort of dress would render him respectable but inconspicuous at court, ordered a suit.

'It will be ready for your lordship in the afternoon,' the tailor said. 'But a young man of your beauty can never be inconspicuous, my friend.'

Marcus, amused by the compliment and the Greek's flowery manner, returned to their tavern, where they ate olives and anchovies and a hard white cheese, and then little pastries rich with honey and pistachio nuts. Then, while they were taking their ease in the heat of the day, they were approached by another tavern-loiterer who had been watching them from a corner of the room.

'You look,' he said, 'to be young folk in search of a fortune, and I believe I can set you in the way of getting it.'

So, without waiting for further invitation, he settled himself on the bench beside Lycas, while Marcus rested with his arm around Pulcherrima and his back to the window. Their new friend called for more wine, and then began to speak in a Greek dialect which Marcus had at first some difficulty in following.

'I understand, for no secret can be kept here in Constantinople, that it's your intention to present yourself to the Emperor. Well, take it from one as knows, there's no good doing that unless you have something to offer him, and nothing, I can tell you, is more welcome to Great Ones than gold. Now I can tell you where and how to lay your hands on some, and I speak as one who has travelled far, known many lands and many dangers.' Here he touched the black patch which he wore over his left eye socket.

'This sounds interesting,' said Marcus with his habitual courtesy. 'Pray continue.'

'On the borders of India – a fearful place, I assure you – lies a vast desert. It supports little life, save some colonies of huge ants. When I say huge, don't think I exaggerate. Ask anyone and they will tell you that Nicias – that's my name – is a man given to *meiosis*' – which, my Prince, is the Greek word for understatement, for saying less than you mean, a habit of my own, as you will have observed. But I digress.'

Nicias, then. 'So let me reassure you,' he said. 'These ants of which I speak are certainly smaller than hunting dogs, no bigger, I should say, than foxes. They dwell underground, and like our Greek ants, which they resemble in shape, though being, as I have said, somewhat bigger, they throw up heaps of sand as they burrow.'

'Italian moles do the same,' Lycas said, who had understood little of the man's speech though he too had some Greek on account of having spent his youth in Calabria, which is Magna Graecia.

'Indeed yes, so they do. Now, in this desert it so happens that the sand these ants throw up is full of gold-dust. The Indians know this, and this is the method they employ when they venture into the desert in search of gold, for which like all men they are greedy. They take three camels each, which they yoke together with the female between the males. The rider mounts the female camel, and I should say, or should have said, that they take care to select one which has recently given birth. So equipped, the Indians ride out, making sure that they arrive in the desert in the hottest hour of the day, which they do because the ants sleep then, hiding themselves deep in their burrows in the sand to escape the heat, which is then terrible, as I know because I have endured it myself. However, the Indians, being dusky, bear it better than we Greeks can, and so despite the blazing noonday sun, they are able to fill their sacks with the sand thrown up by the ants – the sand which contains the gold dust. Then they ride off as fast as they can. But the ants, cunning creatures, scent them, for their sense of smell is acute as a hunting-dog's – though they are, as I think I've said, somewhat smaller. They set off in pursuit. They move with terrific speed, and, if the Indian gold-gatherers haven't got a fair start, well then, they've had it. But they have a trick or two of their own. During the chase, the male camels which – you may not know this – are not as fast as the females – strange that, isn't it? – begin to flag. So they are cut loose to delay the hunting ants. But the females, remembering the young ones they have left behind, are driven by what is called the maternal instinct to run faster and faster, and so they – usually – escape the ants. And that's how the Indians get their gold.'

'Well,' Marcus, said, 'that's certainly a very interesting story, but I'm afraid I don't see how it can help me in any way.'

'Ah.' Nicias laid his finger flat along the line of his nose. 'I'm coming to that, but before I explain just how, you must excuse me while I answer a call of nature.'

So he slipped out of the tavern by a door that led into the yard.

'Odd fellow,' Marcus said.

85

Then their hostess came across the room

'I hope that man hasn't been troubling you,' she said. 'I've seen him about before, and it's my belief he's touched in the head.'

'That was my impression too,' Marcus said, 'for the story he has told us is ridiculous, past all belief, quite incredible when you think about it.'

But Lycas gave out a cry and started to sob.

'I fear he has his wits about him,' he said, when he had composed himself sufficiently to be able to speak, 'for he has taken our purse with him.'

Their hostess seized Lycas by the hair and ordered him and the boy who was tending the spit on which a kid was roasting to give chase at once.

'Catch the thief and bring back the purse,' she cried.

Marcus would have joined the pursuit, but she detained him.

'Not so fast, my pretty, for I have only your boy's word for it that there was a purse. I've no desire to think ill of one so well-favoured as yourself' – she patted his smooth cheek, for like most who met him she had from the first glance been charmed by his beauty. 'All the same, I am an innkeeper, and so only too well acquainted with the deceits men practise. Many years ago I was persuaded by a boy with curling ringlets, dark liquid eyes and a skin soft and smooth as the finest velvet to extend him credit, yes, and I even invited him to share my bed in the afternoons, for I had a husband in those days who went fishing then, and what do you know? The young villain slipped away in the dark of the moon, leaving me as his only payment the infant that was growing in my womb. And ever since I have been careful who I trust. So sit you down, my pretty, and we'll see what's what when your lad returns.'

Hearing this, and certain that Lycas would fail to catch the thief, Pulcherrima burst into tears. If she hoped to soften the dame's heart, she miscalculated, for her tears had the opposite result, spurring the woman to fury. She clubbed the poor girl with her fist, calling her 'slut, harlot, jade, whore and thief'. When Marcus protested that Pulcherrima was none of these things, she pushed him back on the settle against the wall, and sent the kitchenmaid to fetch the Watch. Lycas soon after returned, out of breath and without the purse, without the potboy either, who had seized the opportunity given him by the chase to slip into a brothel.

Then the Watch, or Municipal Police, arrived, and the hostess gave all three into charge as being, she said, 'common vagrants, strolling players', who had tried to cheat her.

'What's more,' she added, 'this one commanded a new suit from the tailor at the sign of the Wounded Ox, and I'll be bound never intended to pay for it, couldn't indeed, being, as you see, penniless. He is full of big talk about how he is going to present himself to the Emperor, as if His Imperial Highness would give the time of day to the likes of him. What a fool I was to relax my constant vigilance on account of his pretty talk and sweet ways. Lord, how sad that so pretty and neat a youth should prove a deceiver. But counterfeit coin shines ever bright, as we innkeepers soon learn.'

Lycas protested that all could be explained and began to describe the thief. But the policemen merely laughed, clapped irons on all three of them, and carried them off to prison.

XIV

As mere thieves, Marcus and his friends were not accorded the dreadful dignity of cells, but were thrust into the common chamber of the prison, which was thronged with bawds who had cheated their customers, sturdy beggars, housebreakers, pickpockets and other petty thieves, fortune-tellers, necromancers and casual murderers. Some played dice, others sat in wretched silence with their shirts pulled over their heads, some quarrelled over food, children hunted rats, and a few lunatics chanted interminable and tuneless songs.

They were soon approached by an old man who retained a dignity of manner unusual in that godforsaken hole.

'Welcome,' he said, speaking in Latin, for he had either guessed that was their tongue or overheard them talk among themselves, 'welcome to this school of life, this academy of unhappy learning, this university of the misfortunate. Whatever ill-hap has brought you here, you now find yourselves in a fellowship where all degree is levelled, all distinction obliterated, and all are equal in their nakedness. Wherefore, to those of us to whom the faculty of reason is granted, whether by the one true God or by the myriad of deities worshipped by many here, this place is no prison, but rather, as I say, a school of enlightenment.'

'That's as may be,' Lycas said, 'and we're grateful to you for your kind words, sir. But they can be of little comfort to us, since we are victims of a misunderstanding, and so find ourselves wrongly imprisoned.'

The old man smiled.

'I have no doubt,' he said, 'that you speak what you believe to be the truth, for you are all three well-favoured, and candour sits like the dawn upon your countenances. But you are inhabitants of this sinful world. Therefore, though you believe yourselves innocent, you are yet guilty, or you would not be here, but in Paradise. Look on this crowd. Choose any among them and you will hear a tale of like misfortune. That woman there is accused of having concealed the birth of a child. She is a priestess of a forbidden cult. Whether she gave birth to a child or not, whether the child lived or died, whether the death was natural or at her hand, is immaterial. She is here because she was picked out to be here, and would be here were she as pure as the snow on the high summits of the Caucasus. All things are written and must be enacted.'

'But of what crime are you yourself accused?' Marcus asked.

'The crime of being who I am.'

'And who then are you?'

'They call me the Jew.'

'And is it a crime then to be a Jew?'

'In some times and places, but it is everywhere and always a crime to be the Jew.'

'I am baffled,' Marcus said. 'I have known Jews live free and prosperous. And I do not understand the difference between a Jew and what you call yourself, the Jew.'

The old man smiled again and seated himself on the ground, motioning to Marcus and his friends that they should do so also.

'Once upon a time,' he said, 'I was called Ahasuerus, and then I was indeed only a Jew, a shoemaker in Jerusalem, no richer or poorer than my neighbours, and no more learned either. I was born there, in the Holy City, but even then it had fallen on evil days, for we had been conquered by Rome and were a poor, mean subject people. So, many looked for the Messiah, the promised one who would redeem captive Israel, as the prophet Isaiah had foretold. All conquered people, I have since learned, have such dreams, and they need them to feed the flickering fire, Hope. And I did so myself. But because, as a shoemaker, I was of a sceptical turn of mind . . .'

'Stop a moment,' Marcus said. 'Why should being a shoemaker make you a sceptic?'

'What is a shoe,' the old man said, 'but a thing that outwears its sole?'

'That is a vile pun,' Marcus said, 'but I think I understand you.'

'Very well then, being a sceptic, though I looked for the Messiah, I distrusted each who presented himself as that. There was then a certain teacher, Jesus, a Nazarene, who worked miracles and spoke in riddles, so that many thought him the Messiah. Moreover, because he angered the priests, many people were indeed ready to worship him as the Messiah, for you must know that in any country where priests are powerful, there will be good men, devout men and even women, who resent and despise them, for good reasons which I shall not weary you with now. One of his followers was my cousin Judas, a young man of great ardour and high ideals.'

At that name, Marcus crossed himself, and shuddered to think he was in the company of a cousin of the man who betrayed the Christ. But the old man was not offended and continued:

'My cousin Judas was disappointed in his master, who consorted with loose women – such as you can see all around us in this prison – and who also hesitated, whether from timidity or indifference, to defy the Romans. Once indeed, when asked whether it was lawful to pay tribute to the Romans, he produced a coin, asked whose head was shown there, and on being told it was Caesar's, told his questioner to render unto Caesar that which was Caesar's, and unto God that which was God's. 'Then,' Judas said later, 'I realised he was nothing but a collaborator, and a traitor to Free Israel.' So Judas betrayed him to the priests, at the Feast of the Passover, and they arranged for this Jesus to be arrested and brought for trial before the Roman governor, a man called Pilate. Now I must add also that Judas, being intelligent – by far the most intelligent of this Jesus's followers – was, though disgusted, still in two minds, as I have learned the intelligent so often are, and part of him still trusted that this Jesus was indeed the Messiah. So he betrayed him in order to force him to prove himself.'

'One moment,' Marcus said. 'There are two things I do not understand. First, how was he to prove himself? Second, and more puzzling to me, you say you knew this Judas, but all agree that Jesus lived here on earth several hundred years ago. So I do not understand.'

'All will be explained in time if you permit me to conclude my story.'

'Very well,' Marcus said. 'But I must warn you that my friends and I are in no mood for any fanciful stories. Indeed, we find ourselves here precisely because we listened to one, and were cheated.'

'There is nothing fanciful in my story,' the old Jew said, shaking his head and running his fingers through his long white beard. 'Would there were. As to your first question, the answer is simple. Judas thought that if his leader, this Jesus, was indeed the Messiah, he would now be forced to declare himself openly, and no harm could come to him. But if he was a mere teacher and false Messiah, then he deserved to die. So Jesus was brought before Pilate, and I joined the crowd at the court. Now at this season of the year, the governor was accustomed to release one prisoner, as a token of clemency, and Pilate now enquired whether he should free this Jesus or another, a celebrated thief who was called Barabbas. And I was among those who cried out, "Free Barabbas!"'

Again Marcus crossed himself. Again, not looking at the old man, whose history was so sad and fearful, he asked why he had spoken for Barabbas.

'Because I had every reason to do so,' was the reply. 'In the first place, Barabbas was a good sort – a thief certainly, but one who never stole from the poor – and a good son to his widowed mother. Moreover, I knew him personally. We used to drink in the same tavern, and I tell you, he was never slow to pay for his round. When you are a poor man you learn to value correct behaviour of that sort. Then he had a girl who was much in love with him and due to bear his child. That sort of thing can't be ignored, and in any case the girl's father was also a friend of mine. Finally, my cousin Judas had, as I've told you, argued convincingly that if this Jesus was the Messiah he could come to no harm, for otherwise the prophets would have been deluded. Which could not be. So, in shouting that Barabbas – a good type, I repeat – should be set free, I wasn't condemning this Jesus to anything – unless he wasn't the Messiah, in which case he was a vile imposter who had deceived all who trusted him. So my conscience was clear.'

The old man paused. His silence extended itself. He began to play with worry beads. Marcus wondered if he had forgotten the story he was telling, forgotten even his audience.

'Go on,' he said, 'please. What happened next?'

'So it was interesting, you see,' the old man said, now speaking very slowly, as if each word had to be hauled with pain and labour from deep obscurity. 'So Barabbas was to be freed, and sentence of death was pronounced on Jesus, with Pilate declaring that he washed his hands of the affair, and I returned home to tell my wife that the false Messiah would soon be led along our street on the way to Golgotha and crucifixion. And I sent a servant to call Judas to come to watch, but he would not come. He just settled himself with a wine-flask, my servant reported. He was drunk, you know, for three days before he hanged himself in the Potter's Field. I never understood that.'

'But surely . . .' Marcus began.

'Why should he hang himself? He was proved right, wasn't he? That's what I thought then. Sometimes . . .'

'Excuse me,' Pulcherrima said, 'I'm only a simple country girl, and I don't understand everything you've been saying. But Marcus asked a question and you haven't answered it, and I think you should. You see, my grandfather once told me that all this happened long before his grandfather was a boy. So I don't see how you could have been there. People don't live that long and my grandfather was an old man when he died.'

'Oh,' said the Jew, 'usually they don't. I'm coming to that. You're a clever girl, though, are you a Jew yourself? Never mind, no matter, no matter. The passage of the condemned man was, as I say, along our street. As they drew near, with the mob shouting insults the way they do, this Jesus was stumbling under the weight of the Cross. That's a mean trick of the Romans, by the way, to make the condemned man carry the instrument of his own death. He leaned against the wall of my house for a moment, to catch his breath, I suppose, and I called out, just to please the crowd, get a laugh from them, "Come on, Jesus, get on with you, no loitering on the way to Golgotha." And he looked at me. I'll never forget that look, I can't, as long as I live, which looks like being . . . never mind. He'd very dark eyes and they were a bit bloodshot, after his scourging, I suppose, and he said, in a low voice, "I'll stand here and rest, but you, whoever you are, you shall go on and wander and know no rest till I come again."'

'So?' Marcus said.

The old Jew looked past him, no, through him rather, as Marcus later declared.

'So? So I kissed the head of my youngest child and handed him to his mother, telling her to take care of him, and I followed this Jesus along his dolorous journey till we came to the Hill of Skulls, where the Roman soldiers took the Cross from him and laid it on the ground and nailed him to it. Then they swung it up and thrust it into the hole in the ground that had been dug, and piled the earth round its base to hold it upright. There were two other convicts, thieves, hanging on either side of him. I think they spoke for a little but I couldn't hear what they said. They didn't speak long. Nobody does, nailed to a Cross. I stayed there till it was all over, not that there was anything much to see. But somehow I couldn't leave. Jesus drank from a cup his mother passed to him, wine, maybe drugged, I hoped so. It was given her by a handsome boy, one of his followers. He was one Judas had been jealous of. Then a soldier stuck a lance into his side, to hasten death. They sometimes do that, when they are eager to get off duty. Jesus shrieked out. I can still hear that cry, in the long nights when sleep is denied me. He called out to God who had deserted him. Then it was over, and all was grey, then dark – there was no moon that night. I turned to go home, but my steps led me away from the city, without my willing it. They led me wandering as I have wandered since, homeless, friendless, often destitute. Only once did I find myself back in Jerusalem, and the city lay in ruins, only a few wretches living like conies in the cellars or huddled against the roofless walls. And none had heard of my wife and children.'

'Truly,' Marcus said, 'you are accursed.'

And, in fear, he made the sign of the Cross again, to ward off the infection of despair.

*

**(Our author carries this story no further. It would seem as if he had heard some tale of this lonely Jew condemned to wander. He goes by other names, Cartophilus chief among them. What our author's purpose in introducing this story at this point in his narrative may be is not clear. Again, it is possible that a leaf from the manuscript is missing.

However that may be, it is of interest to add to his account.

It so happens that in my youth as I cruised the universities of Europe in search of knowledge, I came on one who had been, while still a boy, servant to the renowned Dr Cornelius Agrippa, greatly feared and held in awe, though also persecuted, on account of his deep learning and his knowledge of the philosophy of the Cabbala. Unrelenting in his pursuit of wisdom and understanding, Dr Agrippa was also reviled as a necromancer and trafficker in the Black Arts. This by fools, jealous of his powers. For indeed he was, contrary to his notoriety, one whose thought soared into the realm of purest Light. So cruelly are the wise and virtuous used by the world, which fears the exercise of the divine faculty of Reason, that he was victim of the persistent spite of the Dominicans and the Inquisition.

One night (my informant told me) Agrippa was working late in his study in Florence, to which city he had been sent by the great Emperor Maximilian on a diplomatic mission. The lovely valley of the Arno lay below his windows, its charms made the more bewitching by the shifting light of the moon as it danced between fleecy clouds. Agrippa sat at his table on which many old folios were strewn in an haphazard fashion, some worm-eaten, strange mixtures of metals conserved in acrid fluids, elixirs, salts and sulphur, ingredients of his deep and pious researches. Skeletons of various animals hung on the walls, and a shelf above his table was stocked with many small vessels, containing, for example, oils, bones, the seed of the black hellebore (which connotes Melancholy) and Fassa, which is the herb Trinity.

There was a rap on the door, which alarmed the boy who waited on him, for he feared, with reason drawn from experience, that his master's enemies were again upon them. But Agrippa signed to him that he should open the door. He drew back the bolt and found there no envoy of the Inquisition but an aged man, once tall, now bent, whose hair hung in dirty grey strands reaching almost to his shoulders. He wore a long gown, faded yellow in colour, with a girdle inscribed in oriental characters and stars of David loosely tied at the waist. In his hand he held a staff such as pilgrims carry, and his filthy feet were shod only in worn sandals.

He stood there and was silent, his gaze fixed on the black dog with foam-flecked muzzle which lay by Agrippa's feet. Perhaps, thought the boy, their visitor supposed, like other ignorant men, that the dog, Tully, was Agrippa's familiar spirit. But the visitor, it seemed, had come prepared for the dog. He threw it a lump of meat, which it received as in friendship.

'Pardon,' said the visitor, in a Latin which sounded antique to the boy, but which, as he soon realised, his master had no difficulty in understanding, 'pardon, I pray you, this intrusion on your studies. But the fame of Cornelius Agrippa, most learned of doctors, has sounded to the limits of the world, all of which have been traced by my restless steps, and I could not leave this city without casting my eyes on one so revered by the wise, so execrated by the ignorant and fearful.'

Agrippa gracefully acknowledged the compliment, remarking, however, that his labours, 'so often vain and profitless', had left him fatigued.

'Is it for you to talk of fatigue,' the old man replied, 'of tedious years and never-ceasing travail? Once, more years ago than I can number, I too, at the end of the day's labour, would gaze on the declining sun and think joyfully of how it would rise again in the east, restored and refreshed, heralding a new day. Now that daily renovation grieves me, like the cycle of the seasons perpetually returning, for it is to me as the symbol of that to which I am myself condemned.'

Agrippa, who was indeed exhausted by toil and thought, now told the boy to fetch wine, for he had concluded that the stranger was a madman who would not be quick to depart, and so he thought his work for that night at an end, and was ready to seek solace and relaxation in wine.

But the stranger waved aside the cup which the boy offered him, and as Agrippa drank, he began to talk, at first confusedly and then with growing clarity, of the Marvellous Mirror which, he had learned, Agrippa had made by his potent art of magic.

'Is it true,' he said, 'that whoever looks in this mirror may see, if imbued with faith, the far-distant and the long-dead and departed?'

Agrippa inclined his head to acknowledge that this was so. 'Rivers reach the sea,' the stranger said, 'solid rocks disintegrate, the snows of winter melt, the works of man decay and fall to ruin. I have known the wolf couch on the deserted Capitol and have seen Jerusalem all dust, but it is not so with me. Give me, I pray, one glance in your mirror so that I may again, for a moment, however brief, recover the reality of my youth.'

'Whom would you see, and where, and when, and in what condition?'

'I pray you, call before me,' the visitor said, and his voice was now soft and urgent, 'that adored Rebecca, daughter of the famed Rabbi Eben bin Ezra. I would wish to see her as she was in youth when I wandered with her in her father's garden on the flowered banks of the brook Kedron, and we talked of everlasting love with the innocence of these lost days.'

Agrippa – my friend told me – grew pale when he heard this request and understood its import.

'Who you are,' he said, 'whether from Paradise or Gehenna I know not. What you ask is hard. Yet I shall strive to grant your petition, whatever may rise from the nether world.'

Then he chanted a verse or verses, in a tongue never spoken by social men, and polished his mirror with the soft fur of the ermine, so that many-coloured lights streamed from it in all directions. He raised his arms to the heavens and lowered them towards Gehenna so that his fingers touched the marble floor. With a burst of glory the mirror sparkled in the dim room like the sun at noon.

'To see what you demand,' he said, 'my wand must wave once for every decade since the maiden walked this earth. Number these tens now since the day you seek and be faithful and accurate in your computation.'

He waved his wand and the visitor counted till Agrippa had made the motion one hundred and forty-nine times. The strain was terrible, ever greater the further back in time he willed the vision to appear. He paused. The visitor told him to wave the wand again, and again, till fifteen hundred and ten years had slipped away, and then the mirror's surface revealed forms, at first shadowy, then shining forth in living brightness. In the distance were high mountains and Ramoth-Gilead, ancient city of refuge. The foreground of the mirror showed a lovely valley with a tumbling stream, and under cedar trees, surrounded by a flock of sheep, was a maiden.

My friend told me that Agrippa, though scarce able to look in the mirror, on account of a chill fear which he had never previously experienced in his experiments, yet averred that she was more lovely than any Madonna painted by the matchless Raphael.

The visitor cried out, in a voice in which anguish was strangely mixed with rapture, 'It is she, as she was, my Rebecca, in the days when the Holy Temple, most marvellous work of art raised to the glory of Him who is not named, could not excel her in beauty or inspire more reverence for the Creator of all things. I must, I shall, I will, speak to her.'

He approached the mirror, and murmured words which neither Agrippa nor the boy could hear; and as he spoke, the black spaniel dog came and rubbed itself against his legs. Then a mist, such as rises of evening in the valley of the Arno, crept over the mirror till at last all was obscured, and Agrippa's visitor sank to his knees and bowed his head, touching the mirror three times with his lips. He held that final kiss till the glass was blank as an unwritten page. He rose, and, in broken tones, thanked Agrippa for granting him this evidence of the co-existence of all things. He offered him jewels, but Agrippa would not take them and asked, as his only payment, that the visitor should tell him his name.

Then the stranger pointed to a panel on which a Florentine artist – but I know not which – had represented the crucifixion of Christ, and indicated a figure standing near the Cross.

'Look,' he said, 'and tell me who this is intended to be.'

'That,' Agrippa replied, 'is a representation, perhaps faithful, of the unhappy infidel who struck Christ on his journey through the Valley of Humiliation, and urged him on, with bitter gibes, to death.'

'I am that man, the miserable wanderer, who now stands before you.'

And with these words, he turned and departed.

Naturally, I questioned my friend narrowly concerning this story which he told me, with some reluctance and the appearance of trepidation, one evening when we found ourselves trapped in a tavern in Lower Bohemia, prevented by floods and landslides from continuing our journey. It required several flagons of the renowned ale which they make in the town of Budwar to persuade him to divulge the tale which I have rendered in a manner considerably more coherent than that in which it was haltingly related to me.

It is necessary to add that I was convinced of its veracity. Had I not been, I would have refrained, despite its congruence with the foregoing episode in our author's narrative, from inserting it here.

It is a commonplace that death is the master of all things. So it is written in the Talmud, that book of Jewish wisdom which all who seek enlightenment much study:

'A mountain is strong, but iron can destroy it; iron is strong but fire can melt it; fire is strong, but water can extinguish it; water is strong, but can be evaporated into clouds; clouds are strong, but the winds scatter them; wind is strong, but man may conquer it; the body is strong, but fear may break it; fear is strong, but wine may expel it; wine is strong, but sleep diminishes it; yet death, which overtaketh sleep, is stronger than all.'

Yet the Apostle Paul assures us that 'death shall have no dominion', and indeed death may be no more than our imagining. The body crumbles into dust, for dust it is and to dust it is returned; but the soul has wings. Moreover, there are cases, well attested, in which death itself may be evaded. Heroes sleep to rise again. The soul, by obtaining mastery over all bodily things, may survive, and there are bodies so animated by the soul that they are not subject to death.

Inasmuch as our author introduces here the story of the Jew condemned to wander for all eternity – a story which is no mere convenient myth, as the evidence of my friend, who was, I have reason to think, that boy who attended on the learned Doctor Cornelius Agrippa, demonstrated – it may be that he intends it, in his subtlety, to be read as allegory: the search for wisdom is itself undying, transcends all ages, and may penetrate the intention of the Creator of all things. Moreover, the figure of his hero Marcus, whether he existed in historical time or not is representative of the quest which never ends, for each new discovery leads the seeker after wisdom into new lands. All that we learn deepens the mystery that enfolds us, and yet also gives us hope that, as in Agrippa's mirror, things buried may be retrieved, things lost may be found, and that from which timid prudence shrinks may be disclosed to the keen and fervent Imagination.

What we seek is the true understanding of this world into which we have been cast by our creation, and in which we stumble at first blindly, ignorant of our innermost reality. Thus we live, the generality of mankind, in nightmare, running ever onward, pursued by the invisible, powerless, as it may seem, to escape, suffering blows, falling into unplumbed darkness, as Marcus fell into that river below the vault in which he was imprisoned. Sometimes it seems that we are thrown into the air, tossed on wild winds of misfortune, and lacking wings to bear us up. Other times that we are killing or being killed, smeared with the Blood, not of the Lamb, but of our friends and family, or with our own. But we seek, through heroic study and adventure, to escape from dreams and enter into the pure light of Being.

And is not the condemned Jew the guide who bears the lantern to lead us through the dark forest?)**

XV

One morning, before first light, the warder, a red-headed hunchback of vile temper, shook Marcus from his sleep, and told him that he and his friends must prepare themselves to be led to the market, where they were to be sold as slaves. Marcus protested that as a Roman nobleman and free citizen, convicted of no crime, he could not be legally made subject to such indignity, but the dwarf struck him on the mouth with a ring-encrusted fist, drawing blood, and told him that, if he argued further, he should be flogged before being sold.

'And that,' he said, 'will not only make you scream but will leave you in such a condition that you will not attract the sort of bidder who would normally seek to buy a pretty lad like you. So make your choice. I am quite happy to whip you if you please. Matter of fact, I would enjoy doing so.'

'Then I shall deprive you of that pleasure,' Marcus said.

So it was that, in the chill of a winter dawn, Marcus, along with Lycas and Pulcherrima, found himself in the marketplace, shivering (for he wore only a simple shift) and looking, with an anxiety he tried to disguise, to see what manner of man would choose to bid for him.

'I have run,' he thought, 'greater dangers and experienced more terrible things, but this is the depth of humiliation, to be exposed here in the city of the emperors, and displayed for sale as if I was a brute beast or barbarian.'

And when coarse men, stinking of garlic, came and felt his thighs or squeezed his biceps, and made jokes as coarse as their appearance, he was hard put to restrain his offended nobility and prevent himself from striking them. Indeed he would have done so, had not Pulcherrima begged him to hold back. It was not long, however, before the three of them, along with some twoscore others, were knocked down to a one-eyed Greek merchant.

Then, still loaded with chains, they were marched off to a barracks, where they were each given a bowl of pease porridge and a tin cup of sour wine mixed with brackish water. In the afternoon they were led to the port and made to board a vessel. Then, with many oaths and the lashing of whips from the overseers, they were thrust into a dark and stinking hold.

'Is this then at last the worst?' Lycas said.

'Who can tell?' Marcus replied. 'At least we have not been set as galley-slaves to the oars.'

'That is true, and some relief. Yet the oarsmen are in the open air and can see the heavens, while we lie in this filthy box.'

How long the journey lasted Marcus could not tell, for in the dark he soon lost count of the days and nights. Indeed, there was no reckoning of them even by the meals which they were fed, since these came at irregular intervals and were always the same pease porridge and stale biscuit and sour wine.

'They must have barrels of it,' Lycas said.

At last the voyage ended and they were hustled up to the deck. They moved stiffly, and blinked in the sun's light. They saw a little jetty with low white stone houses climbing up a hillside, dotted with windmills. No people were to be seen, but the breeze carried a chant of worship to them. Birds in the sky were ravens. Marcus made the sign of the Cross to ward off the evil influence these birds are known to have.

They were led two days' journey from the coast to a city with seven gates, and there Marcus, Lycas and Pulcherrima were separated from the column of slaves, and handed over to a nobleman who inhabited a great house protected by its own high walls within the walled city. And in this wall also there were seven gates.

This nobleman, whose name was Melanippos, was an impressive figure, very tall, taller by a head than Marcus, and with a long beard reaching almost to his waist. It was dyed purple, according to a fashion of the day, and his lips were stained with purple also, as if he had pressed black grapes upon them. Seeing that he was a gentleman, Marcus made bold to speak, and relate the injustice which he had suffered. So, whether on account of his beauty and noble bearing or the pathos of his story, Melanippos took pity on him. He ordered him to be relieved of his chains, and brought to speak privately to him.

They withdrew to a privy chamber, and Melanippos took a dagger from his belt, and laid it on the table between them, by which action Marcus understood that the man, his new master as he seemed to be, lived in fear of assault.

'I am not surprised,' Marcus said, 'that you do not trust me, but since I know nothing of any enemies you may have, you have nothing to fear from me. Indeed, my state is now so miserable, having been treated as a common criminal and sold to your agent, as I take it, in the slave-market, that my life is yours to command, and all I can do is seek your indulgence.'

'Perhaps, perhaps,' Melanippos said, stroking his beard as if it was a cat. 'At any rate, you speak correct Greek, grammatical and not too vilely accented. So it will not be painful for me to hear the tale of your misfortunes. No doubt they were unpleasant to experience, but when you reach my age, my boy, you will find that other people's ill fortune is amusingly tolerable. So, pray, begin. You were born . . .?'

Marcus therefore told him all that had befallen him, and did so with such nobility of expression that Melanippos could not fail, despite everything, to be moved.

Then Marcus, sensing that he had won favour, asked: 'What land and what city is this, for I see by your dress and manner that it must be old and famous.'

(Creepy-crawlie.)

'Old of an antiquity scarcely to be imagined, famous among all the cities of Greece, and accursed, I believe, above all likewise. This land is Boeotia and this city Thebes.'

Then Melanippos led Marcus from the house and into a garden.

'Do you see that spring that flows so beautifully from the mountainside?'

'Indeed yes, and very pleasing it is.'

'By that spring,' Melanippos said, 'lie the mortal remains of Hector, son of Priam, the greatest of Trojan heroes. I trust, young man, you have heard of the great siege of Troy, sung by Homer and remembered by all educated men?'

'Indeed yes,' Marcus said. 'I have read and delighted in Homer as every man of spirit must. Moreover, through my mother I am descended from the great Aeneas, son of Anchises, whom he bore from the burning city, and also, so I have been assured, by way of my maternal great-grandmother, also from Brutus, Prince of Troy, though neglected by Homer, I don't know why.'

'Yes, yes,' Melanippos said, 'you Romans were all Trojan princes before the Republic.'

'Not all,' Marcus said. 'Only we patricians. Plebeians can boast no such blood. But,' he continued, hurrying lest Melanippos might be offended by the contradiction – for in the interest of the conversation Marcus had temporarily forgotten his degraded status – 'but, tell me, lord, how it comes that Hector should lie here and not in Troy.'

'I wondered when you would ask. But the answer is simple. It is because of the Oracle, which declared:

> "Thebans, in the city of Cadmus,
> Your city shall have all manner of innocent wealth
> If you bring from Asia,
> Hector's bones. So carry them home
> And worship Hector. Such is the word of Mighty Zeus!"

'Innocent wealth! That is something poor Thebes has never known. This spring goes not by the name of Hector, as you might suppose, but by that of Oedipus, King of Thebes; it was here he washed his hands of the blood of his father whom he had killed. For which crime Oedipus was driven mad, but only after he had lain with his mother.'

'But that is horrible,' Marcus said. 'How can you Thebans bear to remember a man guilty of so vile a crime?'

Melanippos sighed: 'How innocent you are, my child. Oedipus

was no more free to act otherwise than he did than . . . But let me tell you the story, so that you may understand the curse that hangs over Thebes.'

They settled themselves on the grass by the spring, and Melanippos, frowning, began to speak.

'Laius, King of Thebes, had incurred the displeasure of Zeus, and was warned by Apollo, the god whom the Thebans honoured above all others, that he would be killed by the son first born to him and his wife Jocasta. Seeking to avoid this doom, he ordered that a spike be driven through the infant's foot, which is why he came to be known later as Oedipus, "Swollen Foot", and then he was exposed on Mount Cithaeron, that he might die.'

'If he was to die,' Marcus said, 'why was the spike driven through his foot?'

'That is a good question, and one that has often puzzled me. Indeed, it is so good a question that I have no answer. You must simply accept that this was done. As it happened, the baby did not die. He was found by a shepherd, who carried him to Corinth. He had heard that the king of that city, Polybus, and his queen, Merope, were childless, and he hoped for a reward if he presented them with a boy to rear as their son. He did receive much gold. So he at least was happy, for the time. Polybus and Merope were also pleased, and brought up the boy with love and care. He grew up handsome and accomplished, and his lameness afflicted him and was apparent only when he was very weary.

'So Oedipus came to man's estate, and then, seeking to know his fortune, journeyed to Delphi to consult the Oracle. What he learned horrified him, for he was told that he would slay his father and lie with his mother. Being a youth of exemplary virtue, he resolved never to see Corinth again; you must understand that he believed that Polybus and Merope were his father and mother, and so he hoped that he could cheat the Oracle by departing from Corinth. Sad and foolish fancy! So he journeyed through Greece and came to the vicinity of Thebes. Outside the city, some miles distant, there is a place where three roads meet. Uncertain which to take, he ventured to question another traveller, who was, though he did not know it, Laius, his true father. Whether something in the lad's tone angered or alarmed Laius, I cannot tell, and none can at this distance in time; but fierce words were exchanged, swords were drawn, and Laius lay dead in the dust. And so Oedipus came to Thebes.

'Now it so happened that in these days Thebes was much afflicted by a monster called the Sphinx, which word means "Strangler". This creature, which had the head of a woman and the body of a lion, used to lurk by the roadside to apprehend travellers, to whom it posed a riddle. Those that could not answer it, it killed; and for this reason there was much hardship and want in Thebes, since traders and merchants declined to carry their wares to or from the city, for fear of the Sphinx. So Creon, brother of Laius, who was now acting as regent, offered the throne and the hand of Jocasta, a woman whose beauty rivalled the milky feet of Dawn, to any man who could rid the state of this monster. And Oedipus, being blithe and courageous, offered to do so. Accordingly, when he had solved the riddle, which so angered the Sphinx that it was consumed in flames of fury, he claimed his reward . . .'

'But what was this riddle?' Marcus asked.

'Who can tell? It is all so long ago,' Melanippos replied. 'The marriage was celebrated, and the years passed, and Oedipus and Jocasta had children, two sons called Eteocles and Polynices, and two daughters, Ismene and Antigone. And he ruled the city with wisdom and justice, no one questions that. But then, there came a pestilence, and much lamentation, for the people believed that they were accursed by the gods. So Oedipus sent again to Delphi, since he had no cause not to trust the Oracle which had warned him away from Corinth and brought him his kingdom, his wife and children whom he loved. And the word came from Delphi that the plague would not depart from Thebes till the murderer of Laius was driven from the city.'

'This story,' Marcus said, 'is too horrible. It is almost beyond belief. And yet, such have been my own misfortunes, that I am compelled to believe it.'

Melanippos let his hand fall into the stream, and lifted it dripping with water, which he brushed against his purple lips.

And it seemed to Marcus that he was tasting the blood which Oedipus had spilled.

'The King,' Melanippos said, 'being zealous for justice, ordered a search to be made for the murderer of Laius. He had never, you see, known who it was he had fought at the place where three roads meet. He questioned now the blind seer Tiresias.'

'Who was he?' Marcus asked. 'And why should he be thought likely to be of help, since a blind man is in my opinion the least credible witness to a crime?'

'He was a citizen of Thebes,' Melanippos said, 'and he was blind because he had offended Hera, the wife of Zeus.'

'This grows complicated,' Marcus said.

'And is life a straight path?' Melanippos replied. 'Zeus and Hera had been arguing about a matter which often occasions dissension between husbands and wives: that is, whether a man or a woman gets more intense and lasting pleasure from the act of love. Tiresias answered by slaying the female of a pair of snakes, and this so angered Hera that she first transformed him, for a time, into a woman, and then struck him blind. Zeus took pity on him for being so cruelly punished and only for being, as Zeus thought, wise in his judgement. So in compensation he granted him the gift of eternal life and also of prophecy or second sight. So you see, he was a good man for Oedipus to question. Still, Oedipus soon thought it might have been better if he hadn't, because Tiresias told him that it was he, Oedipus, himself who had killed Laius. At first Oedipus wouldn't believe this. He thought it was a conspiracy hatched by Creon, who was now jealous of him. But when he talked about it with Jocasta, and she recalled how Laius had looked and what he had been wearing on the day he died, Oedipus was disturbed by the memory of the man he had killed at the place where three roads meet. Even so, it didn't yet occur to him that Laius was his father. But then a messenger came from Corinth and revealed that he had accompanied the shepherd from Mount Cithaeron when he carried the infant to Corinth, and the shepherd was sent for, who confirmed the story. So there was no doubting the truth. Oedipus howled in horror, and took the pin from brooch which Jocasta wore in her hair, and thrust it into one eye and then into the other, rendering himself blind as Tiresias. And when she was told of this, Jocasta hanged herself. So Oedipus left the city and wandered far, weeping from his sightless eyes, and cursing the gods, and came into waste places.'

Marcus said, 'My lord, this is the most terrible story I have ever heard, and yet I am glad that you have told it me, for now I understand that men have always been accursed by fate, and that my own misfortunes are only such as any man making his way through the dark wood of life must expect to endure.'

'What you say, young man, is true philosophy, and yet I have not come to the end of my tale. There is worse to follow.'

'I am tempted to beg that you spare me that,' Marcus said, 'but to hide from knowledge of the worst is to deny oneself enlightenment. Pray continue.'

And, saying this, he too dipped his hand in the spring and brushed the water against his lips; and to his wonder found that it was sweet and pure.

'Indeed,' Melanippos said, 'when the Fates lay their cruel hands on a house, their malignity is not exhausted in a single generation. So, as Oedipus wandered blind over the wastes of Greece, and his loving daughter Antigone searched for him, his sons Eteocles and Polynices came into their own. There are some who say that Oedipus himself had laid a curse on them, but this I do not believe. They were victims of the gods and of their uncle Creon, who still hoped to rule Thebes, sad city of dragon's teeth. Being unable to agree with each other and reign in harmony together, it was arranged that each should be king for a single year and then give way to the other. Eteocles was king first, and Polynices went to Argos, where he married the daughter of King Adrastus. But when the year was up, Eteocles refused to surrender the throne. Polynices sought help from Adrastus, and he sent to his aid an army led by the Seven Warriors, sons of the Seven Champions, and known also as the Epigoni or the Seven against Thebes. And to each of them was assigned one of the seven gates of the city. They attacked ferociously but were driven back, for the courage of the Theban warriors has never been questioned by any man, in any age, that ever I heard of. In the midst of the battle the two brothers encountered each other, and drove at each other with long lances poised, so that each was carried from his horse impaled on his brother's lance. In this way, in the same minute, they killed each other, to the horror of all. But Creon, who now at last seized the throne he had coveted so long, shamefully refused burial to Polynices and the Argive dead, so that, they lay on the open field beyond the city, prey for the fowls of the air. And, since they were refused burial, they could not enter the Chamber of the Dead, which is the Kingdom of Hades, but their souls must wander, unwilling ghosts, till the end of time. Which is why, in the dead hour of noon and on nights when the moon rides high, the clash of swords and spears breaking on armour, and the cries of battle, echo round the walls of accursed Thebes, city of dragons' teeth.'

'But what crime was Oedipus guilty of?' Marcius asked. 'Since he did not know that Laius was his father and Jocasta his mother, how can it be that he should bring such great evil on himself and his city? I am a Christian and we are taught that we are punished in the afterlife for sin, not for misfortune. And it seems to me that Oedipus was a victim, not a sinner.'

'He was a man,' Melanippos said, 'which is, now I recall, the answer he gave to the Sphinx, and so he was, like all men, the plaything of the gods. I do not know this word "sin". But let me tell you what I think was his mistake. All the other heroes that I know of, when they had slain monsters, took possession of some part of the monster as a guard against misfortune. They closed with the monsters and slew them, and so Perseus for example carried with him the Gorgon's head, so that all who crossed him were turned to stone if he turned its face against them. But Oedipus killed the Sphinx with a mere word, and, when the monster fell into a chasm and was consumed, he was too proud or indifferent to descend there himself and skin it and take to himself its gorgeous scales. So he had no talisman against misfortune to clutch in his hand. He had conquered with but a word, and came away without the spoils of victory such as men have always prized, and without which, it seems to me, battle is a vain thing bringing no reward.'

'But the word, which is Logos,' Marcus said, 'is more powerful than any sword, for the word is not confined in time or space, but travels faster than man, with the speed of the north wind itself, and no mountain pass or river can stay its passage, and no city wall is sure defence against the word.'

'Is that so?' Melanippos said. 'Is that how things are in the world today? Well, it may be. For myself, I never travel from accursed Thebes, city of dragons' teeth, so cannot tell. Yet I have heard that this new religion of Christ has been carried across Greece and conquered Rome itself, though it is a religion of slaves and paupers. Yet, if the word is as powerful as you say, young man, then, since Oedipus possessed it, this would explain why Oedipus was so hated by the gods. For that they are ever jealous of men, no one can doubt.'

'You call Thebes accursed and the city of dragons' teeth,' Marcus said. 'Pray, why do you do that?'

'That,' said Melanippos, 'is another story, and now it is late and we must sleep.'

So Marcus retired to rest, happy that he had found a noble master in Melanippos, but puzzled and perturbed by the stories he had heard.

XVI

Melanippos had a daughter, by name Artemisia, who would have been lovely as the dawn if she had not squinted; for she had hair the colour of burnished gold, a skin as soft as rose-petals and a mouth made for kissing; and her walk was graceful as a lily. But this terrible squint disfigured her, and spoke of a nature that was crooked and not straight. Perhaps this was not so, for it is not always the case that the outward form reveals the truth that lies behind it. Yet no man could see this beauty so disfigured without misgiving, even fear.

Now when Artemisia's cross-eyes lighted on Marcus, she desired him, and went to her father and said, 'This is no mean-born slave that you have bought. I beg you, give him to me, that he may be mine and I his, for I know that my deformity repels men, and therefore I would wish to have this one who has no power to choose.'

So Melanippos agreed, and they were betrothed, to the great sorrow and pain of Pulcherrima. Artemisia hated Pulcherrima, with that deep jealous hatred that beauty and goodness so often provoke in other women, so that Marcus feared for the life of his darling. And for this reason he thought it best to agree to wed Artemisia, lest her jealousy cause her to destroy Pulcherrima.

When they were married, he told her of his misfortunes, and of how he had been prevented from approaching the Emperor. But he thought it wiser to say nothing of Honoria, whose cause he had intended to plead at court, for he said to himself, 'If she is jealous of poor Pulcherrima, how much more jealous will she be of the Princess.' Nevertheless, he urged Artemisia to persuade her father to supply him with the means to return to Constantinople, and this time in a manner more suited to his high estate. He dwelled some time on this, for he was determined that she should understand that in making him her husband, she was not raising him, but restoring him to his proper rank.

But Melanippos would not let him go, and said he still had stories to tell the young man.

One day he asked him: 'Is it better to be virtuous or to be wise?'

Marcus shook his head and smiled. 'There is no answer to that question. Can one separate virtue from wisdom, for is it possible that one can exist without the other?'

'There is indeed no answer to the question,' Melanippos said, 'which is why we keep asking it. If there was an answer, there could be no question. Consider the story of Palamedes, who was both virtuous and wise.'

'I cannot consider it,' Marcus said, 'since I have never heard of him, or if I have, I have forgotten both him and his deeds.'

'But you have heard of Helen, loveliest of women, whom Paris, fair of face, seduced, and stole from her husband Menelaus, King of Sparta, and carried to Troy.'

'Indeed yes. She was the cause of the Trojan War, and my tutor . . .'

'Never mind your tutor.'

'Alas, I rarely did.'

'But listen to me. All Greece felt the force of this insult, and so the Achaeans, as we Greeks were then called, resolved to bring Helen back. The heroes were summoned to the army, and so great was the indignation, almost all responded. But Odysseus, King of Ithaca, wished to evade the summons. So he pretended to be mad, since no commander wants a mad officer in his army. He yoked an ox and an ass together and ploughed the field with them. As he did so, he scattered salt before him, throwing the essence of the sea that bears no harvest on to the earth that would bear no crop. Agamemnon, the great king and his brother Menelaus shook their heads, and would have departed saying, 'Odysseus is no good to us, being mad.' But Palamedes knew better. He picked up the baby Telemachus, the son of Odysseus, tearing him from his mother's arms, and threw him down before the plough. Odysseus stopped. The wise and virtuous Palamedes had outwitted him, and proved he was no madman. So Odysseus joined the army.

'One hero was lacking still. This was Achilles. Word was brought to Odysseus that Thetis, the mother of Achilles, had sent her beloved son to the court of Skyros, disguised as a girl. Odysseus determined that, if he had to go against Troy, Achilles should not be spared the war, and went to Skyros with gifts for the women in their quarters. He laid the basket before them, and the eager girls thrust in their hands, crying out in wonder and excitement on account of the fine clothes and jewels he had brought them. Cunning Odysseus had hidden a shield and sword among the other presents. A lovely redhead seized them, handling them in the manner of one accustomed to arms. So Odysseus knew that this was Achilles, and led him to Troy confident that the war would be won: for who could resist Achilles?

'But Achilles quarrelled with Agamemnon and sulked in his tent. And, while he did so, the war languished. The men gazed at the mountains day and night, or let their eyes fall on the idle sea that separated them from their homes in Greece. It was now that the wisdom of Palamedes saved the Achaeans. He devised games – draughts and dice – to beguile the time, and keep the men happy or contented. He dedicated the dice to Tyche, Goddess of Fortune, in her sanctuary at Argos.'

'I have seen her shrine in Constantinople,' Marcus said.

'It is right that it should be there, for, since Palamedes invented dice, we have come to know that they are the very image and pattern of life. Everything that happens results from the rattle of the box and the manner in which the dice fall. So the soldiers played happily, but Odysseus hated Palamedes all the more.'

'But why?' Marcus asked.

'It may be that he recognised that Palamedes had revealed a truth which he thought was his alone, and so robbed him of the superiority which his knowledge of Fortune gave him. Whatever the cause, he resented and hated Palamedes and now compassed his death. And because Palamedes had exposed the lie of his own madness, he chose to destroy him by a lie which should appear to be the truth. He took and killed a Trojan prisoner and left tucked into his armour a letter, which he had forged, and which was addressed to Palamedes, apparently from Priam, King of Troy. In this letter Priam spoke of gold which he had given in return for a promise by Palamedes to betray the Achaeans and lead them from the siege. Odysseus saw to it that the letter was discovered. Palamedes denounced it as a forgery. Then Odysseus suggested that they search Palamedes's tent. Which they did, and discovered a box of gold under his bed. Palamedes denied all knowledge of it, and indeed spoke the truth, for it was Odysseus who had caused it to be hidden there. But no one now believed Palamedes. So he was stoned to death. Every man threw down the dice which Palamedes had given them for their pleasure, and seized a stone and hurled it at him. He cried out only that he mourned the passing of truth and honesty from the world. But Odysseus smiled, for he knew that his lie had conquered truth, and that wisdom and virtue offered no defence against what we are agreed to call intelligence. And from that day on it is intelligence which matters, not wisdom or virtue.'

'Your story is monstrous,' Marcus said. 'Why, Father – for so I must now call you – do you consider Odysseus to have been a hero?'

'He was the first man not to live in dreams of glory,' Melanippos replied, 'but to judge men as they are. Oedipus slew the Sphinx, as you have observed, by the power of the Word, and Odysseus slew truth, virtue and wisdom in the same manner.'

'I remember now,' Marcus said, 'how I praised his cunning when he deceived the Cyclops Polyphemus, but I never heard this story of Palamedes before. Was Odysseus all of a piece? Do I think worse of him now?'

These questions perplexed him for many nights.

XVII

To those who did not know him intimately Melanippos appeared the happiest of mortals. He was free from all public duties, and the city of Thebes, though decayed from its former greatness, was also, by virtue of that very decadence which saw it abandon the desire for domination, likewise free from enemies and the danger of war. Far distant from the frontiers of the Empire, it seemed to its citizens safe from the threat of the barbarians.

Melanippos himself was rich, but not so rich that he invited envy, most corrosive of sentiments. His cornfields stretched golden from the walls of Thebes to the lower slopes of Mount Cithaeron, and his vines hung heavy with the dark purple grape. The women of his household were chaste, comely and obedient. The coats of his bullocks gleamed velvet, blessed, as he admitted, by Apollo. His flocks were free of breakshugh and tremmlin, and his cattle of murrain. His racing-horses excelled all others in Boeotia. His health was excellent and advancing years had in no way impaired his faculties. And yet, as Marcus soon came to know, he was sore afflicted by mental distress.

Often – too often for these around him – he lamented the decadence of the age. 'Would that I were not of this time,' he would say, or moan, 'that I had died before, or better never have been born. This is the age of base iron, fallen far from the golden days. Now, by day, men labour and grieve unceasingly; by night, they waste away and die. The gods impose harsh burdens on us, provoked by our indifference to them and our forgetfulness of the duties we owe them. Soon, surely, mighty Zeus will bring destruction to this miserable race of men.'

When he heard him speak in this fashion, Marcus strove to conceal his exasperation and tried to comfort him by drawing his attention to the blessings which the goddess Tyche had indeed bestowed upon him. But Melanippos only sighed the more deeply, and said,

'It is but the semblance of prosperity, the mere shadow of felicity. Once upon a time, when Kronos, father of Zeus, reigned on Mount Olympus, the gods created a race of men who lived like gods themselves, with hearts that knew not sorrow and were ignorant of toil and grief. Nor was a wretched old age their destiny but they were ever unwearied in limb and made merry in feasting. They knew no evil, and, when in time they died, it was as if they were merely folded in gentle sleep.'

'Yes,' Marcus said, 'we Christians tell a like story of how our great progenitor Adam lived in happy innocence in a garden called Eden, and how, on account of his woman Eve being tempted by the serpent to seek the knowledge of good and evil, and eat an apple from a forbidden tree, they were driven forth to wander in waste-lands and wilderness where Adam was compelled by harsh necessity to till the soil.'

'I did not know that,' Melanippos said, 'but I think it cannot be true, for it is recorded that the Golden Age was followed by a Silver one and then by one of Bronze in which, as I have told you, the Heroes lived and perished in wars and brave ventures. So that now we live, debased and degenerate, in this Age of Iron itself now dull and tarnished.'

'And can we not escape from that, by aspiring to higher things?' Marcus asked.

'The wise Plato thought so, many centuries before we were born. He said that we must do all that is within our power to imitate the life which flourished in the days of Kronos, and that, in so far as the immortal power abides within us, we must heed its promptings, in both our public and our private life.'

'And is that not wise?' Marcus said. 'For it is, other things being equal, what Holy Church teaches also.'

Melanippos laughed, and his laugh was bitter as wine three days open and left to corrupting air.

'When I look around me,' he said, 'when I listen to the rumours that come to me even here, rumours of wars and barbarian invasions, rumours of murder and corruption at the imperial court, how can I hope that wisdom will prevail? Is it not true that great Rome itself has fallen victim to the ignorant fury of the barbarians?'

'Indeed it is,' Marcus said, 'and to my shame I was carried in their army. Is it possible,' he said, 'that war should one day be no more? Why, my father, are we compelled to engage in war?'

'The most terrible of wars was fought over a mean object, a mere woman. The seduction of Helen by Paris and her removal from the palace of Menelaus, that was the sole cause of the war between the Trojans and the Achaeans. Does that make sense? Is that not proof that men are by nature mad? Why should the Greeks have left their homes, endured hardship, and died for Helen? How could the Trojans endure war and the destruction of their city as the price of a slut, an unchaste woman? How could they die in defence of Paris, a fornicator, adulterer and coward?'

Melanippos turned away as men do when they think grief has unmanned them, and Marcus was left to ponder these matters. He wrestled with the question through many sleepless nights, but came to no conclusion. He is not to be reproached for his failure, since the wisest of philosophers have argued this question, and come no closer to resolving it. Indeed, as the Arab scholar Avicenna wrote, it is 'fundamental to the human condition'.

Consider, my Prince, that no other animal, no created species but man, wars against its own kind. The wolf pulls down the straying lamb and slays it, or invades the sheepfold if the shepherd sleeps; but wolves do not prey on other wolves, but live together socially, in amity and fellowship. Yet we know that the wolf is among the fiercest and most pitiless of the brute creation. When we hear of horses that turn on each other, and kill each other, and eat each other's flesh, as the horses of Diomedes did, we say they are mad, and in that case it was because they had been fed on human flesh, which is contrary to the Laws of Nature, to give flesh to an animal framed by the Almighty to eat only grass; so that this is recognised as a cause of madness.

As for Man, there was no war in Eden, but soon after our first forefather's expulsion, Cain slew Abel, his brother, which we may regard as the prototype of wars. There was a fight, as I read it, between the hunter and the farmer; and it may be that the first wars of mankind were waged between two such groups of people, for it is natural that farmers should seek to deny hunters the entry to their land, lest they destroy the crops. And this we may style an economic cause of war.

We may further conclude that such wars are reasonable. But, whether reasonable or not, war is never haphazard. Men do not kill each other and expose themselves to the chance of death or slavery without cause. There is no war without a motive.

Here you may choose to question my assertion by reference again to the Trojan war, for you may argue that in that case the motive was insufficient.

To say so is however to judge men to be animated only by their needs, and not by passion. Yet, in the ordinary intercourse of life, we see that passion will drive men to actions from which prudence or the consideration of their interests should deter them. How often, in a tavern, have I seen a blow struck, a knife drawn, a man killed, on the account only of some word spoken to which another took offence. For the governing emotion in men of spirit is pride, and not greed, which animates only base spirits. In the Trojan war both armies were held to the struggle by their pride. The pride of the Greeks was insulted by the rape of Helen; the pride of the Trojans would have been lowered had they surrendered her to the demands of the Greeks. No mere material cause could have held two such mighty armies locked in struggle. Reason, that divine gift, would, long before a year had supervened, have caused them to say, 'What we may lose is more than ever we can gain.' And so they would have laid down their arms and made peace, the Greeks retiring thankfully to their ships, the Trojans rejoicing in their departure, having surrendered Helen to her rightful husband. But since the cause of the war was buried deep in the offended natures of both Greeks and Trojans, there could be no agreement and no peace till the tall towers of Ilium were aflame, and so many brave souls ripped from the bodies that encased them.

There is another word for pride, and it is honour. We recognise honour as the most precious possession of Man; and so offended honour is the chief cause of war.

And this explains why the brute creation does not war against its fellows, for all theologians deny animals a sense of honour, though for my part I confess to having seen honour glimmer in the eyes of my French spaniel, Laurie.

If you remain to be convinced, my Prince, then consider the Holy War against the Infidel which was first proclaimed by the Holy Father Urban, and in which your own grandfather, the red-bearded Emperor, perished. Though some say that there were those among the projectors of the war who were not driven by honour, but who, like the base merchants of Venice and Genoa sought riches and the opportunity to capture the trade of the Middle Sea, and though, in the most recent Crusade, the Holy Warriors, enticed by the Venetians, sacked the city of Constantine, yet it was neither greed nor desire for riches that drew all Christendom to war, but rather the dishonour which the Infidel (as he is held to be) had inflicted on all Christian men by his seizure of the Holy Places. And therefore this war is deemed to be just.

XVIII

Winter had passed, and the first flowers of Spring were in bloom before Melanippos at last consented to let them go so that Marcus might fulfil his mission in Constantinople. He had not told the young man all his stories; and indeed it was impossible that he should have done so, for each story that he completed reminded him of another. And this is indeed the nature of stories, sent to console us by the Grace of God as some think, or, as others declare, by the Evil One to divert us. So he made Marcus promise that he would return with the first winds of Autumn; he had never, he said, known anyone so alive to the meaning that lies behind stories as his daughter's husband. Marcus promised as required, but made a mental reservation such as may excuse a man from the fulfilment of an oath.

Melanippos, however, being a wise man who knew that promises may be scattered by the winds of wilfulness or circumstance, and knew also that the young give their word lightly, not yet having learned its value, which is to be weighed as gold and not bestowed more readily, commanded that Pulcherrima remain behind. He had compared her to Artemisia and saw that no man could prefer his daughter to Pulcherrima, lovely as roses. Therefore he was certain that if she remained in Thebes Marcus would return. Moreover, he desired her himself, and he knew that her detention by him would please his daughter. Artemisia indeed looked at him approvingly from her cross-eyes.

So Marcus, Artemisia and Lycas took ship and sailed to Constantinople. Melanippos had supplied them with gold and silver so that they could journey in a manner fitting to their rank and his dignity. Nevertheless, on their first morning in Constantinople, Marcus insisted that he and Lycas should return to the tavern where they had lodged, and there pay their reckoning. The woman of the tavern did not at once recognise them. When she did, she assailed them with angry cries, which, however, were soon silenced by the sight of Marcus's purse. Whereupon she fell on their shoulders, weeping and protesting that she had always known them to be 'quality, the real gentry' and such like, and had never intended that they should come to harm. Marcus smiled and allowed her to kiss his hand. Then he went to the shop of the tailor at the sign of the Wounded Ox to pay him too for the suit of clothes he had ordered from him.

Next day he made ready soon after dawn to go to the palace. Artemisia sighed and said,

'No, husband, it is not safe that you do so.'

'Why should you suppose that?'

'You may imagine, dear Marcus,' she said, 'that my disfigurement is mere chance of nature. But nothing happens in this world without reason and significance; and if I cannot look you directly in the eye, it is because my own are so aligned that they see that which is yet to come. So believe me when I say that it is not safe. You must remain at home today. I have seen the future, and it is red with blood.'

Marcus hesitated. On the one hand, as a Christian, he had been schooled to distrust all divination that was not founded on faith in the Word of God as necromancy, witchcraft, breathing the foul air of the Black Arts. On the other hand, his own experiences had taught him to be wary. And he recalled some of the stories Artemisia's father had told him, stories of divination and awful auguries. So he hesitated, and while he did so, Lycas pulled at his sleeve and urged him to do as his wife suggested.

'You, too, Lycas, have faith in such things?'

'Faith, Marcus,' he replied, 'what faith may be and what it may not be, I don't know, but I do know that when a woman such as your lady speaks in such and such a fashion, it is wiser to listen and obey than to think nothing of it.'

They argued the matter at some length, for both loved discourse and the chop of logic, and, while they did so, there came the sound of a rising wind, and the hangings of the apartment began to waver. Then loud cries rose to them from the street below, and angry howls, and then, swelling like the ocean, came the thud of drums. The noise drew nearer, and they heard running feet and the clash of metal. The chorus drew them to the window, and they saw that the street was thronged with people who by their dress belonged to the meaner quarters of the city. They were preceded by three priests bearing crucifixes and the relics of saints, which they waved aloft while the mob howled its curses.

These were directed at a pagan temple which stood at the end of the narrow street. A big man dressed as a butcher in a blood-smeared smock, and carrying a burning brand, forced his way to the head of the crowd. Now two men, wearing only loincloths, as if they had been disturbed from sleep, appeared at the door of the temple, glanced a horrified and unwilling moment at the advancing mob and made to flee up a side alley. But they were seized and tossed from one rioter to another as if they were sheafs of corn, until they were thrown to the ground and trampled underfoot. Then the mob surged into the temple.

Marcus uttered a cry of horror and rushed from their chamber, closely followed by the faithful Lycas. Descending the stairs two at a time, they emerged into the street to see a pagan priest being dragged from his place of worship. The wretch cried like a woman, and Marcus, filled with pity and indignation, pushed his way through the mob, thrusting people aside as if they were branches that impeded his path through a forest, until he came to the three priests of Christ who were directing these horrid proceedings. He took one roughly by the arm, and besought him in the name of Jesus to desist.

'For,' he said, 'whatever this man may or may not be guilty of, you as a man of God can have no part in this cruel and unruly violence. He is a man and so has a claim on your mercy. He is, I suppose, a Roman citizen, and therefore has a right to a fair trial.'

But the servant of the Almighty would have none of it.

'Do not speak to me of such things. Too long we have tolerated these idolators. Now, when our army has suffered a defeat at the hands of the barbarians, who can doubt that we have been corrupted and betrayed by such creatures as this?'

Turning to the butcher, he commanded that the miserable pagan be hanged from the nearest lamp-post.

The butcher obeyed. A rope was produced and the victim's pleas being disregarded, he was strung up. The Christian priest clasped his arms around the hanging knees and swung from them with loud cries of praise to God for his bounty till Marcus heard the sound of bones cracking, and knew it was over.

The mob, which had fallen silent to watch this spectacle, now surged into the temple to set fire to it. But first they hurled the images and statues of the gods worshipped there into the street.

Marcus, disgusted and sore at heart, would have turned away. But the priest clutched him by the arm.

'Not so fast, my pretty youth. Those who interrupt the Lord's work are friends of sin and idolatry, and must be put to the question.'

So he commanded that Marcus be bound, and then he was led, with the point of a pike under his chin, from the scene of the murder. He stumbled once, and, though he could not look down, knew it was over the body of the first of the mob's victims; and his foot slipped in the blood that had been spilled across the pavement.

Lycas, whose association with Marcus had gone unnoticed, followed closely, to see where his friend was taken, and to be able to report this to Artemisia. He reproached himself bitterly for having failed Marcus.

XIX

At the command of the fanatic priest, and jostled and insulted by the angry crowd, some of whose members hurled dung and stones as well as bitter words at him, Marcus was carried to a Christian church, then thrust down a long twisting stair till he came to a dark dank place, dimly lit by tapers fixed to the slimy walls. Rough hands threw him into a cell, where he fell to the stone floor, bruised and winded, and lay there amazed by the sudden misfortune which had once again struck him. Yet in a little, and for a little, his natural equanimity returned. 'I am,' he said to himself, 'in the hands of the Church and in the city of the Emperor. So I must be brought to trial by due process of law, and not abandoned to moulder in this vile place.' But then he recalled the fury of the mob and the crimes he had been unable to prevent; and knew the temptation to despair. 'Surely,' he thought, 'there is some curse upon me, since each time I try to present myself to the Emperor to plead the cause of his unfortunate sister, my lady the Princess Honoria, some accident occurs to prevent it.'

How long he lay there he could not tell. No food was brought him, and the bonds which held his wrists chafed him as he tried to free himself. Yet he found consolation in the thought that Lycas had been there to see what befell him, and that Lycas and Artemisia would work to set him free. So at last he fell into a sleep, which was, however, disturbed by horrid visions and a nightmare from which he woke screaming. Then he lay and listened to the scurrying rats.

Lycas had hurried to tell Artemisia of Marcus's arrest. 'I could not prevent it,' he stammered, more than once, and dissolved in tears. But Artemisia remained grim-faced. She dressed herself in her finest gown and jewels, amethysts and rubies beyond price, and ordered him to procure the means of transport to the imperial palace. He commanded a litter and they presented themselves there to demand an audience of the Emperor before night fell on the city. But they met with no success. They were detained in an antechamber, being told, first, that the Augustus was at prayer and could see no one, then that he dined and could see no one. But Artemisia refused to quit her post, for her deformity had bred in her a power of will as strong and cold as the North Wind that blows from the mountains, and she had long learned that, being unable to conquer and have her way by means of the display of charms, she must secure her ends by the exercise of an intolerable persistence. So now she said to Lycas:

'Tell those who wait on the Augustus and deny us admittance that I shall not leave this place till I have had the opportunity to lay my complaint before him.'

Then, taking a ruby from her purse, she told Lycas to sweeten her words by bestowing it on the eunuch who kept the door, for, she said, 'I know that base men will do nothing without reward. So assure him that there is a match to this jewel which shall be his when my demand is satisfied.'

The eunuch bowed deeply, being made aware that he was in the presence of a great lady, and not, as he had supposed, of some tiresome suitor of no consequence, one of those who expected something for nothing.

At last Marcus fell into a fitful, feverish sleep in which he was troubled by disordered dreams. Once he woke screaming, and shivered as he lay pressed against the clammy wall. It semed in his half-waking state that a light shone in the corner of his cell, and that from this the figure of a woman emerged. She leaned over him and murmured an incantation. Her eyes gleamed green in the dark, and she spoke to him in Greek, and told him she was Lamia, Queen of Lybia, once loved by Zeus on account of her beauty, and hated by Hera, whose jealousy she had aroused. So, she murmured in a voice that was gentle though the words it spoke were cruel, Hera had pursued her with malice, and killed her children, and condemned her to wander in the waste places of the earth.

He felt her brush her hair aside, and lay a cool hand on his forehead. Then she fixed her lips on his and coupled with him on the wet chill stone. For a moment it seemed to him that he experienced intense pleasure, and then her teeth bit into his neck and drew blood.

'Yield to me,' she sighed, 'and I shall teach you the art of mastering men and making them subject to your will.'

And then he swooned, or woke from the swoon in which he had dreamed, for he could not tell whether he was waking or sleeping, and found himself alone.

On that first night Artemisia and Lycas failed to obtain the audience that they sought. But Artemisia was resolute. She cultivated the friendship or the favour of the eunuch who guarded the door that led to the imperial apartments, for, though without experience of courts, she understood that control of access to Great Ones is a valued privilege of underlings, whose power is for this reason greater than the world supposes. It is, I must warn you, a danger that princes ever run, for, while they believe themselves supreme, and know that their word delivers life or death, nevertheless they themselves may be isolated and kept ignorant of matters of some import, merely according to the whims of their servants. Indeed, the more splendid and remote the elevation of princes above the common run of mankind, the more certain it is that those who keep the gate and determine who shall have the prince's ear exercise an authority that nothing in their station properly grants them, and which even the most mighty prince may not suspect. To this point it has been wisely said, 'The more virtuous the prince, the more easily he is entrapped.' Furthermore, it is observed by all who have studied the ways of courts that in time the prince will come to repose confidence only in those underlings who have by this means secured their position by isolating him from the common run of opinion; and this is why there is often a secret power behind the throne. Be it noted, too, that there is scriptural authority for this state of things, since

Christ gave Peter the Keys of the Kingdom, and said to him: 'Whatsoever thou shalt bind on earth shall be bound in heaven; and whatsoever thou shalt loose on earth shall be loosed in heaven.'

So Artemisia was wise in her understanding that the eunuch who kept the door must be cultivated, and that jewels and silver were the dung which would make the earth rich and bring forth fruit.

Even so, it required several days before he yielded, and unlocked access.

Now it so happened that Marcus was mistaken in supposing that Arcadius, the brother of Honorius and Honoria, still sat upon the throne. Arcadius was dead – poisoned, said some – and had been succeeded by his son Theodosius, who was still a youth, slow-witted and not yet master of the Palace, let alone of the Empire. When Artemisia and Lycas had prostrated themselves before him, and then raised their heads in order to plead for Marcus's life, they saw a slim figure, like a dummy, gazing straight before him, as if his head was held in a vice and could turn neither to left nor to right. The boy seemed to be frozen in this posture, as if any movement, even of the eyes, might betray him. Above the throne, on either side, hung purple banners woven in the shape of dragons and attached to the points of spears glittering with precious stones. A soft air blew through the chamber, spreading a sweet perfume of musk-roses, while the movement of the banners emitted a sound recalling to Lycas the hissing of innumerable serpents. To the right of the throne there was a low stool, and on this sat a woman in a gown of dull gold. She fluttered a fan before her face, and it was she who spoke. Though neither Artemisia nor Lycas knew who she was – and how should they have known? – the person thus assuming this humble station was Eudoxia, the Emperor's mother.

Those who knew her only by repute would have been surprised to see her so placed. She was known to be a woman of a high and commanding temper, who had governed her late husband and was believed to be the controlling force throughout the eastern Empire. She worked in close harmony with the deformed eunuch

Eutropius, a man of infinite guile. But those with a closer knowledge of her would have felt no surprise, since Eudoxia, like the eunuch, combined a relish for power with a fine disdain for its appearance.

When Eudoxia learned whose daughter Artemisia was, she at once declared that she was ready to do her honour; she had heard much of the wisdom and virtue of Melanippos, and knew him to be a man of the most distinguished lineage.

'Indeed,' she said, 'had I been made aware of your birth, you would not have been kept waiting at the door. But the truth is, my dear, that we are so besieged by importunate suitors that it is necessary to exercise great care over who may be permitted to address the Emperor.'

At this speech, the boy twitched, recognising his title; and this was the only sign of life he had given.

'Nevertheless,' Eudoxia said, 'I shall order the doorman who kept you from me to be soundly whipped, that he may learn discrimination.'

But Artemisia begged her to do no such thing, partly because she had a kind heart, and partly because it would put the doorman in her debt.

As the Empress spoke, Artemisia was uncomfortably aware of the close and nervous scrutiny given her by the eunuch Eutropius. However, anxious for Marcus's safety and fearful lest she might soon exhaust the patience of the Empress, she embarked on the story of her husband's disappearance.

'Surely,' she said, 'it is not right that so noble and distinguished a lord as mine should be spirited away according to the whim or command of a fanatic priest. And this at a time when his only purpose in coming to Constantinople was to prostrate himself before Your Imperial Highness.'

To her surprise it was the eunuch Eutropius who replied.

'We understand your perturbation and anxiety. Alas, the city is now in turmoil, and there have been other disappearances which we are also at a loss to account for.'

Artemisia, ignorant of the eunuch's position at court and supposing him to be a mere presumptuous servant, angrily turned her cross-eyed gaze upon him. Whereupon he leaned over and whispered in the Empress's ear. Seeing this familiarity, Artemisia, with that ready intelligence she had inherited from her father, realised her mistake, and would have spoken soothingly to appease him. But she was prevented by the Empress, who immediately declared Marcus's arrest to be an act of monstrous insubordination, and ordered that a search be made for the delinquent priest, who should be brought before her to account for his actions.

Artemisia was as amazed as she was delighted by this speedy success, and attributed it to her high birth and her father's reputation. In this she was mistaken. The truth was that the superstitious eunuch had concluded that she was possessed of the power of the evil eye, which was the one thing, on earth or in heaven, which he dreaded. For this reason he always wore an amulet of bull's horn on a necklace, and Lycas had already observed that his hand flew to touch the horn as Artemisia spoke.

There is much dispute among wise men whether such a power truly exists. Some say that a benevolent and all-seeing Deity would not bestow such a malign gift on any mortal. Nevertheless, examples of its operations – plausible examples – are too well attested for me to doubt its reality, even though the *jettatura* (as the possessor of the power is called in Naples) may not be aware that he, or more commonly she, is so gifted, or, if you prefer, accursed. It is also evident that the mere suspicion that a certain person is a *jettatura* can grant that being an influence over others which he or she may not suspect.

And I may say that Lycas had already concluded that Artemisia possessed this power, since he had seen her throw a disturbing glance at Marcus just as he descended to the street to try to intervene between the rioters and their victims. He did not believe that Artemisia was herself aware of her power, but knowing that the *jettatrice* (as the female of the species is termed) is the most dangerous of all, he rarely, when in her company, now kept his hand far removed from the horn bracelet which he wore round his right wrist. And whenever he felt her crooked gaze upon him, his fingers flew to touch, surreptitiously, the protective horn. And it was thus, he believed, that he had so far kept himself from harm. So now, seeing the effect of her look upon the eunuch, he was confirmed in his suspicion and resolved to alert his beloved Marcus to the reality of his wife's unholy gift as soon as he was in a position to do so.

Fortunately, it seemed that this moment might not be long delayed. The Empress had called for wine, cooled in snow brought from the high Pamirs and stored in an icehouse dug deep under the pavement of the third courtyard of the palace, and they had scarcely had time to down three cups apiece before there came the sound of marching feet, whimpering, yells of protest, and the banging of a mace on the door. It was opened, and the fanatic priest was thrust into the chamber, his wrists and ankles chained. He was hurled on to the marble floor at the feet of the Empress, who, extending a gold-slippered foot under his chin, forced his head upwards, and berated him for his insolence in abducting so distinguished a knight as Marcus. The priest babbled in ignoble terror, and told them where Marcus was held. The Empress then pronounced sentence of death, but Eutropius the eunuch intervened.

'While this wretch,' he said, 'certainly merits death on account of his presumption and lawlessness, yet there are two reasons why the Augusta should, if I may be so bold, stay her hand. In the first place, I recognise him and know that he has devoted followers among the rabble, who will certainly erupt in fury if he is put to death; and the Augusta may think it rash to provoke such a disturbance. But my second reason is more immediate. If he is put to death now, as he so richly deserves, it may be that we shall then discover that he has lied to us, and that the young nobleman is not where he says he is. But in that case we should have no means of obtaining exact information, this creature being dead. So I submit that he should be carried hence and kept under close guard at least till we have ascertained whether he has spoken truth.'

He said this not because in reality he doubted the priest, but because he was a man he had found useful in the past, and was happy to place under a new obligation.

The Empress followed his advice, for she was guided by him in

129

all things. The priest was removed, and soldiers were dispatched to free Marcus and bring him to the palace. Meanwhile Lycas observed that the eunuch's fingers continued to play on the bull's-horn amulet, while the Empress and Artemisia, to distract themselves, discussed the latest fashions.

He noted too that the young Emperor had paid no attention to this dramatic scene, but looked vacant, and occasionally giggled.

'Perhaps,' Lycas thought, 'he is soft in the brain. Well, that may be no great matter, since evidently others rule while he reigns.'

Yet, being tender-hearted, he felt sorry for him. He could not however refrain from comparing this wretched dummy with the Lost Boys among whom he had lived; and so he concluded that the world was ill-ordered, a judgement many have arrived at with little more experience of life than Lycas had then, and which has not been disturbed by a further acquaintance with its ways.

At last Marcus was brought before them. Artemisia wept to see his miserable and exhausted condition, though to one who did not know him, fatigue had given a new refinement to his beauty. He embraced her. She with difficulty restrained herself from display-ing the passion she felt for him. He bowed his knee to the Emperor, who made no response, and then to the Empress, who began to speak in flowered language, deploring his reception in the city, and assuring him that henceforth he would be treated with all the honour and respect due to one of his birth and station. Marcus, though naturally gratified, was also bemused both by the abrupt transformation in his fortunes and by the extravagance of her language, the length of her sentences, and the terminology peculiar to court circles which she employed. He could not know how painfully and with what effort she had acquired this manner of speech, which was not natural to her, since she had been a bareback rider in the circus when she first caught the eye of the Emperor Arcadius, on account, men said, of the length of her shapely legs.

He was further distracted by the eunuch Eutropius. Though this creature was sadly deformed, with a humpback and a lower jaw which extended so far beyond the upper one that his teeth could not meet and the jaws appeared to belong to different faces and to have been cobbled together by a clumsy artisan, yet there was that in his eye and the way in which he regarded Marcus which recalled that other eunuch, John the Adept. This was not surprising, for the two were indeed brothers, subjected to the same mutilation on the same day. Marcus, ignorant of the truth, was alarmed by the resemblance, which he took as an evil omen.

When the Empress had finished speaking, and plied Marcus with wine, she enquired his purpose in presenting himself at court. So numerous had been the young man's misfortunes, so disturbing his experiences, that for a moment he could not recollect why he had come to Constantinople. Artemisia looked at him with dismay. She wondered if his sufferings had deprived him of his wits. His silence caused the Empress anxiety too; she felt it as a reproach, and grew pale.

Lycas, understanding Marcus's perplexity, whispered, 'Honoria, the Emperor's sister, remember.'

Marcus collected himself.

'It is a matter,' he said, 'of some delicacy, which is why I hesitate to broach it. I am a Roman nobleman, formerly in the service of the Emperor Honorius.'

'Formerly?' said the Empress.

'Formerly,' Marcus replied. 'He sent me on a mission to Alaric, King of the Visigoths. At the same time his sister, the noble Princess Honoria, entrusted me with a secret missive to the King. By chance I was led into many misfortunes, and if I was to recount my recent history to you, the seasons would have changed before I had finished. Suffice to say that I am a loyal servant of that princess, who has since suffered cruelly at the hands of her brother. So I have made my way to New Rome that I might call it to redress the balance in Old Rome, and specifically, to come to the rescue of my mistress the Princess. I had supposed that Arcadius, her brother and emperor in the east, would be eager to help her, and that his sword would leap into his hand when he learned of the indignities she has endured, and the danger to which she is exposed. But now I find that Arcadius is himself no more, and so I do not know if my cause is vain, if my plea will be answered.'

The Empress declared herself deeply moved, and eager to assist her dear sister, the Princess. In this she was perhaps sincere, for she detested her brother-in-law Honorius, who had spoken scornfully of her low, indeed disreputable, origins. But she never acted without taking counsel with Eutropius. So she deferred a decision till the morrow, and gave orders that Marcus, his wife, and his dear friend Lycas should be lodged in the palace with all due honour and in the highest luxury.

XX

The three were installed in chambers in the fourth court of the palace. The soft and luxurious furnishings did not appeal to Artemisia, whose taste had been formed according to the classical mode which still pertained in her father's house. But she could not deny that the comfort was welcome.

Marcus thanked her warmly for what she had done on his behalf. He did not love her, and still pined for his Pulcherrima. But he had taken her as his wife, at her father's command, and he recognised her devotion to him. Now he realised that but for her he would still be languishing in that dungeon. Yet, with this thought, his hand flew to his neck and felt the tender wound left there by Lamia's teeth. Artemisia observed the gesture and asked him how he had come by the marks on his throat. He could not answer, and this perturbed him, his habit of veracity being innate. So, at the moment when they should have been united, a shadow fell between them. Marcus knew guilt, and Artemisia suspicion.

Lycas meanwhile wondered how he could convey what he suspected to his dearest friend. But he could not bring himself to tell him that his wife was possessed of the evil eye; and indeed there was no opportunity. So he too was in low spirits. Marcus, observing this, enquired the reason. Lycas first remarked that the atmosphere of the palace oppressed him, then added:

'Moreover, that eunuch is no friend, an I am not mistaken.'

Marcus had come to the same conclusion. Lycas therefore made him only the more anxious.

Yet he preferred not to speak of the eunuch's resemblance to John the Adept, for the thought of that man made him choke.

In another part of the palace the Empress and the eunuch looked long and dark at each other. For a little they did not speak. The young Emperor had been carried off to his bed, and the two were left alone. Eudoxia stretched herself on a couch or divan, and Eutropius, seated on a stool, was permitted to fondle her breasts, his chief sensual pleasure, and one which, he often said, aided thought.

Now he spoke of the fears which Artemisia had aroused. The Empress, intensely superstitious, did not question his judgement.

'There is only one thing to be done,' she said.

'How right you are.'

He smiled, in as much as the deformity of his jaws permitted such a motion. Only one who knew him well could have recognised the grimace as a smile.

'And the sooner the better,' she said. 'Order the slaves to prepare the hot irons.'

'One moment.'

The eunuch held up his hand, the palm towards the Empress.

'The sooner the better, yes,' he said. 'But there is the problem of the young man.'

He was tempted to suggest that the Empress should exert her still considerable charms on Marcus. But fear restrained him. He knew the intensity of her occasional passions. He was sensible of Marcus's beauty. He felt apprehensive lest the young Roman should supplant him in her confidence. Reason told him that this was unlikely; he and the Empress were too deep in too many affairs, had engaged in too many nefarious enterprises, to be divided by a mere youth, however comely. Yet reason is weak against the urgent demands of the flesh; a frail guard against terrors. Eutropius knew that he had no friend, no protector but the Empress, and though reason also told him that she was in so many ways dependent on him herself, yet he listened to his fears and not to his argument.

So they wrestled with the problem, and the sun was red-gold over the Bosphorus before they had determined on a course of action.

In the morning Marcus was summoned, alone, before the Empress. She spoke honeyed words, told him that his enemy the fanatic priest had received due punishment; she expressed her admiration of his constancy towards her dear sister Honoria.

'But,' she said, 'I have learned that she is in no immediate danger, though immured in an Alpine castle. I have no doubt that she gazes from its battlements – for she is an indulged prisoner, confined merely to the castle and not to a cell – that she gazes, as I say, in the hope of espying you, her champion, riding to her relief. And I am anxious that you should do so, just as I hope that, when she is free, we may together remove our brother Honorius from the throne he disgraces, and restore virtue and good government to the whole empire. But, my dear friend, for so I feel I may call you, your journey will carry you into danger, through wild and unruly lands. It is not such as may fittingly be made by your lady. Moreover, when I first saw her, I was seized with the desire to know her better. The life of an empress is lonely, more lonely than a young man like you can conceive, and it would be of the greatest joy to me to have a lady of such distinguished birth, such delicacy of feeling, so fine an understanding, and so noble a nature to reside a while as my companion. I therefore beg you to leave her behind, with me, and I shall treat her, I promise, as if she were my own beloved daughter.'

It was well for Marcus that, ignorant of the court, he did not know that Eudoxia had had her daughter crushed to death between two presses of iron because she had declared her fancy for a captured Gothic warrior, for whom Eudoxia herself lusted.

So now he bowed low in acknowledgement of the Empress's magnanimity. He told himself that the journey he was about to make would indeed be full of dangers, that Artemisia would be safer here in Constantinople, and that it would be good to leave her in the palace to protect his interests. Yet he also could not disguise from himself the relief he felt at the prospect of being free of Artemisia. To be in the constant company of one who adores and who is not loved in return is a sore trial; Marcus's state is common, though condemned by many.

Nevertheless, when Artemisia burst into tears, and asked him if to be abandoned was just recompense for her devotion, he was deeply moved; and would have defied the Empress's will, had it not been clear to him that to do so would imperil them all.

'Very well,' Artemisia said, brushing her tears away with a lace napkin. 'I am not the daughter of Melanippos, rich in olive-groves and horses, for nothing. I shall remain here, a hostage to your good behaviour, for such I see is what I shall be. I at least am not deceived by the candied words which the Empress spoke to you. I observed how she looked on me, and I know she has no love for my person. But, husband, I submit to your will, as a wife must. And I pray only that no calamity may befall either of us.'

Marcus, touched by her dignity and courage, and relieved to find her obedient, wept himself. For a moment he held her in his arms, and endeavoured to stay his tears and speak words of love and comfort.

Then he tore himself away, and with the faithful and loving Lycas at his heel, embarked again on his travels.

XXI

Artemisia wept again to see him go.

'Surely,' she thought, 'Dido, the tragic Queen of Carthage, was not more wretched to see the sail of Aeneas disappear below the horizon than I am now.'

Yet she trusted that the renown of her father Melanippos would serve as her protector; and so she feared nothing more than loneliness and the spite of the Empress, who was, she thought, certain to seek to humiliate her.

In those days great ladies were skilled in the art of writing, and she now settled herself to send an account of their journeying and experiences to her father, 'For,' she said to herself, 'it is my duty; and moreover will occupy my mind and console me in my distress.' And as she wrote, her heart ached to think of Marcus riding forth, and she sighed to remember the sweetness of the gardens of Thebes.

I mention this as evidence that the fears entertained of her even by Lycas were groundless, arising only from the deformity that nature had afflicted her with, and from nothing more. Artemisia was a virtuous woman, such as, the proverb tells us, should be prized above rubies. Had she not been virtuous, then, alas, she might have escaped ill-fortune, since all the world knows that the wicked prosper exceedingly.

Scarcely, however, had she settled herself at her writing-table, where she awaited the return of her maidservant, whom she had sent in search of materials, than the curtain was rudely torn aside, and two swarthy slaves stood before her. She was about to reprove this unmannerly intrusion when her gaze fell on the implements they carried.

Seized with apprehension, yet bold as became one of her breeding, she demanded of them why and on whose authority they approached her with these hideous instruments. But they were unable to answer, even had they been willing to do so, for both had had their tongues ripped from their mouths, that they might be silent executioners of whatever crime they were directed to perform. Only a clicking sound, as of an attempted giggle, escaped the smaller of the pair.

His companion advanced on Artemisia. He took her arms and bound them behind her, and then forced the upper part of her body backwards, so that she was bent over the table on which she had intended to write the letter to her father. The other slave then thrust his hand under her chin and forced her head back, while he advanced the branding iron towards her. For a moment she saw it shine like the gates of Hell, and then it was driven against one eye. Her screams of pain met with no response. She fainted, but this allowed them only to relax their grip before attending to the other eye.

Then the one who held the branding iron made the sign of the Cross against his gleaming ebony chest. His companion did likewise, and they departed the chamber.

The next day other slaves came to the apartment, and taking Artemisia, whose maidservant had bandaged her wounds, hurled her into a mean street which ran behind the palace.

'You may live or die, I am instructed to say,' one told her. 'But if you are to live then you must beg your bread.'

They abandoned her. An old woman, passing by, heard her wails of grief and escorted her to a courtyard, where a colony of blind beggars congregated.

'And this is all that I may do for you, poor soul,' she said.

As to what later befell Artemisia, it is not yet ripe to relate.

When the news that the blinding had been accomplished was brought to Eudoxia, some say that she gave thanks to Almighty God that she had been saved from the danger of Artemisia's evil eye; but others declare that she knew remorse, because she had yielded to the importunate demands and contemptible fears of the eunuch.

Who knows? These things are hidden. It is, however, certain

that it had been no part of the eunuch's design that Artemisia should be thrust into the streets, there to live among hovels and take her chance with the wretched of the city, but that he had commanded that she be immured in a convent. And this is because while he no longer had reason to fear her on account of the power he believed her to possess, he nevertheless feared the vengeance of Marcus, should he learn what had befallen his wife. Therefore he had wished to keep her a hostage, however mutilated. And the proof is that the slaves who conveyed her to the streets were themselves put to death, while the eunuch gave orders that a search be made for Artemisia throughout the city.

XXII

For five days Marcus and Lycas journeyed through a wild and desolate land of mountains and rocky valleys, and in this time they saw no other men but a few shepherds who tended their flocks among these barren hills. Some were old, others young, though already with blackened teeth, but to Marcus their lives seemed enviable, and he spoke to Lycas of how willingly he would exchange his lot for theirs. Lycas smiled and shook his head.

'This is but an idle fancy, my dear Marcus,' he said. 'Do you imagine these men exist like the shepherd-lads in the poems of Vergil that delight you so. I grant you, Vergil is a master of melody, and I too have been lifted to a higher plane when I have listened to you chant his melancholy music, and have even fancied that we two resemble the shepherds Corydon and Alexis. But, believe me, the real life of shepherd-boys is very different. It is rough, hard, cold and full of fear.'

'That may be so,' Marcus said. 'Yet to one who has experienced such malignity at the hands of fortune as I have, dear Lycas, their life appears desirable.'

Then he told Lycas of how the woman who called herself Lamia had come to him in his prison, and of what they had done together. Lycas assured him this was delusion, for the prison, he said, had been close guarded. And when Marcus showed him the marks on his throat, he closed his eyes and did not know what to believe.

Then Marcus spoke of how it had grieved him to be compelled to abandon Artemisia.

'Though I do not love her, as I love you, Lycas, or as I loved our dear Pulcherrima, and believe that I never could, yet I owe her much, and have come to fear also that the Empress intends no good should come to her. I was a fool to trust that empress.'

'Well,' Lycas said, 'be that as it may, there is nothing you can do about it now. The more immediate question is where we may lodge tonight and what we can find to eat for supper. How I long to come upon a friendly inn with a welcoming fire, a round of beef roasting, and good wine to drink'.

They rode on, till dusk crept around them. They followed a path which led them between the flanks of two rocks rising steeply from the plain. They entered the cleft, and it opened out and a wood lay beyond. There, by a trickling stream, stood an altar of rough-hewn stones. It was shrouded by an oleander bush, heavy with fragrant blossom. The earth before the altar was beaten level and was white with the dotted bones of sacrificial victims. Boughs of chestnut trees were hung with offerings, and further on, in the deepest shade, rose two ancient oaks which bore, nailed to their trunks, the bleached skulls of bulls. There was no sound but the breeze rustling the trees and the trickle of water in the stream.

Marcus said: 'Surely this is a pagan altar, long deserted. As a Christian knight it is perhaps my duty to destroy it, and yet, when I find myself before it, I am filled with pious sentiments. I think of my ancestors who worshipped at such shrines, and of how they honoured the immortal gods – as they thought them – who knew neither pain nor grief nor death, while here on earth one generation of suffering men succeeds another.'

He felt both fear and awe. The signs of mortality which met his eyes revived in him love for life. And so, without thinking, he bent back the springy trunk of an oak sapling, and drew it towards him. Then he fixed an earthenware cup, which had hung from his belt, on the uppermost branches, scarcely more than twigs, of the young tree, which, when he released it, carried his offering up towards the sky.

As he stood, wondering what impulse had led him to perform this action, a voice called to them demanding what manner of men they were who had intruded into the sanctuary of the gods. Marcus turned and saw an old man with a high bare forehead bound with a fillet of crimson wool. His beard was a fleecy fringe, white as untrodden snow. His tunic was hodden-grey and his feet unshod. A lyre hung from his girdle, and when Marcus saw this, he let his hand fall away from his sword-hilt.

'We are travellers,' he said, 'and have happened on this place by chance while seeking a lodging for the night.'

'Come,' said the old man, 'let me feel your face, for the passage of years has dimmed my eyes, and now I am as blind as Homer was when he first sang of the wrath of Achilles.'

So his fingers played over the face of first Marcus and then Lycas, and this assured him that they were young, and, as he said, handsome and gentle.

'Do you serve the God here?' Marcus asked.

The old man laughed.

'The old gods whom our fathers worshipped have long fled this place, and all that there is under the visiting moon. Time was when Apollo laughed here and rejoiced in the sacrifices made at this altar.'

Then he enquired whether they were hungry, and on being told they were, gave them supper: bread, pickled cabbage, and cheese made from the milk of ewes, and an amber-coloured wine sharpened with pine resin.

Marcus spoke of Constantinople and the journey they had made, but the old man cared for none of these things.

'Once,' he said, 'once upon a time the Heroes dwelled in these valleys and the meadows were rich in herds of oxen and young white heifers. The doors of their houses were made of ivory and brass and their tables groaned under the weight of pitchers of gold. They were served by many strong and handsome slaves, and the courage of their hearts assured them of wealth and prosperity, which they were proud and resolute to defend all the days of their life. Are you such men as the Heroes of old?'

'We cannot claim to be,' Marcus said.

'In my youth,' the old man continued, 'I served as a soldier and fought in many battles, but, as a poor man, I fought on foot with such weapons as a poor man can afford or is given, and so, being in fear of death as I fought in the trenches beneath the town walls, in the ranks of the pressed men, I won no rich spoils. Yet I observed much: that war gives wealth to men and robs them of it, as it robs others of their liberty. I myself was taken prisoner, carried off, and worked many years as a slave. Yes, indeed, the life of men is hard and its fruits are bitter.'

'Young as I am,' Marcus said, 'I have learned that; and, well-born as I am, I have suffered hardship. But now, old man, it would give us much pleasure if you would play and sing for us, recounting the deeds of the Heroes, that we may be filled with courage and virtue.'

So the old man tuned his lyre, and, as the thin moon rose over the black trees, and the night sky shone deep purple, he sang the old song of the wrath of Achilles. At first his voice was weak and quavered, for he had not sung for many years. But it grew stronger till it broke forth in pristine vigour as Achilles lamented the consequences of his bitter anger, which had brought about the death of his beloved Patroclus, and called out his curse on wrath, 'which stirs up even the wisest man to violence; which tastes sweeter than honey as it swells up in the breast like smoke . . . Agamemnon angered me,' he cried in pain; 'but now let the past slip away like fading memory, let suffering depart with rage, and I shall arise and seek out that Hector who slew my dearest friend.'

So Achilles rose from his bed of grief and put his armour on, and cried out for Hector, killer of Patroclus, and challenged him to battle. They clashed and fought for seven hours by the sun passing its zenith and commencing its decline, and he pursued Hector three times round the walls of mighty Troy, till at last he laid him low. Then Achilles, bitter and unforgiving, harnessed the dead body of noble Hector to his chariot, and dragged it in ignominy round the city whose bravest defender he had been.

It is an old story, my Prince, but one which strikes deep into the heart of men, and of which no virtuous man can ever tire; and no mind can exhaust its meaning.

And when Lycas heard the tale, which was new to him, he wept; and he felt himself to be Patroclus whom Achilles avenged, for angry love.

At last the old man fell silent. Together the three drank wine under the stars, and did not speak more words. The fire which the old man had kindled began to die. He withdrew to the hut where he dwelled, but Marcus and Lycas lay together on the skins of beasts beside the warm embers. Marcus found sleep denied him. The wind rustled in the trees, gentle as a lullaby, and he felt Lycas's sweet breath and the comfort of his trusting body; and yet he could not sleep.

His thoughts turned again to the aged bard's heroic song, and he considered how, in the Latin versions of the tale of Troy which he had known since childhood, it was mighty Hector who shone forth as the true hero, for the Trojans, you must recall, gave birth to Rome itself, by way of Aeneas, Prince of Troy, and son of Anchises and the goddess Aphrodite, whom the Romans term Venus. Yet, though Marcus felt pity and admiration for Hector, and though he could never hear of the degradation of his body without bitter tears, something in his innermost nature, which the Greeks call *psyche*, responded more warmly to Achilles; and this distressed him. For, he said to himself, Achilles was fierce and implacable, selfish and harsh, an ingrate and a man of self-regarding temper. He was far removed from the pattern of Christian heroic virtue which Hector, though a pagan, approached, and which I was taught to strive for. Nevertheless, it is as much Achilles's faults of character as his courage which draw me to him; and does this mean that I am an evil man myself?

Now, my Prince, you are to consider that Marcus, in this musing and self-examination, displayed true virtue, even while he felt himself to lack it. For the truth is that only he who recognises the sin that is in himself, and understands its attraction, and feels keen temptation – even, indeed, he who yields to temptation, some assert – is capable of attaining true virtue and a state of grace.

Moreover, you must consider that in any war such as the Greeks fought with the Trojans, right is never concentrated on one side only, but, by the mercy of Almighty God, is found to be so evenly distributed that all men think their cause is just; else, without surrendering wholly to evil, they could not bring themselves to defend it in adversity.

Furthermore, to recognise the virtue that lies in your adversary is to advance your own virtue, for it is only in honouring your foe, even while you strike him down, that you can avoid that corruption of spirit which hatred engenders.

Therefore, never engage in any war where the cause does not seem just to you; but always consider that your enemy thinks likewise. In this way war may be conducted with nobility, grace and chivalry, though it is of all human activities the most repugnant to the teaching of our Lord Jesus Christ.

You are to consider this: war is sinful, but necessary. And this is a paradox which must be accepted by all who guide and govern the affairs of men.

XXIII

Marcus tarried many days in that enchanted place, which delighted him after the horrors he had known in the great city. Lycas too was content to see his friend and master happy, for Lycas was one of these fortunate souls whose virtue permits them to surrender their will to those whom they love and esteem. Such friendship is a shadowy representation here on earth of the blissful union of the soul with the Almighty. To be the obedient servant of the Divine Will is the highest aspiration of good men, but, being ignorant, few can interpret that will with certainty, and so men seek an earthly equivalent; and this Lycas had found.

Marcus, and Lycas also, delighted in the songs of the old bard. They felt, in listening to him, that they were transported from the dark age of the world in which they were condemned to live and restored to a knowledge of its bright youth and sunlit vigour. Lycas indeed, who, on account of his troubled upbringing, had scarcely received Christian instruction, experienced a sense of harmony which he had never felt before, and, for perhaps the first time in his life, could conceive of a world which was well-ordered and proceeded according to an agreeable and measured rule.

Yet Marcus, even then, questioned the happiness he had found, and one evening, as the smoke of the offering the ancient bard had laid on the altar rose purple in the pale sky, he enquired of the old man whether, as he thought, happiness could ever endure.

'Wise men,' said the bard, 'have debated that since the dawn of the world and have come to no firm conclusion. So it is not given to me to answer. But I shall tell you a story.'

He passed the wine-flask, drank deep himself, scratched his chin, and began.

'Croesus, the great King of Lydia, was rich beyond measure and boasted himself the happiest of mortals. He said as much to the wise Solon, famous as the giver of laws to Athens, which, as you know, was the city of the Goddess of Wisdom. Solon shrugged his shoulders and would not at first reply. So the King pressed him. "If I am not the happiest of men, then tell me who is." Solon smiled, and said: "A long life such as mine gives one the chance to witness much, and to experience much that one would not choose. A man lives some seventy years, and in those seventy years there are more than twenty-six thousand two hundred and fifty days, and not one of them will fail to differ from the rest. So I have learned that chance or accident govern man all the days of his life. As to your questions concerning yourself and your own claim to supreme happiness, I can give no answer till you are dead. Call no man happy till that day, but only at best fortunate. Remember, however, that fortune is fickle, changeable as the winds that blow, now from the north, now from the south, gentle from the west, or bitter-cold from the east, and that the gods in their jealousy permit the sun of fortune to shine constantly on few men. Very often the gods grant a gleam of happiness, then the clouds gather, and we are plunged in darkness." These were the wise words of Solon.'

'Indeed,' Marcus said, 'though I am still young, I have seen the truth of Solon's words.'

'But what of Croesus?' Lycas asked.

'Ah, Croesus,' the bard sighed. 'Croesus was angry. He thought Solon had insulted him. But soon afterwards he had a disturbing dream. He had a son, called Atys, distinguished among all others for his beauty and valour, as is often the way, you must know, with kings' sons. Now Croesus dreamed that the young man was dead, killed by an iron weapon. So, to avert such a calamity, he first ordered Atys to take himself a wife, and forbade him to lead the Lydian army into battle. He also had all the swords, spears and javelins removed from the young men's apartments in the palace, and had them stored in the women's apartments. In this way he thought he had secured his beloved Atys from danger.

'Now it happened that soon after a man came to his court, a Phrygian of royal blood. He sought purification, saying he was stained with blood that he had shed. When he had followed the customary rites, Croesus asked him what crime he had been guilty of. "My name is Adrastus," he replied, "and by misfortune I slew my brother. So my father the King drove me into exile, and I arrived here, naked and accursed." Croesus pitied him, and gave him leave to remain at his court.

'In a little, ambassadors came from Mysian Olympus telling of a great boar that was laying waste their fields and which they had been unable to slay. They sought help from the King and asked that he should send his son Atys, of whose valour they had heard so much, to deliver them from the boar. But the King would not send Atys, explaining that the young man was just married and could not leave his wife to lead the hunting party.'

'But,' Marcus said, 'it was his duty, and besides, Atys cannot have been pleased, for everyone would think him a milksop. Indeed, I cannot imagine that his wife would respect him.'

'Yes indeed, Atys was very angry and told his father he had put shame on him, for it had always been the custom that such hunting parties were led by the King's son. He spoke just as you think he should have spoken, young man. Then he asked why his father had denied him this opportunity to display his courage, and Croesus told him of his terrible dream. Atys laughed and said there was nothing to fear. "What iron weapon does a boar wield? Had your dream said I would be killed by a tusk, there would be good reason to keep me here, but a boar has neither sword nor spear. Your fears are foolish, Father." Croesus was overborne by this argument, but as a precaution he ordered Adrastus to accompany his son and guard him against the dangers of the road, for the country was infested with brigands and wild broken men.

'So they set off . . . but I am thirsty,' the bard said. 'Pass me the wine. Where was I? Yes, they reached Olympus and found the boar and encircled him. Adrastus hurled his spear, missed the boar and struck Atys. So the King's son was killed by an iron-tipped weapon, and the prophecy the King had dreamed was fulfilled.'

'I thought it would turn out like that,' Lycas said. 'Boar-hunting is a dangerous business.'

'They carried the youth's corpse back to Sardis, and Adrastus shed many tears. He confessed his guilt to Croesus and said he could no longer bear to live. Croesus, in his nobility, tried to dissuade him, for he saw that it was fate, of which Adrastus was the mere instrument, that had killed Atys. But Adrastus would not have it, and after Atys was buried, he cut his own throat and let the blood flow on the Prince's tomb. As for Croesus, he recalled his boast that he was the happiest of men, and knew that he had angered the gods.'

**(Though our author does not seem to know it, the destiny of both young men was determined before Croesus dreamed his dream, which in truth did no more than reveal it: for the name 'Adrastus' is interpreted as 'the doomed' or 'the trapped man unable to escape', and Atys as 'the youth under the influence of Ate', which is Fate, or 'the man judicially blind'.

The relevance of this story to that of Marcus is hidden. It may be intended as a warning to the young prince not to presume he is master of his own fortune. Or it may be that our author merely indulges his inordinate love of digression.)**

Then Marcus asked, 'Was it not this same Croesus who was so cruelly deceived by the Oracle at Delphi?'

'I have never heard of that,' Lycas said. 'But this is not strange, since I had never heard till today of this unfortunate man who was rash enough to suppose himself happy,' and he laid his hand on Marcus's thigh, and pressed it, as if for reassurance.

'Indeed yes,' the bard said. 'When he had put off mourning for his son, Croesus considered whether to make war on the Persians, whose empire was daily growing more powerful. So he sent to various Oracles that he could determine which advised him best. Not only Delphi, then, but the Oracles of Abae in Phocis, Apollo at Dodona, the Oracle of Amphiarius, the Oracle of Trophonius, of Brachiae in Milesia and of Ammon in Lybia, all received his emissaries. And to each Oracle he set a test, for his agents were first enjoined to demand of the Oracle what Croesus was doing at that moment. The replies of the other Oracles are lost, since they failed to satisfy the King, but the Pythoness at Delphi answered thus, speaking as was her way in hexameters . . .'

'What are hexameters?' Lycas said. 'I have never heard of them.'

'A poetic metre,' Marcus whispered. 'Sh-sh.'

''Tis mine to number the sands, mine to measure the ocean,
Mine to hark to the silent, to know what the dumb man speaketh:
Lo, in my nostrils there striketh the smell of a shell-covered tortoise
Boiling now on the flame, with the flesh of a lamb in a cauldron,
Brass is the vessel it cooks in, brass the cover upon it . . .'

The bard, who had recited the verses in a stirring tone, paused to gather breath.

'If I was wearing a hat,' Lycas said, 'I would take it off to anyone who could make sense of that.'

'Oracles were meant to be difficult to understand,' Marcus said.

'Ah,' said the bard, 'but this one was not, despite what our young friend thinks, obscure. On the contrary, the Lydians reported the words which they had taken down as the Pythoness spoke or chanted them, and Croesus was astonished. He had conceived as his test the most improbable of actions, and had taken a tortoise and a lamb and boiled them together in a brass pot, and now it seemed that the Oracle had seen what he did secretly and in another country.'

'If you ask me,' Lycas said, 'there was trickery somewhere. It stands to reason.'

'Very probably,' Marcus said, 'but let us hear the rest of the story.'

'So Croesus put the question whether he should war against the Persians and was told that if he did so he would destroy a great empire. This answer pleased him, and he was further satisfied when the Oracle told him that his kingdom would endure until a mule was emperor of the Medes and Persians.'

'I can see why that pleased him,' Lycas said, 'but if you ask me, the first answer should have made him think a bit. Which empire, he might have asked.'

'You are a bright child,' the bard said. 'It fell out just as you suppose. He was defeated in battle, driven back on Sardis and taken prisoner. The Persian emperor Cyrus condemned him to death and, laden with fetters, he was placed on a pile of faggots to be burned alive. Then Croesus remembered what Solon had said to him, and gave vent to a mighty groan. Cyrus was inquisitive and asked why he groaned . . .'

'I would do more than groan if I was to be burned alive,' Lycas muttered, and would have said more, but Marcus placed his hand over his mouth.

'When he heard what Solon had said to Croesus – call no man happy till he is dead – Cyrus was struck by the truth of these words. Reflecting that all that is human is insecure, he considered how he too might meet misfortune equal to that of Croesus, and ordered him to be set free, and received him into friendship. But first he asked why Croesus had chosen to break the treaty between them and make war. To which Croesus replied: "What I did, Great King, was, as events have proved, to your advantage and not mine. But if there be blame, it lies rather with the gods of the Greeks than with me, for it was they who encouraged me to make war. But now I know that no wise man is so foolish as to prefer war to peace, for in war, instead of sons burying their fathers as is the law of nature, fathers bury and must mourn their sons. But the gods willed it so." Saying this he wept, on account of his folly in believing the Oracle.'

'What he says of war and peace is no doubt very true,' Marcus said. 'Nevertheless, there are wars that must be fought, just wars, when it is one's duty to defend one's home or to avenge wrongs.'

'Did the Oracle have some smart answer?' Lycas said.

'Indeed yes, a message was sent from Delphi. Croesus had no cause for complaint because when he received the words of the Oracle he should have sent to enquire which empire would be destroyed. If he neither understood the words of the Oracle correctly nor sent for further enlightenment, then he had no reason to bewail as the malignity of the gods what was merely the fruit of his own folly.'

'You can't quarrel with that,' Lycas said. 'If you ask me, the moral of this story is that you shouldn't be quick to believe anything you want to hear.'

'You could be right, child,' the bard said. 'Nevertheless, men will never do as you advise. The Oracle also told him that he should have considered that Cyrus was the child of parents who belonged to different races, his mother a princess of the Medes and his father a Persian; and that therefore Cyrus was indeed a mule.'

Lycas thought a moment, scratching his leg.

'Did this Cyrus have children himself?' he asked.

'I believe so.'

'Then he was no mule. A mule can't, I mean you can't breed from a mule. You'd think the Oracle would have known that.'

XXIV

There is no temptation like that of ease. Marcus experienced it now. Enchanted by the bard's tales of the Heroes and great kings who had lived long before Christ, he would have lingered there, had not his strong sense of duty urged him forward. Moreover, as he said to Lycas, he suffered anxiety concerning the well-being of Artemisia.

'Precisely because I don't love her, as I love you and our dear Pulcherrima,' he said, 'I feel myself the more responsible for her.'

'That makes no sense to me,' Lycas said. 'Surely it is love that breeds the duty to care for others.'

'Well, I grant you that may normally be the case, and indeed I do not fully understand my own feelings. I know only that, because I took Artemisia as my wife not on account of love, but because it seemed advantageous for me, I cannot escape the disturbing thought that I owe her more than if we had been joined in the most romantic passion.'

'Be that as it may,' Lycas said, 'in my opinion you married as most great men marry, and I have never heard that this inspires them with any great sense of duty to their wives.'

Then they took their leave of the bard, who remarked that they were fools to venture into the world again, but that young men could not be anything but fools, and so they must be on their way.

So Marcus left, eager to search for the Princess Honoria, who was also known as Gallia Placida, and whom he was uncomfortably aware of forgetting at least six days out of every seven.

'Nevertheless,' he said to Lycas, or perhaps to himself, 'she is the lady whom I promised to serve all the days of my life.'

For three days they travelled through mountains in a land deserted of people. Sometimes they saw a burned hut, roofless and solitary, where a mountain shepherd had once lodged. But now there were neither folk nor flocks in these desolate hills; and only the birds of prey hovered in the crystal sky.

'Surely,' Marcus said, 'some strange and terrible calamity has befallen this land.'

'That may be so,' Lycas said, 'and your judgement is better than mine, but it appears to me no worse than many we have journeyed through.'

Towards evening on the third day they were following the course of a stream that led them into a long dark valley, from which the sun had already fled. The water ran deep, surging peat-black over waterfalls and jagged rocks, and the path they followed was rough and narrow. More than once their horses stumbled, losing their footing, and all but tumbling into the waters.

At last they came to more level ground, and saw on the flank of the hill in the valley beyond a mighty castle rear up before them, its battlements a sultry purple against the evening sky.

The path led to a ford across the stream, and on the other bank they saw a mounted knight.

He sat tall on a horse full seventeen hands in height. It was clothed in a burnished breastplate and a jewelled robe that covered its hind-quarters. The knight's armour was green as early summer grass, and his visor hid his face. As they approached the stream, he called out to them to halt.

'Who are you that dare to trespass on my lands, so meanly dressed?'

Marcus, acknowledging his right of enquiry, shouted that he was a Roman prince on his way to the court of the Emperor.

'I know no emperor,' the knight said, 'save myself, whose empire this valley is.'

Lycas, speaking softly, said to Marcus:

'There is no need to cross the stream here. Though the path we have been following leads to this ford, I remember that not half a mile back another path branched off, and I am sure it too will follow the stream, if at a higher level. And so we may continue on our way and find another crossing-place without having to answer this bully.

Marcus, however, replied:

'I have no doubt, dear Lycas, that what you say is true, and that you give this advice with my best interest at heart, as you always have. But never let it be said that one of my birth shirked to meet a challenge.'

'That's as may be, but you have often told me that your birth was uncertain, and your parentage unknown, at least on your father's side.'

'The more reason to prove myself now.'

With these words he touched his horse lightly on the flank and descended to the bank of the stream, allowing the beast, whose sagacity he had learned to respect, to pick its way through the black and treacherous waters. Meanwhile, when he looked up, he saw the Green Knight waiting, lance at the ready.

As soon as Marcus reached the further bank, the knight advanced at a rapid trot, bearing down hard on him. Marcus kicked his horse sharply and it surged forward, so that Marcus got himself under the lance and was able to strike at the knight's body with the flat of his sword as he passed. Then, on level ground, Marcus turned to face the knight, who had been carried into the stream, where his steed, weighed down by its armour, slipped and floundered.

Lycas let out a cheer and hurled a stone at the knight's head. It struck him on the casque and he would have fallen if he had not managed to seize hold of his horse's mane. In doing so, he let the lance slip from his grasp. It fell into the water and was carried away.

The Green Knight, bewildered by this turn of events, turned his gaze towards Marcus, who, however, took no advantage of his discomfiture, but indicated that his adversary was at liberty to regain dry land. Then he commanded Lycas to throw no more stones, and so the knight emerged from the water and, drawing his sword, fell again upon Marcus.

But Marcus, in full command of his mount, again nimbly evaded the charge, and as the Green Knight careered past him, smote him lustily on the back, so that, with a yell of rage or pain or surprise, he fell from his horse and lay helpless on the bare earth.

Lycas had meanwhile taken advantage of the moment to cross the stream himself and tie his pony to a thornbush. Now he ran forward and picked up the knight's sword, which had fallen some distance from his body. He advanced on the fallen foe, while Marcus again sat still as the great mounted statue of the Emperor Marcus Aurelius which you can see in Rome; he looked serenely on the enemy who a moment previously had seemed so formidable. Lycas placed the point of the sword at the knight's throat and asked Marcus whether he should make an end of him.

'For,' he said, 'a bully who so uncivilly receives innocent travellers is one that in my opinion the world would be well rid of.'

'What you say is true,' Marcus replied. 'Nevertheless, I am a Christian knight and a Roman nobleman, and it offends me to slay one who is at my mercy.'

So saying, he dismounted and approached the Green Knight. He very gently pushed Lycas's sword-arm aside, and extending his hand to his adversary, would have helped him to his feet.

'As a Christian,' he said, 'I am commanded to succour the weak and defenceless, and, though you were not such a few minutes ago, I must treat you as such now. In any case, prudence invites me to enquire the meaning of your uncivil behaviour.'

The knight allowed Marcus to take him by the right hand, but then swung his left arm round and caught Marcus a mighty blow on the back of his head. Now it was our hero's turn to find himself hurled to earth, and he saw the gleam of the terrible green visor loom over him. But the knight in his fury at the humiliation he had suffered had forgotten all reason, and Lycas too. The boy, seized with rage on account of the knight's treachery, swung the sword round in a wide arc and sliced through the knight's hamstring, so that he fell again to the ground and lay there cursing (in several languages, as I believe), while Lycas helped Marcus to his feet.

Seeing him still dazed, and fearing that when he recovered his senses he would again command clemency to the defeated, Lycas seized the opportunity to tear off the knight's helmet, and was just about to hack his head off when Marcus again cried out, and ordered him to stay his hand.

'Well,' Lycas said, 'you must have it your own way, but for my part I think the world would be a cleaner and better place without this brute.'

Marcus merely smiled, and again extended his hand. He would have raised the knight to his feet, but the severed hamstring caused him to shriek with pain. So Marcus commanded Lycas to help him, and together they lifted their enemy on to his horse, and, leading it between them, advanced towards the castle.

(One cannot but observe, though our author does not seem aware of it, that this action of our hero's marks the first instance of the Age of Chivalry. That time too has now passed away, on account of the revival of that species of egoism which professes as the principle of all action the procuring for oneself of whatever advantage seems to hand, and of whatever personal objective is most expedient. The spirit of chivalry was, in contrast, founded on self-denial such as Marcus displayed in this encounter. That chivalry was to attain its highest point in the tales told of King Arthur and his Knights of the Round Table, and of the great Emperor Charlemagne.)

XXV

It was a steep and rocky path that led from the river to the castle, and as they mounted it, they rode all three in silence. Marcus felt an unusual heaviness fall on his spirit, as if, in subduing the Green Knight, he had committed a transgression. Reason told him this was not so; and yet he could not accede to the promptings of Reason. As for Lycas, it was the occasional glimpses of the castle, towering dull green and foreboding above them, which dismayed him. Twice he tried to persuade Marcus that they should abandon their defeated enemy to find his own way home, and should themselves ride off in the other direction, 'For I fear,' he said, 'that no good can come to us in this place.' But Marcus was deaf to his pleas.

The knight meanwhile sat his horse like a dull thing, or as a dead man propped up on the beast and supported by some invisible means; he answered never a word to the questions Marcus put to him, but kept his gaze lowered.

'Perhaps,' Marcus thought, 'it is shame that keeps him silent.'

The evening sun had commenced its decline before they came to the summit of the hill and level ground on which the castle reared before them. And they now saw that what they had taken to be a mighty fortification was not that. Rather, the castle itself was a great mound, grass-covered, and what from a distance had seemed battlements were no more than rocky outcrops.

In the middle of the mound was a door cut in the turf, and without speaking, they entered through this and found themselves in a cavern lit by burning torches. Their horses, alarmed, began to paw the ground and would not advance further, but the Green Knight's steed, without guidance from its rider, who still appeared to be in a trance, continued at a steady walk, and raised its head and whinnied.

As if attracted by this signal, there now emerged from the darkness at the further end of the cavern half a dozen little men, no taller than the withers of Lycas's pony. Two seized each horse by the bridle, one on either side, and with much chattering in a tongue unknown to Marcus, and with vigorous gestures, they indicated that they were to dismount. Lycas looked at Marcus, who shrugged his shoulders, as if to say there was nothing to do but obey, which they did, only the Green Knight himself remaining mounted.

Now more little people, elves or fairies as they seemed, came forward, and took Marcus and Lycas by the hand and led them through twisting passages to another chamber. There they found meat and drink laid out for them on a trestle table, which was lit with candles that gave off a green flame. There were pies of golden pastry and loaves of bread, and a tureen of broth, cheeses, a platter of cold meat, open tarts rich with mountain berries, jugs of wine and of milk, jellies, syllabubs, and dishes of clotted cream. Their escorts gestured that they should fall to and eat, and both were tempted, for they had not eaten since early in the day.

But Lycas said, whispering to Marcus, 'If these are indeed fairies who have brought us here, then this is fairy-food, and we must not eat, for it was well known in the district where I was brought up that to eat fairy-food was to condemn yourself to enthralment.'

'That's as may be,' Marcus said, whispering too, for fear that what he said might be overheard, 'though I know nothing of fairies, and indeed did not believe there were any such beings.'

Aloud, he said:

'My dear Lycas, welcome though this feast is, it would be rude and unseemly of us to fall to in the absence of any host or hostess.'

And he turned to one of those who had brought them there, and smiling, in his most willing manner, and speaking first in Greek and then in Latin (which was the language in which the Green Knight had addressed them), explained that, according to the manners of his country, it was deemed a discourtesy to eat before they had met the master or mistress of the feast.

He spoke these words and they were suddenly alone except for one boy who, from his height, might have been a child of five, but whose face was as fully formed as that of a boy of fifteen. His skin was dark, his features comely, and his smile was sweet and ingratiating. As if to encourage them he took a bone from a platter and began to gnaw it. But neither Marcus nor Lycas moved to eat.

Then the Indian boy took a jug of wine and filled three goblets, which were made of fine silver, delicately encrusted. He drank from one, and with that same sweet smile offered the others to Marcus and Lycas, as if they were his guests and he the host. But again they would not take them from him.

Their refusal did not seem to displease the boy, who, however, desisted from this invitation, and went and lay down on a couch. There he pulled up his tunic to reveal his private parts, which were well formed as those of a boy past puberty. He stroked his thighs, which were shapely and gleamed golden-brown in the candlelight, and then began to masturbate, all the while still gazing at them and bestowing on them the same beckoning smile. When they did not move, he paused for a moment and gestured that they should indeed come and share the couch with him. Lycas took a half-step forward, for the temptation worked strongly on him. But he recovered himself and, turning to Marcus, said that this was some trick or devilry. That word aroused Marcus, and drawing his sword, he advanced upon the boy, and smiting him with the flat of the blade across the buttocks, ordered him to cease his devil's play. With a shrill yelp the boy leapt from the couch, and vanished from the chamber.

No sooner had he gone than music sounded, sweet music of flutes and strings, and three maidens appeared, who danced before them, at first decorously, with movements that were languid and graceful, and then, as the music quickened, so too their dance grew lascivious. One, who appeared to be their leader, detached herself from the dance and put her arms round Marcus's neck, so that her raven tresses fell over his shoulders as she buried her face in his, and made to kiss him. She slid down his body and fell on her knees, and her hands closed on his thighs and she thrust her face between his legs. For a moment it seemed as if he might yield to her ardour, but Lycas seized her by the hair and threw her backwards so that she sprawled on the floor and lay there cursing.

Even as he did so, Marcus cried out in a loud voice, 'No, in the name of the Christ I abjure thee, no!'; and for a moment Lycas feared that the anguished words were addressed to him, but when he saw Marcus cover his face with his hands, and saw his body shudder, he knew it was repugnance for the woman and for the act she had tempted him to permit that called forth his protest.

Then a black shadow as of an enormous hand descended upon them, extinguished the lights, and covered all. And they fell asleep, and slept without dreams as if they had been drugged.

When they awoke they were in another chamber, where the walls were of green silk, and where sweet odours wafted a perfume about them. Both felt a delicious and unaccustomed languor. They stretched out their legs, and felt the stiffening replaced by a pleasing softness.

The silk hangings were parted, and their old adversary, the Green Knight, entered. He had removed his armour, and was now dressed in loose garments such as an Arab wears in the zenana or harem. Like his armour, they were green in colour, but of a sumptuous softness. He walked easily, despite the wounds inflicted on him, and this astonished Lycas, who knew that he had cut through his hamstring. Now he approached Marcus and took him by the hand, and hailed him as an honourable adversary.

'Two against one, of course, but those are odds at which I would back myself nine times out of ten – no, I am too modest, ninety-nine out of a hundred would be more exact.'

Lycas said he was surprised to see him walk so easily, but was pleased that he had not suffered a severe hurt.

The knight laughed.

'Yes indeed,' he said. 'You caught me a fair blow, squire, but I have always been a quick healer. I use a little-known herbal remedy originally concocted by my grandmother. I'll give you a bottle if you like; useful if you are carrying on this errant trade of yours.'

Marcus, delighted and surprised to find the knight now so

affable, asked him why he had opposed their crossing of the stream.

'It's what I'm paid to do, old sport,' the knight replied. 'We don't want every Tom, Dick and Harry coming to the castle. Mind you, sometimes I think, have to admit it, that I'm getting a bit long in the tooth for this challenging business. Not that it often gets beyond a challenge, you know. My reputation scares most off. And my appearance, I suppose. Fact is, you get mostly a pretty poor quality of knight travelling the roads these days. Present company excepted, of course. Now, what do you say to a jar?'

'A jar?'

'Mug of ale, you know. Decent enough stuff, if not as good as we used to brew at home. Still, make do with what you've got, that's what I say. Don't suppose I'll ever drink a jar of good Yorkshire beer again.'

'Yorkshire?' Marcus said, politely.

'Where I come from, no county like it anywhere. And I'm a well-travelled man, as you'd expect. Daresay you're surprised to meet an Englishman in these parts.'

'An Englishman?' Marcus said. 'I must confess, and I hope it doesn't offend you, that I don't know what that is. I never heard the word before, I'm afraid.'

'No offence taken. You Romans – I take it you are a Roman, though your Latin sounds a bit old-fashioned to me – you Romans call us Brits, bit behind the times you are.'

He got to his feet, crossed the chamber and, pulling aside a curtain, revealed a barrel, from which he drew three foaming tankards of straw-coloured beer.

'Lager's what they call ale in these parts,' he said. 'It's all right when you have a thirst, and we all three deserve one after our joust. Nimble pair, you are; I suppose it's the new style of fighting. Difficult to keep up with the latest tactics here, especially, as I say, since most knights bugger off when they see what they're up against. Now,' he said, settling himself and draining half his tankard, 'I expect you want to hear my lifestory.'

'That would be delightful, and full of interest, I'm sure,' Marcus said, with his customary politeness, 'but I wonder if you would first be kind enough to explain some of the really rather puzzling things that have happened since we arrived here.'

And, briefly, for he saw that the knight preferred talking to listening, he recited their experiences.

The knight laughed. 'Tests,' he said, 'tests. My Lady places great faith in them.'

'Your Lady?' Marcus said. 'Who is your Lady?'

'Not for me to say. She'll make herself known to you in time; in her own good time, that is. But you passed the tests, you'll be pleased to hear. Otherwise you wouldn't have the pleasure of my company.'

'Those little people,' Lycas said, 'were they fairies?'

'Fairies, elves, gnomes, what have you. Little devils, some of them, but all right when you learn how to handle them. As I can. They're the old inhabitants of this valley, been here goodness knows how long. Useful as servants, now, nothing more.'

'And the Indian boy?' Lycas asked.

'Oh yes, him. Little swine, needs kicking. Mind you – this is between you and me and the gatepost – I'm never certain he really exists. Maybe – no, more than maybe – he's just something she conjures up. But the girls, they're real enough. Little minxes, but choice pieces of Eve's flesh. Not that I have anything to do with them. Girls have always spelled trouble for me, and nowadays I know to leave them alone. But drink up, lads, and I'll tell you my life-story.'

'Yes indeed,' Marcus said, 'but first would you please answer two questions?'

'Delighted, I'm sure,' the knight said, rising to refill his tankard, and frowning slightly when he saw that neither Marcus nor Lycas had drunk more than a quarter of theirs.

'First then, did you have to undergo these tests?' Marcus asked.

'Of a sort, of a sort, framed a bit differently mine were.'

'And how do you come to be here?'

'Well, that's part of the story, but I don't mind beginning there, though I'll have to backtrack a bit later. I was searching for the Grail, of course. It was a quest. I suppose you're doing the same thing, aren't you?'

163

At the mention of the Grail, Marcus thought of the eunuch John the Adept. So much had happened to him since his dealings with John that he had given little thought to what had been the eunuch's obsession. But now the word which the knight pronounced made him shiver. It was the sensation often described as someone walking over your grave.

But Lycas said, 'The Grail? I've never heard of that.'

'Well now,' the knight said, 'that's asking, and I must admit it's not so clear to me as it was when I set out on my quest. Some say it's the Cup from which Jesus Christ drank at the Last Supper, and that's what I believed then. Those who think that believe that whoever comes upon the Grail will be redeemed, incapable of sin, and assured of everlasting life. Well, I don't know about that.'

'Yet you left your home and went searching for it,' Marcus said.

'That's so, and sometimes it puzzles me. It was an adventure, you know. More than that really. You must know – well, you may not, but I've had time to think of it since I arrived here – that what we knights really seek is not salvation, which to be frank is a notion rather beyond our understanding, but renown. So, when this priest came to the court of my then master, the Emperor Gratian – you'll have heard of him, I suppose, pious fellow, good athlete but more given to church-going than seemed right to us, right or wise, I might add – where was I? Need a spot more ale, don't I . . .' he muttered, and suited the action to the word, while Marcus and Lycas exchanged glances in which amusement mingled with impatience.

'You were saying,' Marcus prompted, gently, 'that a priest came to the court . . .'

'That's right, scrawny little fellow he was, but with a voice like a great bell, you'd never have thought so great a voice could have emerged from a runt like him . . . well, he appeared when we were all relaxing in the Great Hall after dinner – after dinner and a good battle against some pirates, as I recall – and he preached at us. You don't expect preaching after dinner, and few of the boys were willing to give him a hearing. Understandable, that, of course. But, I don't know how, he quelled them. There was something about him, little black-robed runt that he was, that forced us to listen. That voice, like a bell, a melodious bell. And his message . . .'

His voice drifted away, and he closed his eyes, as if journeying back into that lost time which we call memory, and which cannot be recaptured (according to the wisest philsophers) by an act of will, but only by its surrender.

'If we found the Grail, the priest said, then the Empire would be redeemed. So it was resolved that the Emperor himself would ride forth, and he chose me to accompany him. So he bade me be ready to ride with him at dawn. I was young then, and anxious, and fearful that I would oversleep. So I lay down in the hall in my riding-clothes among the mastiffs, spaniels, and meaner curs. And they kept me warm, for it was a night of hard frost. Unwillingly, I drifted into sleep, and dreamed as I so often did of fair women. And when I woke there was no sign of the Emperor, but it was light. So I saddled my horse and rode out after him, as I supposed, following the track of a horse, which was not easy, the frost having been so hard. It was a steel-grey morning, snow hanging in the heavy clouds. At last I came to a chapel, set in a clearing in the forest, with gravestones around it, and the Emperor's name on one of them. I entered the chapel, and I would tell a lie, which is against my nature, as well as being sinful, if I said I did so boldly.

'But the chapel was deserted, and a veil of red samite hung before the altar. Then an old man appeared, who told me he was a priest, and I asked him if the Grail was to be found there. And he said he knew nothing of it. And then I asked why the Emperor's name was on a tombstone when I had seen him hale and well in his court the night before. And he told me that it was his business to bury the knights who came to that chapel and never departed, and that the tombstones were ever ready for them, with their inscriptions. Hearing this, I turned and fled from the chapel, and searched among the stones to see if I should find my name there. Which I'm glad to say I didn't, and so I rode off and did not dare to return to court, though I am as brave a knight as any ever horsed. But I feared that I would be held guilty of the Emperor's death. So I crossed the sea, and after many wanderings came here, where I was pressed into that service that you know, guarding this castle at the command of my Lady.

'And who is your Lady?' Marcus said.

'Some call her the Perfect One. But this is gloomy talk,' the knight said, seeming to rouse himself from the reverie in which he had spoken while telling his tale, and resuming his former tone. 'It's honourable work, but dry. More ale is perhaps best.'

He drank, and closed his eyes, and opened them in a little while to drink again. Then he said, speaking very slowly now, and occasionally hiccuping,

'I've had more adventures than you lads have had hot dinners, and I've talked with many knights who like me set off in search of the Grail. And if you want my opinion – which is worth something, since I've lived in more lands than you could count – it doesn't exist. It's an Idea. Nothing more. It's the image of our journey through life, which starts in hope and ends in disappointment. Not that I don't make the best of it, you understand, being an Englishman. We are said to be bulldogs, you know. When we get our teeth into life we don't let go. But, lads, as for the Grail, if you take my advice, you'll forget about it and save yourselves heartbreak.'

Saying this, he slept, and soon snored.

'What a pig,' Lycas said.

'But an agreeable one.' Marcus, ever generous, amended his friend's judgement.

*(Is our author ignorant, or errant, or merely careful? We must suspect the latter; else why put his versions of the mystery of the Grail in the mouths of, first, an unscrupulous, foul, greedy and vilely sensual man whom he calls John the Adept – and is not that sobriquet a word ironically delivered to the wise who may read? – and then of a buffoon, an English lout, bully and drunkard? Why do this, save to conceal knowledge which he dare not admit, and perhaps to tease?

But truth will out, and the knowledge of the Grail is the utmost man may achieve. 'For then I saw through a glass darkly, but now face to face,' wrote that apostle who declared also that he had been 'caught up in the Third Heaven'. He who seeks the Grail by the practice of the appropriate ritual, and is rewarded, will experience the departure of the soul, which is immortal, from the body, which is corrupt, and for three days it will wander through other worlds, both good and evil, and view the bridge that must be crossed to attain paradise.

The quest is the story of an initiation, a translation, if only temporary, to the astral plane, an escape from corruption.

For this, which can be confessed only secretly, and written only here in the seclusion of our preceptory, and which I write trembling, in danger of the rack and the flames, is the true light that lighteth the darkness of this realm that is Satan's.

The beginning of Perfection is the Gnosis of Man, *but* the Gnosis of God is perfected Perfection.

There are two Mysteries: the lesser, which are those of the fleshly generation, and after initiation into these, the initiate must pause before seeking admission to the Great and Heavenly Mysteries, whence ... [*The next lines of the manuscript are illegible.*]

It is in the Mysteries of the Great Mother that we obtain revelation of the Universal Mystery, of which the True Gate is Jesus the Blessed. And of all men, we alone, calumniated Knights of the Temple that has been destroyed, who now live out our earthly existence in hiding and disgraced before the eyes of all others, yet we alone are Christians, accomplishing the Mystery of the Third Gate.)*

**(Our poor Brother, stumbling towards Enlightenment in a dark age of the world, oppressed by fanaticism!

But we Brothers and Knights of the Rosy Cross see the flickering of a New Age of Enlightenment when Universal Wisdom shall be enkindled, and spread its beams throughout the whole world, as the radiance of the Sun reaches from the east to the west; and this enlightenment will awake gladness in the hearts of men, and transform their wills.)**

XXVI

Trumpets roused Marcus and Lycas from the languor into which they had sunk, and sweet scents of rose and honey were blown through the chamber, as if by a wind, though they felt no breeze. There followed six Negro slave boys, of about the middle height, and each carried a wing in either hand. These wings were made of the feathers of pink birds, or of feathers coloured pink, and it was – Marcus thought – the flapping of the wings which moved the perfume. But Lycas interpreted the flapping differently, and thought that the Negro boys were seeking to fly; and so despised them, this being impossible.

The trumpet sounded again, and heralded the entry of a lady, whom they understood, correctly, to be the Lady of whom the knight had spoken as his mistress. She wore a gown of white silk embroidered with red roses, one on either breast, and her face was chalked white but there was a red rose in each cheek.

She lifted her hand and there was silence, and the Negro boys all knelt, one knee touching the ground and the other bent, and they covered their faces with the wings. Then the Lady commanded Marcus and Lycas to approach her, but when she had looked at them, she dismissed Lycas as a mere squire and told him to remove himself to the dark corner of the room, and fixed Marcus with a keen and level gaze, which he returned, but politely.

She enquired of him why he had presumed to penetrate her valley and how he had overcome her champion. Marcus smiled, and with that courtesy which ever distinguished him, explained politely that he and his squire, 'who is also my friend', were travellers who had lost their way.

'It is the common lot of man,' she replied. 'Only the enlightened ones may walk according to the map.'

'As for your champion,' Marcus said, relieved that she spoke Greek in a fashion that he could understand, though her accent was harsh, 'he fought gallantly, and if it had not been for the help of my squire, I misdoubt me he would have proved too strong for me.'

Then, since she did not answer, he explained that he was in the service of the Princess Honoria, and was on his way from the imperial court to rejoin his mistress.

'We take no note of princes, emperors or princesses here,' she said. 'They belong to the world of flesh.'

Marcus, remembering the trials they had been set, thought that he and Lycas had received a sufficiently strong invitation to participate in that world of which she spoke so scornfully; but thought it wiser to keep this reflection to himself.

'You will think us,' she said, 'sadly inhospitable.'

'I think you careful, and do not doubt that you have reason.'

The Lady examined the nails of her right hand.

'The Princess Honoria,' she said, 'And do you serve her loyally?'

'To the best of my ability.'

'I believe you may be virtuous, as virtue goes in the world you inhabit.'

Marcus bowed his head in acknowledgement of the compliment, noting however the reservation it contained.

'Yes,' she said again, 'I would like to think you virtuous, for you are well-favoured – not that such a consideration influences me, for I am a Perfect.'

Marcus, though unable to understand what she meant, bowed his head; he was loth to think she spoke mere vanity.

'But you come from Constantinople, from the palace of that she-wolf Eudoxia – that devout she-wolf.'

'And was compelled to leave my wife there, as a hostage,' Marcus said, with the flush of guilt he felt whenever he remembered Artemisia, which was but seldom.

'And yet you withstood the trials,' she continued as if he had not spoken. 'And so did the pretty boy, your squire, though he was sore tempted.'

'I have read,' Marcus said, 'that there is no merit in resisting any temptation unless you feel its attraction. When the Devil led Christ to the rock and showed him all the kingdoms of the world spread before him, and offered them to him, is it blasphemous to suppose that he longed, if only for a moment, to possess them?'

'It is not blasphemous,' she said, 'it is common sense.'

She clapped her hands, and the Negro slaves rose as one, and removed the wings from in front of their faces, and stood at the ready.

'You have given me much to think of,' she said. 'We shall talk again in the morrow.'

XXVII

Marcus and Lycas lay together in the chamber that had been assigned to them. It had not escaped their notice that the door was bolted on the outside.

'So we are prisoners again,' Lycas said. 'What was it you once told me? That as long as we can say this is the worst, the worst is not yet on us? Something like that, wasn't it? I didn't understand it then, but I'm beginning to see the sense of it now, and that gives me hope.'

'To despair,' Marcus said, 'is a sin. Or so my confessor told me.'

'Then it is better to dream,' Lycas said. 'In dreams, men say, the old gods cross the open frontier with the world of men and women. Did that woman have designs on you?'

'She remarked, rather pointedly, that she didn't.'

'Then let us sleep and hope to dream.'

But whether they dreamed good dreams that night is unknown.

In the morning the door was unbolted and their old adversary, now perhaps their friend, for so they thought of him, the Green Knight entered. He had not yet put his armour on, but was clad in a night-shirt, and carried bowls of goat's milk, and a tankard of ale for himself.

'You made a good impression on the Lady, old sport,' he said to Marcus. 'I've had instructions that I'm to escort you up the mountain to the monastery. To be enlightened, she says. You'd better get a move on, I'm to be on duty at the stream by first light. Not that any bugger is likely to approach it so early, but rules is rules.'

It was a stiff climb to the monastery, up a winding track that a donkey or a mule might manage, but not a horse. The Green Knight – Sir Gavin he had told them to call him now – was panting by the time they rounded a ridge and saw the monastery huddling wet-grey against the black rock.

'Getting old,' he said, '*anno domini*, y'know,' and shook his head, stroked his moustaches, mournfully.

'That fall yesterday won't have done you any good,' Lycas said. 'And how's the leg? I'm sorry I had to do that to you.'

'All part of the game,' he replied. 'I don't hold it against you, lad.'

Two brothers in black robes greeted them. They said a boy had been sent up early to tell them of their coming. They didn't look them in the eye, not till Sir Gavin said he must be off back down the mountain, to take up his post. Only when he had gone did they offer Marcus and Lycas black bread and goat's milk.

Marcus and Lycas stayed some weeks in the monastery, being given instruction in the brothers' faith, as the Lady had commanded. This is what they were taught.

The world is divided into two kingdoms: the Realm of Light and the Realm of Darkness. The first consisted of five elements – Air, Wind, Light, Water and Fire – and was also where the Tree of Life was to be found. In the Realm of Darkness, five devils presided over its own five elements – Smoke, Fire, Wind, Water and Darkness – and from these sprang five trees that formed the Tree of Death. This realm was governed by the Prince of Darkness, who had the head of a lion, the body of a serpent, the wings of a bird, the tail of a fish, and the four feet of creeping beasts; but this Prince of Darkness was able at will to transform himself and appear in human form, either as a lovely woman or a handsome man.

On account of Adam's disobedience and his fall, men were condemned to live in the Realm of Darkness, governed by the Evil One. Yet the soul belonged to the Realm of Light, and to the one True God, and it was the goal of all good men to escape darkness and free the soul that it might be united again with light. But only those who practised denial might escape the world of flesh; those who were unable to do so were condemned to be born again, but in the body and not in the spirit. Only the perfected ones attained that freedom which was loss of Self, but the others, the believers, moved towards it, and on their deathbeds they were consoled by the perfected ones, so that in their next reincarnation they might come mercifully closer to perfection.

'But Christ came to save all men,' Marcus said. 'Do you then deny the Christ and the salvation he offers?'

'The Church tells lies about Jesus Christ,' said the brother who instructed them, a perfected man in his black robe tied with a girdle. 'It says he assumed a material body, but how could he, being divine, and the flesh evil? It preaches that his incarnation, passion, crucifixion and resurrection are historical facts, but we know they are only symbolic. They say, "men killed the Messiah, Jesus son of Mary and of the Holy Ghost". But this is impossible. There was no crucifixion. It is only a metaphor.'

'But this is heresy,' Marcus said, 'to deny the teaching of the Church founded by St Peter, the Apostle of Christ.'

'Heresy clerisy. Are your bishops rich or poor? Do they have great possessions? Does the Pope in Rome live like an emperor in a golden palace? Does he claim to be a temporal power because of the so-called Donation of Constantine?'

Marcus was silent. There were answers to these questions, he knew, but for the moment he could not formulate them.

'Your Pope,' the brother said, 'is no man of God, for all that he claims to possess the keys that open the door of the Kingdom of Heaven. He is of this world of darkness and acts in collusion with its prince.'

Lycas said, 'I understand very little of what you have said. And I know nothing of popes or bishops. It seems to me from what I have observed that men strive for power to exert their will and impose it on others, and so satisfy their natures, and I dare say that is evil as you seem to suggest, but it is also, it appears to me, natural. It is the way of the world.'

'And does not that prove that this world is evil, since the exercise of power leads to cruelty, murder and war?'

'That is as may be,' Lycas said. 'I am only an ignorant boy, and I'm sure you can defeat me in argument, for you are clearly a man of education who has thought deeply about these things. Never- theless . . .' His voice tailed away; he wasn't sure any longer what he had wanted to say. He looked at Marcus, whose brow was furrowed as he thought about the brother's teaching, at the long elegant fingers that lay on his thigh; and he found courage and words. 'There's a lot in this world that feels good to me,' he said; and blushed because he sensed that the brother knew what he was thinking as he looked at Marcus. 'To be outside on a starry night,' he said, 'and to feel the wind on your face. And eating when you're hungry, and drinking and good company and making love.'

The words now came in a rush, and again he felt the colour flood his face.

'Intercourse of the body is sinful,' the brother said. 'We perfected ones abstain from it therefore. But in this world of the Devil it is indeed natural, and therefore practised. In truth we believe that for those who are not perfected, one act of sex is the same as another, and some say that sex in marriage is the most culpable, because husband and wife are taught by the Catholic Church that this sex is not sinful. Therefore, believing that they do not sin, they compound their sin.'

'I do not understand the word "sin",' Lycas said. 'I know only what feels good and what bad.'

'My poor boy, you are very ignorant,' the brother said, and turned to Marcus to continue his exposition of their faith.

*(But this is incredible, the daring of our author; a double daring indeed.

Remember that this narrative is written for the young Emperor Frederick, ward of His Holiness Pope Innocent III, who, however, like all Popes for many years, regarded the young man, then, we must assume, no more than a boy, as a viper hatched in the viper's nest, for so he had been known to describe the imperial family of Hohenstaufen.

And our author dares to offer him – with some sympathy, yes indeed, with considerable sympathy – an argument in favour of that heresy (as the Holy Church deemed it) which had aroused the anger and apprehension of His Holiness when it flourished in Languedoc; so that he raised a crusade against it, and ordered the extirpation of the virtuous Cathars (as they deemed themselves to be).

To further his crusade, of which our author cannot have been ignorant, the Pope created the Dominican Order of Preachers, who were instructed to imitate the Perfect Ones among the Cathars by making an outward display of poverty, so that they seemed – to the ignorant – to walk in the steps of the Apostles and to live in their humble and frugal manner. But this was from the first a deception.

Furthermore, he created the Holy Inquisition, blasphemous epithet to apply to a devilish institution; created it for the better persecution of the wretched but honest Cathars, humble folk. And the Inquisition spread lies about them, for it declared that the Cathars were given to the practice of spitting on the Cross, and of obscenely kissing the sexual organs of cats; that men lay with men and with boys, and thought no sin of this; and other stories too monstrous to relate.

Be it noted, however, that these accusations were identical with those brought against our holy order of the Knights of the Temple, and while it is to be admitted, with melancholy regret, that the love our brothers bore to each other was at times expressed as our author tells us the love of Marcus for Lycas was expressed, the other accusations were mere diabolic inventions. And as for the love between men, or between men and youths, there is scriptural authority for that, since the Gospels speak of the disciple whom Jesus loved, on whose breast he laid his head at the Last Supper. But for my part, and I write this in exile, my life forfeit, and must therefore speak the truth, being in sight of the Heavenly Gates, I forever abstained from all carnal activity once I had taken my complete vows, which included that of celibacy.)*

XXVIII

Lycas chafed at life in the monastery, all the more so because Marcus appeared to listen to the instruction they were given, and to be impressed by it. To Lycas it meant nothing; he could attach no importance to theological argument. He looked out of the narrow window and saw a hawk hovering in the slate-grey sky. He watched it for a long time as it hung in the air, and then it dropped faster than a stone let fall from that window, and when it rose again, a small animal – rabbit or young leveret – was clutched in its talons. When it wheeled and disappeared from sight, Lycas felt abandoned.

He took comfort in the visits Sir Gavin made to them of an evening. The monks viewed these with disfavour. They warned Marcus against the knight; he was, they said, a creature given to carnality and vice. They looked coldly at Lycas as they said this. He knew that they were eager to separate Marcus from him. He told Sir Gavin that he feared they were bewitching his friend.

The knight pulled at his long grey moustaches.

'Hrrumph,' he said, thoughtfully, and pulled a flask from his girdle and drank from it. 'Concerning witchcraft, I could tell you a tale or two.'

'What do they want of him?' Lycas said, disregarding the bait.

'My Lady has taken a fancy to him, no question of that,' the knight said. 'But she has taken a vow of chastity. It makes an exciting contrast to the life she used to lead, I suppose. Between you and me and the doorpost, dear boy, she used to be notorious for lust. As for her lovers, well, horribly dead, most of them. Less said about that the better, I think. Indeed, yes. Silence is golden on that particular subject. As for the bewitching you speak of, you're not far out, dear boy. But it is, I fancy, of a different sort than that which you imagine. Tell me truly now what you know of witches.'

177

'Why,' Lycas said, 'they are night-hags, in communion – men say – with evil spirits, though as for me I have no idea what such things might be. And they concoct potions and poisons, and the potions may change men's natures. Or so I have heard tell.'

Sir Gavin drank again from his flask, which contained a liquor that he said was distilled mountain dew and unfit for a lad of Lycas's tender years, and shook his head, sagely.

'To be sure,' he said, 'such creatures are to be found in every village, wizened, evil-smelling, ill-wishing old besoms. But it is a higher sort of witchcraft that my Lady, who, between you and me and the North Wind, I have come to fear greatly, is wont to practise. When you say that she seeks to bewitch your friend . . .'

'More than friend,' Lycas said, lowering his gaze so that Sir Gavin should not see the tears start to his eyes; but though he hid them, the blushing cheek and quivering lip betrayed the depth of his feeling.

Sir Gavin sighed, pitying the boy.

'As I was saying,' he said, 'before you interrupted me, when you say that she seeks to bewitch your friend, I answer . . . what do I answer? That you are right, and yet also wrong. For it is no vulgar spell such as those you speak of that she is casting on him. Let me tell you a story to make things clear.'

'Very well,' Lycas said. He spoke doubtfully, for he had found that Sir Gavin's stories, being interrupted by recourse to his flask, as often muddied the waters of his understanding as they clarified them. 'Tell,' he said.

'There was a certain man, an African, called Apuleius,' the knight said, 'who was accused of witchcraft in Tripoli. I must tell you that it is well-known that Africans are given to the black arts, some say on account of the number of serpents that infest their country. He offered as his defence – now, what was it? Ah yes – first that magicians were priests. That was all. Theirs was an art acceptable, he said, to the gods, with whom the magicians enjoyed communion of speech. Oh dear me, that was a rash thing to admit. But he was also charged with having bewitched a boy by means of an incantation – and the boy lost his wits. Well, he said, he hadn't done any such thing, not he. Nevertheless, nevertheless

. . . This is thirsty work, cranking up my old memory. Where was I? Yes, he admitted that he had heard tell that a young lad, provided he was beautiful, healthy and intelligent – which we can all agree our friend Marcus is – could be charmed into a trance, and, if so charmed, could be reduced to his primal nature, which is, he said, immortal and divine, and would then be capable of predicting the future.'

'And is that what your Lady seeks of my friend?' Lycas said.

'No indeed, it is more than that. She wants to take possession of his soul, to make him her creature, obedient to her in every way, forgetful of himself, his history and his very being; to be her absolute slave, subject to her will.'

'Then I shall lose him for ever,' Lycas cried.

'He is to be the exhibition of her own inner evil nature, and in this way, she believes, she will free herself. For though she is reputed a Perfect and has declared herself such, yet in her heart of hearts, she has doubts; and therefore seeks this, which she calls the left-hand or sinister route, to join herself to the Godhead.'

Lycas, horrified by the fate that attended his friend, dissolved into uncontrollable sobbing.

The knight watched him and said nothing, till at last the boy's first transport of misery abated.

Then he said,

'You take things too much to heart, laddie. And you mustn't believe everything you are told.'

Lycas looked up, suddenly indignant.

'Is this all then some jest that you are playing on me?'

'Not so, not so. What I have told you is just what my Lady intends. But it's all pish and tush. I'm an Englishman, and I don't hold with such stuff. I don't say it can't be done. I've lived in more countries and through more experiences than I care to remember, and so I've come to know better than to say anything is impossible. And I've seen enough to know what she's capable of. Devilish arts, no doubt about it. But, dear boy, it's fiddle-faddle for all that.'

'Fiddle-faddle?' Lycas said. 'Please, I don't know what that is.'

'A lot of trumpery nonsense then. Bullshit, if you like. Bullshit and balls. I've taken a fancy to you and to your friend, even if he is what the Greeks, sod 'em, call an intellectual. You bested me at the stream. It wasn't what I'd call a fair fight, two against one, though I've won against longer odds than that. And stone-throwing, I don't hold with that, you know, it's not the English way of jousting. Still, you're a foreigner and a nice lad; so I forgive you. And, like I say, I've taken a fancy to the pair of you. I do that sometimes. I've a generous, impulsive nature, you see. So I don't hold with this monkeying about with the boy's mind, don't hold with it at all.'

Lycas was delighted to hear this. He felt that the knight was an ally. All the same, he said he would be happier if they had a plan of action.

'Well, that needs thinking about,' the knight said. 'Staff-work's never been exactly my forte.'

The difficulty, as Lycas soon realised, was not merely the deficiencies to which the Green Knight had confessed, but, far more seriously, Marcus himself. He seemed to have withdrawn from Lycas. He would spend hours at a time sitting cross-legged on the floor and gazing at the blank wall. Perhaps, Lycas thought, he saw pictures there. When Lycas spoke to him, he gave no sign of hearing him. He remained wakeful much of the night, and, if Lycas timidly advanced a hand towards him, would make no response. In short, it was impossible to rouse him from what was either apathy or a sort of trance. Very often poor Lycas found himself in tears.

Matters were made worse by the monks. If they had ever had designs on Lycas, as they too clearly had on Marcus, they had set them aside. They spoke roughly to the boy, cuffed him about the ears, and set him to work on menial tasks. They kept him busy now from dawn till dusk, digging the kitchen garden, splitting logs, washing the stone floors, and such like. It was cold. He got chilblains on his fingers and toes, and spent much of every day in tears.

But his misery made him only the more determined to rescue his friend. Yet when he reminded him of his duty to the Princess Honoria, or even reminded him of poor Artemisia left behind in

Constantinople, Marcus could not be roused. Every day he seemed to sink deeper into his trance, to be less and less Marcus. Indeed, there were moments when Lycas could scarcely recognise him, so completely had he lost all animation of countenance. Lycas said to himself, 'Is it possible that he is being changed utterly? Is there no solid reality to our Being?'

He did not know, of course, that in asking this question he had stumbled on one of the fundamental problems that perplex philosophers.

For, though those who were holding Marcus were what Holy Church terms 'heretics', and therefore it may be argued that their object was to deform him; yet, by their light, in subduing his soul (as was their intention) they were also committed to its liberation from the envelope of flesh; and they were so successful that the fleshly Marcus now denied and did not perhaps even recognise the fleshly Lycas. In their assertion that matter was evil, they went beyond what Holy Church teaches; yet its teaching will also have it that the ways of the flesh are indeed evil, though not the flesh itself. These matters, my Prince, are deep, and to be pondered, for it is the Apostle Paul who speaks of putting off the corruptible body and taking on the incorruptible.

Naturally Lycas, who had no philosophical training, could not argue these points. His standing was more simple. He said to himself: 'If Marcus withdraws himself from me, and is altogether absent in mind or spirit, and if he becomes unrecognisable to me, then is he still Marcus? How can he be Marcus still when he is not the Marcus I have known and loved? And yet in some way he must still be Marcus, since, even if I no longer know him, yet I continue to love him.'

Such thoughts went round and round like an angry whirlpool in the poor boy's head. Meanwhile, as his perplexity deepened, time flew, irretrievable time. Only courage remained with him. Yet, since even the most courageous among us only rarely has the courage for that which he truly knows (or thinks to know), how should courage help Lycas now when his assurance of any knowledge was crumbling? Yet he held on, saying, 'I at least have not been destroyed, and what does not destroy me makes me stronger.' It was the utterance of a noble spirit.

He grew nevertheless impatient and anxious. For some days Sir Gavin did not visit him in the monastery. He feared that either some evil had come to him or that his courage or determination had failed; 'Which in itself is an evil,' he said.

At last the knight appeared. He explained that he had been suffering from a disorder of the bowels, the consequence, he said, of the vegetable diet to which his Lady had compelled him to submit.

'Which,' he added, 'makes me more eager than before to be quit of this place. An Englishman needs beef to function; failing beef, mutton; and failing mutton, pig. How is our friend?'

'Every day,' Lycas said, 'he is less and less. I do not think his will – if it still is his – remains alive. I fear that I cannnot persuade him to escape with us.'

'Hrrumph,' Sir Gavin said, twisting his moustache, 'tricky. Still, not to despair. As I once heard a wise man say, "All good things approach their goal crookedly, like cats, that arch their backs and purr."'

'What does that mean?' Lycas said.

'It means, why it means . . . I had the meaning but a moment ago . . .'

'Then please think hard, try to recapture it.'

'Silence, boy.'

The knight took the now accustomed ruminative pull at his flask.

'It means,' he said, 'that if our friend will not save himself, we must save him from himself, in order also to free him from those who hold him in their devilish clutches. That's what it means.'

'But how?'

'Listen, I have a cunning plan.'

Two nights later, at what should have been the end of his visit to the boys – undertaken, as Sir Gavin explained several times to the monks, only because his Lady commanded him to ascertain – 'check up' was the vulgarism he actually used – that they were well and healthy, otherwise, he remarked, I would have nothing to do with a pair of little beasts like that, being an Englishman, you understand – he was making his way to the door of the monastery in the company of two silent brothers who scarcely responded to his quips and jests, his grumbles and complaints, when, from the chamber they had just left, they heard Lycas begin to howl like a dog. The howls grew more and more frantic.

'Bless me,' Sir Gavin said, 'the boy's gone mad.'

The monks looked at each other, astounded. They looked at Sir Gavin. There was silence, a silence pregnant with possibility. Then the howls resumed, this time like the howling of a wolf.

Sir Gavin made the sign of the Cross, involuntarily, as it were.

'Bless me,' he said again. 'They're both mad. This will never do. What have you done to them, what magic have you performed? This is not what my Lady wanted, not at all.'

The howling now mingled with a mighty crashing, and then the sound of a body being hurled about.

'They'll do themselves an injury,' the knight exclaimed. 'My Lady will never forgive us if harm comes to them in this way. Fetch a couple of straitjackets that we may restrain them.'

The brothers, by now thoroughly alarmed, and incapable of rational thought, hurried to obey the knight. (So it is, my Prince, that in a crisis, decision is all, and he who knows his own mind commands the day.) The three then ran back to the chamber, where they found Lycas rolling about the floor, howling and tearing at his clothes, while Marcus huddled in a corner, wide-eyed, his mouth open, whimpering and emitting low moans. Blood trickled from his upper lip.

'Bolt the door,' the knight ordered; and one monk obeyed.

'Seize the boy's legs and sit on them,' he commanded, pointing at Lycas.

Again the monks did as he ordered, and when they were engaged in holding down the thrashing limbs, he unbuckled his small mace and struck each sharply on the back of the head. One blow was sufficient. Both monks fell face down on the floor.

Lycas struggled to free himself from the bodies which had fallen over him. Then, with Sir Gavin, he stripped the monks of their habits, and encased them in the straitjackets. They forced gags into their mouths, so that, when the first of the monks recovered from the blow which the knight had dealt him, he could only sit, open-eyed and helpless, amazed by the reversal of roles, as he watched Lycas dress himself in the brown habit.

All this while Marcus had not moved, but still sat as one struck dumb. Lycas took a cloth and wiped the blood from his mouth.

'I hit him,' he said, 'to try to get him to start up a sound, Lord forgive me.'

'He looks truly out of his wits,' the knight said. 'I pray God we are not too late.'

But they got him to his feet, and dressed him in the habit of the other monk, and pulled its hood well down to conceal his face, while Lycas did the same to the hood of his own habit.

'He's further gone than I thought he'd be,' the knight said. 'We'll have to change the plan' – for that, as put together, had had him feigning drunkenness and being escorted out of the monastery by two caring monks.

Instead, they had to prop Marcus between them and support him out of the chamber, down the long corkscrew staircase towards the gate, where the porter on duty challenged them. Sir Gavin explained that their poor brother had been taken ill, and they were carrying him to the castle to be tended by their Lady's physician; and when the porter questioned this, struck him too on the head with his mace, so that he fell unconscious to the ground.

And so in this way Marcus escaped a great danger to his soul and body.

XXIX

For two days they rode through a dark forest. When they lay down for the night the darkness was alive with the howling of wolves. Marcus spoke scarcely a word, and Lycas could make little sense of the few he uttered. He feared for his friend's reason, and would have given way to despair if it had not been for the robust support of Sir Gavin, who said, 'The lad is but disturbed. Give him time. Time's the great healer.'

But on the third day Marcus fell from his horse in a swoon, and they carried him into a mean hut made of the branches of hazel-trees bound together with reeds and mud from the nearby lake. The old woman who lived there, a crone with straggling hair and a skin blackened by winds and smoke, received them grudgingly at first. She spoke a tongue neither could understand, and, when Sir Gavin offered her silver, looked at the coins as if they had no meaning for her. However, when she saw that Marcus was sick and that they had come in peace, she made ready a bed of reeds and twisted grasses for him, and, when they had laid him there, wiped his face with a damp rag and muttered words that sounded more gentle to Lycas. She prepared a thin gruel and held a cup to Marcus's lips, but he would not drink.

The knight ordered Lycas to prepare a fire in the clearing, and took his bow and strode into the deeper forest. Before the sun fell, which it did early, for it was now winter, he returned with a young roebuck slung across his shoulders. He butchered it and cut its gigot into collops, and they roasted these on the fire. The old woman ate with them, and smiled and nodded and chattered in the tongue they could not understand. Then all lay down for the night crammed together in the hut.

But Lycas could not sleep on account of the anxiety he felt for his friend, and also because he was disturbed by the knight's snores and by the old woman, who continually muttered and ground her teeth in her sleep. He rose from the floor where he was lying wrapped up in his cloak, and went and knelt by Marcus, and ran his fingers over his brow, which was cold as ice and yet damp with sweat. He would have prayed, but he did not know which gods he should address his words to. So he stepped outside the hut, and his feet crackled on the frosty grass, and he looked up at the bright immensity of the sky, and felt utterly alone.

In the morning Marcus still gave no sign of life, and indeed for a moment Lycas thought that he had passed away; but he held a feather to his lips, and it fluttered feebly; then he leaned over and brushed Marcus's lips with his own and tried to breathe life into him. But there was no response. And so it continued for two days.

Then towards noon on the third day, when the sky was the colour of slate and heavy with snow, Marcus opened his eyes.

'The fever has passed,' Sir Gavin said, and made the sign of the Cross.

Now, when the old woman passed Marcus a cup of her thin gruel, and held it to his lips, he allowed a few drops of the liquid to enter his mouth, and swallowed twice, with difficulty, before he gave a little shake of the head and closed his eyes again.

In the afternoon he was stronger, and in the evening he spoke. But his voice was falsetto and it was the voice of a young girl which they heard; and what he said made no sense to Lycas or the knight.

'He is wandering in his wits,' Sir Gavin said, 'and that is not uncommon after a fever.'

He gave him some broth, which they had made from the bones of the roebuck, and Marcus drank and fell asleep again.

'In the morning he will be stronger,' the knight said. 'In the morning he will be himself.'

It was what Lycas wanted to believe; and yet he could not. He knew too that Sir Gavin was trying to persuade himself that all would be well and that they would soon be able to resume their journey. The knight chafed at their delay, partly because his flask had long been empty, and there was not even beer in the old woman's hut. His nerves were jangled, and it was only because of his good nature and the affection he had come to feel for Lycas and Marcus that he was endeavouring to restrain his impatience.

Lycas, however, was more doubtful. He could not believe that Marcus would recover so quickly, and he was disturbed by the memory of that girl's voice in which he had spoken. It was as if someone had taken possession of his friend's soul, and made him other than that which he had been. As for himself, he felt that his life was suddenly without direction. He had travelled far with Marcus, and for Marcus; and if Marcus was taken away from him, he would not know what might become of him. He was like a fragment of ice being carried rapidly and helplessly along a swollen river, ice that would melt as the river bore him out of these wintry climes into the sunlight, until at last, reaching the sea, he too would dissolve and be lost utterly in the salty water. He took Marcus's hand in his and pressed it, and there was no response. He even imagined there was a drawing-away.

The next day Marcus opened his eyes, and when he had drunk some broth from the cup that Lycas held to his lips, began to speak. Again he spoke in that high-pitched girl's voice, and in a tongue that Lycas could not understand. Lycas addressed him in Latin, and Marcus looked at him blankly.

'His wits are wandering,' Sir Gavin said.

'I think he is bewitched,' Lycas said.

That conviction grew stronger as Marcus regained strength. His gestures were now effeminate. His voice remained girlish. He affected a modesty of manner which it pained Lycas to see. Meanwhile the snow fell and lay deep around the little hut. Lycas and the knight had to struggle through the snow to find fodder for their horses. Marcus kept to the hut and was tended by the old woman, to whom alone he smiled.

Lycas said to the knight: 'His wife Artemisia whom we left in Constantinople is possessed of the evil eye. I believe she has ill-wished him.'

But Sir Gavin shook his head.

'When you first said he was bewitched, I didn't believe you. It's not natural, I said to meself, even though a man of my experience has seen many strange things in his time. But, fact is, I didn't want to believe you, dear boy.'

'Why was that?'

'Stands to reason, don't it? If the lad was bewitched, there's only one person who could have been responsible. Milady herself. Well, I yield to none in courage – you'll grant me that, I'm sure – but the truth of the matter is, which I've admitted to no man before and which I'll thank you to keep to yourself, Milady scares the shit out of me.'

So they argued the matter for many days while the snow kept them fast in the forest hut, and every day Marcus grew in strength and became more girlish in manner and speech, till Lycas was near to weeping whenever he looked at him.

'If it was indeed your Lady who cast this spell on my friend to charm and, as it may be, possess his soul,' Lycas said, 'then we have no choice but to return and compel her to remove it.'

When he said this, Sir Gavin grew pale and trembled with terror, for, he said, having once escaped her clutches, all the devils in hell could not carry him back to her.

'Then I must do it myself,' Lycas said, and when the thaw came and the snow melted, he set out on his mission, so great was his love for Marcus. Meanwhile Sir Gavin promised to guard Marcus.

XXX

Lycas had many adventures on his journey, and most of them do not concern us now. He travelled in apprehension and doubt, for he was in great fear of the Lady he had gone to seek, and moreover he could not think how he could persuade or compel her to lift the curse which she had laid on Marcus. He did not know either if she could do so without returning with him to the hut in the forest, and he could not imagine how he could get her to do so. Even Sir Gavin had been unable to think of one of his 'cunning tricks', but pulled at his moustaches and looked doleful.

One night Lycas came to an inn which was full of company. He sought, as ever on his journey, to escape notice, and settled himself in a corner of the room with his supper of bread and ewe's-milk cheese and a sour greenish wine.

In a little, a trumpet sounded, and then a young man began to play on a stringed instrument. He lifted his head and sang. He was blond and beautiful and blind and his song was one of deep longing which cut Lycas to the heart, for it spoke of desolation and solitude and of a great despair. Then the trumpet sounded again, though Lycas could not discern the trumpeter in what was now a great company, and another, an old wizened man with a black beard streaked with grey, played on a fiddle, a dancing tune and mocking; and the company commenced to dance. At first they paired off in couples, and the dance was decorous. The music quickened and the dance grew wilder, and first a young girl in a white gown slashed from the waist approached Lycas and offered him her hand, and when he refused, a boy, slim as an arrow and dark as the shadows of evening, took her place and made the same offer, which Lycas also declined. The boy looked at him sorrowfully, and smiled, a smile, as it seemed to Lycas, of the utmost sweetness, so that he felt temptation, but yet turned his head away, and would have stopped his ears to the music. Which, however, waxed wilder and more intoxicating until with whooping and howling the company tumbled out of the inn kitchen to resume their dance on the grass beyond. They leaped and cavorted and shrieked as they did so, and dancers twirled dancers in frantic circles. Then some of them fell to the ground and coupled, indiscriminately, men with women, women with women, boys and girls intermingled in couples, trios and quartets. The girl who had first approached him lifted her white gown over her head and was entered by a tall man dressed only in goatskins, and the boy, slim as an arrow and dark as the shadows of evening, languished before a sturdy lad, whom Lycas recognised as the ostler who had taken charge of his horse when he arrived at the inn; and then they were joined together in an embrace and the dark boy swivelled round and offered his buttocks to his companion.

Silence fell and darkness with it, and it seemed to Lycas that all the company had vanished into the night.

He felt utterly alone and empty, and scarcely raised his head when there came the sound of a mighty rushing wind and the beating as if of many wings, and the cry wavering on the night of a departing host.

It was then that he observed that he was not, as he had thought, alone, but that an old man in a saffron robe with a rope girdle round his waist sat in the inglenook by the kitchen fire, reading a book; and as he read, his lips moved as lips move in prayer.

The old man closed his book, stretched out his hands to the fire, rubbed them together, and addressed Lycas.

'It is godly to resist temptation,' he said. 'For you felt it, did you not?'

Lycas felt himself blush, for the old man seemed to see into his heart. But he said only that he travelled on a grave business from which he could not allow himself to be distracted.

'Not to feel temptation is not to be human,' the old man said. 'We would not be tempted to evil if it was not attractive.'

'I have never thought on such matters,' Lycas said. 'They are beyond me.'

'But see, you resisted, and now the temptation is like the chaff of the summer threshing floors and the wind has carried it away. These fools seek knowledge where no good knowledge is to be found. Do you know what they desire? It is to escape time. But we are all subject to time. It is not good for the unlearned to question deeply. What says the sage? "Whosoever ponders on four things it were better for him if he had never been born – what is above, what is below, what is before time, what will be hereafter."'

'Indeed,' said Lycas, 'these questions have never troubled me. I had no schooling, but since it seems to me that such questions cannot be answered, it is foolish to ask them.'

'You are wise in your ignorance,' the old man said. 'Fear God and honour and obey His commandments. That is all the wisdom you need to possess. And yet I see that in other respects you are deeply troubled.'

'That I am,' said Lycas.

'Tell me your trouble,' the old man said.

At first Lycas was loth to do so, for he thought that the music and the dancers might be a device created by the Lady's magic to divert him from his task; and that this old man might likewise be such a device, sent to seduce him since he had resisted the first temptation. So he sat silent.

The old man smiled, and said,

'I see you do not trust me, and that you think yourself wise to be cautious. And perhaps you are right. That would be the judgement of many wise men deeply versed in the ways of the world. There are many stories told of the malignity of travellers and of the unhappy fate that befalls anyone rash enough to put his trust in chance acquaintances. But consider this, young man: you are young and I am old; you are strong and I am weak; you have long years of life before you, and I tremble on the verge of the grave. Which of us, do you suppose, has the greater reason to distrust the other?'

These words made Lycas feel ashamed. Nevertheless, he still hesitated.

'Do old men fear death more keenly than the young?' he asked.

'If it is death you are afraid of, then there is nothing I can do to help you,' was the reply. 'Fear of death corrupts reason.'

Saying this, the old man turned again to his book and seemed ready to ignore Lycas.

Silence hung heavy over the inn kitchen. It seemed to Lycas that the whole world had been withdrawn from him, that he was marooned in time as in space. He gazed at the fire, and the flames no longer danced and flickered, but hung motionless. The fire gave out heat, and yet he shivered. In the red glow of the fire he saw Marcus's lovely face. It stared at him with a pleading intensity, and then the wind blew through the chamber and the face died away, leaving him like a vanishing dream. The image of himself as a fragment of ice being carried to the melting sea recurred to him. He thought of the miles he had travelled, and of the forbidding castle that was his goal; and he knew the temptation to despair.

Then he sensed that the old man had looked up from his book and fixed his eyes on him; but he could not lift his to meet his gaze.

From without came the cry of a cock summoning up the dawn. The old man said,

'I have been condemned to live and to wander, and many times I have thought my life to be a curse. I have stood by my daughter's grave and heard her call me faithless. I have aged with the moon, and regained strength as its crescent grows, but never escaped its waxing and waning. Death has been denied me. You ask if the old fear death as the young do, and I must answer that they do, but that their fear is often mixed with longing. I see now that you, though a young man in the prime of life, also dream of death as you gaze into the dying fire, but I tell you, it is the duty of every man to live out his destiny, no matter the fears he may experience and the hardships he may encounter. That is all we learn in life: that we are bound to the wheel of destiny. Do you know your destiny, young man?'

'How can I,' Lycas said, 'since I have never thought of such a thing, but have lived from day to day? But you are right that I am tempted to despair, for I am on a mission on behalf of my friend whom I love, and who is sick and has been, as I believe, bewitched, and when I looked into the fire, I saw his face, and then it died; and I thought this betokened his death, and if he is dead, then I do not wish to live.'

'What you saw in the fire was but fancy, the image of your bad dreams,' the old man said. 'It was not your friend you saw die in the fire, but your own faith, and so you flee in your own mind from the mission on which you tell me you are engaged, wishing to seek refuge in some desert, or to escape from the world.'

Lycas began to weep.

'That is so,' he said. 'I am a coward.'

'Fear is not cowardice. Only surrender to fear is that. You proved yourself a man and a brave one when you refused to surrender to the temptation of the dance, and to lose yourself in bestial pleasure. So do not abandon courage now, for courage is the virtue without which all others are worthless.'

Lycas could not answer. He had never thought of himself as being brave. Perhaps he had never truly thought about himself at all, in this way.

'We are born in the dark,' the old man said, 'and we struggle to find a path through the dark forest of life. There was a Greek philosopher who saw the image of man as one carrying a lamp by the light of which he hoped to find someone or something which was truly good. But the wind blows and the lamp is extinguished. Does that mean that the good itself is extinguished, or merely that we must be courageous and light the lamp again?'

Lycas did not understand what the old man was saying, and yet he was strengthened by his words. The old man returned to his book. He moved his lips as he read, and his expression was serene. Lycas lay down and composed himself to sleep. Day was almost upon them, and it would not be long before the sun rose and he had to ride to make as much as he could of the short winter day. But he felt at peace now, as not before, and the last thought in his mind as he fell asleep was 'I am no longer afraid of the Lady.'

*(Our author does not tell us who this old man was. Perhaps he did not know. Reading what he has written, it first occurred to me that Lycas had again met the wandering Jew whom he and

Marcus had encountered in the prison in Constantinople. But if so, clearly Lycas did not recognise him.

However, in my travels, I have conversed at length with rabbinical scholars, masters of the Kabbala, and from them I have learned that, according to one legend, there is not a single solitary figure, the Wanndering Jew, but that there are in truth thirty-six of these beings, known as the Lamed-Vaw Tzadikim or the Thirty-Six Righteous. Their number is known to few because each travels alone, and so each is called a 'Nistar' or 'Mysterious One'. The Nistar manifests himself as poor, lowly and aged. He is humble. It is, say the rabbis, by his humility and goodness that the Nistar may be known, though never with certainty; for this reason, it is meet to treat with reverence any old man who is poor, good and humble, since he may be one of the Thirty-Six Righteous, for whose sake, according to the teaching, the world is preserved.

May not Lycas's companion have been a Nistar?)*

XXXI

Throughout the long journey to the castle, Lycas thought deeply about the manner in which he should approach the Lady. He was still afraid, but the blind terror he had felt and which had come close to unmanning him had departed, blown away by the old man's words of wisdom. He whistled as he rode up the track on a morning that was turning from sapphire to turquoise, and not even the first sight of the battlements frowning over the treetops could daunt his spirit. Before they parted, the old man had laid his hands on his head and given what seemed like a blessing, though Lycas was ignorant of the tongue in which he spoke it; it had fortified his spirit, and he wore the memory like armour.

He rode across the bridge over the moat, and hammered on the iron-studded door with the pommel of his dagger. A wicket gate was opened. He explained his business to the porter or sentinel and was admitted. Then he was left to kick his heels in the courtyard, where girls were washing linen at the well, and had to endure their speculative scrutiny.

It was noon before a thick-set fellow in a purple livery approached him, and, in an insolent tone, demanded to know why he sought an audience with his Lady.

Lycas smiled, courteously, as he had often seen Marcus smile, but would give no answer.

The question was repeated. Again he remained silent.

For the third time the question was put to him, and now Lycas slipped his hand into his jerkin and withdrew a lace napkin spotted with blood which had belonged to the Green Knight and been given to him to serve as a password.

The man in livery blenched, took the napkin without a word, gave Lycas a long assessing stare, and, returning into the castle, left him again. Lycas whistled an air that he had often heard the

Green Knight chant in his cups. The girls washing linen at the well nudged each other and giggled. Jackdaws squabbled on the battlements. Lycas waited, outwardly calm, till the servant came back and commanded him to enter the castle. He led Lycas through long dark corridors and up a twisting stair to an apartment high in a tower. He ushered Lycas in, and stationed himself as a guard at the stairhead.

The room was dark, though the sun was shining in the courtyard and was now high in the sky. The walls of the apartment were covered with black hangings, like so many dusky shrouds, and the Lady, herself dressed in black velvet, sat at the narrow slit-window with her back to Lycas. He hesitated, waiting for her to address him. But she said nothing. So he advanced and turned to face her, and at once felt her eyes directed on him, as if they would penetrate and take possession of his soul. He resisted his first impulse to speak, for he guessed that if he compelled her to break the silence he would gain an advantage.

In this he was wise, for it is written that he who preserves silence retains mastery.

So they remained a long time, minutes passing, while they were engaged in a wordless duel, and he accustomed himself to meet her gaze, steadily, and not to flinch.

At last she spoke:

'You are presumptuous,' she said, 'and greatly daring to force yourself upon me.'

He inclined his head in acknowledgement, but still said nothing.

'Where is my knight?' she said.

'I think Milady knows where,' Lycas said, for he was convinced that by her terrible power of magic she had kept track of their journey.

'Why have you come here?'

Lycas smiled to hear the question direct.

'Milady knows why I have come, on account of the love I bear my friend, and on account of the magic you have wrought on him. He simpers like a girl and does not know who he is.'

'And you have come to plead.'

The scorn in her voice cut Lycas like the North Wind that blows from the mountains.

'Pleading were vain,' Lycas said, as the knight had instructed him.

A wintry smile crossed her face.

'But I am remiss,' she said. 'You have doubtless journeyed far, and I have offered you neither wine nor meat.'

She clapped her hands and the servant entered from the stair-head. She ordered him to bring bread and wine.

Lycas said, 'I shall neither eat nor drink here,' for he knew that to do so would give her power over him. 'I have already broken my fast at the inn where I passed the night.'

She frowned, seeing he was well-armoured. Then she passed her hands over a dish of oil that sat, simmering, on the little table by her side. She murmured an incantation, in a tongue unknown to Lycas. Dark smoke rose from the dish and formed itself into the image of a figure. The Lady, the Perfect One, as Lycas remembered she chose to be named, continued to murmur her chant, and as she did so, the smoke was dispelled, and the Indian boy whom Lycas and Marcus had been presented with when they first came to the castle stood again before Lycas now. But whereas on that former occasion he had appeared to have the stature of a mere child, now he was tall as Lycas, and as well-formed. He smiled at Lycas, beckoningly, and slipped his long-fingered hands within the loincloth which was the only garment he wore. His smile, the soft moans he uttered, and the sinuous movement of his shapely limbs all promised Lycas delight. Lycas knew temptation, and felt the Lady's eager desire that he should succumb. He knew fear too. The boy stretched out his hands to him, letting the loincloth fall away, and Lycas felt the arms slip round his neck, drawing his head forward to the tempter. But the image of Marcus torn from his true self came to him, and strengthened him, and he cried out in rebuke and denial. His cry seemed to cause all expression to vanish from the boy's face. He drew back with a soft sigh, and slowly, as if in disappointment, was consumed in the smoke from which he had emerged.

And all this happened in the time it might take a man to recite the Lord's Prayer.

When the Lady saw that her wiles had failed, and that Lycas was proof against this temptation too, which she had not doubted would master him, she drew back in her chair. Her face darkened and put on years, and again she asked him how he had dared to force himself upon her.

'I am armed with the power of love,' he said. 'You have stolen my friend's soul, and I am come to request that you restore it to him.'

He spoke politely, as if what he asked was a mere nothing. The his mildness of his manner surprised the Lady, but did not at once disarm her.

'Are you not afraid?' she said. 'You speak of power and yet you have committed yourself to mine. Why should I not have you bound in chains and consigned to a dungeon? Why should I not have you killed and fed to the fowls of the air?'

These were of course questions which had perturbed Lycas on his journey to the castle, and to which he had found no answer. But now he said merely,

'I ask you to restore what it was not yours to take.'

Then he took a small flask from the satchel which he wore attached to his sword-belt. As he did so, the very grace of his body and his gesture, and the mild sadness of his eyes seemed to exert dominion over the Lady.

'You took his soul,' he said again, 'and it is in your power to restore it.'

'You are mad,' she said.

'No,' he replied. 'Not mad, unless it is madness to wish for sanity in this broken world.'

He did not know whence the words came. He had not thought to speak them, but all his fear had gone, and now he knew himself to be master of the moment.

But it seemed as if she was not listening to him, as if her thoughts had floated beyond that tower-room and travelled on the winds of the world. Yet he knew this to be a ruse, as he also knew it was a duel between them. He felt hatred seethe within her, and yet he was unmoved, calm as a summer noon. Now that his fear had departed, he knew only pity for her. Yet he knew also he must not give way to pity.

'I tell you,' she said, 'I know nothing of what you are speaking, nothing of any stolen souls.'

Lycas took the stopper from the flask.

'If you refuse,' he said, 'I must follow another course. You have destroyed a soul, for such theft is destruction, and you will not set right the wrong you have done my friend. So I am now going to destroy your body, and nothing will ever repair it. I am going to destroy your beauty, so that you will never again show your face among men, and never charm another as you have all your life charmed those who came before you. A body for a soul, a soul for a body . . . which, Milady, shall it be?'

He held up the flask, and toyed with it before her eyes as if it had been a precious jewel; and indeed, to Lycas, no jewel could have been as precious as that flask then was.

'A body for a soul, a soul for a body,' he said again. 'The liquid in this flask will burn flesh and bone into hideous deformity. Which shall it be? Restored soul and beauty preserved, or soul and body both destroyed?'

'She is vain,' the Green Knight had said to him. 'There is no one vainer.'

Now he had put it to the test. A dry sound came from her throat, like expiring hope.

'You have won,' she said, and bent over her dish of oil and once again murmured an incantation. Lycas shivered, for suddenly he felt the indecency of what she had done. Her mutterings grew faint and all the blood fled from her face.

'It is done,' she said. 'Your friend sleeps, and will rise himself again. As for you . . .'

'As for me,' Lycas said, 'I have done only what needs be done. And now you must ride with me.'

'Ride with you? Do you not trust me?'

'Lady,' Lycas said, 'do you still take me for a fool that you talk of trust?'

And so, with many sighs and some tears, she submitted, and they set off for the forest hut where Marcus lay.

(We cannot suppose that our author intends that this ridiculous story should be read literally, for he is careless of detail, and unconcerned with probability. It is an allegory in which Light and Dark struggle for mastery of Marcus's soul. It may be that he had read and recalled the temptation of St Antony, as recounted by the Bishop Athanasius, who describes how, 'in his first struggle towards the light', the Devil came before Antony in the form of an Indian boy, dark, slender, and lovely as the dawn, to whom, resisting, the saint-to-be said, 'Thou hast indeed done wisely to appear before me in this form, for thou art black in thy nature, and as pitiably weak as a boy brought low by well-merited chastisement.' As for verisimilitude, if any should dispute my reasoning, let him consider this: that there was indeed nothing to prevent the Lady, had this story been true, from having Lycas confined, as she threatens, in chains, or put to death, thrown over the castle wall, or tortured, or otherwise destroyed. Therefore, I say that this tale, in itself ridiculous, is to be read allegorically, in which reading it acquires great and cogent force.)

XXXII

Lycas was overjoyed to find Marcus restored to his right mind, but surprised that he looked on the Lady with indifference, and asked who she was and why she had come. He was about to explain when Sir Gavin drew him aside and warned him that since Marcus had no memory of recent days, he would be wise to be silent on the subject. He himself – the knight continued – would be happy to see the back of the Lady, who, however, much chastened by her defeat, did not even upbraid him for his desertion. Nevertheless, the knight was agitated by her presence, for he held her in much dread.

When they rode off, they left her, at Sir Gavin's insistence, with the old woman, who promised the knight that she would keep her there for as long as he wished. She gave this promise all the more willingly because she had been charmed by Marcus, distressed by his illness, and was displeased to learn that the Lady was responsible for it. And so they left the sorceress (as Lycas now called her) carrying swill to the old woman's swine.

'She is humbled now,' Sir Gavin said, 'but when she recovers, well, the fires of Hell will freeze, my lad, before she forgets to be revenged on you. On us all, I daresay. It's a pity you did not do as I advised and slit her throat.'

However, they spoke nothing of their fears to Marcus, who was now all the more eager to put delay behind him and seek out the Princess Honoria.

He had not, however, forgotten the duty he owed his poor wife Artemisia, and when they halted at an inn, he wrote a letter telling her something of their fortunes and misfortunes, and assuring her that she was ever in his mind.

'It is not true,' he said, 'but such departures from the truth are, I understand, a necessary kindness such as all who are caught in marriage must find themselves employing.'

'Just so,' Lycas said, who cared nothing for talk of Artemisia.

As for him, he reflected that it was wise of Sir Gavin to have insisted that they lead the Lady's horse off with them.

'I doubt whether she can work magic from the old woman's hut,' he thought, 'and it is a long and dangerous walk through the forest.'

So Lycas lifted up his voice and sang merrily as they journeyed towards Italy.

But, eager though Marcus was to regain his native land and put himself once more at the service of his lady, the Princess Honoria – who had, however, as I shall reveal more exactly at a later moment when my narrative is ripe, utterly forgotten her champion, to whom indeed, such was her fickleness, she had given scarce a thought since he had, as she imagined, failed in his mission to Alaric the Visigoth – yet events now conspired to delay him still further.

It is now necessary to lift our gaze from Marcus and his companions and return to the city of Constantine in order to paint a true picture of the dissension there which would give rise to the next chapter in our hero's story.

XXXIII

You will remember, my Prince, that Marcus had fallen victim while in the city to the turmoil which religion has ever stirred up there. But at the time in which I recounted these events it was not needful and would have been confusing to enter into particular details.

For the art of narrative, of which I am a master, having studied the writing of history for many years, consists especially in placing each event in its proper setting. This I have learned from Titus Livius and Josephus (who wrote a History of the Jews, which I would not recommend, it being partial), and also from the evangelists, Matthew, Mark, Luke and John, of whom the greatest, though not the most lucid, is John, be he for ever blessed and his name revered.

But I digress, which, however, is no sin in narrative, if the way of the digression be pleasant. Rather, you are to think of the digression (when I digress) as a staging post or hospitable inn where you may rest on the journey of the narrative. Though Horace tells us, admiringly, of Homer that he always hastens to the outcome and plunges his listener into the heart of things as though they were already familiar to him – and this is good advice – yet it is also agreeable to mind that other precept of the poet, and hasten slowly, keeping hold of fleeting time, which, when flown, is as Virgil tells us 'irretrievable'.

And so the wise or cunning or 'canny', as we say in my native Scotland, story-teller will vary his pace, now hurrying on, now lingering by the way, now scudding the waves with wind-filled sail, now languishing in gardens of delight. And this is the art and craft of the matter.

So, let us leave this inn where we have rested in our imagination, as Marcus, Lycas and Sir Gavin took their ease at a mountain tavern where they fed on the flesh of lambs roasted on a spit and garnished with aromatic herbs – thyme, marjoram, and fennel-seeds – and drank a green wine of the district; and let us plunge into the fetid cesspit of ecclesiastical politics.

Do not, however, let your eyelids fall in the expectation that this will be dry stuff. Few things rouse the passions more than the quarrels of churchmen, and this is because each supposes that the Almighty God, by means of the Holy Spirit, speaks through him.

Now it so happened that, some years previously, when the seat of the archbishop had fallen vacant, the eunuch Eutropius, moved in a manner that was unaccustomed, had, on a journey in the east, been struck with admiration for the sermons of one John, a priest of Antioch. So eloquent was this man that he was given the name of Chrysostom, which means Golden Mouth. He had studied under the celebrated pagan teacher of rhetoric Libanius, who ever after lamented that his most gifted pupil had been, as he put it, stolen by the Christians. Others, however, saw in John's resistance to the wiles of the Greek sophist the surest sign that he had been chosen by God. And they were confirmed in this opinion by the knowledge that he had passed six years in the desert, where he conquered the lusts of the flesh that are common to all men, and especially urgent in men of the finest and highest spirit, and had there subjected himself to the most austere and painful of penances.

This paragon, having won a mighty reputation for eloquence and piety during his years in Antioch, was, as I say, translated to the see of Constantinople, second only to Rome itself. Eutropius soon regretted his choice, for John Chrysostom displayed an independence of mind and spirit which did him honour, but quickly offended the Empress Eudoxia. It was one thing, she said, to call sinners to repentance, and indeed that was the proper work of a prelate. But it was quite otherwise and reprehensible when the same prelate officiously and insolently stirred up the populace against the court, which he denounced for luxury, cupidity and vice. Moreover, the rash priest even named the Empress herself as chief among sinners.

It was not to be tolerated. Eutropius, now repenting of his

former patronage of the holy man, and fearing that the Empress, on whom alone he depended, would turn against him, bestirred himself to be rid of the turbulent priest. He therefore sent to Theophilus, the Archbishop of Alexandria, in the name of the Empress, whose fury against Chrysostom had been sharpened since he compared her to Jezebel, the wicked wife of Ahab, King of Israel, who had persecuted the prophet Elijah, with whom, it may be, the archbishop had come to identify himself. This Theophilus, corrupt, simoniac, greedy for riches and lavish in ostentation, hated Chrysostom, whose virtues were a rebuke to his vices, and was only too eager to head a conspiracy against the saintly one.

You must know, my Prince, that the quarrels of kings are mild in comparison to the quarrels of ecclesiastics. And the reason is this: that every churchman, once he has attained power, is puffed up with arrogance and pride, believing himself to be the mouth and interpreter of the Divine Will. Furthermore, they are all jealous of superior merit, as I have learned, painfully, and to my cost.

So Theophilus, eager to destroy his rival, landed at Constantinople at the head of a detachment of Egyptian marines, whose task it was to overawe and, if necessary, subdue the populace, who were greatly attached to their archbishop on account of his famed austerity of life, and because he pleased them by attacking the imperial court, and exposing its vices for their delight. Theophilus brought also a company of eastern bishops, all of whom owed their elevation to the bribes they had paid him; and they were sufficient to assure him of a majority in the synod which he convened in the suburb of Chalcedon. It was Eutropius who chose this suburban location, where the bishops might debate insulated from the passions of the mob and free of the terror with which these passions might fill them.

Chrysostom himself disdained to obey a summons to this assembly, which he declared to be illegal. This was foolish of him, since it denied him the use of his strongest weapon, which was his own eloquence. Moreover, there is a Greek proverb of which he should have taken note: 'The absent are always wrong.'

Accordingly, he declined or ignored four summonses to answer the charges, listed in forty-seven articles, which his enemies had devised. The scope of the accusation was wide, ranging from the allegation that he had celebrated the Mass at uncanonical hours to a charge of heretical opinions concerning the doctrine of Original Sin, and another of buggering altar-boys. Some were frankly ridiculous: for instance, he was said to have employed holy nuns from the Convent of St Mary Magdalene to lay ice-packs on his genitals to subdue his lusts; and how this sat with the charge of buggering altar-boys, I do not know.

Be that as it may, his absence acquitted the synod of the need to examine these allegations. He was condemned for disobedience and contempt of the ecclesiastical court, and his deposition was pronounced. Theophilus then hastened to the palace to request the Emperor to ratify this decision, which the Empress Eudoxia, acting as usual on behalf of her imbecile son, was quick to do. She declared that she had never been so deceived in any man as in the erstwhile archbishop; and Eutropius, relieved by the success of his conspiracy and assured of the Empress's continued favour, put it about that Chrysostom had proved himself a 'whited sepulchre', like the Pharisees condemned by Christ himself. Then Theophilus modestly suggested, after prompting by the eunuch, that the language which the deposed archbishop had employed against the Empress showed him to have been guilty of treason, for which the penalty was death. The Empress would have been only too willing to agree, but she feared the anger of the people. Accordingly, she contented herself with ordering his arrest and banishment, and so he was seized in his palace – at his prayers, men said – and conducted to the banks of the Euxine for transportation.

The news soon spread and inflamed the populace. The Empress had been wise to fear their anger, foolish to fail to guard against its explosion. Theophilus escaped their fury, disguised, some say, as a washerwoman. Others were less happy. The Egyptian marines and some two hundred monks, whose dissipation had provoked the anger of Chrysostom and aroused the scorn and hatred of the people, were slaughtered in the streets. (Some of the Egyptians had their genitals cut off and stuffed into the mouths of monks, a vulgar reference to these monastics' supposed sexual tastes or preference.) The mob howled round the imperial palace itself, and the threats which were carried to the ears of the Empress and her favourite threw them into ignoble panic. This was intensified when a detachment of the palace guards, moved either by fear or indignation and religious fervour (though the former appears more probable), deserted their posts and allied themselves to the rioters. In short, for a few hours it seemed as if the established order had been overthrown and mere anarchy would be loosed upon the Empire.

Eutropius, totally overcome by terror, fell to his knees, and clasping his hands round those of the Empress, implored her to rescind the decree of banishment and restore the archbishop to his seat. Eudoxia despised his terror and saw the good sense of his advice. The order was given, the mob was appeased, and, from this day on, the bond between the Empress and her favourite eunuch was loosened, for she saw that in a crisis he was in mind and spirit, as in other essentials, less than a man. Eutropius felt her disdain, resented it, and knew himself to be helpless; there was not a man in the palace or indeed the city who would not have willingly put a halter round his neck. So he who had terrified so many was now condemned to live in perpetual fear and corrosive anxiety. Truly God is just.

Meanwhile the city rejoiced. The archbishop returned in triumph, being chaired into his cathedral on the shoulders of his supporters, who were so filled with delight that it seemed as if they worshipped Chrysostom rather than the Lord he himself so eloquently served. In the general euphoria none noticed that the sentence of dethronement passed by the synod had not itself been annulled, but only the sentence of banishment passed in the name of the Emperor.

Chrysostom, whatever his piety and true religious zeal, was unfortunately lacking in common sense, and, a zealot, rash in speech, he had no feeling for that moderation with which wise statesmen seek to render temporary success enduring. For, my Prince, you must learn that in statecraft there are few moments so perilous as those in which victory appears absolute. So it proved with the archbishop.

Far indeed from practising moderation, he now cast himself loose of the shackles which formerly propriety had bound him with. Remembering only the hostility of the Empress, and overconfident in his momentary triumph, he was blind to danger, deaf to warnings, and oblivious of the fickle nature of the mob. Unable to imagine that they might transfer their enthusiasm to a new hero, he could not suppose that the Empress would set herself to provide them with one. So, no longer content with denouncing vices with at least some restraint or circumspection, he was more free and outspoken than before in his denunciations of the Empress and her immorality. 'Herodias,' he cried out from his pulpit, 'is again furious. Herodias again dances or summons her daughter Salome to the dance. Herodias once more demands the head of John.'

He spoke truth, of course, but it was rash to do so; and this insolent allusion was more than Eudoxia could forgive.

So she determined to be revenged on the audacious priest. But, being a woman of infinite self-control, she was prepared to bide her time, and not only because she knew that revenge is a dish most savoured when eaten cold, but also because she was ready to wait till the mob tired of its adoration of the archbishop and grew weary of his prohibition of the pleasures of the flesh, which, after all, are among the few that the poor can enjoy as abundantly as the rich.

So it was that, while she was pondering on how best to satisfy her lust for revenge, she remembered Marcus. In truth, the young man had often come to her mind, for Eudoxia, though now over forty and with blackened teeth, remained lustful and sensible of the charms of handsome youths. So the image of Marcus was often before her eyes, and in particular she dreamed of his legs, which were, as I may have mentioned, long and beautifully shaped. She therefore now determined to fetch him back to Constantinople to be both her pleasure and her instrument of revenge. And so she sent messengers in search of him.

When Eutropius learned of this, his terror was still more

intense. Unlike the Empress, he had not forgotten Artemisia, and knew that Marcus would at once demand to see her, which could not be permitted on account of the cruelty with which she had been treated. Made for the moment bold by his fear, he reminded the Empress that Marcus had a wife, and of what had been done to her.

'Does she still live?' the Empress said. 'If not, why then, she died of fever in my arms, and if so, then see to her removal. And we shall tell the same story.'

So Eutropius sent slaves to search for Artemisia in the meanest quarters of the city. But they could not find her, for reasons which I shall later reveal. The eunuch did not, however, dare to tell the Empress of his failure, but instead assured her that Artemisia was no more. It was a lie born of cowardice, and such lies return to plague their author.

XXXIV

Marcus and Lycas were taking their ease in the inn, while Sir Gavin snored, stretched out on a window-seat. Snoring, as I have told you before, is commonly described as 'stertorous', a word which originally meant no more than noisy, but has now taken on a more rumbling thunderous sense. Sir Gavin snored as if he had been a very Vulcan (whom the Greeks knew as Hephaestus), who has now been transformed into the patron saint of smiths and all canny workers in metals.

Our hero and his friend found the noise comforting rather than oppressive. That, I may say in passing, was not the opinion of the citizens of Sybaris, famous in the Ancient World for their love of luxury, ease and tranquillity. They indeed were so disturbed by the noise of hammering that they banished the smiths and other metal-workers from their city, sending them to the town now known as Acri in the mountains of the Sila. Acri is still there, and presently is the stronghold of one of the most obnoxious of your barons, Sir Guy de Montalto; but Sybaris is no more, vanished, buried under the sands of time. Some teachers would point a stern moral drawn from this story, but, for my part, I choose not to do so, regarding the fates of the two cities as one of the accidents of history, which are always inexplicable.

But I digress, if only for your better instruction.

As I was saying, Marcus and Lycas found Sir Gavin's snoring agreeably companionable, for they had both grown fond of the knight. Admittedly, their affection was tinged with mockery. So, for example, when Lycas said, 'He is a very mastiff for courage,' Marcus replied, 'And for intelligence also,' whereat they both laughed.

'Do you remember,' Marcus said, 'the knight's story of the Holy Grail?'

'In a sort,' Lycas answered, 'though to tell truth it made little sense to me, and so I do not recall it well.'

'I dreamed of it last night. We were travelling in a land I did not know, you and I – for you were with me in my dream, as in life, Lycas. We followed a white road. It was dark, with no moon, and yet the road was white. It seemed to me that a third person was with us . . .'

'Sir Gavin?' Lycas said.

'I think not, for he did not speak. So it can't have been our friend the knight who is never silent but when he sleeps.'

'Not then either,' Lycas said. 'Listen to him snoring now.'

'Moreover, when I counted, there were always only you and I together, but when I looked there was another by our side, in a dark mantle and moving with a gliding walk. "Who is the third who walks always beside you?" I asked, but you answered each time, "It is nobody, just you and me, Marcus." And yet I felt his presence. So the road climbed and then we came to this hollow in the mountains, and now there was moonlight, faint as the breath of Spring, and there was a sound of murmuring over the short grass, murmuring that was music and near a song. We walked over tumbled graves, with ivy twining round the simple stones, and came to the empty chapel, which a voice told me was the wind's home. It had no windows and the door swung open. So I entered, and you followed me, and, of a sudden, a light shone over the altar – but there was no altar – and a voice spoke, clearly – and yet I cannot remember what it said, and this perplexes me, puzzles and dismays me. Oh, Lycas, if only you had dreamed my dream as you were part of it, we might know what the voice said.'

'I do not think men can dream each other's dreams,' Lycas said.

'No.' Marcus shook his head and stirred a log in the fire with his foot. 'But it was so beautiful and held out such a promise to me. One thing I know for certain. I shall dream that dream again, and one day will live it in reality.'

'Reality?' Lycas said. 'The reality is that we should sleep if we are to ride far in the morning.'

But they were not to sleep that night, for at that very moment there came banging at the inn door. The innkeeper, grumbling, raised himself from the settle where he was stretched out. There was a demanding shout of 'Open in the name of the Emperor.' He unbolted the door and six soldiers filled the room. One of them, a centurion, addressed Marcus, asking him to identify himself, and when he had done so, announced that the Empress commanded his presence.

For an instant Lycas thought they were under arrest, and looked wildly for his sword or some other weapon. But the centurion had saluted smartly, and now apologised for the urgency of his mission, which would brook no delay.

'As soon as my men have had a bite and a sup to drink, we must be on our way,' he said. 'Her Imperial Nibs's command. I count myself fortunate we have happened on you so soon.'

So they roused Sir Gavin, who coughed and snorted and cursed, but, like the old campaigner he was, did not allow his mutterings and indignant complaints to delay his preparation for departure.

'Needs must,' he said to Lycas. 'There's no rest for the wicked this side of the grave. And often not in it either, from all I've heard tell.'

And so they mounted, and under a full moon, with a cold wind at their back, set off for the city.

XXXV

As they rode towards the city, the captain of the guard engaged Marcus in conversation, for he was curious about this youth for whom the Empress had so urgently sent. Marcus replied to his enquiries with the utmost frankness, and had no reason not to do so, even if he had been given to duplicity, which, as we know, was foreign to his nature. He confessed openly that he had no idea as to why the Empress required his presence, assured the captain that he had met her only on one occasion, and indeed scarcely knew Constantinople, was ignorant of the palace and the ways of the court. The captain was charmed by his manner, and the talk soon moved to other, but equally perilous, matters.

The vile persecution which the Christians had suffered at the hands of the emperors had long since, as you know, given way to the imperial enforcement of the Faith which their predecessors had attempted to suppress. Indeed, Christians now had only their fellow believers to fear, and, as we have seen in the case of John Chrysostom, engaged in ferocious quarrels within the Church, such as have enlivened and disgraced the Faith ever since.

(Is this a reference once again to the Cathars, for whom, despite his slanderous portrayal of the Perfects, among whom the Lady he does not name was numbered, we may yet suspect our author of displaying a certain tenderness?)

Moreover, so certain were the Christians that they alone possessed the true Faith, in which judgement they were of course correct, that the intolerance once directed at them was now in turn visited by emperors and bishops on all those who still clung, as wretched mariners seeking to save themselves from shipwreck may put their trust in floating spars, to other older and now prohibited faiths. And indeed Marcus, on his second visit to the city, had been caught up in the frenzy which intolerance of pagan practices could provoke; and, though innocent, had suffered, as I have already narrated.

It was therefore expedient that those who still adhered to proscribed religions should do so secretly and speak of it only to other initiates. But wine is a great loosener of tongues and serves as a key to unlock restraint, and so it happened that in the tavern where they lodged on the first night of their journey, the talk turned to religion.

The captain supposed Marcus was a Christian. His tone was cold, suggesting that he was not one himself. Marcus agreed that he had been brought up in the Faith and believed it to be the true Faith.

'But,' he said, 'since I left home and journeyed far and wide, I have met all sorts of men and women, and I have concluded . . .' He paused. 'What have I concluded? That there is no firm conclusion.'

The captain picked flesh from the lake trout and ate.

'When I was a young man,' he said, 'my father used to tell me of the Emperor Julian, who was reared as a Christian, being of the family of Constantine, but studied in Greece and rejected Christianity as a religion for women, slaves, and milksops. He was initiated into the mysteries at Eleusis, and became a great general. Pity he was killed young. Don't repeat what I say, but the Empire's breaking up. I blame the Christians myself.'

'But why should that be,' Marcus said, 'if, as we believe, our Faith is true?'

'Did not your Christ whom you worship say his kingdom was not of this world?' the captain replied. 'How then can those who profess to follow him guide the affairs of a mighty empire?'

Sir Gavin left off gnawing at a chop-bone, and waved it at the speaker.

'Speaking as a plain man,' he said, 'a Yorkshireman brought up to value common sense, I have learned to pay no attention to what priests say. In my experience, which is considerable, for I've travelled and fought all over the Empire, from the misty Cheviots to the Arabian sands, I've learned that religion is one thing, and the arts of war and statecraft very different. Make a priest a bishop and nine times out of ten you have made yourself a politician. That's what I think, and so I see no confusion such as you suggest. The priests may preach that Christ's kingdom is not of this world, but believe you me, my dear chap, they don't act on that preaching. Between you and me and the gatepost, Christian emperors don't differ a whit from the old pagan ones. You could put the difference in your eye and you wouldn't notice it. That's fact, friend, not theory or theology. All the theology in the world doesn't affect the fact of power.'

That Sir Gavin spoke truly, my Prince, has been proved frequently in my own lifetime by the acts of the Bishops of Rome.

'Besides,' Marcus said, 'weren't the pagan emperors priests themselves? I have read that Julius Caesar was proud to hold the office of Pontifex Maximus, high priest of all Roman cults.'

'Be that as it may,' the Captain said, 'and I honour you for the defence you make of your Faith, nevertheless I hold to my opinion. Your Christian God is a God of peace, and this is a world of war. How then can those who serve your God display mastery in this world?'

'I have no doubt your question is a good one,' Marcus said. 'Yet Constantine, who made Christianity the religion of the Empire, was, as I have heard, no mean soldier.'

'Though Constantine, as you say, betrayed the gods of his fathers, he took care not to be baptised a Christian till he knew he was dying. And that proves to my mind that he knew that the Christian Faith and the demands of power could not be reconciled. You must know, young man, that I have thought deeply on these matters, and that my aversion from your Faith is no vulgar prejudice.'

'Constantine was a shit,' Sir Gavin said. 'I take it we are all friends here and I can speak my mind.'

Lycas sighed.

'All this conversation,' he said, 'is above my head, or beyond my wits. I was brought up a poor country boy and we learned which gods and spirits had to be appeased with offerings. But we had no time or taste for this sort of discussion, and so I am, as I say, out of my depth. But I would be very pleased, sir, to learn something of the religion you practise yourself, and of the faith that you follow.'

'My faith,' the captain said, 'is now proscribed, outlawed, persecuted; and yet why should I conceal it, why should I be ashamed to acknowledge that my master is Mithras, God of the Morning, Light-Bearer, the unconquered God of Battles, the guide of souls whom he leads from this earthly life back to the light whence we have all issued? Even Constantine himself issued coins bearing the inscription "To the Sun, the unconquered", that is, Mithras, giver of victory, god of the soldiers.'

The captain had by now drunk deep of the purple wine, and his voice had become thick, but there was no mistaking the fervency with which he spoke of his god, in a manner which impressed Lycas and moved Marcus, even though he knew him to be in error.

'For his sake and in his honour,' the captain said, 'I have endured the castigations required of an initiate. I have fasted long, swum a wide circle in a grotto black as night, seized fire in my naked hands, lain twenty days in snow on a high mountain, submitted to scourging, and endured other torments too numerous to mention. And is all this now to be thought of as worthless, even – in the quaint language of you Christians – sinful? I have passed through the degrees of raven, warrior, and lion, and have clasped the garland tossed from a sword, and pressed it down on my shoulder, for Mithras himself is my garland and my crown. The legions marched, an ever-victorious army, borne up by Mithras, the god of the rock. And all for nothing? Now the monks, those filthy animals, have decreed a new worship. In the place of the gods they now call on us to revere the most miserable and contemptible slaves, whom they style martyrs, creatures who for a multitude of crimes were justly condemned by the state to an ignominious death. These we are now commanded to honour. Is it any wonder, then, that, while all the frontiers of the Empire are menaced by barbarians – among whom the most recent and most terrible are the Huns – devil-worshippers and, as I have heard asserted, cannibals, at this awful moment in the history of the Empire, Rome should lie in ruins, sacked by the Visigoths, who also profess themselves to be Christians, and that Constantinople itself should be given over to riot provoked by the hatred of a dissolute empress – saving your presence, since she has sent for you, for some reason or other – by her hatred, I say, for a turbulent and insolent priest who presumes to tell princes and generals how they should conduct themselves?'

'But you say yourself,' Lycas said, 'that this empress is dissolute, and certainly on the one occasion I was before her, she appeared to me to be peculiarly horrible, as was the disgusting eunuch by whom, men say, she is guided. So isn't it right that she should be reproved?'

'It's not the business of priests, young man,' the captain growled, 'to seek to govern the Empire. She may be a bitch, indeed she is, and the young emperor an imbecile, as they say, but that doesn't change the facts: that to give authority to priests who have never held a sword in their lives and couldn't draw up a line of battle if you paid them all the gold in Persia is no way to be going on. Besides, these quarrels among you Christians are as ridiculous as they are dangerous to the Empire.'

'It seems to me,' Marcus said, 'that you have some personal animus against our religion which exceeds even your dismay at the damage you believe our Faith has done to the fabric of the Empire.'

The captain drank wine, and sat silent. It seemed to Lycas that he was about to fall asleep. Then he bestirred himself, called to the servant-girl for another flask, and when it was fetched and she had refilled all their cups, he spoke again; and his voice was both hard and sad. There was loneliness in it, and anger, and an echo of desolate places.

'I had a brother,' he said, 'younger than myself, as lively and gamesome a fellow as you could hope to meet. No one was quicker in repartee or with a quip. No one was bolder in love or more forward in war. A Christian priest or monk, a mewling, whining scarecrow of a creature, acquired – how, I can't tell, it is a mystery to me – influence over him, and persuaded him that not only his way of life but the flesh itself was evil. My brother was, as you say, converted. He withdrew from the world. He now lives an anchorite on a rocky islet off Corsica, where it is as if he had been driven by the Furies of old to renounce the way of men. I visited him last year, and found him a credulous exile from all humanity. He mortifies his flesh to save his soul, and takes no pleasure in any of the delights this world offers. In short, he is victim of a creed more vile than the poison Circe fed to Odysseus's sailors. She made only their bodies bestial; my poor brother, for love (he says) of this god of yours, has ... no, I can't go on ...'

So saying, he buried his nose in his beaker. Marcus pitied him, and murmured that even the best religion could take a perverted form. Lycas thought that the brother's self-mortification, though beyond his own understanding, sounded no more absurd that the Mithraic castigations which the captain had boasted of enduring.

Sir Gavin said only, 'What a business, but now we must let the ship go, and sleep on all that we have said and heard.'

But Marcus's last thought, as he fell asleep, was: 'There are more things to admire than to scorn in this man. And yet he is an unbeliever. And yet I feel virtue in him. Well, one either has it or one hasn't, I suppose, and everyone must find his own salvation, whatever that is or may be.'

(I grow more amazed, the further I read, by the audacity of our author. Is he preaching a perfect scepticism to his pupil, the prince? Certainly, his lesson is that the words of priests may clothe a moral nakedness. Alas, how true that is.)

(My predecessor, as editor of these papers, had the knack of missing the target. What is the true message of this conversation so faithfully – or imaginatively – recorded? Is it not that this life is a perpetual quest in which certainty is never to be attained, and that therefore the expression of certainty, from whatever quarter, is to be distrusted? Therefore it is requisite that we be earnest to attain the understanding and knowledge of philosophy, which is an eternal enquiry, much confused by the unclean babblers who lay claim to perfect knowledge when at best – but then how seldom – they do but gaze through a glass darkly. Listen, my brothers, to the beating of angels' wings and to the music of the spheres, for it is in tranquil contemplation of such majesties that humility may give birth to understanding.)

XXXVI

It is common to hate those we have injured. The Empress Eudoxia had done wrong to so many that it was hatred which filled her breast. Indeed it was hatred which fed her vitality. Hatred begets cruelty, and cruelty is an appetite that is never satisfied. All this, as a warning, the captain of the guard told Marcus as they rode towards the city.

'Nor,' he said, 'will she reward loyal service. On the contrary, it offends her. She suspects that it is a mask which conceals disaffection. Moreover, those who are good serve as a standing reproach to her, and it is her chief pleasure to make them feel the cruelty of the world, for that is how she perceives its nature. She had a steward once, a handsome young man, a barbarian. I forget his name. No doubt he had shared her bed – I warn you that she will invite you to do so also, which is why I am telling you this story. Whether it was his virtue that offended her or his beauty that provoked her, no one can tell. But one day, without accusing him of any offence, far less a crime, she commanded two of the guard – men who have served under me, which is why or how I know the story and can vouch for its truth – to seize her steward and bring him before her. Then she ordered the clothes to be stripped from him, and his naked body to be stretched over a table, pinioned at the wrists, which were tied to the table-legs. He moaned pathetically, asking why he was being punished, but she merely smiled. Then the soldiers were ordered to whip him. Naturally, they obeyed, though reluctant. What else could they do. They lashed the young man and he screamed as the leather cut into his flesh, and the Empress smiled, and then she knelt and licked the blood from the young man's buttocks. That's the lady who's requiring your services. Just thought you ought to know, sunshine.'

Marcus was horrified by the story, but thanked the captain for telling it. Beyond that, he made no comment, but rode on, frowning. Though he was still young, he had experienced so much in his travels since leaving home that he had learned wisdom beyond his years. So now he reflected that it is foolish implicitly to believe lurid stories told about the great, for they are always improved in the telling, even when they are not invented. Credulity may bespeak an innocent nature, but is often the mark of a simpleton. No story should be accepted on the evidence of one man's word. He thought that the captain might bear a grudge against the Empress, and so be happy to slander her. Then it occurred to him that he might have been told the story as a test, to prove his loyalty; even on the instructions of the Empress. After all, it was she who had dispatched the man who now slandered her. So he chose to remain silent, and wary. 'After all,' he said to himself, 'I am going to a court where nothing is likely to be clear and straightforward.'

It was evening when, after several days' journeying, during which the captain seemed unnerved by Marcus's reticence and chilly self-control, and himself grew ever more silent, they saw the towers of the city stand out magnificent against a sky of many colours.

'My orders are to take you directly to the palace, no matter at what hour we arrive.'

Marcus smiled in agreement, and asked whether he should come alone or in the company of his friends.

'I have no orders concerning them. They may do as they please, for the time being.'

So, after their passports had been checked at the city gate, Lycas and Sir Gavin repaired to the inn where Marcus had first lodged in Constantinople.

'The woman there will remember me,' Lycas said, 'and since you paid her so generously on our second visit, we may be sure of a friendly reception.'

Marcus was led into the palace by a back way, through a labyrinth of dark dank passages. Sometimes they descended narrow staircases. Once at least they seemed to him to be entering a subterranean prison. At every turn of the way, guards were posted, grim, silent figures who scarcely acknowledged the document which his guide showed to them. There was a sound of running water, and, further off, the howling of wild beasts. Then they mounted another stair, and found themselves before a barred iron gate.

This was opened to them by an unseen hand, without a word being spoken, and they entered a lofty hall. It seemed to Marcus to be peopled chiefly by slaves, dusky Africans, who were engaged in different and sometimes futile occupations. Some stood as if on guard with sabres drawn, but the vacancy of their gaze suggested that they would make but a feeble attempt to repel any aggressor. Others sat, cross-legged, on carpets, as if in the bazaar, and chewed sweetmeats or played games with counters on chequered boards; and these too wore the same empty expression, as if all the animation they might ever have possessed had been drained out of them by some device, and put to a purpose Marcus could not imagine. All were silent. Not a word passed between them and not a glance was given to Marcus and his companion. They were to men as the withered stalks of winter are to the flowering plants of summer.

So, they made their way through a succession of apartments till at last they entered one longer and loftier than the others, with walls coated in marble the colour of mottled flesh. It was but dimly lit, and the oils or gums which fed the lamps gave off a sickly odour, so that Marcus drew his sleeve over his nose and mouth to guard against it.

His guide now commanded that he wait there, and Marcus, using what he knew to be the approved formula, muttered, 'To hear is to obey.'

Left alone, for this hall was apparently forbidden to the African slaves, he employed his reluctant leisure in examining the apartment. At the far end stood a small altar, with a crucifix above it, before which Marcus bowed his head – happy, if truth be told, to remove his gaze from the tormented and all too lifelike figure of Christ, which could be the work only of an artist inspired or excited by thoughts of pain and cruelty. Nevertheless, he made the sign of the Cross and murmured a prayer.

His wait extended itself. He grew chill and knew the first starting of irrational terror. Then he said to himself, 'This is but a charade to impress you. Well, I am proof against that and entrust myself to the care of the Archangel Michael whom I knew as a child on the slopes of Mount Gargano.'

So he steeled himself for whatever might ensue, and not for the first time wondered whether he would find his wife Artemisia with the Empress, who had promised to care for her.

At last the door which had closed behind his guide opened again, and a young man, dressed as a page in a suit of sky-blue taffeta, entered and advanced to greet him. The youth moved with a mincing or willowy walk, and, when he drew near, Marcus first smelled a sweet scent of attar of roses emnating from his person and then saw that his lips were painted gold and his cheeks sparkled with gilt paint and his eyelids were purple-blue. But when he spoke, announcing himself as Nicanor, a confidential secretary of Her Imperial Highness, his Greek was admirable and his voice musical and more manly than his effeminate appearance had suggested.

'You have travelled far, and in rough company,' he said, with a bright smile, 'and I would advise that you eat and drink before your audience, for Her Imperial Highness is eager to meet you.'

'If she is eager,' Marcus said, puzzled, 'would we not be wise to go to her at once? I have only a small acquaintance with her, but that was sufficient to convince me that she would not like to be kept waiting. Which indeed few princes are prepared to tolerate.'

'Oh, you are right,' the exquisite replied. 'Nevertheless, you must do as I say. In the first place the Empress is at her worship, and in the second' – he laughed and – 'I do assure you that you will need all the strength you have, and so must eat and drink. I do have your best interests at heart, I assure you.'

So saying, he took Marcus by the wrist and led him into a side-chamber where two curly-headed slaves, boys of a dozen years or so, attended a table laden with dishes.

'Let me recommend the lobster,' Nicanor said. 'Nothing is a

choicer accompaniment to this wine from Chios, and besides, it is well known that lobster provokes ardour. Or these pastries, stuffed with calves' brains and sweetbreads, are, I assure you, of a very acceptable delicacy.'

Marcus, surprised to find himself hungry, ate heartily, while his young guide chivvied and teased the slave-boys, even while continuing to press dishes on Marcus, enquire about his journey, warn him of the dangers of the city, add that it had delights also which he would be only too happy to have the opportunity to reveal to Marcus, and examine his appearance in a hand-mirror which he withdrew from his belt.

'You must think I'm vain,' he said, blushing to observe Marcus regard this activity with what seemed like scorn. 'Well, I confess I am. But it is not merely vanity, I assure you. My looks are my only recommendation. I am not well-born and have no great talent or intelligence. I must please by my appearance, and if the Empress takes a dislike to it, then, poof, it's off with me.'

He accompanied these words with a radiant smile and a mischievous look in his eye which made it impossible for Marcus to believe him sincere.

'I assure you,' Nicanor said, reading scepticism in Marcus's look. 'But now we must to Her Imperial . . .'

So he led Marcus again through a veritable maze of corridors, the walls of which were covered with marvellous tapestries depicting scenes from Christ's life, imperial triumphs, strange and wonderful animals, any one of which Marcus would have been happy to pause and admire. But Nicanor was now impatient of any delay, evincing a sharper nervousness the more closely they approached the Empress's sanctum. They came to a door of beaten gold at which he scratched three times. A voice charged them to enter, and they obeyed, Nicanor falling prostrate on the marble floor and crawling towards the Empress.

She was alone, sitting modestly on a stool placed on a dais before the throne. This was of the utmost magnificence, studded with gems – rubies, amethysts and sapphires – and, like Solomon's of old, flanked with two lions, couchant and made of gold or at least gilded metal. Behind the throne rose up a golden tree, in the branches of which were birds, cunningly made and enamelled, and fruit composed of precious stones.

But the Empress herself wore a simple gown of dark and heavy material, and her head was covered with a woollen scarf such as village girls wear when they go to fetch water from the well in winter. Her face was streaked with dust or ash, and tears had made little rivulets through the grime.

Nicanor lifted his head to announce Marcus, who, however, himself astonished by the appearance which the Empress presented, and amazed to find her alone, did no more than bow, stiffly but not awkwardly (for he was incapable of any movement or gesture which was not graceful).

To Nicanor's amazement, the Empress did not appear offended by Marcus's failure to observe the etiquette of the court, but addressed him gently, and – for she was a consummate actress – in near-broken tones welcomed him to Constantinople. Then, in the same halting voice, she commanded Nicanor to go stand by the door and refuse admission to anyone, 'Even,' she added, 'those dearest to me.'

Then she bade Marcus sit by her on the edge of the dais.

'I sent for you because I need your help,' she said, 'and I had hoped that our meeting would be joyful. But, alas . . .' She paused and dabbed her eyes with a kerchief, 'Alas, I have first sad and lamentable news to give you. No doubt you looked eagerly to see your dear wife again. I say "dear", for she has been like a daughter to me. But soon after I sent for you she received word that her father, whom I know you respect, was gravely ill and desired her presence. So, torn between love and duty . . . what would you?'

'She chose duty,' Marcus said, 'as any true Roman would.'

'Indeed yes. She set sail for Greece three days ago, and only this morning . . . how can I tell you – no, it is too terrible . . . I had word that the ship had run aground on dangerous rocks and been sunk with the loss of all aboard. My poor, poor boy . . .' and, saying this, she let her hand lie lightly on Marcus's head. 'There is no comfort,' she said, 'that I or anyone can offer for such a loss. Believe me, it grieves me second only to you yourself.'

So complete a hypocrite was this empress that she moved herself to real tears and nobody could have believed that her emotion was not genuine. Marcus himself wept, and if his tears and sobs were called forth as much by the guilty feelings he had always entertained for Artemisia as by the tepid affection in which he had held her, he cannot be blamed. Love takes its own way and cannot be directed by the will.

'I scarcely dare intrude my business into your grief,' the Empress said, 'and yet I must. Nicanor, fetch us wine.'

She paused, her hand still resting on Marcus's head and now toying negligently (as it seemed) with his hair. When Nicanor had brought wine, and, without requiring a command, had tasted it himself, pronounced it good and safe, and poured goblets for her and for Marcus, she again ordered him to withdraw to the door and stand guard, out of hearing.

As for Marcus, are we to think the worse of him because this news of Artemisia's death and of Melanippos's sickness awoke a surge of hope that he might once again be reunited with his darling Pulcherrima? I think not, for, as I say, the passions are involuntary.

Now the Empress said again, 'I have no comfort to offer you, dear boy. The task I summoned you for is delicate and dangerous. It is an ill moment to speak of it, and yet perhaps not so, for if there is no sure remedy for grief, no balm, yet action and the performance of perilous duty may serve as a drug to ease the pain.'

And then she recounted what I have already narrated: the turmoil in the city occasioned by the impertinent and treasonous (as she called him) archbishop John Chrysostom.

XXXVII

Meanwhile Lycas and Sir Gavin had settled themselves in the tavern, where, as Lycas had expected, the woman who kept the inn had greeted him with enthusiasm. Indeed, she covered his face with happy kisses, enquired anxiously about Marcus, said yet again how much she regretted the misunderstanding that had spoiled their first visit, asked what had become of the pretty girl who had been with them then, and so on. She talked so volubly that Lycas had not time to answer any of her questions, but that did not matter. He understood that they were not really questions but merely expressions of her delight to see him again. She pinched his cheek and called him her pretty darling boy, and all went merrily as a marriage bell, and much more merrily than most marriages themselves prove.

She brought them a great fish stew in which there were all sorts of bony and finny creatures such as that which in Naples we call the *guarracino* but which in Constantinople is known as the *korakino*, the name being derived, as I understand, from the Greek word for raven, which is *korax*. And there were also octopus, squid, scorfano, lobster, huge prawns, crayfish, mullet, and many other delights. The soup was heavily flavoured with garlic and saffron and served with black bread soaked in green olive oil and toasted in the oven.

'A dish fit for an emperor,' cried Sir Gavin, falling to with a will.

The good knight also relished the tavern's retsina, which he quaffed as if it had been the much-praised bitter beer of his native Yorkshire, which is indeed beer that is as superior to the thin beers of Italy as our sun-smacked Falernian or deep-purple Sicilian wines made from grapes grown on volcanic soil are to the sour and incorporeal vintages of the Rhine.

And as he drank, Sir Gavin chanted, unmelodiously, a song of his own composition in praise of wine and women, listing those to whom he had paid court and by whom he had been favoured. Truth to tell, it was but poor verse, and therefore I shall not weary you with it, but the knight's mood was such that it sounded cheerfully in his listeners' ears.

But at last, overcome by wine, the good knight lapsed into sleep, snoring lustily, and, as their hostess, whose name was Dorcas, remarked, 'no less tunefully than the good man's singing'.

Lycas, who as was his custom had drunk but sparingly, though sufficient to do honour to their hostess, now asked her what was the news of the city; for he had been anxious for Marcus's safety since they had received the imperial summons, and so wished to be well acquainted with what was happening. Being an intelligent youth, who had formed careful habits of observation in his travels with Marcus, he had learned that knowledge is power.

When Dorcas heard that Marcus had been recalled to Constantinople at the express command of the Empress, her first excitement at seeing Lycas again having abated, she frowned and bit her lip.

'To speak ill of great ones,' she said, 'is not my habit, for it is dangerous, and so in my position I have always found it expedient to keep my head down and my opinions to myself, yet nevertheless . . .' and here she paused, and refilled Lycas's cup. 'Nevertheless,' she continued, lowering her voice to a breathy whisper, even though they were now alone, but for the snoring knight, in the inn parlour, 'I would sooner put the baby I suckled at my breast into a cockatrice's den than have one I care for having dealings with that one.

'I knew her,' she said, 'when she was a common whore. She used to drink here, and bring her young men to do so, and it's my opinion that she fleeced them something rotten. Not, you understand, that she denied them the favours they sought. She would go to it as eager as a ferret. But the truth is that almost every young man of birth and breeding who fell into her honey-trap ended up lost, desolate, and much poorer than the day he met her. Of course that was twenty or more years ago, when she was a mere slip of a girl, and would appear on the stage raising her skirts over her head, and then peeking out in the most provocative manner. I'll admit that she could make me laugh, that was why I put up with her, that and the trade she brought to my house. She was even more shameless behind the scenes of the theatre, as I know well since my sister – now dead, poor soul, died of drink she did, I'm sorry to say, but she always loved a nip and in the end lived for nothing else – my sister, as I say, was a dresser there, and she would tell me how Eudoxia would undress in the sight of all and arch her back, displaying all her charms like a peacock, equally to those who had already had her and those who had not. And with all that she was jealous of the other actresses, and savage as a scorpion. Talking of which, what became of your friend's wife, the Greek girl? I could see he didn't feel for her as he felt for the little beauty who was with you on your first her visit, but he spoke of her with respect, which was proper.'

'She remained behind here in Constantinople,' Lycas said, 'and the Empress promised to care for her.'

'I don't like the sound of that.'

'Nor do I, after what you have told me,' Lycas said.

So Lycas went to bed anxious for his friend, even more anxious than he had been when they rode back into the city and were separated. And, thinking of what Dorcas had said concerning Artemisia, he resolved to make enquiries about her, and to go first in the morning to the house where they had lodged. It was true he did not like her, and indeed feared her, on account of her possession, as he believed, of the evil eye. Nevertheless, on account of his love for Marcus and the debt of loyalty he owed him, he thought it right to discover what had happened to his wife, and vowed that if she had come to some evil, the knowledge would at least serve to put Marcus on his guard. So, in the morning, he told all this to Sir Gavin, and they set off together.

**(In writing of Eudoxia, our author either displays ignorance or gives way to fancy. Either way he takes gross liberties with recorded history. While little is known with certainty of Eudoxia, there is reason to think her intelligent and pious. She is reputed in old age to have lived in Jerusalem, where she wrote commentaries on the Scriptures and a biography of St Cyprian, martyred in the reign of the Emperor Valerian, and himself author of a tract denying that the Bishop of Rome could rightfully claim to exercise a judicial authority over other bishops. Is it probable that a lady so given to theology and study should have been the shameless and wicked wanton here portrayed?

Moreover, much that our author relates of this Eudoxia, who in his hands appears a mere fictional figure, is lifted, borrowed or stolen from the Secret History of the Greek author Procopius, inveterate critic of the Empress Theodora and her husband the Emperor Justinian, who ordered the great codification of Roman Law which has been a boon to all civilised men since.

Is our author then ignorant or malicious? Or does he transpose these empresses merely to amuse his pupil and add spice to a narrative that otherwise shows signs of flagging?)**

XXXVIII

The Empress Eudoxia led Marcus up a high mountain and showed him the Kingdom of the World, and so dazzled him. She lured him into the dark pit of lust and bewitched him. Her mastery of the art of love far exceeded anything he had experienced or imagined. Whereas the monstrous woman of the litter, whom her deluded followers took for the earth-mother of all things and beings, had demanded that she receive pleasure, and, ignorant in her selfishness, had no thought of giving, Eudoxia, though doubtless subject to that horrible erotomania which takes possession of so many women, yet understood that whoever gives in the act of love will receive the more abundantly. Her practices were perverse if not perverted, and would be repulsive to read were I to describe them fully; yet they brought Marcus to a pitch of unimagined ecstasy such as he had never known in earlier and more innocent couplings with the lovers of his tender youth, with Lycas or Pulcherrima, and certainly not with Artemisia, frigid to the point of chastity, poor woman. And so, like others before him, he became the very slave of love. As Ovid writes, 'things practised become second nature'; and it may be said that in these ecstasies he for the time being forgot his first nature. And he is not to be blamed, for Eudoxia knew more of the art of love than the poet Ovid himself could write. So he was subdued to the Empress's will.

When she had thoroughly subjected him to her will, and knew him to have been reborn as her creature, she held out a glittering prospect.

'Glory,' she said, 'which all brave young men seek, and power, which wise men – and women – value as gold.'

She toyed with him as she spoke, as if her words were merely idle, and then she pleasured him again and drew him on to pleasure her.

Their silken bed of imperial purple held them for hours while censers emitted sweet fragrances, wood of aloes and smoked violets. Then, as Marcus experienced that sweet sadness which in all men of sensibility and spirit succeeds the act of coition, the Empress revealed her will for him.

Her son, the Emperor, was, she said, a near imbecile, though sweet-tempered. Governing the mighty empire was beyond him. He could no more lead troops in battle than asses can fly. Consequently the whole weight of empire had been thrown on her shoulders; she struggled like Atlas to hold up the globe. For some years she had taken as her coadjutor the eunuch Eutropius. Many blamed her for this, but where could she find a man worthy of her trust? Eutropius was clever, ingenious, subtle; yet like all members of his maimed tribe, he lacked nerve. He was unfit for moments of danger such as afflict all empires. 'And never more,' she said, tracing with her moist finger the exquisite curve of Marcus's lips, 'than now.' To preserve the Empire, she required – and here she paused, and smiled (taking care as always when she smiled not to expose her blackened teeth) – she required a young man of mettle.

'I have waited long,' she said, 'near to despair. Now Heaven has sent me the answer to my prayers.'

And she smothered his face with kisses.

So she expounded her plan: that Marcus should marry her, and be hailed as emperor, jointly with her poor son.

'You will protect him,' she said, cooing the words with soft lovingness, 'and under your guidance Rome will be great once more, and I shall be content to be your ever-loving wife, your stay and support, but free myself from the burden of government.'

Could Marcus resist? Could any man resist such an offer, from one who had already afforded him unimagined delight? Alas no! Man, as the poet says, is like a sleepwalker, and in his sleep climbs dangerous ledges and scales impossible heights.

So Marcus, as one who is drugged, forgot Artemisia, whom he believed dead though he had no time, nor great inclination, to mourn, forgot the callipygous Lycas, forgot Pulcherrima, fairest of his darlings; and consented.

'But first,' she said, 'we must rid ourselves once and for all of this turbulent priest, John of the Golden Mouth, who defiles me with filthy insults and spreads malicious lies about me.'

Truly is it said that man, on account of consciousness, is a diseased animal; for Marcus, even in his enchanted state, knew that he sinned against his own nature and was thereby corrupted; yet consciously pursued his bewitcher's policy.

(Our author is confused, as confused as his hero whom he so determinedly seeks to exculpate. For consciousness, far from being, as he hints, a disease, is what first elevates man, and so makes transcendence of personality possible. To escape being one must first know and acknowledge it. But our author lived in a Dark Age and is not therefore to be chided for his ignorance of what we, the enlightened ones, have come to know.)

So on the vigil of Easter, Marcus, at the head of a detachment of barbarian troops, Goths and Germans for the most part, who had been brought secretly to the city for this purpose, invaded the cathedral of St Sophia where the archbishop was administering baptism (to naked catechumens, after the primitive fashion of the eastern church, since repudiated by Rome as an encouragement of lascivious behaviour). He met the reproving question of the reputed saint with equanimity, charged him with being a disturber of the peace, a usurper of his episcopal seat – all this in language dictated by the Empress – and carried him off to prison, the barbarian guards beating off bloodily several attempts at rescue made by the infuriated populace. So the quondam archbishop was led to a mean cell, to await the Empress's pleasure. She, meanwhile, hesitated, tempted to put him to death, restrained by fear of the mob, who had broken out in riot, setting fire to the senate-house and seven churches.

It was not till, satisfied by this evidence of Marcus's calm valour, Eudoxia declared their marriage and raised him to the purple as co-emperor that the fury of the people was changed to joy. They had longed for a 'real emperor' and recognised Marcus as a worthy and God-given Augustus.

Now I am aware that many will censure this passage in our hero's history, and not without reason. But I plead with them to consider how many great heroes have been deceived and led astray by women. Your ancestor Aeneas himself was tempted to turn aside from his divinely appointed duty on account of the loveliness and wiles of Dido, Queen of Carthage. And the Holy Scriptures tell us how Samson, mightiest of men, most heroic judge of Israel, was stripped of his powers by reason of his infatuation for the Philistine woman Delilah. Indeed our first progenitor, Adam, was expelled from Eden because he listened to the sweet pleas of Eve. Truly is it said, though by a cynic, that Woman was God's chiefest blunder.

XXXIX

The disorders occasioned by the arrest of the archbishop were soon suppressed. Ringleaders were suitably punished, some put to death (by hanging or beheading, depending on their rank), others blinded, some exiled, others cast into prison and forgotten. Dissidents muttered that Constantinople had become a killing-house, a graveyard, or a dungeon. But the populace was soon appeased. In honour of their marriage, Marcus and Eudoxia held the most splendid Games that had been staged in the city since the days of the great Constantine himself. For a week also free banquets were provided throughout the poor quarters of the city. It was not long before the exiled archbishop was forgotten, or even reviled; 'A dull Puritan who gave us sermons to eat, not lobster patties, and the cold water of doctrine rather than fountains flowing with wine,' said the citizens who, a few weeks previously, had rioted in his defence. Truly, my Prince, the mob is fickle and keeps its attention on a matter for the summer of a dragonfly. Whosoever depends on popular support builds his house upon sand. The wind changes, the waters rise, and its foundations are washed away. That stern emperor who said of the people, 'Let them hate provided they fear', was wise.

As for the execution of those who were deemed rebels, which took place in several public squares of the city, the barbarity of these spectacles at once appalled and pleased the people – who can never see enough blood flow.

Did Marcus, our gentle and noble hero, have no doubts? You may well ask.

He did indeed more than once plead with Eudoxia that the killing should stop. Order, he said, has been restored. Why therefore should we persist in further repression? But she soothed his awakening conscience and laid his doubts to rest by procuring evidence of further and still more dangerous treasons. Only when the wicked have been extirpated, she said, will the Empire be safe.

Moreover, she drew his attention to the danger gathering like a thundercloud on the frontiers of the Empire. There the Huns were mustering, terrible and terrifying enemies, led by their king, Attila, who delighted to style himself 'the Scourge of God'. Who were the Huns? you ask. Fear not: I shall give you a full account of them and their king at a later appropriate date. Meanwhile I have other matters to relate.

I said that the archbishop had been exiled. Such indeed was the sentence. But it had not yet been executed. The truth was that Eudoxia, who still feared this John, on account of his virtue and his golden-mouthed oratory, preferred for the moment to let it be assumed that he had departed the city for his allotted place of exile, the remote and desolate town of Cucusus on the slopes of Mount Taurus in Armenia Minor, while keeping him chained in a dungeon in the bowels of the palace, where she hoped he might expire, though, owing to superstitious scruple (for she had received a warning from an astrologer she trusted), she did not dare to order his murder.

One night when the Empress was drunk – for this remarkable woman sometimes relieved the nervous strain to which her unprincipled pursuit of power subjected her by indulging in deep potations – Marcus slipped from the imperial bedchamber, being nauseated by her stinking breath; and summoning one of the mute slaves, an African boy whose devotion he had speedily won by acts of kindness and the grace of his manner, had him guide him to the dungeon where the archbishop was confined.

He found the saintly prelate on his knees, engaged in his devotions. The famed eloquence of his sermons was displayed in his prayers also. Believing himself to be alone in the presence of the Almighty, the archbishop entreated his Lord for mercy not for himself, but for the poor benighted people who had been his flock. To Marcus's amazed embarrassment, he heard his own name invoked, not angrily, but with pity, as one who had been led astray.

Overcome by this generosity, which appealed to his own noble nature, Marcus burst into tears and threw himself on the wet and malodorous stone flags before the archbishop, craving pardon for the wrong he had done him. John Chrysostom, thus disturbed in his prayers, was for a moment taken aback to find the co-Emperor before him. He rose to his feet, stiffly on account of the rheumatism that plagued him, and bade Marcus rise also. Then he took him by the hand, and looked him in the eyes.

'Father, forgive me,' Marcus said again, 'for the evil I have done you.'

'Forgiveness is the Lord's,' the archbishop replied. 'But, my son, you have done me no evil, for you have brought me face to face with the Lord. You have pulled me from my throne and left me naked before the Almighty, and for that I thank you.'

This was a speech which in other circumstances might have seemed to Marcus an expression of the utmost hypocrisy. Yet the archbishop's voice was so gentle and loving, its tone so calm and assured, that Marcus could not doubt his sincerity. And this again reduced him to tears. He knelt before the archbishop and besought him to speak a blessing.

'Later,' John said, and took him by the hand and led him to a corner of the cell where there were two stools, and sat him down.

'You are but an instrument of the Lord,' he said. 'All that happens, whatever befalls us, is in accordance with the Divine Will, part of God's plan for mankind and the world. He raised me to the pomp of the tiara, and He has cast me into this prison that I may learn the wretchedness of Man's lot on earth, and be preserved from the sin of Pride. Blessed above all men are the martyrs, who are granted the ineffable joy of bearing witness to the goodness of God. There are two kingdoms on Earth, and one is Christ's.'

'I have been named emperor,' Marcus said. 'Is mine the Kingdom of the Wicked?'

'Your kingdom is what you make of it,' John replied. 'In itself it is neither good nor bad. But power such as you now possess presents choice opportunity for Satan, who is the enemy of Mankind. Few men – and no women – are to be trusted with power, for our natures, being corruptible, are subject to all temptation. The more you feel free to indulge your lusts and passions, as the possession of power makes you free, the more surely you are a prisoner of the evil one. Therefore power is a snare and a delusion. Truly it is the meek which shall inherit the earth and attain salvation. That miserable woman the Empress . . .'

'She is my wife, God forgive me,' Marcus mumbled.

But John paid no heed, or appeared not to, and continued,

'Miserable woman, as I say . . . Had she remained in a private station such as she was born to, she would doubtless have even then been in thrall to her carnality and a cause of sin in men. But her scope would have been small. Then, awakening the lust of the late emperor, she found herself in a position where the only Law to be observed, as it seemed to her, was her own will. And of course she became its captive. For this is the lesson of life: that surrender to self imperils and in time destroys the soul, but surrender to the will of God sets us free. Truly, my son, I enjoy more liberty in this cell than the Empress in her palace. I am more at ease on this mattress of straw than she in her silken sheets.'

'Is it then impossible,' Marcus said, 'to have power and use it justly?'

'It is not impossible, but it is hard, for where there is power there is no silence, and it is in silence that Man hears the voice of God. The descent to Hell, which the pagans called Avernus, is an easy and inviting road; but the path to Paradise is stiff, steep, and beset with thorns. You walk, my son, on a narrow ledge, and below you on either side great gulfs yawn.'

So Marcus left him, his mind much troubled, his soul disturbed; and yet a faint hope stirred in his heart; for John Chrysostom had lit the way for him, and would serve henceforth as his beacon.

XL

Lycas was at first surprised that Marcus had not sent for him. Then he was anxious concerning his friend's safety. Depression followed. He learned of Marcus's favour with the Empress, for rumours ran fast in Constantinople; and felt the stirring of jealousy. Nor did Sir Gavin's philosophy bring comfort. 'As men rise in the world,' the knight said, 'I have observed that they shed their old acquaintances.'

'I am, I was, more than an acquaintance,' Lycas said.

'To be sure, dear boy, to be sure; it makes no difference.'

So Lycas sank near to despair, and was the more irritated by the knight's easy acceptance of the turn of events, the comfort he found in the hostess's good wine, and indeed in the hostess herself.

Poor Lycas was deceived. Marcus had indeed dispatched messengers to fetch him and Sir Gavin to the palace. But they had been intercepted by the eunuch Eutropius, who, having lost the ear of the Empress, was determined to regain it. For a little, Eutropius had been undecided. He had, at their earlier meeting, observed the looks which Lycas directed at Marcus and those which were returned. So at first it had seemed to him good that Lycas should be brought to the palace, where he and Marcus might be led to an indiscretion which would turn the Empress against her new love. But then it seemed better that Marcus be isolated from his friends, the more easily to be destroyed. So Eutropius caused a wall of obstruction to be raised round his enemy, and prevented the messengers from setting out in search of Lycas.

So, neglected, heartsore, Lycas threw himself into debauchery as so many young men have done in his condition. He haunted low taverns and the brothels that lay in mean streets behind the harbour. Through sensation, he sought to kill true feeling. By nature temperate and loving, he subjected himself to all forms of abandonment. He drank deep and found oblivion. He woke some mornings in the gutter to see the world with a startling and novel clarity. He allowed himself to be embraced by all sorts of women, from tarnished girls younger even than himself to filthy and painted hags. In this way, he who had a horror of female flesh, shape, and smell, indulged in that self-mortification which is sometimes the uttermost sensual vice, sometimes the route to purity as fire burns away alcohol. In sailors' taverns too he submitted to rough embraces and extreme degradation, finding release in humiliation. Often he insulted those he drank with in order to provoke them to violence, and returned to the inn where he still lodged with bruised and blackened face and puffed and bloody lips. One night he even permitted a Greek nobleman who frequented these low haunts also in search of extreme sensations to take him to an inner room, bind his ankles and wrists, and then whip him till the blood ran and he screamed with pain. But in none of these excesses did he find the release he sought, and nothing could banish Marcus's image from his imagining eye.

One night, disconsolate, he sat alone in the corner of a mean tavern, which was all but deserted. The hour was late. Curfew had sounded, and the host, an Armenian, had barred the door, not choosing, however, to eject his few customers. He had earlier made advances to Lycas, which had been met with indifference and then repulsed. The Armenian did not take this amiss. He was a man of generous carnality, and was now caressing a curly-headed youth who lay across his knees with his tunic rucked up to reveal long, soft and dusky boy-legs. The Armenian laughed and called over to Lycas, 'See these legs, one for each of us if it pleases you.' But Lycas smiled, sadly, again declined and devoted his attention to the wine. Drinking, he found that evening, carried him gently into a happier past. For the moment the anger that struggled with pain and grief to possess him was stilled. He knew an unaccustomed peace, and as he drank, that sense of peace deepened. He remembered how Marcus had spoken of his devotion to the Princess Honoria and the vow of service which he had made, and he thought, 'If his true devotion lies there, then it was never mine, and never his dear Pulcherrima's, and so cannot be this monstrous empress's either.'

And he remembered too how Marcus had spoken so longingly of the Holy Grail and of his conviction that, as the descendant of Aeneas, whose story he had so often related to Lycas, he was born to accomplish some great task. Thinking of these things, Lycas knew for the first time in many days a certain happiness.

It was at this moment that his attention was caught by a pile of rags in the corner of the room. To his surprise, the rags stirred, and then a sound came from them, a thin, plaintive wheedling note, as of one accustomed to beg bread.

For a little, Lycas watched, silently. But the rags too fell silent and did not move again. He looked about him. Two of the other topers had fallen asleep. The Armenian and his ephebe were locked in an embrace, oblivious of all else. Lust may not be love, Lycas thought, but it serves as a substitute; and perhaps it is preferable, for it does not bruise the heart. To think harshly of a friend is, doubtless, what the Christians call a sin, and it is certainly unkind, but too often it proves to be true. I have been thinking harshly of Marcus, and though, while sitting here over my wine, I have marshalled all arguments to excuse him, yet the thought recurs to me inescapably that he has forgotten me, and such forgetfulness is a sort of betrayal. What's sad, moreover, is that I can't bring myself to betray him in my heart, and all my acts of treachery are meaningless.

His thought was confused. It ran round not in circles but in elaborate arabesques. One moment his love for Marcus was more intense than ever, on account of his absence; the next, it turned sour as wine two days opened.

The rags stirred again. Something pale emerged from the dark shadows. Lycas was again diverted from his whirling thoughts. He saw a foot and an ankle, and the ankle was delicate and shapely. There came again the sound of moaning and whimpering.

This time Lycas rose, and, taking the lantern from the table, came and stood over the bundle of rags.

'You are in distress of some sort,' he said, gently. 'It would please me if I could be of any help.'

The rags gave a convulsive shiver, but made no answer.

Lycas knelt and placed his hand on the ankle, which was cold as chastity. He applied a gentle pressure and spoke again, offering assistance. He spoke first in Latin, then repeated himself in halting Greek.

The rags stirred. The head of a woman emerged. The hair was grey and matted, the brow furrowed, the cheeks sunken and streaked with ash, and where there should have been eyes there were no eyes but bruised sockets, violet-black.

Lycas uttered a startled cry, then bent forward and touched the woman's cheek.

'What do you want?' he said.

'I want to die.'

'Death surely is not hard to find. He follows hard on our heels in our passage through this life, and, it is said, refuses none who seeks him. You have clearly suffered much, and yet you have not made an accommodation with Death. So I judge that you have still some persistent purpose to pursue. Come,' he said, putting his arm under hers, and raising her up, 'come to my table, drink wine to restore you, and tell me your story.

'I am weary of my own thoughts,' he said, when he had settled her on a bench with her back to the wall, and had held a cup of wine to her lips and made her drink. 'I have been bewailing my misfortunes, but see that your state is more to be pitied even than my own. How true it is, what my friend has so often said to me, that the worst is not yet on us so long as we can say, "This is the worst."'

At these words, the woman lifted her head and would have looked at him if she had had eyes to see. Even so, Lycas felt that these orbless sockets gazed into his soul. For a moment he was petrified, and thought of the Gorgon and the story of Perseus which Marcus had told him as they lay under the winter moon.

'The worst is not yet on us so long as we can say, "This is the worst,"' she repeated, slowly and wonderingly. 'I too knew a man who was used to say that, but he spoke the words merrily, for he was light of heart.'

'Come,' he said again, 'tell me your story.'

'Are we alone?' she said.

Lycas looked around the room. The Armenian and the curly-headed boy were still in each other's arms, but they had subsided to the floor, and, satiated, slept.

'There is no one to hear you but me,' he said.

'But do I dare confide in you? How can I tell if you are not an enemy, or a spy sent to seek me out?'

Even as she spoke, she seemed to gain in assurance, which contradicted the uncertainty of her words, and her voice took on the tone of one who had formerly been accustomed to command.

'When did you last eat?' Lycas said. 'Not for ages, I'd guess. Wine on an empty stomach will make you sick. Wait a moment.'

He slipped through to the back room which the Armenian used as a sort of kitchen, and returned with bread and cheese. He broke bread and put a piece in her hand, and then gave her a sliver of cheese too.

'Eat slowly,' he said. 'Take your time. We've all that's left of the night for your story.'

She nibbled and swallowed and coughed, a spluttering cough. But the bread and cheese stayed down and her hand felt for the cup of wine. At last she said,

'I wasn't always what you see now.'

None of us were, Lycas thought, but kept silent.

'They put my eyes out,' she said. 'I think they thought I would die. I don't know why they didn't kill me. I have lived on the streets, in cellars and hovels, ever since. In the early days, for food, I sold myself. There are men, I found, who like blind girls. They are husbands who must cheat their wives and are afraid to do so. They find safety in doing it with a blind girl. Of course I didn't know that at first. That went on for a long time, though I don't measure the passing of time now. But the day came when no one desired me, I was too degraded even to be a whore. I daresay you didn't know there were women lower than whores.'

She essayed a smile in which Lycas discerned the shadow of former smiles. Now that she was talking freely, if at a distance from him, she had a beautiful voice; and her Greek wasn't the demotic of the woman who kept the tavern where he lodged, but, like Marcus's, pure and classical.

'It is strange,' she resumed. 'I would have been accounted a beauty but for my eyes, which were crossed. They put them out, and though I can't look at myself in a mirror, I know my beauty has deserted me. I can still feel my skin, and it is rough.'

Lycas said, not believing what he said, 'Artemisia.'

'That was my name,' she said. 'Artemisia, daughter of Melanippos, rich in horses and vineyards. But that was in another time.'

She pulled the rags over her face, as if to hide tears. But without eyes she could not weep, and her body shook with dry sobs.

'Artemisia,' he said again. 'I am Lycas, friend of Marcus.'

She did not answer, and he wondered if she had heard. So he said again what he had said before, and, searching among the rags, found her hand, withdrew it, and pressed it to his lips. For a long time they did not move, and sat without speaking.

'I think you did not like me,' she said.

'I was afraid of you. And I was jealous, forgive me.'

'Is Marcus with you?'

She spoke haltingly.

'He is in the city,' Lycas said.

'He cannot see me like this,' she said. 'Ruined. Leave me be. Let me return to the darkness where I have learned to live.'

'No,' Lycas said, 'he cannot see you as you are. But we can remedy that. Come.'

And so he took her by the arm and, with gentleness and pity, led her to the inn where he lodged, and called the woman, Dorcas, and bade her tend to Artemisia, wash her, and clothe her in decency.

And he sat long, pondering what should be done next, and wishing that Sir Gavin would rise from his drunken sleep that they might discuss the matter. He valued the knight's opinion, at least when he was half-sober.

XLI

Marcus would have liked to renew his conversation with the deposed archbishop, but Eudoxia, though he supposed her ignorant of that meeting, had had John Chrysostom transported to his place of exile on the flanks of far-distant Mount Taurus. There he would win more golden opinions for the assiduity with which he pursued a Christian life, and cared for the flock of shepherds and rude mountaineers for whose company he had perforce exchanged the sophisticated intellects of Constantinople. He extended his pastoral care to the missions of Persia and Scythia, and retained to the full his independence of mind. To proceed further is to depart from the narrow course of my narrative, but perhaps I may add that, at a later date, the jealousy of Eudoxia still bore hard upon him. An order was given that he be removed to the inhospitable desert of Pityus, and the journey was so arduous that he died, in the sixtieth year of his age. But this is to anticipate.

In passing, however, I may add that though future ages would honour his name, extolling his innocence, piety, and acute intellect, yet, though John was good and Eudoxia may be considered evil, in their public quarrel, the scales were more evenly balanced. For John Chrysostom displayed to the full the arrogance in his public stance too often found since in the Bishops of Rome. It was his ambition, as it has been theirs, to make no distinction between the secular and the religious, or at least only such a distinction as is ridiculous: for, like the Bishops of Rome, he assumed the right to order the public affairs of the Empire and to treat the secular power as his mere vassals. And this is, as I say, absurd, since the security even of Christ's Church depends on the support of the sword. Christ himself, when asked whether it was lawful to pay tribute to Caesar, took a coin and asked whose portrait was there displayed. Render unto Caesar the things that are Caesar's, he told his questioner, and unto God the things that are his. Therefore there is a clear distinction between the two powers – the temporal and the spiritual – and a community is well governed when the two are properly balanced. But the arrogant ambitions of the Papacy have blurred this distinction, upset this balance, with evil results, as your own illustrious father, my Prince, learned so bitterly. A prince who neglects or persecutes Holy Church is evil; but so also may we style a Pope who seeks to subject a prince to his will.

But I digress.

Soon after his conversation with the archbishop, Eudoxia began to disgust Marcus. Perhaps the two things were connected. I do not know. But it is well-known that licentious sexual activity provokes satiety in the virtuous, and Marcus was also repelled by the association in the Empress's mind between pain and sexual pleasure. Yet he could not desert her bed. His position as emperor depended on his continuing ability to please and satisfy her. He knew that she would not hesitate to have him put ignominiously to death if he revealed his altered feelings. Another in his shoes might have struck first, which would indeed have doubled his already soaring popularity. But the thought never occurred to his virtuous mind.

Instead he busied himself with his duties. He administered justice with sublime impartiality. He occupied himself with reforming the army in preparation for war on the frontier against the terrible Hun. He dispatched ambassadors to the west, calling for Honorius to join him in this campaign for the defence of Christian Europe. In short, in a few months he showed himself to be the most energetic and capable emperor since the ill-fated Julian.

But he felt his loneliness, as Great Ones may. Time and again he longed for the company of Lycas and Sir Gavin. Yet all his efforts to discover where they had gone or what had happened to them were vain. So true is it that even an emperor's power is limited, being dependent on the service he can command and the information he may obtain. Apart from the mute African slave whom he had made his personal page, he had no friend in the palace; and this friendship was unequal, and limited on account of the boy's inability to speak. Marcus found some comfort in confiding in him, certain that his confidences could not be spread abroad. But often in the waste hours of the night he sighed for Lycas.

In his loneliness he began to consort with his co-emperor, the young Theodosius. He discovered that the boy was not, as he had feared, an imbecile, though this was how he presented himself to the world and therefore how the world, which takes things at face value, regarded him. In truth the world could not be blamed. The boy was timid, awkward, given to headaches and fits of weeping. Moreover, he suffered from an impediment in his speech, which caused him to stumble over words, and often reduced him to impotent silence. At such moments his lips moved convulsively, the veins on his pale forehead stood out as if ready to burst, sweat coursed down his cheeks, soon mingling with helpless tears; and indeed he seemed a very idiot. Compelled, even when such fits were on him, to present himself before others, while his mother looked sourly on before taking the management of the occasion upon herself, he would afterwards be prostrated in an agony of shame and terror. He held Eudoxia in such awe that when alone with her he could scarcely speak, and never a coherent sentence. She was then inspired by his abject fear to break out in cruel and cutting speech, calling him 'cripple, imbecile, girly-boy'. Yet in other moods she displayed an intense maternal tenderness, cooing over him and addressing him as her 'poor benighted lambkin', stroking his pale cheeks (which were painted with gold-leaf for his public appearances), caressing him, and covering his face with kisses.

Marcus, finding the boy too timid to speak, would play games with him, first simple ones, such as dice and that which the Romans called *micatio*. Discovering that the boy enjoyed these, he was emboldened to teach him chess, for which Theodosius displayed an unexpected aptitude. He had an eye for the pattern of the game and was soon thinking several moves ahead. It was not long before he would beat Marcus two times out of three. As he gained confidence, the boy relaxed, and was even able to converse, at first hesitantly, with much stammering; but then more fluently. Marcus discovered that, though shy, the boy had ideas of his own. For instance, he detested cruelty to animals. For this reason he hated having to attend the chariot-races. Marcus had never before heard anyone complain that the danger the horses ran, and the injuries they suffered, made the sport unjustifiable, however popular.

'You mustn't speak like that to anyone else,' Marcus said. 'The people demand that the Emperor should delight in the Games.'

'Oh, I know that, and I do my best to pretend to. But it's too horrible. I wish I wasn't emperor.'

'Unfortunately you are.'

'I've often thought I would like to retire to a m-m-monastery. I would like that. D-d-do you think it might be possible one d-d-day?'

'Perhaps,' Marcus said, though he knew otherwise. No emperor can retire and live safely, because his successor will always regard him as a danger, will forever be afraid that partisans may seek to restore him to the throne. But he saw no reason to say this to the boy. So he said merely, 'Perhaps,' and pitied him.

At first Eudoxia was pleased to see Marcus paying attention to her son. But when she found that he was avoiding her bed, or was cold in his response to her embraces, she became suspicious. The eunuch Eutropius was not slow to observe her altered mood, or to seek to turn it to his advantage. He was morbidly jealous of Marcus, and now lost no opportunity to poison the Empress's mind against him. Did she not see that Marcus was corrupting her son? Did she not perceive that his intention was to exclude her from the government of the Empire? Wasn't it the case that he went to all lengths to cultivate the guards?

Yet neither Eudoxia not Eutropius dared to move against Marcus, though the Empress's lust was turned to hate. The news from the frontier was too alarming. The Huns were on the warpath, and already ravaging the northern provinces.

XLII

I promised you, my Prince, that I would speak fully of these Huns; and yet my pen fails me. This is not for lack of knowledge, but rather because what I have to impart is such as strains belief, for the Huns were like no other men.

So, for example, whereas the other barbarians who for so long had threatened the Empire, invading it and laying waste, were tall, fine-looking warriors, as you might expect, seeing that your own German forefathers were doubtless among them, the Huns were squat and yellow of skin, their eyes narrow, and their lips cracked by the harsh wind of the eastern grasslands whence they emerged.

All other barbarians were capable of receiving the blessings of civilisation. Indeed, it was on account of the desirability of city life that they burst the boundaries of the Empire. But the Huns feared and despised cities, and, if a Hun was imprisoned in a stone dungeon, he would be raving mad within a seven-night. For this reason they sought to destroy towns and cities with fire, which some say they worshipped.

All barbarians were cruel, but the Huns exceeded all others in cruelty as a great river exceeds a mountain stream. It was their habit to slit the noses of captured children, but only as preparatory to raping them. Some say that it was also their custom to sear the limbs of these infant captives before their camp fires, and then cut collops from the living legs and eat them. And this I believe, though it is too horrible to contemplate.

The Goths became Christians, even if choosing a heretical form of the Faith, for which, it is proper to believe, Alaric and his followers rot in Hell. But the Huns, being deprived of reason, were incapable of receiving instruction. Their gods were devils, whom they conjured up from the wastelands of the northern desert, whence they derived themselves. What they sacrificed to these devil-gods has not been revealed; but we are told by good authorities that slave-children – that is, children taken when towns were sacked and then enslaved – were habitually stretched on their altars and their throats cut.

Their king, Attila, was proud to designate himself the Scourge of God.

Their army was very terrible. The soldiers were all mounted on sturdy and shaggy ponies and they rode as if man and horse were a single beast, like the Centaurs of the ancient world. They had no infantry-men and despised all who fought on foot. They moved with an inconceivable rapidity. Behind their army stretched miles of dust. They carried a short sword which could both stab and cut, and their only defensive armour was a small round shield made of horsehide. They wore leather caps and tunics made from the skins of dormice. All this is well-attested.

When Marcus drilled his legions and the Gothic mercenaries who fought on horseback, he found that he first had to overcome the fear that even the word 'Hun' inspired in them. He knew from his study of History, for he had read deeply in the Greek historians as well as in Livy, Sallust, and Tacitus, that an army which goes in fear of the enemy is defeated even before it joins battle. Soldiers as they advance are already seeking the route by which they may escape.

He therefore addressed his assembled troops as follows:

'Romans: I call you that to remind you of our heritage. You are the heirs of the legions who conquered the known world, from the misty island of Britain to the deserts of Parthia. You are all citizens of the Empire, though you come from different stock. There are Greeks among you whose fathers marched with Alexander, Africans who crossed the Alps with Hannibal, as well as descendants of the legions led by Caesar and Trajan. And among you also, today, are our brave Gothic allies, once our foes, now our friends. They will show themselves worthy of Alaric as you of Alexander and Caesar.

'I know that some of you are afraid. That is nothing to be ashamed of. Fear itself is not shameful. It is surrender to fear that makes a man a coward whom all shun.

'Some of you, many it may be, are apprehensive about the battle we are going to fight. You know that the enemy have defeated many armies, and you may think that they are invincible. But think of this: they have never encountered the full might of Rome till now.

'They have had fortune in the past, but fortune is fickle. We should remember that accidents may happen, but real courage never alters, and those who have it never use lack of experience as an excuse for being anything but courageous.

'Consider this: they are far from home, fighting not in defence of their hearth and loved ones, but merely to satisfy the ambitions of their king. His war is selfish and without meaning. Ours is just the opposite.

'There are solid advantages on our side. We are more numerous than the enemy and better armed. In war, victory usually goes to the big battalions if they are well-equipped as we are.

'But war is fought not only with equipment, but with the heart and spirit. And there we have the advantage, as I have said. We fight also in the name of Christ, the one true God, who will succour and protect us and see that right triumphs.

'I have never led you in battle before. But, though I am young, I have never lost a battle in which I have engaged. I respect the strength of the enemy, but I do not fear him. I am supported by my faith in the Almighty God and in the heroic tradition of Roman arms.

'So we have prepared for battle in such a way as to leave no one the excuse to play the coward. Should anyone do so he will be punished as he ought to be, and his name will be remembered with shame, but the brave will be honoured with the rewards that are due to courage.'

So Marcus put heart in his men, and then he drew up his line of battle.

He formed the legions on the flank of a hill overlooking marshy ground, and gave stern instructions that they were not to attempt to advance, but must allow the enemy to come to them. The Huns were horse-archers, but the range of their bows was short, and Marcus calculated that they must cross the marshy ground under a hail of javelins before they could fire their bows. Moreover, the distance between the fringe of the marsh and the slope where the legions were drawn up in line was no more than fifty yards. So the Huns would be crammed together once they were through the marsh, and would not be able to deploy. Only the front ranks, Marcus thought, could shoot their arrows.

Then on his left, out of sight behind the ridge, he had positioned his Balearic slingers, who would hurl stones on that flank of the enemy, while, also behind the ridge, but on his right, the heavy cavalry of the Goths was drawn up, ready to charge into that flank of the Huns and force them back to the marsh.

'It is all a question of timing,' Marcus told his staff.

The Huns descended the hill on the other side of the valley. The little ponies advanced at a brisk trot. Marcus had expected they would dash forward with loud barbaric war-cries, but they came on in silence. And this unnerved his front line, made up of raw recruits, who wavered at the sight, and would have broken. But the second and third lines were veterans, who stood their ground, and denied the young men the retreat that in their hearts they sought.

As the Huns reached the marsh, they hesitated, and that hesitation restored the confidence of the Romans. They saw that the enemy too was doubtful, and no longer felt them to be invincible. The ponies were pricked forward into the marsh, but they had to cross it carefully, for a few horsemen who urged their mounts forward at a sharp trot strayed from the firm paths that led through the marsh and were swallowed up. When the Romans saw this they gave a cry of triumph.

But the Huns were experienced warriors and soon a good half of the host was making its way through the marsh and approaching firm ground. Marcus now gave the signal to the Balearics, some of whom hurled flat stones from their slings, while others threw light sharp-tipped javelins.

The Huns hesitated a moment, surprised by the assault. But, being experienced warriors, they soon rallied, and rode carelessly over the fallen to get within range of the legions drawn up in line, who now came under fire from their bows. On Marcus's instructions they had formed a shield-wall, with the shields raised high, and little execution was done. Nevertheless, the wild cries, high-pitched as those of demons in Hell, which the Huns gave vent to now that they were engaging the enemy caused the first line of Romans to waver. Some were for breaking ranks to fight the Huns hand-to-hand, while others would have turned and fled but for the staunchness of the veterans drawn up behind them. A few, disobeying the centurions, did indeed dash forward, and were all cut down, but the gaps they had left in the shield-wall were straightway filled by men advancing from the second rank.

So for a little, as the pagan poets would have put it, the gods watched over the equal balance and promised victory to neither army. More and more Huns pressed forward across the marsh and against the line of the legions, which was compelled to yield a few paces. But at the same time the javelins and stones hurled by the Balearic slingers continued to wreak havoc among the now congested enemy, whose ponies also felt the stabbing swords of the legions when they were pushed forward into range. Yet the cries of the Huns grew louder and more exultant as they forced the legions to yield ground and themselves advanced over the bodies of the fallen.

Marcus, conspicuous on a grey horse atop the hill, watched the fluctuating encounter with a serenity which was marvellous to behold, though he maintained it with difficulty. He looked across the marsh to the plain beyond, where the black tents of the Hun were dotted like a herd of fine cattle. He looked down on the battle, and waited. In every battle, he had read, comes the decisive moment, and the victorious general is he who seizes it. He held his breath till he judged that moment to have arrived. Then he turned to Athalric, the royal commander of the Gothic cavalry, and said, quietly and with no note of excitement in his voice,

'Now, Athalric, now's your hour.'

The trumpet sounded and the gaudy chivalry of the Goths, tall men with glittering breast-plates mounted on heavy steeds, themselves protected by body-armour, descended the slope at a sharp trot and was launched against the unsuspecting left wing of the Huns. The momentum of the charge, made by heavy cavalry with lance at rest, was irresistible. The Huns were unhorsed, thrown back, trampled underfoot. Those at the rear who had just crossed the marsh, unable to see what was happening, continued to press forward, throwing their comrades who sought flight into still greater confusion.

Marcus now gave the signal for the legions who had held their line so firmly to advance, slowly and still in order. And they pressed hard on the Huns, so that gradually the compressed mass was forced back into the marsh, where thousands perished, while the fortunate ones gave their horses their head and disappeared in ignominious flight.

As the sun dipped behind the western hills, there was not a Hun left on the field of battle, but for the innumerable dead.

At that moment Marcus ordered the trumpet to be sounded to halt the action. And he was just in time, for already some of the braver spirits among the Romans – or rather, the most rash among them – were advancing into the marsh in pursuit of the fleeing enemy. But they obeyed the signal, and the line was reformed. Meanwhile Athalric, with more difficulty, halted his Gothic cavalry. Some grumbled and protested, saying that now was the opportunity to finish off the Huns once and for all, but Athalric reproved them.

'I have fought many battles against the Huns,' he said, 'and I have seen them rally often in retreat. Believe me, your Hun is like the wolf, never so dangerous as when wounded.'

And he had impressed this on Marcus before the battle.

Marcus now ordered his light cavalry, who had taken no part in the fight, for they had not been needed, to ride and cross the river some miles downstream, and then, circling the Huns' camp, take up position on the heights behind them and above, that they might be ready to harry their retreat.

And then he addressed the soldiers, as follows:

'Soldiers,' he said, 'you have done bravely. You have fought in a manner worthy of your ancestors, who did great deeds in their time. Every man has his appointed day, and all men have but a short span of life. It is the task of brave men to extend our fame beyond that term; and this you have accomplished today. Your heroic deeds will live for ever in song and memory.'

*(Investigation of the records of Byzantium, when I sojourned there and enjoyed leisure while recovering from a wound, yields no evidence of this famous battle; or so I was assured by the clerk I employed to research these records on my behalf. On the other hand, it bears a distinct resemblance to an encounter against the Saracens fought by the Crusading army led by the Plantagenet king of the English, Richard, named the Lionheart. That victory was gained, in desperate straits, by a like charge made by my own glorious and godly Order of the Knights of the Temple, a charge in which I had the honour to fight in the vanguard. It is therefore my opinion that our author, seeking a suitable vehicle to serve as testimony of his hero's prowess in battle, has remembered stories which he must have heard of the great feats performed by the Templars in this battle, and impudently transferred them to the Gothic cavalry under his hero's command.

No doubt, though no warrior himself, but a mere scholar, he hoped to stimulate his princely pupil's zeal for war by supplying him with such an example of courage and skill.

But his story must be accounted a mere Romance, when ascribed to his hero.)*

XLIII

Marcus remained wakeful that night, his gaze fixed on the flickering lights that came from the Hun encampment. Several times he sent out scouts to try to discover whether the Huns were slipping away, leaving their camp-fires burning to mask their departure. But the scouts reported that though there was movement, there was no evidence of a general retreat.

'They don't know how to cope with defeat,' Athalric observed. 'I doubt whether they can organise an orderly withdrawal.'

'You have fought against them many times,' Marcus said. 'What will they do? Will they fight again when it is light?'

'We gave them a good bruising, but we have only scotched the snake, not killed it. Attila is a man of infinite guile. You may think him a mere barbarian, my lord, and a monster, but . . .'

'A monster indeed, horrible, misshapen, huge,' Marcus quoted.

'Not huge, my lord, for his head comes no higher than my breast-bone; and a monster only in cruelty, but with a keen intelligence, when it's not drowned in wine, mead, or ale. He has a sharp wit, which women call pretty.'

'But what will he do?'

The Goth raised an eyebrow, gave a half-smile, and muttered, 'Nobody can tell what a crafty bugger like that'll do.'

'What do you think?'

Marcus turned to his chief-of-staff, a white-haired Roman noble of the old school, L. Aemilius Scaurus.

Scaurus sniffed.

'Who can judge the thinking of a man without a history, and ignorant of the ways of civilised men?'

Athalric's colour rose.

'That's like you Romans,' he said. 'We Goths have beaten you in countless battles, *not* least at Adrianople, but you still think yourselves superior to us, because you have wasted your time reading books.'

'Gentlemen, friends,' Marcus said, 'there's no call to quarrel. Scaurus has merely confessed himself ignorant, which is the speech of an honest man.'

'I'll tell you this,' Athalric said, 'from my reading of the Hun. He'll try something different. Where force has failed him, cunning will step in.'

'Good,' Marcus said. 'That sounds reasonable to me. So we must prepare ourselves to meet cunning with intelligence. Meanwhile, we wait and watch.'

Dawn came, not as the poets send it with rosy fingers touching the sky, but damp, misty and chill; it was still half-dark an hour after sunrise, for no sun was visible, and the lights of the campfires still glowed.

An outrider returned from the light cavalry to assure Marcus they were in position to impede and harass any withdrawal of the Huns.

They waited. They could now discern movement in the horselines across the marsh, but no sign of general advance. Nevertheless, Marcus ordered the legions to stand to, and prepare for a renewal of the battle.

Meanwhile, when he had given orders that the men be fed as they took up position in the lines, and seen this done, and had shown himself to the troops, and spoken to many individually, praising their conduct yesterday and encouraging them to show the same courage, if it was called upon, today, he broke his own fast with bread dipped in olive oil and a cup of wine mixed with water.

'What will the Huns eat this morning?' he asked Athalric.

'Strips of horse-flesh dried in the wind and washed down with mare's milk.'

'Are your men in good heart for another battle?'

'Battle is to them as the dew is to the grass.'

But there was still no sign of forward movement from the camp of the enemy.

Then, towards noon, two horsemen were seen to ride out of the

258

Huns' lines, approaching the marsh. They carried a flag of truce, but at the far edge of the marsh hesitated, as if uncertain whether it would be honoured. Marcus therefore dispatched two of his officers, with a Gothic nobleman who spoke the Hun language, to assure them of safe conduct. Then he waited while they parleyed on the Roman side of the marsh.

'It's some trickery, I'll be bound,' Scaurus said.

'Perhaps, perhaps not. I suspect that by now they have discovered that their line of retreat is endangered.'

Word was sent that Attila proposed a meeting with the Roman commander on an island a mile downstream. Each was to be accompanied by only four others, and all unarmed.

'Never,' Scaurus said. 'Never, there's some devilry planned. You can't trust a Hun. If you ask me, you can't trust him till he's a corpse lying at your feet. And even then you should be careful.'

'I accept the proposal,' Marcus said. 'Tell Attila I shall be there two hours before sundown.'

Scaurus turned on him as soon as the message had been conveyed to the emissaries of the Hunnish king.

'It's folly,' he said. 'We have them in a trap. All we need do is sit here, and leave them to rot and starve. It's evident they have no stomach to fight again.'

'Nevertheless,' Marcus said, 'we shall speak with Attila. I am a Christian knight, and it is a Christian duty to prefer an honourable peace to the continuation of the war. To seek glory in battle is honourable, but to seek to destroy a defeated enemy is vanity; and the bitter fruit of vanity is shame. Who knows? Even Attila may accept baptism. We shall take a priest with us. You will accompany me, Scaurus, and Athalric also.'

He chose to take Scaurus with him because he did not trust him if left in command of the army.

'Does Attila speak any Latin?' he asked Athalric.

'As a dog with three legs runs, he gets along in the language.'

'We must take him a present,' Marcus said. 'What would be acceptable?'

'Half a dozen virgins, from what I've heard tell,' Scaurus said. 'But I doubt if you'll find any among the camp-followers.'

'Gold and jewels,' said Athalric. 'They say he's a perfect magpie for jewels.'

So it was arranged, and in the afternoon, as a pale sun pushed aside the swirling misty clouds, they went down to the little boat that would carry them to the island. As their puntsman pushed off, they watched the Huns set out from the farther bank. The wind was cold. Marcus drew his furs about him.

He said to Scaurus, 'You have a dagger with you?'

Scaurus nodded.

'You must leave it in the boat. That was the stipulation. No weapons.'

'Don't be green,' Scaurus said. 'I know that is no way to speak to the Emperor, and you may have my head for it, if we emerge safe from this meeting, but believe you me, if you think Attila and these devils are going to come unarmed, well, what can I say, you might as well expect your Christ to get down from the Cross and walk.'

'Your Christ? My Christ? Which do you mean?'

'I've a tenderness for the old ways.'

His eyes slid from Marcus's gaze. He looked out on the cold brown river. His profile was sharp, and his nose like a heron's beak.

'No weapons,' Marcus said. 'We don't cheat when I'm in charge of the game.'

'On your head be it,' and Scaurus, drawing the dagger from his belt, sent it spinning to pierce the wood between Marcus's feet.

They disembarked, and stood waiting for the other boat to reach the island. Marcus said,

'Are you sure Attila will come himself?'

No one answered his question, which was indeed directed to himself, or to the empty air.

Four people came towards them: two small, squat, yellow, with bow-legs; a taller man with grizzled hair and a sword-cut on his cheek; and, to Marcus's astonishment, a woman, her face hidden behind a scarf.

The older of the two small men stepped forward, smacked his fist over his heart, and said, 'Attila.'

Marcus glanced, questioningly, at Athalric, who nodded his head. He then advanced two steps himself.

'I am Marcus, Emperor of the Romans.'

Attila nodded, spat on the ground, then squatted, took a blade of grass and sucked it. He then spoke rapidly in a tongue Marcus could not understand; nor indeed could he distinguish a single word. When he had finished, the grizzled man interpreted.

'The King congratulates you. He says he got careless. He had not thought to meet a Roman commander who understood the art of war, and you so young. He says to tell you he admits he is in – how shall I put it? – the devil of a pickle.'

Marcus clapped his hands. Attila looked up, alert. His hand flew to his sword-belt. Then he smiled, spread his hands, to show that he wore no sword.

'I trusted you,' he said. His Latin was guttural, but clear enough. Marcus's African slave-boy, the fourth member of their party, now fetched wine from the boat. Attila laughed.

'You think to get me drunk to get your way, but you no make me drunk. Attila drinks with devils, and like the devils.'

He laughed again.

Marcus said, 'A courtesy merely, to show you that we mean well, and that I believe we can reach an agreement, a concord agreeable to us both.'

They sat on the damp ground and drank wine. Then the negotiations began. They went on for a long time, on account of being conducted through the grizzled interpreter, a German who had been captured by the Huns half a lifetime ago, and instead of being enslaved or pulled apart by wild horses (which was a punishment very popular with the Huns, who watched it with the same avidity and enthusiasm as the citizens of Constantinople watched the chariot-racing that the young emperor so hated; and the Huns would bet on the outcome, how far the horses would travel before the man's limbs were separated from his trunk, and which would come off first, arms or legs. Sometimes it was one, sometimes the other, so interest was intense), instead of this, as I say, he had been made a household, or rather camp, pet by Attila's father, and indeed reared as Attila's foster-brother, for he had been a mere child when taken captive. But his rendition of Attila's rapid Hun into old-fashioned Latin was slow and seldom clear. Moreover, the matter was complicated further by the interventions of Athalric, who conversed from time to time with the German in the Gothic language, in which exchanges they argued points in considerable and tedious detail. But this is the way of diplomacy, which is never rapid, and which habitually complicates whatever is already complicated, so that to follow the course of diplomatic negotiations is like finding one's way to the centre of a maze.

Attila sat patiently, drinking wine, his eyes sparkling. Sometimes he laughed. He seemed to Marcus neither the ogre of rumour and legend, nor indeed like a general whose army had been defeated and who now found himself in a perilous situation. Occasionally he glanced at Marcus in such a fashion that he seemed to be inviting him to share a joke; as if it was a comedy that their representatives were playing out.

Marcus found himself liking him. It is absurd, he thought. This is the Scourge of God. He is proud to be known as that. He has brought ruin and devastation to Christendom. Scaurus is right. He cannot be trusted. He is cunning as seven devils. It was all true; and yet he liked him.

He looked at the woman. Who was she? Why was she here? Her forehead, all he could see of her face, was white. She was too tall to be a Hun. Was she one of Attila's wives? He was reputed to have wives and concubines without number.

Marcus recalled the story of Croesus which the old bard had told him: call no man happy till he is dead. It was a pagan story but he had felt its truth. And yet, in defeat, the King of the Huns behaved as if he was happy.

At last the negotiations were concluded. The Huns would be permitted to withdraw. Attila promised to retreat beyond the Danube, not to trouble the eastern frontier of the Empire again.

'Nor the west,' Marcus said.

Attila giggled. 'Nor the west.'

Scaurus muttered, 'Promises are easy.'

But Attila would leave hostages, seven of his sons. They would be brought to the Roman camp in the morning.

Then Marcus ordered the presents to be produced: gold dishes, finely wrought, and many jewels, rubies, topaz, amethysts that glowed rich as toads' eyes.

Attila smiled, thinly, but did not grab for them as Marcus had thought he might. Instead, lazily, he picked up a single topaz and held it up to the light. He observed Marcus looking at the silent woman, and spat out a single word in his own language. Very slowly, and with a weary grace, she unwound her scarf to show herself. Marcus felt he was falling from a great height. It was the Princess Honoria who stood before him.

'My best wife,' Attila said. 'You will want to talk.'

He sat, cross-legged like a tailor, letting the jewels run through his hands, juggling with them.

Marcus drew the Princess aside, while Attila watched them, mockery in his eyes.

'It is true what he says? You are his wife?'

'And why not?' she said. 'I was willing to be Alaric's. You remember that? You remember delivering my letter to him?'

'But,' Marcus said, 'you are a Roman, a Christian. How can this be?'

'Oh,' she said, 'when you came to me in Milan, I thought you were charming, a charming child, and now they tell me you are married to that witch Eudoxia, my sister-in-law as was.'

'How do you know that?'

'You mustn't think that we who live in "barbarian camps"' – she paused around the words, dwelling on them as if they expressed a delightful absurdity – 'are ignorant. Why, we have devils whom we summon from vasty depths to retail the news of the Roman world. So you are married to Eudoxia and yet you find it strange that I should be Attila's wife. Really, it's too absurd.'

'But,' Marcus said, stammering like the poor boy-emperor, his wife's son. 'But,' he said again, and could find no words to follow.

'Come,' she said, more kindly, 'recall our earlier meeting. You came to the imperial court at Milan, and you were dispatched on an embassy by my brother. My brother – the Emperor – a nasty little pervert who shared his bed with depraved children he had debauched, who started in terror at his own shadow, and then submitted to being whipped by his priests to expiate his sins, which the next week he repeated. A creature whose gaze was fixed on Heaven and who suffered nightmares in which he believed he was in Hell, where, if such a place exists, he richly deserved to be. And this was the thing that occupied the throne that was once that of Augustus, of Trajan, of Hadrian, of Marcus Aurelius, of Diocletian, of Constantine. Because I knew him for what he was, he feared me and caused me to be imprisoned, immured in a mountain convent, and that only because he dared not have me killed – on account of what his astrologer had foretold. And it was from this convent that, in the full glory of his warlike vigour, Attila rescued me, bore me off, delighted in me and I in him . . .'

She paused, sighed, touched Marcus's cheek with a light forefinger.

'You still don't understand, do you, dear boy, poor dear boy? It's finished. Rome is finished. The great adventure is over. Those whom the gods promised empire without end, without limits, have proved unworthy of that promise. Night falls on Rome. Christendom is but a dream, a womanish dream that has unmanned Rome. And in this Dark Age of the world it's only what you call barbarism that has a right to flourish. The world is to the strong, and the weak must go down under their flail.'

'But yesterday,' Marcus said, 'under my command, Rome vanquished barbarism.'

'A mere incident,' she said, and laughed again, a cold, clear, echoing laugh chill with mockery. 'Can you turn back the tide? Can you stay the deluge? And, besides, who won the battle for you but your Gothic cavalry, barbarians themselves?'

'Barbarians who acknowledge and worship Christ,' Marcus said.

'And who destroy even what they seek to make theirs. Dark, dark, dark, that is the night we inhabit. In the black night, it is each for himself, or herself. So I shall ride north with Attila, and you . . . you may return to the city and see what my fine sister-in-law has in store for you.'

XLIV

As they rode back to Constantinople, the Princess's words lay on Marcus's spirit heavy as a stone in the belly. His companions, not understanding, were perplexed. They muttered that the Emperor did not look like a general who had won so great a victory and was returning in triumph to the city.

Dark shapes of birds hovered over the line of march, ominous to his eye. Was doom, long pronounced, now imminent?

He remembered that, as he advanced with Alaric on Rome, he had wrestled with the question of how the pagan city had stood inviolate, while now that it had embraced the true religion, it was exposed to sack and pillage. He had found no answer then; he found none now. And yet, he said to himself, ours is the one true Faith, and that of our forefathers was false.

He was wise in his perplexity, for there is no good answer to such a question. Heavy burdens are imposed on the godly, while, in the words of the psalmist, the wicked grin like dogs and run about the city. Even had he read the Book of Job, he would not have been comforted.

Scaurus did not hesitate to reproach him for having granted the Huns free passage from the Empire.

'You do not know how to be great,' he said. 'You have forgotten the great watchword of empire: to spare the subject and subdue the proud. For the Huns, this defeat was no more than a check, and you have let slip the chance to destroy them utterly. You have wounded the wild beast, but you have not tamed him.'

Marcus made no reply. He set his face against the rain which slanted in from the east, as the horses splashed through puddles and slipped sometimes on the inclines.

In the city all was apparently joy. The citizens, accustomed for some years to live in fearful expectation of the barbarians, gave themselves over to nights of pleasure. The considerations which made Scaurus frown disturbed them not at all. The poor live ever in the present, and give themselves over to the emotions of the immediate day. Their horizons are short, and cannot be otherwise. It is enough to know that they will have a full belly when they retire for the night. Now they were overjoyed to learn that the Empress had decreed two days of holiday and chariot-racing – to which admission would be free – in celebration of her husband's victory.

Yet, though she decreed public rejoicing, she knew fear in her heart. It was provoked by the eunuch Eutropius. He had taken advantage of Marcus's absence to insinuate himself again into Eudoxia's confidence. His manner was as ever artful. First he praised the wisdom she had shown in choosing Marcus, according him her trust, and raising him to the purple – and here he paused before adding, almost under his breath – 'and to power'. This victory, he said, was truly glorious. No emperor had achieved so much in his memory. Marcus had revealed that he was a true successor to Augustus, Trajan and Constantine. He was indeed worthy of the name of Caesar. His lustre shone before men.

He continued in this vein for a full half-hour while the Empress picked with growing impatience at a loose thread on her dress. When Eutropius remarked, in a tone of calm approval, that it was now commonly said in the city that Marcus's glory exceeded that of all other men, he saw the Empress frown and bite her lip.

'Is that indeed the common report?' she said.

'My lady,' he replied, 'Augusta, the people are as chaff. They blow where the wind listeth. Marcus is the hero of the hour and they have eyes for none other.'

From the palace they could not hear the excited tumult of the city; and yet the silence that followed his words was full of it.

'He is co-emperor,' the eunuch said, musingly, as if speaking to himself. 'But for how long can the Empire be shared? All previous divisions of the imperial power have resulted in struggle, the triumph of one emperor, and the elimination of another. This Marcus went to war a boy. He will return a man. Will he consent to share his glory with your son Theodosius, his nominal partner in empire? Will he still consent to be guided by . . . you?'

So the eunuch dropped his poison, delicately, in the Empress's ear, and guided her thoughts in the direction he desired.

She said, 'I made him.'

'Do not expect him,' Eutropius replied, 'to feel gratitude. All men resent those who have given them the hand that raised them high.'

So this subtle barrator worked on his lady, who, being herself a stranger to virtue, drank his poison as if it had been sweet liquid honey. And by the time Marcus returned to the city, she was certain that he was now her mortal enemy who must be destroyed.

Yet she did not dare move against him on account of the enthusiasm of the people and the love they evinced for Marcus. Like all those whose power is founded in fraud and not in justice, she feared the indignation of the mob. Therefore, following the eunuch's counsel, she received Marcus with a semblance of love. It was easy for her to play such a part, for she was the most accomplished hypocrite, and indeed delighted in deception. So, having embraced him, she sat herself on a stool below the throne which he shared with Theodosius, lavished praise upon him, and made it seem to the people that her adoration was equal to theirs. And so it continued throughout the days of the Games held in his honour. But, secretly, she considered how to be rid of him.

Eutropius meanwhile cultivated Scaurus. Though that flinty aristocrat despised the eunuch and all his tribe, he was nevertheless susceptible to flattery. Eutropius, with that delicacy of manner that he could so easily assume, suggested that, though Marcus was hailed as the hero of the hour, both he and – he hinted – the Empress did not doubt that credit for the glorious victory belonged in truth to Scaurus himself. Marcus, after all, was but a novice in the art of war, a boy without experience; it was inconceivable that one who had never previously commanded even a small detachment of troops in the field should have devised a plan so masterly in conception, or have exercised so acute a tactical control over the battle itself.

'Such mastery of the art of war is not given to beardless boys,' the eunuch said. 'I suppose he relied greatly on your experience and your advice.'

'Oh, as to that,' Scaurus said, frowning, 'as to that, it is not for me to claim the laurels that wreath the brow of the Emperor.'

Eutropius saw that Scaurus was feeling his way cautiously, fearing that the eunuch was trying to trap him in expressions of disloyalty.

'Come,' he said, 'I assure you the Empress knows the truth of the matter. Naturally, she had to entrust the supreme – or shall we say nominal – command to the boy, he being her husband – for the time being, you know. But when she appointed you as second-in-command she said to me, "He will keep the boy straight and will have the true management of the business." It couldn't be otherwise. She knew that, and she is very grateful to you for all that you have done.'

'As to that,' Scaurus said, 'only my duty, you know. Only my duty. If I have acted in a manner worthy of my ancestors, and have earned the Empress's gratitude, that is reward enough. Let the . . . boy . . . enjoy the plaudits of the mob. He acquitted himself bravely, and well enough. In the battle, that is.'

'Yes, in the battle,' Eutropius said. 'No one doubts that the lad has courage. But after the battle? That's another matter. Between you and me – and mention this, I pray you, to nobody – what happened after the battle has left the Empress dismayed.'

'Dismayed?'

'Dismayed, puzzled, and displeased.'

The eunuch smiled. It was the smile of a conspirator. It invited collusion. Scaurus shifted in his seat. Eutropius read doubt, hesitation, suspicion in the movement. He pressed more wine on the Roman.

'She respects your loyalty, as she values your services and your opinion. That is why she has asked me to speak with you. I am, as you might say, her confidential agent. You understand. She trusts my discretion absolutely, because she knows I rely utterly on her continued favour. Whatever you choose to say to me will go no further . . . no further than her ears.'

'I am not easy with this matter,' Scaurus said.

'Your reluctance does you credit. Of course, we are not certain of the facts. That is why we are holding this conversation. Let me put it this way. It seems to the Empress that the happy outcome of the battle, this great victory which you master minded, gave us the opportunity to destroy Attila and his horde of savage barbarians, utterly and for ever; that his retreat to the waste-lands beyond the Danube was, or could have been, closed to him. And yet it was then laid open to him. This is what puzzles the Empress, puzzles, dismays, and displeases her – if these are indeed the facts. Are they the facts? Is this a true statement of the case?'

'A true statement of the case?' Scaurus frowned, drawing his heavy eyebrows together. 'I was trained in philosophy, you know. As a Roman nobleman of my generation, you understand. It has left me uncomfortable with the idea of truth, that there is ever, I mean, the true statement of a case. Nevertheless, and insofar as it goes, yes.'

'Aaah ...' The eunuch sighed deeply, and an expression of ineffable and sinister content lit up his face. 'Just as I thought,' he said. 'And why?'

'Why?'

'Why this ... treason?'

He spoke the last word quietly, delicately even.

'Treason?' Scaurus blinked, twice. 'Treason? I don't know about that. Nasty word, treason. I would say, from some sense of magnanimity. Mind you, I told him it wasn't our Roman way.'

'Magnanimity? Misplaced magnanimity, surely. And not, as you say, our Roman way. The Empress will be distressed to have her worst suspicions confirmed. She was fond of the boy. To allow the Empire's greatest enemy, a man proud to be known as the Scourge of God, to escape scot-free from a trap is rankest folly or, as I say, treason. Who knows what was secretly colluded between them? Is it not true also that the renegade Roman princess, Honoria, sister of the late emperor and of the ever-glorious Honorius, who governs the western half of the Empire, is now Attila's concubine?'

'Alas, it is true.'

'And is it not also the case that this Marcus, this presumptuous upstart, who has wormed his way into the Empress's favour and her very bed, is devoted to this Honoria?'

'So I have heard him say.'

'So. So indeed. A nest of conspirators, a very nest of vipers. My lord Scaurus, the Empress is in your debt. She will not forget. Your services will be honoured in the appropriate fashion.'

Smiling, he bowed deeply and scurried off to report to the Empress.

'It is as we supposed,' he said.

Yet still Eudoxia hesitated. This was not because she retained love or even desire for Marcus. Since he had been unable to conceal the distaste he now felt for her embraces, she had come to hate him. Moreover, she was jealous of the influence he exerted over Theodosius, who indeed was attached to him with all the passion that a shy, neglected and backward boy may feel. But Eudoxia was wary of the mob and its unpredictable fury. Eutropius, however, now fully restored to favour, assured her that he would attend to that.

'The mob is fickle,' he said. 'Fickle and credulous. What it believes is what it is told – if the telling be skilful.'

So he sent agents among the people to spread rumours concerning the secret alliance Marcus had made with Attila. The Huns, it was said, had withdrawn only to return in greater strength. Marcus had promised to divide the Empire with Attila and his concubine Honoria. True religion would be persecuted; paganism and worship of devils restored. Every Hun warrior had been promised that he could satisfy his lusts on the wives and daughters of the citizenry. As for their sons, they would be sold into slavery. Marcus, far from being a hero, was a traitor.

The poison worked, as poison always does. Scepticism, the mark of an honest mind, is alone a guard against calumny, and the people are never sceptics.

*(How true this is, we, the suffering remnant of the noble Order of the Knights of the Temple, now lurking in obscure refuge in the cold north, may affirm. It was calumny, and nought but calumny, that brought grief and ruin on us, destroying the goodliest

fellowship of noble knights ever seen since the dawning of the world. Malice and mad bestiality are stirred up by the cunning calumniators; and the world gives eager ear to their lies.)*

So the mob which one day hailed Marcus as a hero sent to deliver them from fear and slavery now cried out against him. And when she heard this cry, Eudoxia felt safe to order his arrest. He was seized in his bedchamber as he rose to greet the morning, and hurled headlong into a dungeon. Eutropius urged that he be put immediately to death – 'painful and humiliating death' – but the Empress demurred. He should first be narrowly examined, she said, with all the most refined instruments of torture, and then put on trial that he might openly confess his treason. So it was agreed.

Meanwhile Eudoxia's eye and favour lit upon Scaurus, and she commanded him to her bed. Eutropius, knowing that she could not subsist without an object of her lusts, assented, for he was certain he could manage the Roman.

But Scaurus, though stupid, was a man of antique honour. He was horrified to see the result of his incautious speech, and therefore cast about for a means to rescue Marcus. Moreover, the thought of being subject to Eudoxia's lusts disgusted him.

XLV

Meanwhile, in their poor tavern in a mean quarter of the city, Marcus's friends learned first of his glory, then of his disgrace.

They had passed the time of his absence pleasantly. Sir Gavin ate well and drank deep and shared the bed of Dorcas, the tavern-keeper. Neither was lustful, both easy and comfortable in the autumn of their days; they took undemanding pleasure of each other. Lycas exerted himself to restore Artemisia to health and confidence; pity had altogether expelled the distrust and indeed dislike he had previously felt for her. She for her part, as she recovered from the ordeal she had endured, knew a strange contentment. She had learned much in her months of degradation; learned her own strength, learned too that the most wretched of the earth may yet display kindness and generosity such as are rarely found among the mighty. Now she felt for Lycas an abounding gratitude; it amazed her that she had formerly been jealous of his influence (as she thought) over Marcus, and had despised him as a catamite. Realising his true goodness of heart, she sought a means of repaying him, and found it in cultivating his intelligence. She spent hours teaching him to speak correct and classical Greek, and she recited the epics of Homer, which, to her own great comfort in her worst days, her father Melanippos had long ago insisted she commit to memory. Lycas responded to the heroism of *The Iliad*, though he professed himself dismayed by the arrogance and folly of the chiefs of the Achaeans, and by the childish mendacity of the gods – who do indeed lie as children do, stupidly. But he was still more entranced by *The Odyssey* and its matchless and unscrupulous hero.

'I remember,' he said to Artemisia, 'how, when we were held in a cave by the vilest of our enemies, our dear Marcus recalled that strategem by which Odysseus deceived the Cyclops, and how it pleased him, even in our extremity, to quote the lines which you have just recited to me. Of course I did not understand them then, as I do now, thanks to you, but he translated them for my benefit, though, as it happened, the device or trick was not one that we could repeat to our advantage.'

So they passed the time, and Artemisia regained her confidence.

It was necessary to keep her hidden, or at least her identity concealed. It was known that the Empress had taken Marcus as her husband – 'How could he?' Lycas said; but since Artemisia was his lawful wedded wife, this second marriage was no marriage at all. Therefore, as Sir Gavin said, the Empress would kill Artemisia soon as look at her – if she was ever apprised of her continued existence.

'Pish and tush,' Dorcas stoutly said. 'There'll be no killing in my house. I run a seemly establishment, as all the world knows. Just let the lady bide quietly here, and she will come to no harm. I'll cudgel any rogue who threatens her with injury, for she's a sweet lady, as is easily seen, and has been most villainously abused.'

Sir Gavin took her hand and kissed the tips of her fingers.

'Well spoken, my plump partridge,' and he fondled her breasts while she giggled, 'Leave off, will you.'

Lycas attended both days of the Games held to celebrate Marcus's triumph. Able to afford only a cheap seat among the citizens whose breath stank of onions and fish-sauce, he had no hope of catching Marcus's eye. Neither he nor Sir Gavin had ever believed that Marcus had deserted them of his own will; both were certain that he had been told lies about them, and so Lycas had no doubt that if Marcus happened to see him in the crowd, he would find some means of sending for them. But there was no chance of that. He reported, however, that Marcus seemed pale and weary, looking a victim rather than a conqueror.

'Poor lad,' Dorcas said, 'I'll warrant that bitch of an empress has sucked the guts out of him. Never forget, I knew her when she was a common strumpet; and she's no better now she's an uncommon one.'

Then came word of Marcus's fall, disgrace, arrest. It came, as news comes to the poor, first as wild rumour. Some said he had been found in Theodosius's bed; others that the Empress had laid his back open with the whip to which she was known to be devoted. (Artemisia and Lycas both yelped and shuddered at the thought.) Then it was known that Marcus was in secret alliance with the Huns; that there had been no battle; that the battle had been a terrible defeat; that the account of the victory was doctored; that Attila had bribed Marcus with gold, or maidens, or with gold, jewels and maidens; that the Huns would even now be at the gates of the city if the Empress had not acted. In short, everything was said. Everything was believed as gospel truth, and retailed eagerly. Nothing was believable.

One night, as they sat huddled in the tavern in low spirits and confusion, the former in Sir Gavin's case not elevated, and the latter muddled further, by great draughts of retsina, there came a knock at the door (for Dorcas had closed the house, it being the hour before the Lord's Day and she not wishing to attract the notice of the priestly police).

She made no move to answer. The knock was repeated, gently.

'Admit him,' Sir Gavin muttered. 'A man demanding entry to a tavern and being refused will attract more notice than the same man admitted privily.'

So Dorcas did as he advised, though telling the visitor that the tavern was closed for religious reasons. Nevertheless, murmuring politely, he entered.

Their visitor stood without speaking. The lower part of his face was muffled with a scarf. A beaky commanding nose surmounted it. The eyes were hooded.

'It has been hard to find you,' he said.

Nobody questioned his knowledge of who they were.

He bowed to Artemisia. Was he unaware that she had been blinded? The bow was at least recognition of her quality.

'You have the advantage of us,' Lycas said, 'for, though you seem to know who we are, we remain ignorant of your identity.'

'It is enough to say that, like you, I am a friend of Marcus. I employed a Negro page who is devoted to him to seek you out. The boy is dumb, but he knows the byways and dark corners of the city, and has his own means of acquiring information. So I know that this is Artemisia, daughter of Melanippos of Thebes, and our friend Marcus's only lawful wedded wife. That you, sir, are an English knight, by name Gavin, once renowned in martial combat, but wanted by the imperial police for nefarious acts too numerous, and in some cases, revolting to mention now. What say you?'

'Calumny, sir, nothing but calumny and vile rumours. I'm a man as has lived life to the full, and in such living has acquired enemies, scores of 'em, some beneath the sod, and others still, unhappily, above it.'

'And, you, madam,' the stranger said, disregarding Sir Gavin's protest (which he accompanied with a swig of retsina), 'are the keeper of this low tavern, described by the priestly police as a notorious bawdy-house; but, long before that, you were a dresser in the theatre in the days when the Empress herself graced, shall we say, the stage.'

'Say "graced" if you please, my man,' Dorcas replied.

'And you, sir, are Lycas, servant, bedfellow and catamite of Marcus.'

'Say, rather, lover and faithful friend,' Lycas replied. 'So, sir, we cannot doubt that you know us well, and that we are in your power. Which is what, I assume, you intend us to feel. But why are you here? You say you too are a friend of Marcus. We hear that he is in danger, condemned perhaps to death. Why have you come here?'

The stranger settled himself at the table. Dorcas set wine before him, but he did not drink.

'A good question,' he said, 'to which I shall give you a true answer: to wit, that I do not know what impulse prompts this visit, since it can be of no conceivable benefit to me.'

'If we acted always only for our own benefit,' Dorcas said, 'this world would be a sadder place than it already is.'

'True,' said the stranger, and sniffed deeply. 'Your friend Marcus has been foolish, rash, ill-judging, careless of good advice. And yet is that sufficient reason he should die?'

'Marcus die?' Lycas said.

'As surely as the sun will rise tomorrow, unless . . .'

'Unless what?'

'Unless his friends act, at the risk of their own lives, to rescue him, and carry him safe far away from Constantinople.'

'And we are those friends?' Sir Gavin said.

Meanwhile, Marcus endured many torments. He was chained to the wall of a deep dungeon where the stone ran with water and the chill was extreme, sharp as the coldest quarter of Hell. He could move neither arm nor leg, and a necklace of lead attached him more closely to the wall. For three days he was denied food and water, and then was led from the prison-house to the council chamber to be examined by hooded judges. But in this examination no charges were laid against him; nor was anything said which accounted for his torment.

It came to him that he was punished not for anything he might have done or left undone, but for being who he was. And in his confusion of mind this seemed just to him, for – the words ran round and round in his fevered brain: 'Here pity lives when it is altogether dead. This is the judgement on me. For who is more impious than he that first questions, then sorrows at God's judgement?'

For what was accomplished was this, that all torturers seek to impart in the softened minds of their victims: the fear that whatever awful now befell him was his due, ordained by the sublime and unknowable Almighty will. For it is the triumph of torturers to lead their victims first to acquiesce in their misfortune, and then to love it.

So Marcus suffered; and his gaolers reviled him.

Once, he believed, the eunuch Eutropius himself appeared before him, and his appearance was transformed, so that he seemed to Marcus not the malignant and deformed creature that he was, but a golden angel carrying the sword of vengeance. And he laughed to see Marcus as he now was; and ordered him to be whipped, for his own pleasure and for Marcus's further debasement.

'You will long for death,' he said, 'and therefore it shall be long denied you.'

*

276

On the third night the stranger again appeared in the tavern, and now revealed himself to be Scaurus, Roman nobleman and chosen by Eudoxia as her next husband.

'Which,' he said, 'though all men of ambition may rightly aspire to govern the Empire, is nevertheless a fate I am eager to escape. But our friend is in sore straits. Sometimes he weeps and sometimes cries out to the Lord to end his torment. He raves and would fall to the ground if the chains did not prevent him. Or so my informants report, and therefore there is no time to lose if we are to save not only his life, but also his reason.'

Artemisia wept from her sightless eyes, but Lycas comforted her, saying that by Scaurus's account they were not yet too late, and that in any case Marcus had a better hold on reason than any man he had known. And this was kind of him, for in truth he was as dismayed and heartsick to hear what Scaurus said as Artemisia herself.

Then Scaurus told the ladies, Artemisia and Dorcas, to cover their heads with their cloaks, and follow the African page, whom he had brought with him, to the third landing-stage of the fourth dock, where a vessel was waiting.

The captain, he said, was a Sicilian, nevertheless to be trusted, for he owed Scaurus his life, though there was no time to tell why this was so. And they were to board the vessel and go below deck and wait.

Artemisia demurred, for her misfortune had rendered her suspicious of anything arranged by any other, but Dorcas took charge of her, and told her roundly they had no choice but to do as Scaurus ordered.

'And to prove it,' she said, 'I'll remind you that I am sacrificing this tavern which has been my home and livelihood these twenty years, and doing so because I see we are all subject to Necessity.'

When the ladies and the page had slipped out of the tavern through the yard and then out of the gate which led on to a maze of twisting streets – this being a poor and criminal quarter of the city – and when Scaurus's own bodyguard had returned to report that they had got away and not been followed, Scaurus led the others by a twisting route to a house some five hundred paces from the palace. He knocked twice at the door, which was opened at the second knock by an old Jew in a yellow robe, who extended his hand, into which Scaurus pressed gold. Then, without speaking, the Jew escorted them down a corkscrew staircase to the cellar of the house, where he drew back a handle, and by the light of the lantern which he carried, they could see a portion of the wall open before them. Scaurus then gave the Jew more gold and he left them.

'That opening in the wall will lead you by secret passages into the heart of the prison of the palace,' Scaurus said. 'Keep turning to the left and you will approach the dungeon where Marcus is confined. The guards have been drugged, and if any have proved insensible to the drug, you, Sir Gavin, may be trusted to deal with them. This key will unlock the chains which hold our friend. You will please leave it in the lock when you have released him. Take then the second opening, again on the left, and that will lead you to the outer gate. You will present the guards there with this seal, which is your authority, and while they are examining it . . .' He looked significantly again at Sir Gavin, who inclined his head in understanding. 'That gate opens on the dock where the vessel is moored. When you are underway, the captain has instructions to raise the plague-flag, that other vessels will give you a wide berth. And may the gods look favourably on your enterprise.'

'And are you yourself deserting us at this point?' Lycas cried out in surprise.

Scaurus heard the note of reproach in the boy's voice.

'My duty,' he said, 'is to Rome and the Empire. If that requires me to wed the bitch-empress, whom I detest, so be it. *Roma super omnia*, Rome above all else, such is the motto and the watchward of my family, to which I am faithful, as my ancestors, sixteen of them consuls, have been before me.'

Saying this, he embraced them, and departed.

'Come,' Sir Gavin said, 'he has done more than we had any entitlement to look for. Now it is up to us. One for all and all for one, as we used to say when we were a company of young knights.'

'I was never a knight,' Lycas said, 'but I would give much to have in my possession now the ashes of the burned body of a blind cat, for, as Marcus told me and himself proved in one of our extremities, that is a sovereign remedy which never fails.'

'Be that as it may,' Sir Gavin said, 'I have a strong right arm which you may rely on. But we must waste no time in chatter, for in any affair of this sort, as in a battle, right timing is all. Now may the gods be with us.'

And so, calling on the pagan gods, he crossed himself, to make, as he muttered, 'assurance doubly sure'.

Then they entered through the hole in the wall, which was low so that even Lycas had to stoop, and Sir Gavin must bend himself double, and they descended a steep staircase, feeling their way by the slimy wall; for it was dark as the road to Hell, and they dared not display the lantern which Lycas carried. So they came at last, deep in the bowels of the earth as it seemed, to level ground, and before them was a door under which a light feebly shone. Sir Gavin advanced boldly and threw open the door, and they entered on a narrow chamber with an arched roof. There was a table in the middle of the room, and three guards sat at it, but their heads had fallen so that they rested on the table. At this sight both knew great joy. They had feared, though neither had dared to speak of his fear, that Scaurus might have deceived them, or that his plan had gone a-gley. One of the guards stirred, as if the drug had not rendered him quite senseless. Sir Gavin, obedient to his instructions, swung the mace which he wore at his belt, and brought it down heavily on the guard's head. He picked up the lantern from the table, and Lycas uncovered his, and they passed through by the other door, which led to the dungeons.

In the first they found an old man with a beard that hung below his waist. He was naked and chained to the wall, and his lips moved in a silent babble. When he became aware of their presence, he whimpered and his head jerked as if to avoid a blow. In the second there were two children, a boy and a girl, of perhaps ten years; and they had been blinded. The third housed a burly fellow who wrestled hard against his chains and cursed freely. The fourth held a man who seemed alive only by the motion of his throat, in which his Adam's apple jumped; but his face was dead as crumbling plaster

So they moved through horror, and were unable to speak, sickened by the evidence of what men were reduced to. Lycas indeed wept, but Sir Gavin took him by the arm and urged him onwards, till at last they reached the cell where Marcus was confined.

He hung from his chains and his feet did not touch the ground, so that his weight was supported by his upper body. His face was bruised and swollen, and his tongue lay on cracked lips. Both eyes were closed, and for a moment of anguish Lycas feared that they had arrived too late. But Sir Gavin stepped forward, and with the key that Scaurus had given him, unlocked the chains, and Marcus fell into his arms. Lycas, now unable to restrain his tears and sobs, stretched out his hand and touched the bruised face of his beloved. Then Sir Gavin hoisted Marcus over his shoulder.

'We must hurry,' he said. 'We must get him to the boat before the guard is changed and the alarm raised.'

And so, Sir Gavin bearing Marcus, they prepared to leave the dungeon. Before they could do so, however, Lycas turned to the knight and said,

'Give me the key with which you unlocked the chains. I cannot endure the thought that we must leave those blinded children in this hellish place. Perhaps the same key will free them from their misery.'

So the knight gave him the key, though loth to delay, and Lycas returned to the other cell and found that the key served there too, and released the children and brought them with him, holding each by the hand that they might not stumble in their blindness.

'Artemisia will care for them,' he said. 'Like tending like.'

A cynic might say that Lycas liberated these wretched children to provide distraction for Artemisia and so leave the care of Marcus to himself. But the cynic would be wrong. Lycas was prompted by the noblest of instincts, which is pity.

So they came to the outer gate, where the guards – bull-necked Bulgars – challenged them. Sir Gavin proffered the seal which Scaurus had given him. They examined it narrowly, turning it over, passing it from hand to hand, and frowning. Then they fell to disputing its meaning; and as they were so occupied, the knight, who had set Marcus against the wall, where Lycas hastened to support him, again drew his mace and with quick blows laid out the guards. And so they passed safely from the palace and came to the boat.

They laid Marcus on the deck. Lycas entrusted the children to Artemisia, who was divided between the desire to care for her lord and the pleasure which she at once received from these unfortunates, once she realised that they were blind like her. Meanwhile, Dorcas wiped Marcus's broken face with a cloth dipped in oil of hyssop and vinegar, and as she did so he seemed to revive, and sighed,

'Where will my journeyings bring me? Lord God, what have I done, what sin did you find in me, that you have loaded me with such a yoke to torment me? Why am I thus plagued to wretchedness and madness with this stinging terror? Oh that the grave would open before me. I cannot tell how otherwise to escape from pain and dread.'

But Dorcas soothed him with cunning fingers, and first Artemisia and then Lycas kissed his brow and then his lips, and he fell asleep, as the pilot guided the vessel out of port and they made for the open sea, where, obedient to his orders, the captain raised the plague-flag. So, ghostly, the ship glided into the dark of night.

(This account is, I fear, purely fanciful, for I know the imperial palace and its prisons well, and I may aver that there is no gate that opens on the dock; nor is there any record of prisoners held in the deepest dungeons ever again seeing the light of day, or sniffing the winds of freedom. But our author will have his way, and will write his own myth.)

XLVI

For the first two days of the voyage Marcus slept, not peacefully. He babbled in his delirium, cried out that monsters, strange beasts with the heads of men, were threatening him. Dorcas and Lycas tended to him. Artemisia occupied herself with the blind children.

She said to Dorcas, 'I have longed to have Marcus, my husband, restored to me, and now that it has happened, I find I care nothing for it. Misfortune teaches one thing only as far as I can tell: that you must be truthful to yourself. And the truth is that he never loved me, he married me for convenience, and he deserted the girl he truly loved in order to do so. Did I steal him from her? Perhaps. In moods when I feel more kindly to myself, I say that I did not know, that I was then blind to the truth as I am now blind to the world. Is it a judgement on me?'

'Stuff and nonsense, my poor pigeon,' the older woman answered. 'You made a marriage like most marriages, and I should know, having buried three husbands and lost or mislaid two others. Nobody knows husband or wife till they've passed years together, and if they learn then that they were never suited, so be it. No use crying over spilled wine or bitter words. We must just make the best of things as they are. Now you have these poor abused children who need you, and that's more than many of us can hope for. Life's a matter not of making good, as the young think, but of making whatever happens for the best, which may be bad enough.'

Marcus himself was still held in the world of dream beyond sense. On the third day the evil dreams departed from him, and he dreamed instead, first, of his lovely Pulcherrima, walking with him in springtime meadows among flowers. Her hand was clasped warm in his, her long hair brushed his cheek. They were silent, with no need of words.

He woke and opened his eyes, and they were blue again. The wind was soft, gentle from the south, warm from Africa. Lycas held his hand and carried it to his lips, then fetched him wine mixed with water from the barrel they carried on deck, sweet rainwater from the hills; and he smiled at Marcus, and, as he grew stronger, told him all that had befallen him, and how Scaurus had planned his rescue, and what brave deeds Sir Gavin had performed in its execution.

So they sailed towards the west, they passed by Crete, and the mountain called Ida, within which stands upright an Old Man whose back is turned to Egypt and who gazes towards Rome as if it was his reflective glass.

'Crete,' murmured Marcus, remembering lines of Vergil, 'the cradle of our race.'

And he seemed to see the Old Man, whose head is made of fine gold, his arms and breast of silver, his middle parts of brass, his legs of iron save for the right foot formed of baked clay; and yet it is on that foot that he plants his weight.

And he represents the decline and fall of Rome itself, and the clay foot is the Pope, that successor of St Peter, Vicar of Christ, who forged that donation by which it is alleged the great Emperor Constantine himself granted him temporal power, and sovereignty over all princes.

Which is a lie, for his power is spiritual and not temporal, and it is from Almighty God and not from his so-called Holiness, the Bishop of Rome, that princes derive their authority to rule over states and mete out justice.

(So our author prepares his pupil Frederick for his long career of enmity towards Holy Church and his defiance of the pretensions of the Papacy. A mischievous master and an apt pupil; and yet, as our founder, the Knight of the Rosy Cross, has written: 'Although we cannot be by any man suspected of the least heresy, or of any wicked beginning or purpose against the worldly government, we do condemn the West and the East (signifying the Pope and Mahomet), blasphemers against Jesus Christ, our Lord, and we offer and present with a good will to the Princeps, head and chief of the Most Holy Roman Empire, our prayers, secrets, and great treasures of gold. And in the Reformation that is to come, we acknowledge ourselves truly and with the utmost loving sincerity to profess Christ, condemn the Pope, obey the Emperor, addict ourselves only to the true Philosophy, lead a Christian and obedient life, and daily call, entreat and urge such others as may be worthy to enter into our Fraternity, should the same Light of God, which is Knowledge, shine upon them.' Thus all men of wisdom and insight may attain to the wished-for happiness and sweet content of the Fraternity of the Rosy Cross. And, though born and flourishing in an age before our founder R.C., and therefore with eyes dimmed by ignorance, it appears to us that, howsoever uncertain, lascivious, capricious, misinformed (or ignorant), sometimes mischievous our author may appear, nevertheless his gaze was turned to the light which, thanks to our founder and brother R.C., now shines in the darkness of superstition and false belief, illuminating them for what they are, that the wise and aspirant may judge truly. So help them God!)

As he grew stronger, Marcus kept his eyes fixed to the west, and with each day his beauty was born anew.

He thought often of Odysseus, or Ulysses as the Romans knew him, and of how neither his love for his son Telemachus, nor his reverence for his sire Laertes, nor the love and duty he owed his wife Penelope could conquer and subdue in him the ardour he had to win knowledge of the world, and of all that man can do for ill and good.

Like him, he thought, I am launched on the deep sea, with a small company of faithful friends, alert to its dangers. Like him I approach the Pillars of Hercules, with Spain on one hand and Africa on the other, those Pillars set by the hero to hinder or deter man from pressing beyond them to the unknown ocean. Yet we approach them and shall dare to pass beyond.

So he turned to Lycas and, taking him by the hand, spoke as follows:

'My friend, brother, and lover, who has been faithful to me in all extremities and dangers, will you, now that we have attained the west and approach the gates men were forbidden to pass, hold with me yet. Let us not, for whatever time remains to us, shrink from experience of the unpeopled world behind the Sun. Consider our origin, our nature, and our many noble deeds, and the dangers we have met and overcome. We were not formed, you and I, to live like dull beasts, but to follow virtue and knowledge wherever they may lead us.'

When he heard these words Lycas was seized with joy, for he understood that Marcus was restored to himself, and to him.

But Sir Gavin, who had also overheard him, smiled, as an elder may smile at the zeal of boys, and said,

'All this rhetoric is very fine, my friends, and does you credit. But when we pass through what you call the Pillars, which look like ordinary rocks to a plain Yorkshireman, and turn the ship's prow to the north, we shall reach a fair land, not yet called England, though that is what it shall be, but Britain, once a Roman province, now fallen to barbarism, and waiting for a bold man with a keen sword to conquer it. Though I am old and would happily settle by the hearth with my good lady, as Dorcas has consented to be, without, she says, benefit of clergy – "stuff the priests" were her exact words – still I'm ready for one last campaign. Britain or England have it as you choose – is waiting for a sword, a saviour, a deliverer. And you're the man, Marcus, the man, as we say in Yorkshire, of the hour.'

So they sailed north, for many days, through rough winds and high seas, till they came within sight of the white cliffs, above which the noble castle of Dover now looms. Then they nosed into the estuary of a great river called the Thames and sailed up to what had been the fine Roman city of London, but which crime and anarchy had made again one of the waste places of the earth, so that the wolf whelped in the great church of St Paul and the few citizens who survived lurked in the fallen masonry like conies in the rocks.

And they disembarked there and rode west till they came to a city called Winchester, where the King, who had once been a Roman general, was sick and dying. And Marcus was welcomed there and received with great joy, and became king, or rather emperor, in his place; and the land flourished exceedingly. So he reigned in glory all the days of his life, and the land knew prosperity, Artemisia knew happiness devoting herself to the blind children and other works of charity, Dorcas kept a fine inn, Sir Gavin achieved his ambition of dying in a tavern, and Lycas grew grey and wise in Marcus's service.

But of what befell next, and of the story of Marcus's true heir, and (as some think) his reincarnation, Arthur, I must speak in another volume.